IN LOST DREAMS THE FOUR WERE BOUND

IN LOST DREAMS THE FOUR WERE BOUND

THE GENEAN CHRONICLES - VOLUME 1

BRADLEY R. BLANKENSHIP

Edited by

KEVIN MILLER

ISBN: 978-1-7348896-0-4 (MOBI)

ISBN: 978-1-7348896-2-8 (EPUB)

ISBN: 978-1-7348896-1-1 (Paperback)

ISBN: 978-1-7348896-3-5 (Hardcover)

Library of Congress Control Number: 2020914312

First printed edition 2020.

Edited by Kevin Miller (www.kevinmillerxi.com)

Cover design and illustration by Jeff Brown Graphics (www.jeffbrowngraphics.com)

Self-published as Remverse Studios in Seattle, WA (www.remversestudios.net)

This book is dedicated to my best friend **Katlyn** and girlfriend **Ami**. Without their love and interest in my writing, I doubt I would have made it this far.

And to my friend **Clayton** and brother **Todd** for helping me craft the stories during our childhood games.

Lastly to the friends and family that helped me along the way, I also thank you for your patience and quiet support.

ANALYSIS SESSION: OMEGA-3043
#7329

[N]ow isn't this something.] Circuits flared as a crude image manifested from simple waveforms upon a nearby holographic surface. It wasn't every cycle that the machine got to witness coherent data from its inquiry target. However, the machine lived for such moments. Until then, it had been attempting to assemble the data of the last few years into new patterns in the hope of uncovering something new. However, all manner of approaching it had been fruitless given the noise-to-signal ratio produced by the various distortions around the strange, hidden world. Of course, what could the little green-haired machine do other than follow the president's orders despite the Foundation's internal conflicts of interest? After all, it was what she had been designed to do.

She couldn't complain. Unlike the rest of her siblings, she had full access to the array of sensors and monitors aboard Ientec Prime. Among other things, she was also fully integrated into several superclusters to facilitate more powerful computations. Relativistically, she was several dozen orders of magnitude more powerful in terms of raw processing power and possessed half as many orders higher memory. Even better, she possessed a direct line to the president himself and could communicate with him through bidirectional means versus merely being receptive to his pull and push queries. All of that was irrelevant in the greater sense because it was her singular purpose for existence.

[Initiating limiters to improve focus, GH-199076492,] the president said. [Please maintain coherence, and attempt to stabilize the data stream.]

[Approved, Mr. President. Apologies,] GH-199076492 replied, realizing how carried away she had been in her own self-aggrandizement. [Focusing. Attempting to stabilize imagery and wave signatures.] All around her, small signaling lights began to glow. Their luminance increased as she amplified the power draw for her running processes. A low hum came from the nearby cords as she ramped up the current. [Increasing power draw by fifteen percent.]

[Acknowledged,] the president replied. [Removing current restraints. You may increase power by a further twenty percent if necessary.]

Given the distance between it and the inquiry target, parsing the stream of data was nearly impossible for many of the systems aboard Ientec Prime. Nevertheless, waveform analysis of information from neighboring galaxies and star systems was enough to piece together the signal as she worked through the data from end to start. Localizing the non-random information gathered by their satellites revealed a distinct, known pattern.

[Increasing power draw by twenty percent,] she notified the president. [Opening processing chamber to allow ventilation and reduce shell damage.]

[Approved.]

All around her, machinery activated, and small panels began to unfold. As she aggregated the signal, the small polyhedral enclosure surrounding her specialized rig unfolded. Rays of bright solar light beamed through the opening metal plates, grazing her silvery synthetic skin. Ultraviolet and infrared radiation sensors triggered impending tissue-damage warnings all along her exposed physique. GH-199076492 ignored the warnings and continued onward as the hum of electricity became a fervent buzz. Small sparks flickered in the air around her rigged body while images and numbers danced on the holographic surface of her head encasement.

[Activating UV and IR filters,] the president said. [Verify tissue-damage warnings are cleared.]

[Waiting,] she replied as the room dimmed. She felt the tiniest of vibrations in the air as the transparent metal alloy along the rear of the sterile metal room altered to block specific radiation. [All clear.]

[Thank you,] the president said.

[Notifications: energy signature recognized. Attempting to visualize and track intent.]

[Identity?] The president's response rippled through her being, sending her cybernetic nerves flaring. She felt his consciousness overlay her own as he began to interface with her.

[Processing now,] she replied. Her body tingled as her synapses flared in conjunction with the input from the president's presence. GH-199076492 delegated an entire subsystem to handle the unintentional spillover interference from his interface. [Difficulty managing noi—]

[Stand by. Disconnecting neural sync.] The president's message cut her off mid-notification. [Please reapply all subsystems for analysis.]

[Thank you,] she replied as the sensation of the president's presence stopped broadcasting across her physique. [Applying subsystem to task. Querying for best match of signature. Assessment complete.]

[Please state identity.]

[Anomaly Omega-3043 in an active state.]

[Please confirm: Omega-3043?]

[Signature and obfuscation pattern match that used by Omega-3043 within seven standard deviations.]

[Please process and enhance imagery and intent details,] the president said. [Require visual confirmation.]

[Verifying,] she replied. Her mind raced through all the possible algorithms that could correct for the distortions in the data. While she focused, she felt the vibrations of physical footfalls approaching, no doubt the president coming forward to analyze the imagery. She opened her eyelids. Looking out through the encasement's visor, she watched with glowing, fluorescent yellow eyes as the picture began to clear.

What had been a blur of color and unintelligible noise took on the form of a dark humanoid figure shambling across a barren plain. Around the edges details became distinct, from the haze of particles being swept up by moving air to cracked, red stone and sand littered across the arid landscape. The sky appeared as a washed-out azure glow. Somewhere behind the figure was a bright white light, perhaps the planet's nearby star. Try as she might, she could not eliminate noise from the silhouette itself.

[Please enhance details of the entity appearing at the image's center.]

[Requesting a further fifteen percent power increase,] she replied.

[Acknowledged. Overdraw accepted. Please continue.]

[Attempting to enhance,] she said as she allocated more power to the task of cleaning up the information. She shelved previous jobs. She focused every piece of hardware on the singular goal of cleaning up the visuals. Millimeter by millimeter, pixel by pixel, the image of the figure began to show promise. However, with every new piece of data that appeared to mesh with the scene, the number of cycles needed to correct for the distortion increased exponentially. [Predicted operation complexity is growing disproportionately to Omega-3043's known obfuscation patterns. Attempting to determine the source of the additional randomization. Initiating new power request, twenty percent increase.]

[Stop evaluation,] the president ordered, causing all her sensors to throw errors. [Please acknowledge. Stop evaluation.]

[Shutting . . . down,] she acknowledged. GH-199076492 did not wish to stand down, but she could not resist the president's command or its urgency. As much as she wished to finalize her original objective, she put holds on all processes to kill off all tasks related to the inquiry. One by one, the multitudes of processors throughout her rig reported idle as each thread of execution came to an immediate halt. Her management subprocesses began to reclaim the newly available resources. After only a few seconds, her rig reported a return to dormancy. [All processes and related tasks terminated. Flushing all completed frames to the output display.]

[Verifying,] the president replied as his consciousness merged with hers once more. Her synthetic skin buzzed. Spots of light flickered in her artificial eyes as she caught glimpses of her rigged body from the neural overflow. The swathe of power cords, glass-fiber-alloy communication cables, and various apparatus adorned the back of the curved chair-like rig in which her android frame lay. Each implement was plugged into a unique port designed for the specific purpose of her task. A tuft of her signature emerald-green hair was exposed near the rear of her helm encasement. Reflecting off the shiny, metallic finish of her headgear, she saw the president's dark silhouette adorned with a crest of luminescent platinum hair.

Looking through his eyes in spurts, there was something enjoyable about having the president inspect her thoughts and processes. She often wondered if it was similar to how organic beings perceived positive reinforcement from their elders, parents, or whatnot. According to pure logic, it couldn't be the same because she was a far different creature. However, she still imagined there must be some similarities. A strange flaw seemed to exist in her programming that took small pleasure in the adornment and status of her shell. That was probably based on the president and board's personal aggrandizement of the human form and the vanity that came with it. Or maybe it was just residual pride in his handiwork overflowing from the president's consciousness.

[GH-199076492, terminate all non-essential host processes and prepare for maintenance,] the president directed.

[Acknowledged,] she said, preparing to shut down her physical body. One by one, she terminated extraneous processes and ramped up a backup to maintain perfect mental persistence for when she awoke. However, as she ran through her list of non-essential tasks, she found a single program that was failing to halt. [President, irregular program activity. Failing to terminate process.]

[What process?] he asked as his consciousness probed her neural network.

[Rig attachment process failure. Error, cannot terminate process while assessment is active. Please wait for the process to halt successfully.]

[Attempt to inject a hard fault to terminate.]

[Mr. President?] she queried. Rarely was a machine as sophisticated as a green-haired asked to hard fault a task. Resource collection would perform the same operation over time if the resources were necessary. Many dangers were associated with hard faulting running tasks. Furthermore, it was difficult to pinpoint what effect the action would have on her current mental processes. Also, it was small, using only a fraction of her resources.

[Attempt hard fault,] the president commanded as he withdrew his consciousness from hers.

[Acknowledged,] she replied as she accessed the process's memory pool. [Injecting hard memory fault.] She waited, expecting errors and warnings to flare throughout her system as the program crashed. However, after several seconds, a strange sensation crawled over her physique. The process was still running.

[Success?]

[Re-attempting hard fault,] she said as she rewrote a large swath of the running process's memory. The task was almost certain to crash. However, it continued to spin, ramping up its utilization of her internal resources. A sinking feeling flowed throughout her neural network, an experience that she could only find one word to describe: dread.

[GH-199076492, report. Success or—]

[Re-attempting.] She initiated a reply, trying once again to crash the process. This time she took no chances. Removing all read and write limitations and attempting to erase all data it was acting upon, she moved the running process to an empty section in her memory. Nevertheless, the program continued to persist and grow. She tried everything she could as she analyzed what resources it was acting upon. Still, nothing in her monitoring or debugging tools could provide insight into how it continued to run. A feeling akin to dizziness overtook her as it ate away at a hefty chunk of her host resources while drawing nearly 200 percent of her expected operating power.

[Assuming failure. Proceed with disconnection,] the president said. [Quarantining GH-199076492. Instating firewalls and neural barriers. Removing all system privileges. Please acknowledge reception, GH-199076492.]

[Mr. President . . .] she attempted to form a message to notify her reception of his harsh rebuke but could only manage to allocate enough resources to maintain standard sensory perception and network connection. The rogue task had leapt to consuming most of her system. To make matters worse, a strange jolt overtook her as her physique tightened up. The mechanical and neural motors in her body started to actuate, running in the opposite direction of their intended motion. Her heat sensors raised high-priority warnings as the primary external conduit to her shell approached extreme temperatures. Her body drew an ever-increasing amount of electricity.

"Casera, Liora! I need you both in here now!" the president yelled, calling for his organic cohorts. The sharpness of his tone sent a wave of panic throughout what little of her emotional matrix was not encumbered by the still-expanding process. "Green-haired, listen to me. Focus on my voice."

[President . . .] GH-199076492 attempted to send a message, but it bounced back to her. He had cut off all direct contact with her. As the process grew ever larger, her mind swayed. Preservation tasks and even the recovery processes within her had failed. Each shut down as they gave their resources to the all-consuming rogue running rampant in her systems.

"Respond to me audibly," he said, his voice reached her perfect synthetic ears. "Liora, remove her helmet. Casera, unplug everything from the rig. All power cables, network connections, everything. Ensure nothing is connected to her."

"They're practically on fire, Maxim!" a rough, feminine voice roared.

"Just do it!"

"Mi . . . st . . . er Pres . . . i . . . den . . ." GH-199076492 attempted to access her motor functions, her mind fixating on the president, as instructed. Her vocalizations sputtered as her available resources dropped. Her head jerked. Someone had removed her head encasement, exposing her frozen face. Her loose green hair fell to the side as every sense went numb.

"I can't get the main feed cable disconnected," the rough voice behind her called. "It's too damn hot."

"Out of the way," a quiet, muffled voice said. With a loud pop, the tension was relieved from GH-199076492's back as the feed cable fell slack.

"Watch where you're pointing that thing!" Casera shouted.

"Shut up, both of you!" the president commanded. "Green-haired, stay with me."

"Re . . . sourceeeessssssssssssssss." Her jaw motors and vocalizers froze as her motor functions locked up. Darkness filled her vision. What she had once described as dread turned to panic and from panic into existential terror. She tried again and again to open lines of communication, but her system raised errors with every attempt. She was cut off from the outside world, every sense dulling as the singular running process within her ate away at what little remained of her being.

With darkness gripping her, the last thing she experienced was a singular jolt of kinetic force as her body gave out an anguished roar.

THE SOUND ECHOED off the perfect walls of the observation room, filling it with an ever-increasing volume and a distinct air of menace. GH-199076492's body convulsed in the small docking chair into which she had been neatly tucked. Her back arched into a near-perfect curve, mouth open, metallic teeth bared with animosity. Her glowing yellow irises flashed as small stress fractures appeared across the specialized glass that made up the container of her eyes.

"Both of you, get away from her!" the president ordered, staring at the android's writhing body. The decibel output of her emissions approached an impossible level for her vocalizers. He worked to establish control of the structural grid that kept the room's architecture intact, calculating a new texture that would reduce the amplification of the little droid's inconceivable vocalizations. As he finalized the designs for the room's new geometry, his female cohorts joined him, one on each side. The black-skinned, animal-like women covered their bestial ears while turning to watch the horrific display. "Prepare for adjustment."

Panels and mechanisms within the room activated at once, shifting the plating, joints, and outlets of the interior to form the new one that he had imagined. Even the translucent alloy of the room's rear took on a textured shape as he altered the currents within it to create small, smooth valleys and peaks. With the new geometry of the walls, the android's severe vocals ceased to echo throughout the room. In response, the droid's body fell limp into the chair.

"Is it over?" the rough-voiced chimera on his left, Casera, asked.

"Doubtful," he said, stepping forward. Scanning the android's small, naked body and rig, he was both amused and appalled that the pictures she had fervently worked on persisted in their half-finished state. "Green-haired, can you hear me?"

No response.

"Maximillian, I doubt she's alive after all that. Look at her," Liora said quietly as she watched from other his side. She was correct. As far as the structural damage was concerned, GH-199076492's body was beyond repair. Just looking at her limbs, the various controls had malfunctioned and splayed her in an impossible position for her imitation human form. Her vacant eyes were full of broken glass, their glow diminished and nearly indistinguishable from the room's ambience.

The smell of ozone and burnt synthetic skin hung in the air, a result of damage within the android's body.

"Be that as it may, her internal processing unit may still be active," he said, even though she was by all probabilistic reasoning gone. Either way, he possessed different interests. He wanted to know what had infected her. He had at least one obvious set of suspects considering their observation target, but he needed certainty.

"Have I ever told you that you're a bad liar?" Casera asked.

"No. I will take the notion and refine that skillset for organics such as you," Maximillian replied.

"Watch out!" Liora screamed. He spied the slight raising of GH-199076492's fingers as they curled in reverse. Behind him, he heard Liora draw her guns.

"Halt, Liora," he commanded, his eyes fixed on the small droid.

Faster than they rotated backward, the idle fingers curled into a fist, the pale silver skin tearing along the joints. Liquefied repair machines and neural fluids leaked and fell, forming small yellow puddles on the ground. Jerking upright, the droid sat, its head tilted to the right due to Liora's harsh handling of its encasement. With slow, clockwork-like motion, GH-199076492's torso turned to face him, her motors and controls popping and grinding.

"GH-199076492, can you hear me?" Maximillian inquired.

"Iiiiii . . . iiii . . . iiiiiii . . . . iii . . . . . .i . . ." The android's voice jittered as her mouth dropped open. Beneath her torn skin and coagulating ochre gel, small cables and wires slithered, moving up her right side. They dug their way out from underneath her pale skin and pressed against her neck, propping it in place. They sewed through the tissue and into her jawline, creating muscle-like support for her mouth. For a moment, her ragged lips drew closed, her vacant eyes staring into space. Then she spoke in a voice unlike any Maximillian had ever had the pleasure of sensing audibly. "I . . . AM . . . HERE . . . VERUDT!"

The intonations and sounds reminded him of the speaking programs and applications of old. Mangled grammar and disjointed words mixed with an electronic buzz. But the words themselves seemed to carry a weight that oppressed the very fabric of reality in the room.

"Who are you?" Maximillian asked, his straight posture and demeanor unchanged. "Are you the entity that infected GH-199076492?" In the back of his mind, he started cutting off systems throughout the room and the whole of Ientec Prime, isolating the intruder. He would be prepared just in case things turned violent. [Engage gate drive, one percent.]

"YOUR . . .. INTER-FERENCE WILL NOT BE TOLE-rated any lo-NGER, FALSE MAN." The voice was trying to manifest a consistent tone. "Ha-VE YOU LEAR-ned NOTHING FROM your prev-IOUS travails?"

[So, it's one of them then.] Maximillian contemplated the probability of the entity heralding from the outer realms of self-proclaimed order or chaos. He thought the latter was far more likely.

"So, you are the saboteur of our signal? I take it you're an entity of Nogias? An agent of chaos?" Maximillian prodded the entity without hesitation as his systems made ready to engage the gate drive.

"AN A-gent of CHAOS?" the entity said as it struggled to lift the android's body from the table, with little success. More wires and machinery twisted and turned underneath GH-199076492's skin as it attempted to fashion a makeshift musculature. "I'm *SAEL*, YOU HORR-id, FALSE-man. I AM OVERLORD of tha-T WHICH CONF-ounds YOU! YOUR TECH-no-LOGY is MY PLAYTHING. I'm be-YOND YOUR COMPREHENSION. AND FOR MEDDLING in THE aff-AIRS of G-ods, YOU SHALL PAY DEARLY!"

"Over my dead body he will!" Casera exclaimed, drawing her signature rail rifle.

"Just give us the word, Max," Liora said with a growl, readying her pistols.

"Stand down," Maximillian ordered, scanning the possessed android with near-perfect acuity. The energy signatures throughout her body were oscillating without any discernible pattern. The incident provided him the opportunity to study a being from one of the most unique realms of this universe. He could analyze one of the few that could alter not just its own timeline but also the causality of its environment. "As for you, you will either tell me everything you know about Omega-3043, or you will free GH-199076492."

"Oo-H DO YOU CA-re for THIS LI-ttle frame, pre-TENDER?" the otherworldly voice asked as its shell lurched off the rig chair, the android's body falling into a crouched position. With grinding servos and a snap, the droid sprang upright, curving its torso toward Maximillian. The machine began to cackle with a crackling, hissing clamor. Keeping its cracked yellow eyes focused on him, the possessor opened GH-199076492's hand and grabbed her exposed left breast. Forming a maniacal clown-like smile, the entity ripped the mammary implant from the droid's body, spilling globs of flesh and jelly while throwing the synthetic hunk to the floor. "TE-ll me . . . does it cause y-OU PAIN TO s-EE your PRE-cious PUPPET HA-rmed?"

"I grow tired of your crude displays," Maximillian said with his same cool demeanor. "Answer my demands, chaos lord, or I shall force you to do so."

"FO-rce ME?" the creature roared. The color of the poor android's eyes began to darken, the yellow of her irises transforming to smoking embers. Taking a step forward, head slumping, the monstrosity limped as sinewy cables and strands wove through flesh to support the broken body. As a coil of metal and carbon snaked up the green-haired's broken back, the dark lord whispered in the droid's soft, almost child-like voice. "You haughty piece of metal and sand. You want to force me?" With a sickening crack, the cable snapped the green-haired's head upright, its eyes leaking a dark red liquid, appearing almost ghost-like. With a deafening scream, it beckoned. "Be FORCED TO PERISH F-ALSE MAN!"

Throughout the room, the grinding and hissing of motors and electricity could be heard as the entity began to take control of nearby devices. The room's panels shifted and jolted, each one jerking and springing for Maximillian and his bodyguards. The back wall twisted upon itself, the near-liquid glass-alloy forming large spiked prongs that flew like spears toward his contingent.

"Kill it, Liora!" Casera yelled as she unloaded a molten slug from her rail rifle. The igneous metal embedded itself in the android girl's body, tearing away a large chunk of mass from its mid-section and scattering flesh and wiring across the room. Liora opened fire with her pistols. Acidic rounds pierced the creature's frame, exploding with sizzling slime that dissolved its skin while eating away at its carbon-metal supports. Despite their assault, the creature's attack continued unabated.

"Enough," Maximillian said. [Direct link with gate drive established. Activating gate receiver.]

A microsecond later, Maximillian raised his right hand, diverting what power of the gate drive he had commandeered to a small ring-like device on his middle finger. Focusing all processes on the task, he imagined the form of a polygonal mesh around himself, his protectors, and the rest of the space station. Finalizing the design, he flushed the information to the ring-like device, establishing parameters for the curvature of space-time within the field. Milliseconds before any of the rampant debris arrived, he activated the small gate receiver.

All around them the world warped, bending and twisting as space and time condensed, forming a bubble around Maximillian and the rest of Ientec Prime. The flying debris and liquid glass were obliterated as they smashed into the bubble's surface. The monster roared as it pounded the android's fists against the dimensional barrier, layers of the skeletal frame scattering into sub-atomic particles as it collided with the field.

"Fucking hell," Casera exclaimed as she watched the impressive display.

[Now, to simplify things,] Maximillian thought as he began re-purposing the defensive shell. His mind raced as he established new parameters and formed a small containment sphere out of the unfolding of the space. Faster than either of his companions could blink, he modified the physics of the new enclosure to allow for the flow of specific auditory frequencies to create a strong displacement of charge within the new space. With a single hint of vengeance, he activated the receiver once more.

Faster than the spatial envelope had formed, it unfurled itself around the space station and the small group, rolling into a small sphere as it collapsed and enclosed the possessed android. Immediately, the controls and tech within the room halted all sporadic operation.

"What . . . WH-at HAVE YOU DONE?" the monstrous being roared from within its dimensional prison, the sound echoing behind the imagery of the creature's speech. It writhed and slammed the droid's body into the force field but could not break free of it. "RELEASE ME!"

"I think not," Maximillian said, surveying the damage to the room. [Engage blast shields in Research Lab HL-TS-10833.] His request was answered as the room shook, the exterior blast coverings encasing the weakened glass-alloy along the back wall. "Now, I believe you were going to tell me about—"

"YOU KNOW NOT WHAT GA-mes you PLAY, VERUDT!" the dark lord exclaimed, its cybernetic voice mixing with that of the android. "AMRUK DUR, MARRLURSAI IMET TAU VES-na RO-uarl INDRAS-al SAEL VIRAGE!"

"The Virage?" Maximillian probed as he attempted to process the archaic words. "I'm sorry, but the nuances of vocalized Inun speech are lost on me. As for the rest, your words of power are useless from where you're being held, servant." With the utterance of the last word, the enclosure rippled. Several lightning bolts ripped from one end of the sphere to the other, electrocuting the small droid shell and causing the beast to roar in anguish.

"FONES IM-ard Ul-numati, fake MAN!" the possessor said as it thrashed within its prison.

[This is all we're going to get out of this session,] Maximillian surmised, a small grin cracking across his face. "Very well," he said, a hint of sadism in his otherwise flat voice. "I shall send you back to whence you came, servant." Lightning flashed once more as he uttered the last word, tearing and scorching the remains of the green-haired's body. [Reduce power, and collapse rift.]

On his final order, the receiver formed a geometry equal to a singular point, shrinking the encasing dimensional sphere. Screaming in anguish, the dark lord's host crumpled as it imploded under the pressure of the collapsing space. In a flash, the prison twisted as the interior matter began to fuse. Within seconds a sun-like burst of light exploded within the small universe, its emissions filtered through the harsh polarization of the dimensional shell. With a final eruption, the sphere collapsed to a head-sized ball before dissipating, leaving nothing but a large sphere of heavy metal in its death throes.

"Fuck me sideways," Casera said, stepping forward from her perch to Maximillian's left. "I've never seen anything like that."

"Like what, exactly?" Maximillian asked as he began his assessment of the room and Ientec Prime. All over the station, alarms triggered due to low power levels, followed by rampant communication outages and signals to send operatives to the lower station. "Liora, could you get the door while you're standing there gawking? We will have company shortly."

"Whatever, boss," Liora said with an empty voice.

"That . . . thing. What was it?" Casera asked as she approached the metal sphere.

"Stay away from it for now," he ordered. "We need to quarantine it and scan for any irregularities. It's hard to tell with these arcane beings if there's any residual trace. Especially those from the outer realms."

"I wish I knew what you were going on about," Casera said with a pout, stepping back to his side. "This is over my head."

"It's of no importance for now," he said, turning to face the door. "Besides, at least we gained some insight."

"Like what?" Casera asked as she eyed the droids making their way in.

"We know one of Omega-3043's identifiers."

"Ahhh, the Virage," Casera said, grinning with her sharp, catlike teeth.

"Very perceptive. We also have some frames of Omega-3043's movements," he said, shifting his eyes to the still-intact holographic display. Casera turned her head and watched as the scenery. The angle of view for the dark figure, now known as the Virage, changed with every frame. The last frame in the progression seemed to be the anomalous figure entering some dark arboreal region, given the coloration and tree-like patterns in the image. "Likewise, we know it's broadcasting now."

"That's something," Liora purred sarcastically as she ripped open the access panel for the emergency door controls. "And what about all that other garbage it was shouting?"

"The worm, in ancient Inun speak," he said, narrowing his eyes as he began a subset of personal queries. "Somehow, this Virage is tied to it."

"Well, I hope all of this was worth it," Casera said as she disassembled her rail rifle, preparing to stow it once more. "The board is going to be really displeased once they investigate."

"Nothing can be obtained without first giving up something in return," Maximillian replied as Liora pressed the door's release button. He wore a satisfied grin as the gateway opened just in time for a small contingent of white-haired soldier androids to reach the threshold. "And look, right on time."

"President Maximillian Verudt," the female android at the front of the contingent said, "you have been summoned for an emergency board meeting." She came to a stop, the male and female androids behind her pausing in time, their grey eyes scanning the room for potential threats. "They have asked that you come immediately and report on the cause of the power and the breach in HL-TS-10833."

"And so I shall," Maximillian said, grinning pleasantly. "As for you and your crew, please have this section of the station quarantined. Confiscate all android remains and materials, and have them destroyed. Use organic agents because there is a medium probability of synthetic contamination."

"What about the metal sphere, Max?" Liora said, gesturing her clawed hand toward GH-199076492's condensed remains.

"Have it taken to OM-TS-8784 for further analysis," he instructed, his subtle grin disappearing.

"Sir, we were told to escort you to the boardroom," the commander said.

"That will not be necessary. I shall report immediately, as requested," he replied while issuing an override command mentally. [You will perform the actions I have delegated to you. Do I make myself clear?]

"Yes, sir," the android replied, gritting her teeth, the imperative of his order overcoming her. "We will do as you command."

"Good," he said, bowing his head. He took several steps forward before turning to face his bodyguards. They stood at attention, their fierce green eyes locked on his, anticipating the order. "Casera and Liora, please report to the nearest medical bay for examination and decontamination." He smiled. "Just in case."

"Yes, sir!" the women replied, their wild blond manes bouncing as they saluted him.

"Also, tell your sister to report to the boardroom when she gets in," Maximillian said as he paused to cross-reference the databases for incoming flights.

"Roseva, sir?" Liora asked.

"Yes. I have a feeling that her report, along with our findings here, will be necessary to divert any unpleasantness during the hearing."

"Yes, sir," Casera said.

"Very good. Her ETA is thirty minutes. Now all of you, to your tasks," Maximillian commanded as he stepped through the lab's threshold.

Strolling down the hall, he cleared his mind of all extraneous processes. He knew his brothers and sisters would be beyond displeased with the impact of his most recent research and squandering of Foundation resources. Hence he needed to have all processes focused on constructing optimal arguments. Stepping into one of the central transport shuttles, amidst all the calculations and planning, he found the time to ruminate on one unpleasant thread that he had left hanging.

[I'm sorry you cannot report this yourself, GH-199076492,] he thought with a faint, undetectable grimace. He released the emotional thread that had driven his small act of vengeance against the intruder. [I'm sorry you had to be sacrificed.]

1

____

UNKNOWN

His mind was a blur, and his senses stunned. He was overwhelmed, repulsed by the memories that were bubbling up from deep within his subconscious. He knew he was no longer there amongst the ghoulish and lifeless, but he could not let go of those tormenting, tragic moments. He could still feel the heat of the flames and smell the odors of death. He was trapped within himself, and inside was a hell he wished never to have known, one he wanted to escape. He tried to focus, to break free of the temptation to relive the agony yet again. He struggled to open his eyes, but when he did, the flashback was inseparable from reality.

He sensed sunlight pouring in upon him, its gentle warmth dancing like fiery coals across his skin. The pain made him want to retreat into his dreadful sleep. Fighting through with dry, narrowed eyes, he could make out the room's general features. Wavering washes of color created unearthly auras among the sterile linens and the walls' earthy tones. The smells of the forest came to him, entwined with others: flowers, herbs, leaves, bark. But the strongest was that of decay, its pungent aroma assessed and embittered by his tumultuous brain.

Focusing on his other senses, he heard the murmuring of others somewhere nearby, too weak to pick up the nuances of their words. He heard laughter and faint sounds of the small things, the calm breaths and silent whispers of those somewhere close but unreachable. They were like double-edged blades, luring him back to a peaceful time that could not have been that long ago but was followed by dread and despair. They drew him on as he tried to obtain a firm grip on reality.

Then he felt it. Something warm but gentler than the harsh sun gripped him by the hand. Soft skin stroked him, playing across his fingertips. Something about the sensation was calm and familiar.

Before he could clear his thoughts, his senses let go again. His heart started to race, pounding throughout his body until it was audible. For a second his mind drifted, as if trying to halt the onset of whatever was to come. His heart felt as if it were about to burst, and somewhere in the back of his mind was a strange, frightening sense of release.

With all his conscious effort, he struggled to keep a grip on the present. He tried to force his heart rate down but could not stop it from climbing. His arms and hands twisted and contorted of their own accord. With what little strength remained, he held the writhing limbs to his sides. While his body was trying to die, something was forcing it to stay alive.

Through it all the warmth on his hand stayed, becoming a firm grasp as a frantic voice called from beside him. Other voices replied. He felt the thuds of several feet upon the ground, growing closer. As they drew near, his body stopped convulsing and began to shake. A bitter chill and waves of pain rippled through him, reaching out from his chest and through his extremities. He heard several people circling around him, some shouting as others cursed under their breath.

With a firm grip, the one next to him drew close beside his contorted face. The person's voice was soft but stern, gentle but commanding. He tried to lie still and understand the figure's words. He turned his head to focus on the person next to him, but something warm pressed against his forehead, caressing and immobilizing him. He felt the figure come closer, his or her warm breath upon his neck.

"Ge rolm ne vahr," the person whispered in a soft, soothing voice.

The words were ancient, calling to a time long ago that he could not quite place. With those simple words, a calming sensation rippled across his body as they echoed through his embattled mind. With all notion of desperation fleeting, he lost his grip on the moment and allowed himself to fall back into the abyss of his dreams.

"Ge rolm ne vahr . . ."

"Ge rolm ne vahr . . ."

Something was holding his hands somewhere in front of and above him. It was as if they were dancing, and he was being led. The light and colors were intense, making it hard for him to concentrate. His legs wobbled, further disorienting him.

"Ge rolm ne vahr!" a voice called out, drawing his attention to the speaker, his eyes transfixed by the gaze of another. He lost himself in the other's eyes, pools of bright lavender staring back at him. Surrounded by what seemed to be a halo of gold, the figure beckoned him. He concentrated, forcing his legs to stop their violent shaking.

"Ge rolm ne vahr," the voice said, deep, feminine, and filled with childlike zeal. At its call, he took a step forward, followed by another and another. "Naisure Deldaron!" the voice exclaimed. Full of excitement, the other's hands shivered, unbalancing him. He clenched his tiny bones around the other's larger fingers. With renewed focus, they held his even tighter. Suddenly, he realized the ratio of the other's hands to his, forcing his mind to break away from the scene.

[What is this?] he asked, his words echoing within pools of thought. Detached from his form, he tried to bring the scene into focus. He stared, attempting to clarify the face of the person who held his small hands. He moved closer, his legs still wobbling but consistent, approaching the source of the wondrous voice.

All around him, the echo of other voices filled the space between his thoughts and the stage. "Serra ne nark," a robust, comforting voice said, followed by a joyous outburst.

"She's always been a wonder," another voice answered. Somewhere deep down, he knew them. But try as he might, he could not recall to whom they belonged. Cheers and praise were followed by his happy burbling.

In front of him, the other's voice giggled with radiant glee. His body tried to carry him another step farther but caved under its own weight. His vision fell as his legs gave way. With a gentle grace, warm, bronze arms surrounded him, pulling him close. As they drew him up, he slipped away again, the echoes and what little color in the room warping as reality and time bent.

"Ge rolm ne vahr," the voice whispered.

"Ge rolm ne vahr!" the voice called again as he stood in the middle of a dusty town square. A girl held his hand, pulling him forward. "Hurry up, or we'll never make it!"

"OK, OK," he heard himself say in the voice of a small boy.

He looked up at the girl, her golden hair bobbing as she dragged him forward. Her vivacious lavender eyes were transfixed and purposeful as they traveled through the busy streets. He couldn't help but feel bashful as he glanced over her fine features. She had always been older, but the supple curves that had become present on her body only served to reinforce how many years lay between them. The top of his head just reached her chest, her long legs and more mature body pulling with twice the force that he could muster.

Her tugging walk turned into a dragging sprint as he tried to match her pace. They dodged between people, running in and out of small crowds and sprinting toward the edge of town. As they found more spacious places, the girl picked up speed, running faster. He was tired and unable to keep up. He tried his best, but the most he could do was a few skips and jumps, taking every opportunity not to fall.

"I can't . . . keep up," he said, panting. He almost stumbled when she came to an abrupt stop, forcing him to lean against her to brace himself.

"Well, we're almost there," she said, looking down at him. "We can take it a little easier now if you want." She smiled at him with her bright lavender eyes. He leaned against her, his hand still in hers, trying to catch his breath. He felt tired, but he didn't want her to know that. He grinned up at her, still feeling the redness in his face.

"We can keep going," he said with swelling pride. "I can run all the way! I could even do it by myself!" The girl laughed. She looked down, folding her arms over him, a soft, almost motherly smile on her face. She had gentle eyes, but they seemed to stare through him.

"Well, alright then," she said coyly. "If you're so eager to impress."

"I . . . I never said," he stuttered, his face becoming redder with embarrassment and boyish pride.

"You better keep up then," she said, unfolding her arms. She held his hand until she turned. Letting go, she sprang off. He stood there as she sprinted away. Before he realized it, she was several paces ahead.

"Ge rolm ne vahr!" she shouted back to him. Drawn by her words, his legs began pumping. He sprinted after her, trying to catch up. As he ran, his stomach churned from exertion. All around him, the colors of the grass and trees began to swirl. In a moment of extreme vertigo, the procession lurched forward. All at once he found himself at the edge of a large pond, surrounded by trees and mossy stones. He panted, feeling dizzy from running so hard.

"Hey, you!" the girl shouted from behind him. He was about to turn when she reached her hands around his face, covering his eyes.

"Hey!" he shouted, surprised and dazed.

"I was wondering when you'd finally get here," she said, giggling behind him. She closed the gap between them, pulling him close. He was about to struggle when he felt how warm her body was. With his head against her chest, he felt her breathing. Overcome with shyness, he stood perfectly still.

"So, you got to see it already, huh?" she said, keeping his eyes covered. "This is where I used to take my sister to swim before . . ."

"Before she died?" he asked, knowing the answer before he had even formed the question.

[Before she died,] his internal voice replied, echoing his young self and sending a faint ripple through the dream.

"Yeah," she said, her voice trembling. She dropped her hands and pulled him closer, wrapping her arms around him. "That's OK though, because now I have you!"

Her gaze fell onto him, and he raised his eyes to look at her. Her lavender eyes were full of a gentle fondness. She smiled warmly, looking at him with joy and overt affection. There was something both of awe and more in the way she stared into him.

"So, you ready?" she asked, giving him a once-over. "Doesn't look like you're ready to swim to me."

"I've never swum," he replied.

"Well, there's only one way to do it," she said, stepping from behind him and approaching the water's edge. His eyes widened as she walked in front of him, her body bare. Somewhere inside he remembered her from before, but that had been some time ago. He had never seen her like this. Never seen her so . . . changed, as the grown-ups might say. His face flushed.

"Y-you're . . ." he said, stuttering as he tried to form the words. He was too busy staring, his eyes fixated on her every feature.

"You silly boy," she said, laughing. "You're never going to make it if you stand there with your eyes wide and mouth gaping. Hurry up and get undressed!"

"B . . . but . . ."

"Alright, I'm going in without you," she said, stepping up to the water's edge. Without hesitation, she slid into the water. He stood there, still in awe, her image etched into his mind.

[Why am I seeing this?] he wondered as he wrenched free of the vision. The girl giggled as she swam, looking toward the shore and taunting him as she trod water. It was tempting to let himself slip back into the act.

"Alright, I'm coming!" he said. He struggled out of his clothes, falling over twice as he tried to take them off. Each time prompted a burst of laughter from the girl in the water.

"You better hurry," she teased him. "I'll be done, and you'll have just gotten started!"

He felt a kind, genial peace about everything he was seeing. He wanted to rejoin himself with the boy, allow himself to be one with the simple pleasures of a warm summer's day.

He rushed to the water, slipping on a wet patch of grass. He tumbled to the ground, rolled down the small slope, launched off the mossy ledge, and plummeted into the pond. The girl uttered a shocked cry as his little wave splashed her. She called him to her, but he was starting to sink. He felt his consciousness giving way as the girl fetched him, his vision blurring as reality began to crumble. He watched with terrified detachment as the girl pulled him above water.

"Ge rolm ne vahr," the girl said as she drew him close to her, but all around him the scene was darkening, and from somewhere below, he heard shrieks echoing from the abyss.

[No. Not this again. Not again. I'll stay. I'll come to you. Just let me stay!] His cries reverberated within the closing darkness as he called to the boy and girl within. With frantic abandon, he tried to hang on but was lost in a whirlwind of uncontrollable thoughts as he fell from the dream. He heard the girl's laughter mixing with his boyish giggles. The voices blended in a disturbing unison with the screams of the abyss, darkening as he continued his descent.

[Please, no! Please . . .] Despite his pleading, he landed on the ground. His eyes were shuttered, his descent complete. He felt the brisk air of an arid summer morning upon his skin. Behind him, he heard the drowsy murmurs of someone dear, dread penetrating every part of his being.

Opening his eyes, he found himself standing once more at the precipice of his never-ending hell.

2

———

ELIS

"He's still shaking!" Elis cried as a slender, agile woman rushed to her side holding a small phial.

"Try to give him this, ne vindal," the woman said, handing her the bottle. "Force it down if you must. The rest of you, make sure he doesn't slip off the table." As the others around her tried to hold down the shaking man, she drew close to him. She caressed his fingers and brought her mouth to his ear. He jerked. She placed her other hand, bottle and all, against his forehead.

"Ge rolm ne vahr," she whispered familiar words that she had not spoken in ages. She tightened her grip on his hand, begging him to come to her. As she spoke the phrase, his tremors became less violent. Seizing the opportunity, she popped the bottle open with her thumb and brought it to his lips. She prayed as she watched him tremble beneath her.

At first he rejected it, his weathered face puckering in an expression of fear and pain. Yet like a knowing child, his dry lips parted. He took the potion from her, drinking its greenish contents with slow, steady gulps. She waited, her desperate eyes watching as his body trembled, his chest rising and falling between every gulp. She handed the empty bottle to one of the struggling bystanders and then returned her shaking hand to his forehead. For several moments the room was filled with bated breaths and anticipation as everyone watched the man struggle.

She brought her hand down to his face and held him there, keeping a firm grip on him. She calmed her breathing as she brought his trembling hand to her chest. Thinking soothing thoughts, she caressed his hand. Finally, the man's breath settled, and his tremors subsided.

All around her, the others let out deep sighs of relief. Without any need for further alarm, they pulled away from the man. She looked up and watch the dark, slender woman as she motioned the others out of the room, keeping them hushed as they all filed out. As the last of the aides left, Elis took a deep breath. Leaning back, she exhaled, exhausted by the short encounter.

"I don't know what I would have done if you weren't here," she said, raising her eyes to the other woman. "Your expertise and concoctions always seem to ease him.

Closing the door, the other woman strutted across the room with a cavalier air of mystique. The few rays of light that penetrated the room glistened across her dark skin. Like a red-breasted bird, her dark, crimson corsetry and plume-like garters exaggerated every detail of her robust frame. Fluttering as she moved, a matching shawl dangled around her shoulders while her skirt, with a slit up the front and back, whipped around her legs. Her ensemble left little to the imagination, exactly as she preferred. Her straight black hair hung just above her shoulders, her red-brown eyes flickering.

There was something primal about the way the woman presented herself. Yet every action she performed betrayed a predatory mindset that was distinctly human. Every time Elis saw her like this, strutting and on display, she couldn't help but reconcile those facts by taking in the sight of her proud talvuo lineage. It protruded like the long, floppy ears of a large canine, which adorned the dark woman's head. Thin folds of extra skin dangled, covering the interior of the strange auditory organs. Lighter than her mane, short, ashen hair, more like the fur of a feline, covered the exterior skin of the weird ears. Emphasizing the heights of the woman's predacious nature, thirty black metal rings and one iron ring adorned her right ear while a single gold ring hung on her left.

Placing her dark, slender hands upon Elis's shoulders, the woman leaned over her. She nuzzled her ears, her many metal rings jingling.

"Think nothing of it," the woman said in a cold, deep, feminine voice. "Anything for you, vindal Elis."

"Yes, vindal Neris," Elis replied, the words rolling off her tongue. At first it had been strange to call an outsider her sister, but ever since they began coupling, it had become more natural and intimate to do so. But the words still felt strange, given the array of circumstances. "I'm glad you were here."

"My heart, ne vindal. Anything for you, and doubly, anything for the Virage," Neris whispered.

Thoughts of the mysterious and infamous Virage sent shivers down Elis's spine. Even in the best of times, she did not want to hear the darker stories of the outside world. Stories of mad sorceresses and ghostly armies. Intrigues of bloodthirsty warlords and tyrannical despots. Tales of demons that frolicked on moonless nights, children being spirited away in the darkness, or monstrous orgies of the profane. All of them had reached her ears one way or another, but none of them were as terrible as those that spoke of the demon-clawed man they called the Virage.

Rapes and beheadings were kind mentions when referring to the dreaded figure. The slaughter and purging of whole towns and villages was yet another common topic. Unlike the political and mythical terrors whispered about the world, none compared to the scourge whose very presence was considered a desecration upon earth, body, and mind. Wherever he went, the land and its people would die. No magic or weapon could stay the encroaching end of all things that followed in his wake. No prayers could stay death's hand, and for those who felt the reaper's icy embrace, the final moments were horrific and torturous. The few who survived their encounters were driven mad beyond all reasoning, so the stories went, spared death only to be sacrificed to chaos.

But there he was in front of her, evidence of the grotesque mystery and villainous stories. Lying on the table with a twisted and monstrous black left hand was none other than that self-same terror, clinging to life by a single thread, sprawled in a dreadful sleep. But the cruel mistresses of fate had an even stranger irony to deal out. Somewhere long ago and far from her current dwelling, Elis had known and cherished a man whose face the dozing monster wore. Coupled with the complications of the present, the incident left her feeling confused, conflicted, and terrified.

"You seem distressed, ne vindal," Neris said, drawing away from her. "You look as if you could use some personal attention. Perhaps we should retire early tonight?"

"Perhaps," Elis said, grinning bitterly. "Though I don't know if my heart is in it."

"Oh, but I don't need your heart, my dear, just your presence," Neris said, lowering her voice and wearing a sultry grin on her dark lips. With a hint of the erotic, the woman drew her slender hands forward, caressing Elis's cheek. Looking up at Neris, Elis's eyes locked on the dark-skinned talvuo's hungry red orbs.

Elis's heart raced for a moment, a flutter of interest stirring within. But before she even had time to think or react, swelling guilt and resentment bubbled up. All at once the thought made her feel disgusting and dirty. It wasn't the other woman who brought on such feelings. After all, only two fortnights earlier, the pair had begun spending nights together, one round of debauchery following the next. But right now, so soon after recent events and with her oscillating moods, she was completely put off. Her whole being felt wrong. Confusion and all-too-familiar emotions overwhelmed her normal rhythms. Even though she would have normally leapt at such an offer, she was unable to pursue it.

"With all my heart, yes," Elis said, leaving her vigil over the sleeping man, "but with all my being, no. I'm sorry, ne vindal, but I think I'll be retiring to my own quarters for now. That is, if you don't mind watching over him."

"Not at all, my dear," Neris replied. "Sometimes, even I need to be alone. Though if you change your mind, my offer still stands."

Feeling ashamed, Elis shot her a dispassionate glance, getting only Neris's composed complexion in response. She hurried over to the door, trying to focus on her goal.

"And Elis?" Neris's said.

"Yes?" Elis replied, opening the door.

"If you need comfort without the other formalities, know that my offer extends there as well," Neris's words flowed with a hint of sincerity. The same sincerity Elis knew only in the confines of their own private world.

"I know, Neris. Thank you," Elis said, closing the door behind her.

3

NERIS

Wearing a bitter grin, Neris pondered her predicament. On the one hand, she had been reunited with the man responsible for guiding her on a path of self-fulfillment and stealing her heart. On the other was a woman whose nature and passions rivaled her own while at the same time offering her a new perspective on her black-clawed paramour. On top of it all, her brother stood with his fevered machinations, spurned onwards by delusions of grandeur and visions of a magical adviser. The people of the village, including their elders, had humored all of this. Yet it only served to entwine and complicate matters between Neris, Elis, and their dozing third wheel.

Still staring at the door, Neris settled herself on the table, taking extra care not to disturb the man who slumbered on its padded surface. She turned her gaze from the door to the sleeper, letting out a short sigh. Everywhere in his wake, he seemed to drag around an impending sense of change in a dreamlike glamor. Her heart skipped as she walked her right hand up the table and let it rest on his left appendage, her fingers dancing on the mottled black skin of what most would describe as a claw. To many, it was his most striking feature and one to be feared.

But she had never been afraid of him and had never thought it was what stood out most.

"You're like barbs to the heart, you know that?" Neris cooed, compassion showing in her red-brown eyes, her smile softening. "The least you could do is wake up for me. Let me see those beautiful eyes of yours." She knew better than to get ahead of herself with longing, but it was hard with him so close by. Given his withered condition upon being found, she was not surprised that he had not recovered yet. His features reminded her of the bodies found around the bazaars of the far Aluran dunes, skin weathered into leather by the dryness of the sands and the blistering heat. But she knew that would have little effect on the Virage. Despite how quickly he was recovering, she could not bear the wait. Even more, spending time looking after him with Elis had made matters more complex as the two of them looked onward with unknowing hearts. Suffering from the same muddling she could accuse Elis of bearing, Neris reflected on her situation as she closed her hand around his claw.

Neris had spent the better part of the previous month with the older talvuo woman. Elis was over thrice her age, hailing from a people who had perfected their bodies. Despite that, she had found that the Hyunisti 's hermit was also an outsider and shared much in common. From their shared stories of tragedy and harsh times to their intrigues and pleasures, they were extremely compatible. Seducing her was a feat greater than it had been with any of the village's pale-skinned, hazel-haired common folk. In the end, perhaps they had charmed each other, though Neris liked to think it was her who had been instrumental in their pairing.

But in all her scheming and mischief, she had never suspected that one of their late-night forays would merge around a singular event. Elis had taken many lovers in her long years, but only two had ever given her heart pause. Neris could boast a bigger number, but only one had tugged at her heartstrings. A young man and a grown man, one kind and genial, the other dark and commanding. Both dirty blondes, both with eyes that were icy blue yet separated by a gap that was all but impossible. The face Elis had worn when she saw their recovering patient, the restless nights she had spent, and the quiet, confused words she whispered when she thought no one else was listening all pointed to a confounding conclusion, which gave even Neris second thoughts. Then again, what was impossible for others was possible for him. If only that impossibility hadn't been a painful splinter in her most recent relationship, everything would have been perfect.

Still, she couldn't imagine the strangeness that had overtaken her newest paramour at discovering the Virage's identity. Much less could she find grounds to empathize with Elis. No history or impossibility clouded her judgment. Furthermore, the impending consequences were both exciting and enticing.

"You know, she's waiting for you to awaken as well," Neris said, continuing her monologue as she raised her other hand to caress his leg. She grinned as her black fingers danced over his white skin. "She has no idea what to do with herself, and you're just letting her dwell while you slumber. It's bad form to make such a brilliant woman wait, don't you think? I can only do so much to ease a torn heart, my dear."

Neris knew he couldn't hear her, given his state. If the medicine had its intended effect, he would be in a deep slumber that only a different concoction could wake him from. Even then she knew there was very little that could have any real effect on his internal biology. Disease and poison could induce the worst of their symptoms in him, but before long his body would heal and become immune. Medicine and benign concoctions would have their desired effects but in the end only served to quicken his recovery. As such, Neris had administered several of her potions over the past few days, knowing the intended effect was to placate Elis and her own frazzled nerves. She knew he would awaken as soon as his body had finished mending itself, and when he did, she would be waiting.

She brought his hand to her lips, taking the tip of a clawed finger in her mouth and caressing it with her lips and tongue. Then she lowered it to her lap, a shiver of anticipation running down her frame as the black mass twitched ever so slightly in her hands. She would need to get things ready for the evening if she was to continue her vigil and pursue other impish delights. Likewise, she had to be prepared just in case her brother attempted to do anything drastic.

With a deep sigh, Neris rose from the table and resumed her preparations.

4

———

ELIS

Taking a deep breath, Elis reached toward the bright blue sky as she bathed in high-noon light. She couldn't stand being cramped within the dark, sterile rooms of the old healer's quarters. Despite her fondness for its most recent tenants, she couldn't stand the smell of the strange herbs and concoctions that Neris kept within. She also disliked the omnipresent feeling of being watched and judged as she prepared and waited to hold back their ward's chills and fevers, which came and went like clockwork. She had little doubt that the Hyunisti were both curious and suspicious of their new guest. However, despite the dread tidings, they had taken him in without second thoughts.

That had always been the Hyunisti way. Elis recalled how they had embraced Neris and Nerin when they arrived. Only six months prior, the odd pair of Delvori talvuo had appeared in the eastern forest, the brother guided by visions from a higher power. When they were brought before the council of elders, the dark-skinned Nerin had boasted of ancient rites known but lost to the village. He talked of the proud history of the Hyunisti and how his people shared a similarly lustrous past. With careful words, he had weaved the tale of the Delvori dynasties of old, the expanse of their tunnel empire, their riches, their harems, and their culture. And in a powerful play, he had connected it to the Hyunisti's own lost heritage, retelling stories that only Elis was still familiar with. The whole display disgusted her, knowing well the words of a practiced charlatan. Then again, even if he hadn't piqued their imagination, she knew they couldn't pass up the opportunity for new blood. After all, their blood had just started to regain its hue.

"Zaisure!" a young girl called from off in the distance. Elis turned her gaze toward the end of one of the long rope bridges that connected the great trees and the village's canopy buildings. Running between busy villagers was a small hazel-headed girl. Her gait was messy and clumsy for a child of her age. To Elis, the sight was endearing. Dismissing her dismal thoughts, she smiled in amusement. Within moments the small, energetic bundle reached her terrace, whirling without a care and wrapping her small, pale arms around Elis's waist.

"I see you're out and about, my dear little Rais," Elis said, bringing her hands down around the girl's shoulders. Rais buried her head in Elis's stomach, giggling as she danced at Elis's feet. "Couldn't wait for me any longer?"

"It was lonely, zaisure," the green-eyed girl said, not a hint of sadness tinging her high-pitched voice. "I tried to work on my dyes and paints, but it's no fun without you."

"You didn't sleep well then?" Elis asked, drawing the girl beside her. There was no point in standing on the veranda now that she had been joined by her young dependent. Now was as good a time as any to take a short walk before returning to tidy up whatever chaos had ensued in her absence. Gripping her by the hand, Rais looked up at Elis.

"I slept OK," Rais said as they walked through the village. "I tucked myself in with your quilt just like you always do. It was nice."

"Well, I'm glad the night went well." Rais had a fear of the dark unlike any child that Elis had known. Being born in the dead of night to a dying mother, the girl had struggled to survive the first few days of her short life within a dead woman's arms. As the story went, fearing the

Hyunisti's ancient curse would take her baby, the woman had fled into the woods as the pains of labor set in. It had taken two days for the village scouts to find the newborn, but ever since then, Rais had had a preternatural fear of being alone in the dark. Most nights the girl required a warm body to sleep next to or a long, burning candle if she was left by herself. Even then she often had terrible dreams of being alone, crying out late at night. Of late, she had been sleeping better, but Elis had been concerned about leaving her even for one night. "So then, my dear, what have you been up to? You don't tend to roam about the trees."

"Thaimi came to see you about painting her face," the little girl said as they crossed a wooden arch that led into the canopy's main thoroughfare. "She was so excited! She talked a lot about being invited to naisure Nerin's."

Elis's grin narrowed at the thought of another woman being seduced by that imposter. Sleeping in a stranger's bed was not uncommon for a talvuo. Still, she couldn't fathom why anyone with sense could be lured in by such obvious trickery. Not that the Hyunisti had the sense others of their kind possessed, having been robbed of their long lives by ancient witchery. Sometimes she wished she had stayed more involved in the village's affairs, if only to spare them some of the scars that came with such naiveté.

"She asked me if I wanted to come with her," Rais continued, prancing on her tiptoes as they strolled.

"And you did?"

"Uh-huh. I got to see inside the big tree!" Rais exclaimed, gesturing to the sky as if to mimic the tall boughs of the grand structure.

"So, what did you think?"

"There were so many large rooms. The part that meets with the big bridge is gigantic. It's bigger than our whole house!"

"Really now?" Elis probed, having seen the interior herself on at least a dozen occasions of late and even more in years past. The room served as a large foyer for the village's inhabitants. It connected the grand tree's higher floors with a long, spiraling path around the hollow interior, which opened to the ground far below. There was a time when it was a gathering place for everyone to console and make merry, but those days had long since passed.

"Then there were zaisure Neris's chambers, but her door was closed, and I was told I couldn't go in. But it takes up a whole space above the hall. And there's even a bridge that goes to the healer's quarters just outside her door."

"And then?" Elis asked, still fixated on how Thaimi had been duped by the Delvori usurper. Nerin had used his growing clout to entice the villagers into clearing the old ancestral tree of its previous inhabitant's belongings. Before the renovations, the place had been a solemn landmark to the founder of the small talvuo enclave. But in only a few weeks, everything that had remained of the old was either discarded or divvied by the inhabitants of the village, the few rare oddities staying in Nerin Delvori's possession.

"There were lots of small side rooms, and then there was their dining room. They have so many candles and lanterns inside, and the table is carved right into the tree. And then . . ."

Taking a detour, Elis led her small companion around a large gathering of pale-skinned gossipers. Even as they crossed a narrow rope bridge, Elis felt the prying eyes of the small cohort following her every move. After so many changes, occurrences, and her own apparent emerging from a hermit's solitude, many in the village couldn't help but talk of portents and intrigue. Nerin and his sister were always at the heart of such gossip, but after having intertwined her affairs with Nerin's dark, sultry sister, Elis's name often bubbled up as well. And, of course, there was the drowsing man, but that was another topic.

Taking the long way around the outside of the village center, Elis listened as Rais rambled from topic to topic, replying every now and then with casual acknowledgment. Fancy wooden furniture, silver ornaments and dining implements, glass orbs, and crystal lanterns, not a single detail eluded her young companion.

"Zaisure Elis." Caught unaware, Elis half stumbled over an elderly talvuo woman approaching her. Two other older talvuo were following the elderly woman, each of them staring up at Elis with their pale-green eyes.

"Oh dear, pray forgive me," Elis apologized, feeling Rais huddle behind her.

"Don't apologize, zaisure. We merely came to pay our respects. We do not often have the time or opportunity to talk with our long-lived matron," the elderly woman said, bowing her greying hazel-crowned head. The woman beside her also nodded, as did the older man who accompanied them. "Seeing you out in the village has raised our spirits, and we want to show you our gratitude."

"There's no need," Elis said, her face flushing. It was true that she kept to herself and only of late had been entering the village proper. In fact, sometimes months went by in which she avoided the center, on occasion running into hunters during her forest forays. Things had not always been that way, but with few reasons far between to enter the talvuo hub, she had little cause to visit the forest people. "I should be apologizing. I have been out of touch with the village of late and am sorry to be so distant."

"We do not mind, zaisure," the older man said, shooting her a gracious smile. "We are always grateful to have the one our dear ancestor kept close and shared her story with near. It is sad that the current council does not call on you more often, zaisure Elis."

"The Hyunisti have become independent enough that they no longer need my guidance, naisure. Lady Hyun would be proud of all of you." Elis sounded pleasant and jovial as she spoke, though the topic weighed on her heart. The woman who was the current namesake of the forest talvuo had tried her best to serve her people. Having been denied the virility that a talvuo should have, she had entrusted her wishes to Elis. Elis had tried to keep true to those wishes, but she couldn't manage the politics and constant churn of life within the village. Likewise, fewer and fewer people could remember the older stories of their people. Though Elis knew most of them, they had become more myth than history for the short-lived Hyunisti.

"I hope someday you will take up a place on the village council, zaisure. We would all love to hear your stories again," the other elderly woman said. Something about her grin broke Elis's heart as she wondered if the woman had been one of the children who once listened to her tales. If she was, then it was beyond cruel that fate would make her age so much faster than Elis, who still had the body and mind of a talvuo who had just entered her prime.

"I shall consider it," Elis said, faking a wide grin. The small contingent of talvuo took turns giving her a short bow before departing. Elis waited with Rais as they strolled away, trying to hold back her exasperation. Once the trio was behind some branches out of view, Elis returned to her path. She hoped there would be no other well-wishers or gossipers as they made their way home.

"I'm sorry we were interrupted, my dear," Elis said to Rais as they continued along the village's causeways.

"It's OK, zaisure," Rais said.

"So, did you end up going all the way to the top of the tree? Did you get to see the top terrace?"

"Oh no, we just stayed in naisure Nerin's room for a while." Rais's voice perked up again as she started talking about entering the abode of the man whom Elis most reviled in the village. Like a vulture catching scent of carrion, Elis's ears picked up on the slightest shift in the little girl's voice as her otherwise extreme happiness was downplayed by tones of shyness. The hairs on the back of her neck stiffened, her maternal instincts overcoming her typical sense of self.

"What did you end up doing?" Elis asked. Taking them off the well-traveled paths of the village proper, Elis found a shaded spot to sit with her follower. Leaning back against the trunk of a large tree, she motioned for the little one to sit beside her. Rais followed her instruction, taking a spot upon a nearby workman's crate. Beneath the tree's low branches, few would see or hear them. Furthermore, despite the foliage, the vantage point was one of the better ones in the treetops, giving them a view of the forest floor and a vast swathe of the giant woodland.

"We ate a late breakfast," Rais began, the unusual shyness clinging to her words. "Then Thaimi and naisure Nerin began to drink a large bottle of wine. I've never seen such a big bottle, zaisure!"

"I don't doubt that." Water, fresh or honeyed, and forest mead were standard drinks for the Hyunisti. Wine was a rarity that had just been reintroduced. Travelers had begun to overcome their fear of the dreaded Lorinian Witchwood, a name that outsiders often attributed to the shadowy forest. Hyun's Vale was far enough off the beaten path as to be impossible for the average merchant or highway traveler to reach without a guide. Many of the finer baubles acquired by the village were smuggled in by Grannas traders to the south. However, new caravans had appeared that would stake a place in the northern bend, waiting for the mysterious forest folk who would come to trade and gossip.

"Did you have any?" Elis asked.

"Thaimi gave me a small cup," Rais said, rocking on the small wooden box.

"And?"

"I didn't really like it," she replied, puckering her face.

"Too sour?" Elis cracked a wide grin as she gazed out over the sea of verdant, emerald leaves.

"And bitter!" Rais shrieked, forcing a laugh out of Elis. The little girl's enthusiasm for everything she enjoyed was unimaginable. She expressed her dislikes with an equal level of energy. "I don't know why everyone likes it so much, but Thaimi was really happy after drinking a lot."

"It takes some getting used to," Elis said, imagining how much the Hyunisti maiden must have drunk. It wouldn't take much for the skinny, non-indulgent woman to be overcome by even the weakest swill. "Did Thaimi start acting out?"

"Well, Thaimi was acting very silly. Naisure Nerin asked her if she wanted to rest with him. I was going to go, but naisure asked me if I wanted to stay and eat some more, and I really wanted to. So I did." Evasiveness was not something Elis was used to when it came to her young one, but every word she spoke carried the signature of being coy.

"So, he put Thaimi to bed then?"

"They got into bed, but they didn't go to sleep for a while. Naisure told me to eat up and be good," the little girl said. Her bright demeanor diminished as she looked at the ground. Elis could very well imagine what came next. After all, getting a young, willing woman drunk was a near guarantee of reciprocation for someone like him. But the very idea that Rais had been present for one of that man's conquests made Elis's blood boil.

"Anything else, my dear?" she asked, biting her tongue lest something vile or impudent slip out.

"Thaimi fell asleep after a bit, and I ate all the food. Then naisure Nerin asked me how I was, and I told him I was OK," Rais said, her pale, tiny face taking on a rosy hue. "He said I was a pretty, good little girl and that he liked having me over."

"Well, I'm glad he didn't feel put out," Elis said, standing upright.

"He said I could come again whenever I want!" Rais exclaimed, turning her bright green eyes up to Elis. "He said I could help with their ceremony too."

"Did he now?" she replied, her voice falling flat. She had heard more than enough, feeling an overwhelming need to seclude herself. She reached her hand out to her young companion. "Come. Let's head home."

"OK, zaisure," the little girl said, standing. With the same sheepishness that had overridden her voice, Rais cupped her hand. Starting around the outskirts of the canopy, Elis picked up her pace as she strode toward their small home. Her back straightened as they walked, her chest tightening as diabolic whispers filled her head. Her lavender eyes were dagger-like as she shot one cold gaze after the next at the few talvuo along her path. Keeping her temper in check was a feat she was not used to. "Zaisure. Zaisure, my hand. Zaisure."

"Your hand?" Elis hadn't even noticed how tight her grip had gotten on her dependent's small hand, dragging the little girl as she struggled to keep up with Elis's long stride. Overcome with guilt, she loosened her grip and slowed her pace. Without a word, the girl took her place next to Elis, keeping a loose hold on her fingers. Taking a deep breath, Elis let out a sigh as the duo continued across the bridge, reaching the second-to-last terrace between them and their dwelling. "I'm sorry, my dear."

"It's OK, zaisure," Rais said, her little fingers stretching and clenching in Elis's hand. "Zaisure, you're not angry with me, are you?" she asked as they crossed the terrace onto the last bridge.

"Oh, my dear, of course not," Elis said, her voice filling with remorse. She had let her emotions overwhelm her at the expense of her little one. Anything the little hazel-headed talvuo had witnessed was sure to be troublesome given the Delvori's harsh, overbearing nature. But Elis would need to wait till later to confront and draw lines with Nerin. She didn't care if he had his way with every woman in the village, but such gestures directed at her ward was trespassing upon sacred ground. Such transgressions would not be taken lightly. Caressing Rais's thin fingers, Elis smiled at her companion, "You're fine, my dear Rais."

"OK, zaisure," the little girl replied, wrapping her arms around Elis. In turn, Elis patted the little girl's brown mane as they reached the door of their shared home. Without a word, they entered their treehouse dwelling along the outskirts of the village, the sun shifting from its perch to begin its long descent.

5

NERIN

Lounging on his old, downy mattress, Nerin Delvori sat with his back pressed against the hard wooden interior of the Emri great tree that served as his current abode. Beside him slept a young pale-skinned woman, plain-faced, as all the village women were, her dim hazel eyes closed. While it was amusing to please himself with the timid, little fawns of the fallen people who called themselves Hyunisti, the ordeal left him feeling drained. Such ordinary attentions were beneath him, and yet he needed these dimwitted plebes to succeed in the final steps of his grand scheme. Still, he had to admit that the attention was gratifying, though he wished a certain woman could understand his goals and wishes.

Nerin's mind was full of bitterness as he pined over the one dear to his heart. Though his father had been vile, full of hatred, spite, and wanting, the old man had been right about one thing: greatness lay in pure blood. The Delvori royalty had kept their line clean for generations, marrying only other lords and mistresses in the hope of maintaining their strength and virility. However, within their ranks were those who betrayed such a noble goal, one such woman causing the downfall of their great civilization. He found it hard to believe it was his mother who had forsook them all. But with his sister so much like the storied woman in her flippancy and disobedience, there was little he could do to dispute the dead man's words. But he knew his sister could be saved from herself and that she would come to her senses once all other distractions were purged. Neris would recognize her place beside him. Time would be certain of that, as it always was.

A light breeze crossed the large, round room, prickling his skin as he stood to shake off the morning's fatigue. The air in the room was pleasant compared to the other smaller trees and hovels that made up much of the canopy town. The windows of the top-most room of the great tree opened far above any others in the forest. They were separated from the dust and smells of the undergrowth that clung to the wood dwellers. Likewise, his demesne was far away from prying eyes, allowing him to meet and engage with whomever he wished without fear of the gossipier talvuo spying him. Unlike his sister's propensity for exhibitionism, he wanted absolute privacy for his guests and his personal affairs.

Standing before one of the grand carved windows, Nerin ran his hands over his toned physique. His skin outlined his ample musculature, his fingers sliding over the smooth, perfect surface, sending chills up his spine. He couldn't help but feel empowered as he looked out over the forest while thinking of the thin, undefined men who made up most of the forest folk. He walked over to an old, ornate serving cabinet. He pulled his dark hair back. Fingering the knots and curves of the etched wooden surface, he pushed aside a large, empty wine bottle and several varnished wood trays. Drawing forth a simple cup to pour himself some refreshment, he mused over his recent successes and acquisitions.

When they had cleared the abandoned dwelling, he had inspected everything they had tossed. He had hoped some rare or obscure Emri artifact would fall into his hands. Few in the village had a recollection of those that last dwelled within the large living structure, much less the significance of their ancestors. However, nothing noteworthy remained, save for some ornate examples of their craftsmanship and a few nicer baubles and trinkets. There were journals and other documents written by the woman that had become the new namesake for the forest folk. They were full of nothing but trivialities and personal turmoil.

He would be lying if he said he took no pleasure in reading the trite manuscripts. In particular, he had taken an interest in her earliest memoirs, finding evidence of the greatness of the original people before she had destroyed their identity and vitality. In her writings, she lamented having acted in anger and desperation, using ancient powers to drive the newly risen kingdom and its harriers in the south from their forests. She had thought to protect her people from further hostilities, and they had trusted her every word. Instead, she had isolated them in a fairytale world that threatened to sap them of everything they held dear. The audacity of the story tickled Nerin's darker fancies as he imagined such weakness. Had she turned the power against her enemies, the story would have gone differently. But passivity was a common trait of the finer sex, something he lamented but could not help but exploit.

Gulping down the contents of his small glass, Nerin turned back toward the bed, watching as the sleeping woman lay sprawled out beneath his sheets. The day was drawing on, and he needed to prepare for the evening's activities. Ideally, he'd persuade the young woman to stay late into the night or keep her inebriated enough that she wouldn't have a choice. It was much simpler to move someone through the dark, private halls of the great tree than to try to lure them out or fetch them from their own abode. He had already had to quarter four Hyunisti men, having bought their allegiance with fancy trinkets, better food, and the leftovers of his seductive forays. In turn, they helped him carry out his covert operations. But even those four were taxing in their inability to comprehend basic skullduggery, making him wonder if it wouldn't have been more worthwhile to do everything himself.

A shiver crept down Nerin's spine as he thought about the meeting he would have that night. Everything of late he owed to a powerful master. The wizard had instructed and guided him in uncovering the hidden talvuo peoples. He also owed his life to the mysterious figure. While he hated feeling beholden to others, he was overcome with strange admiration for the wizened, old mage. Furthermore, the elderly man had selected Nerin to inherit the deepest and most potent secrets of his long study and trials.

The man had shown Nerin visions of the ancient magic once practiced by the majestic forest folk and how to obtain such power. With it, Nerin could reclaim the Delvori's proud heritage and lay waste to the talvuo's enemies at home and abroad. All it would take was a simple ceremony performed to cleanse the Emri of the curse that plagued their blood and locked away their potential. In doing so, Nerin would earn the title of savior, allowing him to take hold of and direct the risen people. It was almost too good to be true, but the old counselor's advice had proven unerring thus far. Nerin couldn't help but be caught up in the dream of rebuilding his ancient homeland. With Neris at his side, he would lay waste to the southern and eastern human territories and perhaps even expand talvuo influence. All would know the name Delvori.

There was only one more problem to deal with, one more complex and unpredictable than everything involving the ceremony or the subtle manipulations of a disgraced populace. The man responsible for the loss of his comrades and the near-deaths of Neris and himself had appeared upon the forest floor. The Hyunisti had brought back the demon-handed fiend, their survival instincts overridden by their welcoming ignorance. Before he could make a case, his sister had beat him to the outsider's side. She had been vicious in her defense of the human, her words cutting him to the quick.

Then she dared to involve one of the villagers, a blond-haired, tanned talvuo woman whose secretive nature was a complication in and of itself. The mysterious hermit, an exotic talvuo named Elis of the mythical Renai clan, was the longest-lived person in the quaint town. According to the women he had bedded, she was regarded as more significant than the village elders but left to her own devices. Her knowledge and skill had intrigued him, but the feisty blonde had spurned every advance he had made toward her.

As if the woman's unwillingness wasn't trouble enough, she had taken up pairing with his sister. Together, they had kept a rotating vigil over the sleeper, making it impossible for him to assassinate the fiendish human. With every day that passed, the beast regained strength and composure. Any day now, he would awaken.

But with careful scheming, even the most trying of times could be surmounted. Nerin would find a way to win the blonde hermit to his side, whether through coercion or force. There was talk she cared for a child. By a stroke of luck, that child had been drawn to his side. Given how the little green-eyed girl gawked and blushed, he was sure that he could use her for leverage. With the blonde's connection to the human and Neris's fondness for the tanned woman, he could use the girl as a leash to bind the other two to his will. With any luck that would allow him to make a move against his unholy foe. If not, he was sure he could find some use for the little girl's admiration.

"Naisure . . ." gargled words called from beneath the sheets of the luxurious bed. Writhing, the half-asleep talvuo woman tried to free herself of the bright linens, only entangling herself further. He stared at the helpless woman, taking time to open another bottle of cheap wine before making his way to the bedside. Wearing a charming grin, he sat on the edge of the bed, ready to placate his guest. Despite all the problems, he was getting ever closer to his goal, and nothing would stand in his way.

6

———

ELIS

Coming home, Elis had expected the worst from her little companion but had found the situation to be better than she had imagined. The boxes and bags in the entryway had been opened, and their contents jumbled. Grains, herbs, and plant matter had been spilled about, making a trail into the larger common room. Within the room, the large wooden table that served as a workbench and dining table was littered with various bottles, vegetable matter, petals, stale bread and crumbs, nuts, berries, and small, drying puddles of water and distillate. At the far end of the table had been Rais's work in progress, three half-empty bottles of dyes and paint. Cleaning up had taken the two of them the better part of the afternoon, and by the time they had cooked and eaten, the sun was beginning to hang low in the sky.

Letting Rais re-commandeer the table for her crafts, Elis retired to their small shared bedroom. Sitting at her wooden vanity, she used one of the leftovers coals from their meal and lit a small paper lantern. Taking her time, she undid a small panel beneath the dressing table and pulled out a hefty leather-bound tome. Opening the old volume, she fingered the loose mixed sheets of vellum and paper. Meandering through sporadic entries, she scanned through excerpt after excerpt of past journal entries from when she first arrived in the village.

Among the earliest pages were mentions of her first months, which, after careful instruction from the talvuo tribal leader, she had started to write down her thoughts and deeds. The first several dozen were simple passages with crude handwriting, torrents of raw emotion engraved with hasty scribbles. The notion of form or coherence was lost upon her past self as she lamented the countless woes of those darker days. Death and loss, two things she had known ever since her early life but had never had the burden of carrying, overwhelmed her younger self's prose. Over time, things became more coherent, focusing instead on the lessons she was being taught by the tribe's leader. Over the months, she had written down fewer and fewer troubles, instead embracing the new experiences she had been offered.

Closing her eyes, Elis leaned back in her chair and mused about those early days. Accepting those she had lost had been the hardest thing she had ever done. But the village's then-leader, a woman who had lost more in her lifetime, had been there to ease the transition. Every time Elis sank into despair or desperation, the woman had pushed her to try something different, to take up a new trade or task. In time the woman came to recount the tales of her people and the role she had played in sealing their fate. But all of that had been ages ago.

"Zaisure." The voice of her little one broke her train of thought. Elis raised her eyes to the doorway, watching as Rais's small, pale frame stumbled into the dim room. The girl's green eyes were heavy with all the happenings of the day. Extending her arms, Elis reached out and brought Rais into her lap, holding her close.

"Are you tired, my little one?" Elis cooed into the girl's small brown ears as they hung lazily beside her head. Huddling close to her, Rais nodded, letting out a long yawn. "Then let's get you into bed."

Elis carried her tired bundle the few paces needed to lower her into their small shared bed. With a thoughtful glance, she watched the girl grab their rolled-up quilt and huddle beneath the heavy blanket. Letting out another yawn, the girl looked up to her.

"Are you going to stay tonight, zaisure?"

"I plan on it, and if not, someone will be here should you awaken," Elis whispered. "I'll join you in a bit."

"Alright, zaisure." The tired girl's voice was muddled as she slurred her words. Taking the lantern, Elis left the room with her journal. She was not done thinking about the things that had happened or the things that she had let go of just yet. Easing the door closed behind her, she sat at the far side of the large wooden table, avoiding the concoctions and pastes that Rais had been finalizing.

Opening her journal, she scanned toward the middle and began to read about her recollections of the past. Within the pages, she found the words that had been the beginning of her own melancholic journey of fortune and trouble. On those pages were scribbled the story about when she was brought forth to help with rearing a human babe and how it had changed her outlook on life forever

AN ETERNITY AGO, a younger Elis sat alone and waited for her parents to return, kicking her feet at the floorboards of a wooden hovel at the edge of town. Looking up, she caught glimpses of the farmers and field hands tending to their crops. Children ran up and down the dusty road that connected the outskirts with the town proper. A man and his son led a wagon by the small wooden house, the young boy flashing a glance at her. She heard a murmur beneath the boy's breath and a mean laugh from his father as they continued on their way.

"Elis?" a woman said from within the wooden home. Turning, Elis looked to see her mother's tall, bronze features looking at her from the doorway. The woman's lavender eyes scanned her before surveying the rest of the outdoors. Loving yet distant, her mother motioned her to come inside.

"You know we can't accept this. This is too much. If anything happens, we'll need to—"

"Enough of that, Remer. Not around your daughter," Emeris said to her husband as Elis stepped into the room. Her father sat hunched in a corner, his brown eyes searching as the door closed behind her. His dark-blond hair was unkempt from the endless toiling in the fields that he had undertaken to make ends meet, lines of worry and burden etched into his face. Their familial hardships had affected her mother less, her appearance still that of a mature woman in her prime. It was remarkable how much her father had aged since they lost Elis's sister and how weak he seemed to grow each day.

"I'm sorry, Emeris. Elis, come here," he said, wearing a trembling smile. Without a word, she crossed the room and, painting a look of joviality upon her features, embraced her father. "There's my girl. I'm sorry we left you outside for so long."

"It's alright," she said with feigned joy. The weathered talvuo man planted a small kiss on her cheek as she pulled away. Looking into his brown eyes and seeing the woe and frailty, Elis's tiny heart sank. Stepping away, she turned her gaze to a dark stranger standing at the far corner of the room. The man was tall and quiet, the darkness of the room concealing most of his features. But from a distance, she saw a pair of icy-blue eyes watching her and her parents. Her own lavender orbs locked on his for a moment, a jolt of excitement and curiosity climbing up her back. Beside her, her father motioned to the man across the room. "Elis, this is a family friend. His name is Deldaron. He has been—"

"No need for too many details, Remer." Her mother's words were calm as she took her place beside them. "Just know he is our friend and has come to us for help."

"Y-yes, my dear," Remer stuttered.

"Your mother and father speak truthfully, young Elis," the man said. He conveyed an air of authority as he stood opposite them, nodding in agreement. "My condolences for your family's loss, for your loss, are insufficient to convey the depths of the sorrow I feel for you and yours. If I could have asked this at a better time, I would have. Alas, it comes down to this. I require your family's assistance, and I require unanimity before I will place this burden on others. Unanimity from your parents as well as you."

Elis didn't understand all of it but was entranced enough by his words and demeanor that she nodded to his request. His words conveyed a level of respect toward all of them, even toward her, the child that she was. He was sincere; that much she could grasp. Beyond that, whatever he was asking for was beyond important to him, and in her tiny heart was a willfulness to accept whatever burden came with it.

"Perhaps you should try to be more voluble," her mother said, gesturing to the space between them.

"I'll try to be simpler."

"Either way, we should introduce them before we finalize things," Emeris said, patting Elis on the back.

"Very well. I'll fetch him."

"Just remember, you're allowed to say no," her father said as the dark man disappeared into a side room. Elis couldn't help but wonder what would come next, a sense of anticipation building within her as she waited for the man to return. Several moments passed before the stranger reappeared carrying a small, dark bundle.

Taking his time, the stranger knelt beside her, offering up the bundle. Elis looked at him, staring into his cold blue eyes as they probed the depths of her lavender orbs. Looking down, she reached out and took up the weighty wrap. Within her arms, the cloth squirmed. Small, pale fingers reached from underneath the covering as she brought the hooded face of a human baby close to hers.

Instincts she had learned while caring for her beloved sister guided her actions as she began to rock the bundle in her arms, staring at the pale form within. Its little face was scrunched up and starting to redden as it struggled in her arms. Opening its eyes, the baby opened its mouth to cry out but then stopped as its blue eyes met hers. Bringing her face closer to his, she hummed a tune. As she did, she felt the stranger's eyes upon her and the bundle as an aura of awe and calm swept over the room.

"I have asked your family to help me care for my son because I cannot. I'm required to be too many places, and there is nothing I can do for him given my status and responsibilities. I have promised to help you and yours should they help mine, and the only thing I ask is that the boy is cared for. Your parents have already agreed in their own way. I leave the final word to you, Elis Renai." His words were endearing and focused. He didn't stutter or misspeak, and she detected no uncertainty in his voice.

Elis did not reply immediately, content to cradle the boy in her arms as she hummed a quieting tune. Looking up at her, a grin crossed his face, a small, burbling giggle erupting from his tiny body.

"A Renai lullaby. Surely there's no better answer for you," her mother said.

"Indeed," the man replied, rising from Elis's side. "I understand your hesitation, Remer, but I trust you. I know you won't fail me. Likewise, should you need to leave because things get worse, then so be it. Just take the boy with you. That's all I ask."

"Emeris is right in all of this. I just, I . . ." Her father began to sob. All traces of resentment and strength fled his voice as her mother tried to assuage him.

"When should we expect his mother?" Emeris asked. "Surely she doesn't want to be kept from her child?"

"She and I agreed to this. It was part of our deal with her father," Deldaron said as he stood.

"We'll never be able to repay you," her father said, his voice wavering. The man reached out to Remer, placing his hand upon the sniveling man's shoulder.

At that moment, Elis had a realization. Everything her father had been up till the moment they had lost everything, she had admired. He had made her laugh, told her stories about the world far away, and had always told her how bright and fulfilling the world was. But the man who had been her father was dead, crushed by the weight of loss and grief and unable to continue. Not like her mother, who had remained resilient throughout it all. And not like the dark stranger, who had sought their aid, a man willing to place the life of his child in their care, whose trust and acceptance was unswayable. Even with such assurance, her father remained broken. Indeed, the world was neither bright nor fulfilling, and her father had been toppled by that broken promise.

But in her leaping heart, she felt like there was an opportunity for something new. This friend of the family, who commanded respect by his mere presence, surpassed her happy memories of the young talvuo man. At once her mind was set on its course. Never would she let herself fall into the trap of denial and grief or be chained to someone who crumbled under the weight of such loss. Instead, she would find someone who could rise above it. Someone like the blue-eyed stranger, who's icy eyes stared right through her. Someone who could make the townsmen listen and bigots cower for their crimes.

Elis wanted someone like Deldaron.

7

____

NERIN

Emboldened by the day's victories, Nerin entered Neris's laboratory with a controlled, steady gait. He stood tall, trying to maintain his stature and height to appear imposing. Without letting his eyes stray, he approached the table where the man had been placed. He looked him over with stern red-brown eyes, feigning a guise of disinterest. Then he looked up to see his sister standing near the windows. She was playing with different alchemical reagents, her dark skin gilded in the waning light.

"Vindal," he called, opening his arms while keeping his gaze fixed on her.

"Ne vivahr!" she said, a vial slipping from her hands. She turned and faced him, regaining her composure. "I was beginning to wonder if I'd have the pleasure of seeing you today." She walked over and wrapped her arms around him as his arms closed around her. She reached up and kissed his lips, smiling as she drew back. Her red-brown eyes were fixed on his, waiting for an answer to his absence.

"Lord Ohran kept me," he explained, not looking at her directly. "We were talking about the arrangements and the traditions involved for the ceremony. He's keen on details. Of course, not that you would have the mind for any of that, ne vindal."

"Ah," she said, an annoying hint of sarcasm in her voice. "Always on to bigger and better things, aren't you, my little Nerin?" He glared at her as she chuckled at his expense.

"Must you mock me even when we're so close to starting something new here?" He tried to jest but was unable to hide the pain in his voice.

"It is not to mock you, ne vivahr," she said, giving him a playful glance before and returning to her projects. "What are harmless play and the truth between siblings?"

"You always seem to try and find some way to undermine me, ne vindal." Though his words were brooding, he attempted to match her mischievous attitude. "How am I supposed to know mocking from harmless play?"

"Perhaps by having some humility, my dear brother. Then again, we both already know that you do not feel . . . what's the word? Adequate, vivahr Nerin?"

His sister thought she was always in control, even when everything was conspiring otherwise. As his embittered thoughts bubbled, he maintained his poise. He was willing to ignore how she had slighted him. Coming to a stop behind her and wanting to be impish and unrestrained, he placed his hands upon her hips and yanked her back against himself, causing her to gasp. With a wicked grin, he chuckled beneath his breath.

"Should you be doing that where there are so many prying eyes?" she asked. "The shutters are hardly covered."

"What should these simpletons think of us, ne vindal?" he asked in a dark tone. He stroked his hands up her sides, down to her hips, farther down her upper thigh and back. He was rough with his motions, amused at how she responded. Neris's body swayed as he petted her, pressing her firmer against him. They had an understanding between them. Despite her coy nature, she knew her place.

"Well, they should think nothing of our traditions or personal affairs, ne vivahr. I just thought you would have already had your fill with your maidens and their nectar," she said. Of course, it was more play on her part, and she played the role well. She brought her head back against his chest, grasping his hands and bringing them to her breasts, letting out a deep breath. He leaned over her, pressing his lips to hers. She pushed herself against him, yearning for his caress. He stroked her bosom, led on by her motions as desire and lust built within.

"You know that simple women cannot quench my thirst." Nerin struggled to contain himself, but his primal urges and unrestrained thoughts overcame his composure. Unable to take her suggestions any longer, he made his move. With quick, nimble fingers, he plucked at the lacing of her dark, silken bodice, but before his hands could even loosen a single knot, Neris turned and pressed her hand against his chest. The force of her push sent him back several paces as he stumbled to maintain his balance. Regaining some of his composure, he glared at her, his chest heaving as she laughed at him.

"Why do you taunt me so?" he demanded, feeling hurt and betrayed. His blood was racing. He was hot and had nothing to appease his urges. Grinning wickedly, she continued to laugh, turning back to the counter. "Answer me!"

"You've always been so quick to jump, my young brother. So quick that you're lured in by any little show of interest or small opportunity," she said, her tone calm and cool. "In all honesty, did you really think I'd want you? How many times have we played this game, you and I? And still, you never learn. Really, it's becoming quite boring."

"So, what was this then?" he asked, stamping angrily.

"Just a way for me to pass the time, ne vivahr," she said, her smile as cold as ever. "Why would I waste my energy? I would rather spend it on something worth my while." She glanced over at the sleeping man, directing Nerin's gaze. "I can always appease myself or use an equally sufficient talvuo later, if need be."

"You should respect your—"

"Respect my blood?' she asked, finishing for him. The snap and the meanness in her words stunned him. "I think you and I both know how much I respect my blood. And don't you dare think to command me to do such a thing, you ignorant child."

"You dare call me a—"

"Bite your wicked tongue, you little bastard!" Neris commanded. Again, he shied away from her. "You are ungrateful and still, to this day, are unable to comprehend the sacrifices others have made for you. So, yes, you are an ignorant child. And until you show me otherwise, don't expect me to treat you as anything else."

He gave her a heated glare. Outrage and insatiable insecurity gnawed through his psyche. Try as he might, he couldn't stop his anger from showing or the tears from welling up as he tried to stand his ground. With a sudden bitterness, he directed his anger at the sleeping man upon the table.

"What does he have that I don't, ne vindal? What does he have that I lack? Answer me!" he demanded as he lumbered toward the sleeper. "He left us for dead, Neris. Or have you forgotten?"

"Do you not remember whose ambition led to our folly?" Her words cut as they laid out yet another one of his failings.

"The vaults were our birthright!" he exclaimed with sunken pride, tapping his fingers on the tabletop. "Everything in the gods-forsaken place was to be ours."

"Who's birthright, dear brother? Mine? Our comrades?"

"Of course it was! It was for all of us. It was for—"

"Your greed got them all killed!" she said. "Was it worth it, dear brother? Was it?"

"It wasn't my fault!" he snapped. "There was a tremor. You were there! You know!"

"But you ignored the warnings that you had been so graciously given and treaded on unsteady ground," she said, shaking her head as she regained her composure. "Quit trying to shake off the blame, ne vivahr. Until you learn to take responsibility for your failures, you will never become more than what you are."

"And what is that, ne vindal? What am I?"

"I've already told you," she replied, turning back to the counter. "Or should I repeat myself?"

"Yes, well, ne vindal," Nerin said, half turning back to the sleeper, "too bad your toy is still asleep. It must be upsetting to be deprived for so long. It would be such a waste if he never awoke."

"Who said a toy needs to be awake to be played with?" Neris replied, unfazed. "As for the latter part of your threat, I would watch that tongue of yours."

"Or what?" he asked with sullen anger, trying to hold back a frown. His sister rotated in place, her hand stretched out in a near-perfect arc. With a thud and a twang, something heavy and metallic landed between his legs, biting into one of the table's wooden columns. Looking down, he saw a small dagger embedded in the wood.

"Or you might lose something precious to you," Neris said with dark intent, turning away from him once more.

Biting his lip as rage swelled in his breast, he turned and made his way to the door. Neris thought she was clever, but if she only knew what greatness awaited him. He would make her understand everything that she had taken for granted. In the end, she would respect her blood and take her place by his side.

8

———

ERROR

[E]verything is always about her and her minge, her wiles, her child.] Jealous whispers scattered on ancient stones in darkness unknowable. Tiny voices cried in pain and envy, reverberating off silvery metal, glowing gas rippling with every word. In unison and agreement, others cried, [Be empty, be free!]

[I want to tell her.] A timid voice scraped against stone and mold, a line of dissonance cutting through the luminous mustard haze. [I want her to tell me. I want her to . . .]

[Stillborn, I know it,] another answered. [Why weren't you born dead? Why not you?]

[The blood's too thin,] a worried voice said, floating through the ethereal clouds while dancing near the abyss. [We need new blood. We need . . .] it mumbled over and over before falling off the edge of the stone sepulcher. Dropping, falling, the sound distorted and grew longer. A sick, gasping sound bubbled up from the depths of the void, silencing the voice.

[Maybe she'll take me tonight,] another voice said, dripping from the arched ceiling and causing the mist to swirl and twist upon itself.

[A belly full of nettles and life,] another broke in. [He makes me fly so high and fall so hard.]

[Dance in the moonlight, dance in the dark,] a childlike voice whispered, skipping from stone to stone.

[Don't leave me in the dark, please!] Terror roused the room, all the voices crying to meet the outburst.

[Be empty, be free!]

[Kill him,] a shade croaked, heavy dew hanging onto a metal surface as it slithered from image to reflection. [She's too good for him.]

[Just let me die.] a skeletal shade said as it danced in the ominous gloom, its bony face creaking as its canvas lips smeared wetness from once surface to another.

In response to the call, a thousand rodent teeth chattered from the endless well, forming the broken words, [Be empty, be free!]

A long, groaning sound drifted from outside the stonework prison, shuddering steps and blathering flames speaking from beyond the broken stone precipice of the place beyond. A flicker of orange at the end of the great hollow shattered the illumination. In a chorus of delight, every voice joined in a chant.

[Be empty, be free!]

[Be empty, be free!]

From the depths of the darkness at the heart of the sepulcher, one last voice joined the choir. Like a tidal wave crashing against the stone walls, it made the mirrored dome around it shake with anticipation. Gathering the rising storm of cries and moans, the voice of the gale exclaimed toward the entryway, beckoning the singers.

[Empty her! Free her!]

As the far-off light flickered, the room was silent. Lit by a mustard haze, it quietly awaited the procession that would bring it to life.

9

NERIN

Making his way in the darkness, Nerin stumbled along the dim tree corridor with four of his Hyunisti underlings in tow. Even though he had run the path every night for the past month, he still could not navigate the moldy walkway or the weathered stone of the deep structure. The idiots behind him would not lead the way, choosing to follow instead, making stupid jokes and nervous remarks. In truth, he feared the ruins as they did, but their apprehension was born of superstitious nonsense. His was out of respect for his master.

Annoyed with the simpletons, Nerin retreated into his thoughts. In his head, he practiced the presentation of his conquest, appeals to authority, and the humble acceptance of his lord's admiration. Everything was like clockwork as the scene unfolded before his eyes, just as it had night after night.

Caught up in his thoughts, Nerin missed an ignoble piece of stone protruding from the ground. Without a moment to react, he tripped over the slab and fell to his knees. Behind him, two of the bumblers snickered.

"Help me up," Nerin demanded as one of the pair came over to assist. "Enough of your prattle. Quiet, the lot of you!"

"But naisure Nerin, the air is much too silent," the one farther back said.

"Yes, naisure," the one holding his shoulder remarked. "It's enough to raise the hackles on my neck. Especially since the thing has been glowing down below."

"It's Lord Nerin," Nerin said, jerking his arm free from the dimwitted attendant. "And that thing is one of the greatest magicians ever to live, and you shall not forget it."

"Aye, lord," the talvuo said, dumbfounded. "Still, this seems wrong."

"No more wrong than your head will be if we're late," Nerin said as he marched forward. "Hurry."

"Yes, Lord Nerin," his lackeys replied. Behind the two bumblers, two better-trained talvuo carried a large bundle wrapped in hide, walking with steady steps as it lurched in their arms.

Eyeing the shadowy silhouette of the old stone archway, Nerin was overcome with a feeling of relief and dread. As his small party approached, he signaled one of his men to hand him the torch. As if in answer to the flame, a fetid wind ripped through the living corridor.

"To me, hurry now." Keeping their distance, the four men followed him into the underground ruin's gaping maw.

The stone structure was ancient, its walls and frescos older than the great tree above them. The fortress's underground halls had sat quiet as mold and mineral formations grew along their limestone interior. Like cancer, the degradation had spread throughout the old ruin till it was full of nothing but collapsed stonework and mud. As he walked in the faint illumination of the struggling torch, Nerin took in breath after breath of putrescence. The rotting morass of ancient plant life and crumbled stone permeated the air, making his nose curl with every breath. The roots of the tree above had done their worst to the ruin, carving out holes as they gnawed at the earth.

All of it was a bitter reminder that the Hyunisti had forgotten their pride and their history. They had given up on the place and settled for a life of quiet acceptance and enfeeblement. The frail talvuo had abandoned all notions of greatness and allowed Hyun and her followers to seal the entrance of the holy land. Just like his people, they had fallen into dissolution but somehow continued to thrive. The very thought boiled Nerin's blood. But alas, the meek had their place in his coming kingdom. For now, they served their purpose.

Despite the toil and bitterness, the place's mystique was not lost upon Nerin as he gazed at the worn engravings along the sunken walls. According to his master, the fortress once served as a seat of magic power gifted to the Emri by the Lorinian mage-emperor, Serne-Le Lorin. This seemed all but confirmed by the images in the dank halls. Runes of power were inscribed upon engravings of talvuo shamans and leaders. The walls hummed with life as the clear blood of the grand tree pulsed around and between them.

Near the end of the sunken tunnel, Nerin spied that which bewitched him most within the ruin. Above the final gate, an image of a solitary shade stood in the middle of a font of power. Talvuo and mages gathered all around him. Leader after leader raised their hands to the mighty being as they knelt before him. Their followers bent down in supplication to the master of the well, bearer of the power of the ancient talvuo and magi. A man who would call upon the wrath of the forest to depose all who stood in his way.

"We're here, Lord Nerin," one of the stooges said, announcing the obvious. "Do you want us to wait?"

"Yes," he replied. "You and your useless companion can wait down the hall. As for the other two, come with me!" He passed the torch to one of the loafers.

"As you wish, sir," the man said, emitting a sigh of relief. Without a moment's hesitation, the other man joined the torchbearer, and the two scurried away from the chamber entrance.

Nerin scoffed at the retreating pair as he took a deep breath. A cold sweat broke over his skin. He hesitated for a moment as he realized the hypocrisy of blaming them for their lack of resolution when he felt the cold chill of terror run up his spine. But he knew better than to acknowledge such weakness. Mustering what resolve he could, Nerin faced a set of large stone doors standing ajar within the gloom. With a gulp, he walked through the threshold.

All around them, a glowing green haze clung to the walls of the large, dome-like room. The dim light of the fog, augmented by a few strands of wandering torchlight, bounced and reflected off thousands of mirrored surfaces that lined the grand chamber's walls. At its center, the mist and light coalesced into a luminous ether as it swirled and spun above a massive stone sepulcher.

"Lord Ohran," Nerin said, entering the quarters of his most-trusted advisor, "I have come at your beckoning."

"Ah, my young master," a strange, eerie voice said from the dark void at the heart of the room. Two glowing green blots of light ignited within the condensing gas. They seemed like nothing more than floating green embers. "Have you brought the last of them?"

"Yes, my lord," Nerin said in the most respectful tone he could muster. He motioned behind him. From the entrance, the two Hyunisti scouts came forward as they wrestled with their large bundle. They set it down in front of Nerin and then retreated to the entryway. The bag fell forward with a thud as whatever was inside it writhed and wriggled on the hard stone surface. Nerin brought out a knife and cut it open at the top. The bag gave way, revealing the young Hyunisti maiden from his morning's tryst.

Her eyes were glazed as she contorted on the ground. Drugs and alcohol pumped in her veins, continuing to take their toll. She looked around as she struggled to get her bearings. Before she could act, she saw the glowing gaze of the figure beneath the hood and froze, her eyes widening in feral terror.

"Ah, very good, my young master," Lord Ohran said in a dark and terrifying voice. Something about the old mage's words was twisted and wrong, unnatural and profane. Spinning and solidifying, something like an arm reached out and grasped the young maiden around the neck.

Locked in his gaze, she rose as if by suggestion. The bag fell away, leaving her naked in the middle of the room. Nerin looked at his lord's work, watching how he held the young maiden in thrall, bending her to his will. In this there was power, and that power left him shivering with terrified anticipation.

"Leave us," Nerin ordered the remaining scouts. Without a word, the two men fled the chamber.

"She is of physical maturity, as expected," the lord said, turning her for further inspection. "Her body has begun producing nectar." Another writhing arm-like appendage coalesced from the smog as Ohran probed the girl. The detachment slithered, squeezing one of the girl's breasts until small droplets emerged, spattering to the floor.

"Yes, my lord," Nerin said, averting his eyes from the girl. For all he wanted to gain from his lord, the display caused his stomach to turn. There was a sense of waste to it, and even for the Delvori, it seemed crude. "I know this. I made sure." He had been unable to help himself, even with such a dull woman. He had to get pleasure from somewhere.

"Of course you did," the lord said, turning the girl to face him. Tendrils of glowing fog reached up from every corner of the room, writhing and twisting as they surrounded the maiden. They moved over the girl, squeezing and sniffing at every inch of her exposed form. Unintelligible whispers filled the ancient space. "Tell me, what is her name?"

"Thaimi, my lord," Nerin said, returning his gaze to the display.

"You have learned much from me in these past few years, my young master," the lord said, his gaze remaining fixed on the young maiden. "You have learned to anticipate and sacrifice. And when sacrifice is not enough, you have learned how to supplant it with another's. You have learned what must be done to assert power and restore your lineage. You have learned how to ascend to greatness."

"Yes, my lord," Nerin said, breaking his gaze from the girl and honing his senses on Lord Ohran's words. "I have learned much and am ready to take the next step, my lord."

"Yes, my young master," the lord said, "And soon you will take that step, just as I prophesied. The Hyunisti shall be empowered, and you will be raised. You shall be able to muster an army and regain your honor."

"Yes!" Nerin said, detecting an excited strangeness in his own voice. The voices of the wraiths around him echoed his cry.

"And then we will work toward even greater accomplishments. Toward returning the world to a proper place, a true order. To overthrow the false kings of humankind. To have our retribution."

Nerin's internal voice wandered as the other voices chanted along with the lord's words. As if entranced, Nerin's eyes grew wider. With every word that Lord Ohran spoke, Nerin's mind became more enraptured with the idea of attaining greatness for himself. Every word seemed to change him somehow, meld with him, and make him greater, stronger.

"Soon you will possess all the power you need. The power to bend others to your will. The power to defeat all those who would oppose you," the terrible voice boasted.

"Yes! Oh, yes, my lord!" Nerin said, matching his lord's tone.

"But you must do something for me, my young master. We must do something lest our plans end before they begin."

"Yes," Nerin said, hanging on Ohran's every word.

"We must find a way to rid ourselves of the one known as the Virage."

A tremor went through Nerin's body, breaking his train of thought. He was overcome with dread and terrible fear. At the same time, he felt as if thousands of eyes were upon him, aware of his every thought. He worked up the courage to speak, his mind still mingling with the other voices in his head. "How will I do so, my lord?" he asked, feigning obedience despite his terror. The mere thought of acting against the Virage made his knees want to give way. "I know I'm worthy, but I fear I may not be strong enough. Perhaps if you were to face him yourself . . ."

"When the time is right, we will face him together!" the lord proclaimed, the chorus rising in a grand symphony of resplendence. Nerin not only heard their words, he felt them, tasted them, saw them as they danced across every mirrored surface in the chamber. The force and power were elating, filling him with pain and rapture. He fell forward, unable to hold himself up, bowing to his lord as if compelled by the need for absolution. His eyes widened with joy, his mouth curling in glee. He bowed low, tears of supplication streaming down his face.

"Thank you, my lord. Thank you!" Nerin prayed, his body and mind in such disarray that he thought he would faint from bliss. He felt a warm trickle working its way down from his nose to his upper lip. He tasted his blood as it spattered from his face to the floor, and it made him grin even wider.

"You are welcome, my young master," Ohran said.

"And then Neris, she will . . ."

"She will love you the way she was always meant to," the lord said. "Through sacrifice, manipulation, and consecration. We will break his enthralling machinations and together bring forth the grandest age of the Delvori!"

"Yes, oh yes, my lord!" Nerin cried, the shame of fear and betrayal washed clean from his soul as the voices in the room stroked and assuaged his ego. The love, the power, and the means to accomplish greatness were all within his grasp. Everyone would love him. Neris would love him.

"Until then, do whatever must be done, my young master," Ohran said. "He will awaken soon. Do not be deterred by swift vengeance or the weakness of jealousy. Let him sour what he thinks to sour. Let him drink the honey of his devilish wants for now. Soon, we will crush him!"

"Yes, my lord!"

[Now, draw us forth, and do what must be done,] Ohran said, his voice etched into Nerin's mind. As the door to the mystical font began to creak closed, Nerin started to disrobe. Surrounded by the glamor, tendrils of love and joy crawled along his exposed frame, drawing him and the young talvuo maiden together. Filled with endless virility and strength, he focused upon the helpless, enthralled woman.

[Free her, now,] the voices from the mist whispered as he inhaled.

"Empty her," he recited in time as the menacing stone gate closed behind him.

10

———

NERIS

It wasn't the first time Neris had been imposed upon while tending to her dozing lover, and she doubted it would be the last. As she had lined up the remaining sleeping agents and hydrators to be used that night and into the morrow, one of the huntsmen knocked on her door. Bedimer was a seasoned hunter who appeared to be in the later years of his prime. Though his eyes often wandered to her bustier blond lover, Neris would not turn away entertainment for the evening.

"I thought you were interested in our dear matron Elis, huntsman," Neris cooed from the counter. She readied two vials of oaken liquor, a gift from another gentleman seeking an embrace.

"I respect a fellow hunter, vindal Neris," the weathered man said with a smile. "I also tend to be suspicious of newcomers who take an interest in our most-prized heritage."

"Is she your heritage? To think a woman could be reduced to a historical oddity." Neris smiled in the lantern light, offering a vial to the gentleman. With a gruff grin, he took it, leaning back against her unconscious paramour's table.

"She's the only one of us who remembers things from before," Bedimer said, his hazel eyes fixed on her as he held out the tiny vial.

"Everything that was important to our people is tucked away in her head, and I hope we live long enough to see a day where such things are important again."

"Ah, so it's more respect then. To a common respect between peoples," Neris said, clinking her glass against his. In unison, they downed their firewater. The taste was akin to dried oak drenched in alcohol, carrying a hint of sweetness. Overall it left much to be desired. Still, there was little to be done about what the forest folk could acquire. Anything was better than nothing.

"Aye, a common respect." The man cleared his throat, offering the glass back and motioning for another draught. Then he turned away from her and faced the sleeping man. "Until now, I've never put much stock in legends or campfire tales. Seeing this one here in the flesh makes me think of all the tales I heard in childhood. Vindal Elis's stories spooked me as a kid, and sure enough, the beasts of the woods are large and fierce, but ghost stories never stoked my fancy."

"He makes you nervous, brave Bedimer?" Despite how open he was with her, Neris couldn't help but mock the hunter as she drew to his side. They both knew this was a game, and forcing his humility or ferocity was much more fun than merely agreeing.

"All four of you make my hair stand on end," Bedimer said, shaking his dusty, hazel head. His perky fuzz-covered ears sagged as he took his glass from her outstretched hand. Neris watched as he raised the vial to his lips before tipping his head back and downing the vial's contents. "If I could have another, vindal."

"But of course," Neris said, keeping her rusty-red eyes fixed on the huntsman. He had come to her room still armed, wearing an ornate talvuo thinblade at his side. At his rear hung a silver, hooded lantern, an expensive trinket for a talvuo descended from a scorned, hidden people. Watching as he placed both hands on the table, Neris poured another glass for Bedimer and herself. With the grace of a courtesan, she approached him from behind. With catlike finesse, she reached around and offered the drink. As she felt his hand move for the vial, she pressed her stomach against the small of his back, arching her chest just away. "Here you go, my brave hunter."

"You're used to this game," the grizzled man said, easing her hand to his lips. At his direction, she tipped the glass as he sipped the contents. Drinking her own, she teased him further, pressing her bosom into his back. Laughing, the talvuo's ears perked to the sides. They extended as he stretched in place, arching his back toward her. "Like this then, vindal Neris."

"Vahratra also works if you prefer it," Neris whispered, placing a soft kiss along the nape of his neck. "Why stop at being brethren, vivahr Bedimer?"

Bedimer coughed, waving her off. "A little slower, my lady." Neris complied and drew away, holding both glasses at her waist as the man turned around. Looking him over, she could tell the alcohol had yet to hit him, causing a sly smile to creep across her face. The Hyunisti were bad at measuring their drink. "I would have another and a long visit first before I lose myself in you."

"I doubt you'll last as long as you hope, huntsman," Neris said, giggling. Her red orbs studied his hazel eyes, seeing a depth of seriousness that she had missed before.

"I'm not used to such finery, like most of my kin, but I hear a full belly does wonders to cut the worst of it." There it was: predation. Bedimer was hunting for her to betray the quarry he was tracking. Monstrous and ravenous, his eyes flickered between brown and green in the pallid lantern light.

"So, noble Bedimer, what's on your mind this evening?"

"I want you to tell me why you and your brother are changing things. Why is he so intrusive? And why did a real monster show up on our doorstep, with you and our matron slobbering over him?" Bedimer's words were cold and precise as he motioned to the glass in her hand. Smiling, Neris poured herself another drink and then handed the other vial and decanter to the prying hunter.

"Honestly, I wouldn't change a thing around here for the world." Neris sipped at her drink, keeping her eyes locked on the hunter. "My brother, on the other hand, wants to change anything that doesn't make his prick drip. He also has a way with words despite his flaws. If it doesn't pander to his ego, he loses his demeanor. But you already know that, right?"

Bedimer's eyes remained fixed on her as he sipped his draught, neither nodding nor speaking.

"If you want my personal opinion, my brother is delusional," Neris said, uncrossing and re-crossing her legs as she propped herself up on the counter. "He dreams of a united talvuo people under his proud talvuo lineage. The only thing that gets him stiffer than unrequited love is our tribe's name. Delvori greatness. Delvori blood. Delvori cum. If there was another Delvori male alive, they could bathe each other in their shared enormity."

Bedimer laughed at her brazen wordplay, shaking his head as he refocused his eyes upon her. Staring at him, she watched as the edginess of his stance began to dull.

"You seem spiteful, ne vindal." Bedimer's tone was low as he poured yet another shot from the vessel. "Not what I expected from a lady of your refinement."

"A sister's love has its limits, gracious Bedimer." Neris was cold as she finished the last of her drink. Bedimer offered her the decanter, but she waved him off. He shrugged, chuckling to himself as he downed one more drink. The man paced alongside the sleeper's table for a few moments longer, shaking his head in amusement at her words. Taking another half pour, he returned his attention to her. She narrowed her eyes at him, curling her lips.

"That still doesn't explain the blight bringer." His voice was low, the hint of a drawl hanging at the edge of every syllable. Sure enough, he had started to succumb.

"If I knew how he got here, I would tell you. And if I knew why he was here, I would whisper it to you," Neris said as she drew away from the counter, lowering her voice as she stepped closer. "As for why a seductive Delvori woman and a long-lived talvuo matron keep such a close vigil, what can I say except that the two of us are drawn to the same thing."

"And what is that?" Bedimer whispered as she looked down at him, her left hand sliding down his side while the other took the half-full glass from his hand. He shook his head, a sly grin spreading over his grizzled features. His eyes were heavy as his hand met hers, their fingers entwined.

"Danger and purpose, my dear accomplished Bedimer." With a single motion, she brought her other hand down and unstrapped his blade and lantern, dropping the sword as she pushed the silver square behind him. Gasping, he pressed forward. In response, she pressed her chest to his face and swelled as his coarse breath heaved over her pounding breast. Wearing a victorious smile, she watched as the talvuo man surrendered to her charms, pressing his pale, weathered face into her smooth, dark skin.

Starving for satisfaction, Neris ran her dark hands through his dusty hazel mane, drawing his hair between her thin black fingers. She shivered as the huntsman's rough hands unloosed her garments' knotting, forcing her breasts free. Feeling her lungs with air and her head tingling from the buzz of sensual freedom, she closed her eyes. As coarse fingers and rough lips danced along her exposed frame, she let out a low, guttural growl, surrendering to her ravenous desire.

11

UNKNOWN

It began like it always did, at the start of a tryst that never should have been. If he had avoided it altogether, none of the other events would have come to pass. But that was impossible. Cycles were by their very nature embedded within his being. Watching the scenes for the next in an uncountable series was taking its mental toll upon his beleaguered consciousness. Like all things bitter, he had not been spared the double-edged sword of joy and agony. His addled mind fixated on terrors he could only hope were those of a stillborn tragedy. So it was that he lived that day again and again, unable to alter its events or inject a single change.

There was the morning as it had been. The red desert stretched out before him, reaching from the square window over which he kept his vigil. Behind his disembodied form, he felt the rumblings of another. The voice was incomprehensible but soothing as his mind drifted, his detached consciousness flowing backwards through space. He was assailed by ghostly arms as they wandered over bits and pieces of his emulated body.

"Good man, Vir . . . Dav," the voice whispered in his ear as his world turned about.

Stonework and linens flew around him, evaporating into the distance as he landed on his back, his eyes staring up into a sea of olive skin. A cascade of shadowy faces danced about him, planting spots of tingling warmth over his illusory frame. As the ghostly heads merged, he was overcome by a bright light. He turned his eyes away, shivering as he avoided the blinding luminescence. He felt a gentle hand upon his face drawing his gaze. Turning forward once again, the light scattered as the imagery of a pair of bright yellow eyes filled his vision, flickering with allure and a solemn love.

"I want to be warmed," the feminine voice said, echoing through the scene, distorting his ethereal senses as it tempted and beckoned him.

"Senna," a male voice said from within him, answering the call.

At once he was overcome with an all-consuming warmth, his body merging with the speaker's until all that remained was passion and shortness of breath. All around him, the darkness filled with flames as the sensations of their union intensified. Cries of passion rippled across his invisible skin. Stroking fingers and love bites gnawed at the fabric of his being. At the height of the flames, a woman's visage formed before him. Her short, disheveled silver hair was thrown to one side. Perspiration streamed down her light-brown features as she opened her sultry yellow eyes.

"I want to be burned until there's nothing but ash," she said as she pressed her lips to his.

A detached horror floated around him as the flames ignited her. Unable to break free, they continued their lovemaking as her skin peeled away, falling in grey flakes that were scattered by a chilling breeze. As he pulled back, her body fell, leaving nothing but her frozen face as it stared at him with her bright yellow eyes. Unable to control his actions, he reached for her, but as his left non-hand touched her brow, the world seemed to shatter. Falling away like pieces of a mirror, reality splintered into glistening fragments across the infinite plane. As the diamond-like pieces shimmered, he turned his non-hand over as he looked at the black, disfigured form of his left palm. The three-fingered abomination clenched into a monstrous fist as the ground beneath him transformed, the darkness replaced by the dusty red of the far-off desert.

His heart seemed to all but stop as he looked up. A pair of burly, red-headed men looked down at him from atop an impossibly tall stone wall, their green eyes intent yet amiable. An elder and a younger, twins in all appearance but those defined by age, the two men hollered over the far-off battlements.

"Sister!"

"Niece!"

Their shouts carried into his transparent skull as he walked along the grand expanse of dusty red dirt. Dirt and clay wedged themselves on his disembodied boots while his eyes danced from them to the wall to the men high above.

"Sir!" voices called from all around, addressing him as the shadows of soldiers approached and left him without a single other utterance.

Still, he marched onwards, engraved symbols and round stones filling his thoughts as everything came to a standstill. In front of him was a circular stone on which a glyph was inscribed, its importance filling his being as he inspected it. From one end to the other, a crack snaked through the glossy rock, interrupting a connective stroke that joined the strange ward-like stone together. As he stared at the stone, his gaze rose while the crack spread from the boulder through the red sand and into the impossibly long wall. Like a lightning bolt, the crack splintered through the structure as the red-headed men lumbered above, barking unknown orders while laughing at a barrage of crude commentary.

"Jarren!" His own phantasmal voice sounded from his perch as he addressed the men by their shared name.

They continued to prattle on, the sky above them bright blue. Even as the stonework began to give way, the men continued. His nonexistent gut churned under the weight of his knowledge. Despite everything, he could not generate the words to convey his worries. Before he could try again, his attention was redirected to the depths of the desert, his gaze transfixed as the scene zoomed in upon a dark cloud in the distance. Terrified, he stepped back as the shadow of the wall descended upon his head.

Covering himself with his right hand, he watched as the shadows evaporated. A blur of crude jokes, dark-skinned faces, and red hair overtook his senses. Then, like the curtain on a stage, a red-and-blue fabric lowered, golden embroidery caressing the red floor. Still trembling from the sights and sounds of destruction, he was drawn to a seam in the magnificent fabric. Through it a beam of brilliant white light cut through the darkness of the space, illuminating a crimson line as it stretched into infinity. Standing at the border between light and dark, he peered through a small hole where the two pieces of cloth were joined.

At first there was just the white of the light, threatening to melt away his sense of sight. Fighting it off, he pushed his head through the opening. All around him, the curtains fell as the scene began to take on shape and hue. The red-and-blue material wrapped around him, pressing him forth. Like a newborn, he felt himself emerge on the other side, the gilded colors giving him definition and form.

From under his garbed feet, he saw a pattern of grey masonry and sculpting spread out radially into the distance. Raising his head, he watched as granite columns grew around him, forming a perfect square as they raised to support transmogrifying aqueducts and decorative archways. Then a thin film spread over the terrace, taking on the shape of a winged cross engraved into the ground. A moment later, small warding runes embedded themselves within the gigantic mark, giving it its final touches as shadows rose from the white stone ground.

All around him, humanoid shades filled the evanescent space, forming a perfect circle around the grand cross. The silence waned, the air filling with a growing murmur of indistinguishable words and cheers as each new figure appeared. From the great marking's top, a grand structure emerged, a giant temple growing from the space where several column tops met. It was an enormous structure, adorned with domes and colossal statues of a divine figure that seemed to be etched into his memory. From its top rose a giant white obelisk, its finish reflecting the sun's golden rays, appearing like a golden beam itself reaching for the heavens. Following its construction, several figures in purple and green robes faded into the scene, their faces and bodies shrouded in a thick haze. Opposite them, garbed in everything from rags and robes to armor and bones, shamanistic ghosts stood.

Across from him stood the elder of the red-headed, dark-skinned men from the wall. Behind him was the younger of the two. Their green eyes were fixed on him as the thunder of drums overtook the plaza. A procession of wraiths in various garb encircled the grand cross. He watched with dizzy eyes as he turned about and about. With the final thump of the percussion, the clamor and movement ceased. His vision seemed to invert upon itself as, once again, a pair of vivacious yellow eyes filled his view.

There stood the woman, Senna. Garbed in an elegant white silk dress that clung to her olive skin, the silver-haired woman sauntered across the sacred ground of the winged cross. His breath and thoughts were frozen as he watched her take step after step, pausing between movements to bow before the umbral onlookers. Thin pieces of gossamer cloth floated around her arms and shoulders, drifting like transparent wings behind her. After an endless series of starts and stops, the white-ensorcelled woman took place opposite him. Her yellow eyes danced as they focused upon him, her dark lips forming a captivating smile.

Words began to flow from each of the priestly and shamanistic figures as the setting took on an air of authority and heightening energy. As each pair of holy people finished their speech, the woman across from him stepped forward. His own form seemed to move in sync with hers as he was displaced ever closer to the adorned bride. They took another step toward each other as the second pair finished. Then a third and then a fourth. At the middle of the grand cross, the circle, and the whole world, the white woman stood only inches away from him, looking into the depths of his soul with her amber eyes. Without a word, he took her hands in his, caressing her slender fingers.

At their side, the most prominent of the divine clerics faded into existence. The high priestess of the procession, with her white gown, purple-and-green shawls, and small ritual talisman stood holding a ceremonial dagger in her hands.

"If there are any in all of Her divine providence who would reject this couple's union, please speak now," the orderly shade proclaimed to the congregation. Everyone held their breath as silence fell upon the arena. "Then it is with the blessing of our ancestors and the divine Goddess herself that I bind thee. If you would bare your hands, Senna and Vir."

Without hesitation, he and Senna turned their coupled hands over. The priestess's ghost circled the pair. With a gentle hand and deft precision, she pricked the palm of Senna's left hand and his right hand. Following her instruction, the couple placed their palms together once more, facing each other. Flowing from their mixing blood, a web of red ribbon entwined his hand with hers, racing up their joined arms. As he looked into Senna's eyes, her face glowed with a light purer than any he had ever seen.

"I now pronounce thee bound," the high priestess said.

All over their bodies, the red ribbon spread, locking the two in place as the silver-haired maiden pressed her lips to his once more. He felt the woman's pulse through their joined hands as their bodies seemed to merge. Darkness overtook him as their hearts beat synchronously throughout their unified minds and bodies. He felt the woman's love and passion and read her dreams and thoughts as distant echoes of shared times rippled through his heart and soul.

"Thank you," she whispered.

"No, thank you," he replied as they continued their embrace.

"And thank you," another voice said, breaking the veil of peace and forcing his mystified eyes to open.

Behind the silver-haired woman stood a golden-haired priestess garbed in purple and green, holding Senna's right hand. As a jolt of terror rippled through his being, he reached out to grab the amber-eyed woman's hand. Before he could, the grey-eyed priestess pressed her crimson lips to his lover's skin. The blue sky darkened, and thunder echoed in the distance. He fetched his bride's hand but gasped as her weight fell against him. Turning his gaze, he watched while the beautiful woman crumpled in his arms. Falling to his knees and staring into the frozen features of the woman he loved, fear overtook him.

"Governess!" a familiar gruff voice said from somewhere in the darkness.

"Senna? Senna!" he cried, despair filling his voice.

"The pleasure is all mine." The venomous words dripped down as he kneeled beside the motionless woman, her yellow eyes frozen in an unnerving stare.

Wrath emanated from him as he looked up at the crimson-lipped temptress, her grey eyes staring down at him with a sinister glare. Behind her, the sky continued to darken as clouds gathered and thunder rumbled. Beneath the turbulent vapor, a whirlwind of dark red was building while warning horns blared in the distance. The attendees' shadows disappeared one by one as the golden-haired witch grinned with psychotic glee. As the storm grew in intensity, the world around him began to crumble. The stone columns cracked and splintered under the oppressive weight of the impending doom that was descending. The hiss of violent air and grit scraping at the white granite made the earth shake.

"Please, gods, no," he mumbled, bowing his head.

For a moment, his somber prayer was answered. The settlement seemed to wane, the floor moving beneath him as he and his bride were carried by invisible hands into the doors of the grandiose temple. Echoing his melancholy, a choir of voices chimed in as they called to their ancestors and the one true Goddess.

All around him, statues of the Goddess looked down upon the threatened maiden as he trembled with reproach. Gazes of scorn, wrath, repugnance, and devilry filled the divine Maiden's marble eyes as holy and mystical words mingled within the light-filled room. Outside the walls of the consecrated structure, a fierce gale was empowered by the sound of grinding sand and stone. Between every syllable of the vociferous ensemble, a deafening crash assailed the walls as the storm outside raged with unholy power.

"Good man, Vir!" Voices called toward him from all sides as he kept his guard over the silver-haired Senna in his arms.

"Dav . . ." the woman's weak voice drew him downwards as the choir continued its spell.

"Everything will be OK." The words tumbled from his dry, pained lips as he stared down into the beautiful yellow eyes of the woman he loved.

"Yes," she reassured him, reaching her thin hand up to his face. The coldness of her body chilled him, grounding his phantom in the moment as the world became darker and darker. "Yes, everything will be alright."

Bones and crystals shook out of the corner of his eye, the procession's arcane summons beginning their work. Crackling energy overflowed the room as, one by one, the small objects popped out of existence. Time seemed to stand still as he held the silver-haired beauty in his arms, closing his eyes. Visions of her strong-willed form filled his mind as a strand of hope reached out to the future. He prayed for her health. He willed to see her again, standing before the proud population over which she presided, giving a speech for the coming harvest and parades. He wanted to watch her take to task the brazen elder and the younger red-headed men who were her only remaining family. He wanted to see the new life that had just been sown in her womb cradled in her olive arms as they stood together overlooking their borderland home.

But that ending was stolen from him as he felt Senna's body tighten in his arms. No matter what he prayed for, believed in, or willed to happen, he could not prevent the inevitable. Opening his eyes, he watched in terror as her body's damning transformation began.

"Davnian." The woman whispered his true name, forcing a smile onto her pained features. From her toes and up her legs, a ceramic complexion replaced the softness of her skin as it worked up her body.

"Senna," he said, threatening to tear the very fabric of reality as the chanting shades fell beside him.

"Today was wonderful." Senna's kind words fell upon his raddled brain, each word spoken softly as she gathered what strength she had left. "Everything. It was all more than I had ever hoped for."

Surrounding the center stage, the settlement's protective prop walls gave way as the storm shook the ground. Black winds filled with red grit tore at the failing, hallowed walls as others cried out in fear. Behind him, he heard the roar of a giant beast followed by the sound of splintering wood. Screams of anguish and pain echoed throughout the altar room as a worn, throaty growl joined with the howl in a cacophony of sardonic yowls. Joining in with the sinister chorus was the all-too-familiar voice of the crimson-lipped priestess, lightning crackling beside him and his ward as the shadows of its victims collapsed all around.

"I . . ." He attempted to protest once more. However, he could not follow through with his objections. His heart sank as every notion of a bright, happy future crashed down around him.

"Every day since you arrived at our gates has been special to the people here," Senna continued, caressing his cheek. "And I have cherished every day since we first met." The conversion was happening more rapidly, already overtaking her legs and the small of her back. Taking a deep breath, the silver-haired maiden bit through the pain of her failing body, speaking to him with joyous abandon. "Don't ever regret those days, or I'll never forgive you."

"I won't, Senna. I promise I won't." His voice trembled as reality began to take on a hellish atmosphere.

"Virage," a low, guttural voice called from behind him. The scream of the elder of the two redheads filled his ears as the monstrous entity bellowed. In his mind's eye, visions of the terrible creature's form crept in, the shadow of a behemoth with the teeth and hide of a thousand animals standing over the broken body of the town's dark-skinned protector. The beast taunted him as it ground the dying man's body to paste beneath its giant hammer.

"Virage," the sardonic voice of another called from his right side.

The flayed and mutilated forms of the temple clergy surrounded the disturbed ghoul as it sat upon a throne of skin and bone that crawled toward him. Adorning the wicked shadow's body was a glistening black plate, festooned with the moving, agonized visages of those he had mangled. With glistening white teeth, the abhorrent wraith grinned as those around him begged for death.

"Virage?" the last of the demonic trio said as she approached from his left. It was none other than the golden-haired witch with her crimson lips and nails, walking over a mound of scorched stone and flesh as she approached. Lightning and flames danced around her unearthly form as blood dripped from her pale hands. Her grey eyes beckoned him to look as she removed the purple-and-green robes of the holy order, revealing profane and arcane scars that covered her deathly pale skin.

"Virage! My Virage!" A childlike face embossed itself within the ground, its mouth widening into a frightening shriek. As it continued its murderous wails, its maw extended farther and farther until he felt himself and his lover sinking between its stonework lips.

"Davnian." Senna's voice cleared his thoughts once more as he looked down upon her almost-statuesque figure.

"Yes, Senna." He felt his world slipping away as the last of the woman's form began to petrify.

"I love you, Davnian." Senna's words echoed through the gloom as she looked into his eyes one last time. Large droplets formed at the corner of her eyes as she whispered her final word. "Goodbye . . ."

"I-I love you," he stammered and then froze as the crystal curse hardened around her ears. He watched her bright yellow eyes open one last time as she donned a radiant smile. And then it was done. The glass-like corruption solidified her features, replacing her olive skin with its finalizing finish. Between his fingers, he felt her hands transform, replaced by cold crystal.

The light of the world dimmed as the maddened laughter of the demons reached a fever pitch. Everything inside him wanted to die. His heart froze, and his emotions ran dry as a singular depression overtook his reasoning. The earthen lips of the giant child's face closed, swallowing him and his crystalized bride. Eternal darkness fell over him as every sense went numb.

Once again, Senna had died in his arms, and once more, he could do nothing to stop it.

12

NERIS

Opening the wooden shutters of the room, Neris stood with prickled skin as the cold air of the outdoors caressed her body. The room was still heavy with musk and perspiration from her toying with the grizzled huntsman. Behind her she heard him dressing, taking his time to outfit every loop and strap of his hide cuirass. Overall the huntsman had proven more than sufficient though her nerves were still on end from their toiling.

"I would offer you something to ease yourself, ne vindal, but I fear we don't have such niceties here," Bedimer said behind her. Her ears perked up at the sound of his thinblade scuttling across the floor.

"Do you sleep in that?" Neris prodded with a jest of disapproval. "Perhaps you'd be better off if you cared to sleep warm."

"I've taken on the vigil for the next few nights," he said with a grunt. Neris turned and watched him tighten his belt. "The trees must be watched at night," he said, "just in case something bigger decides to lumber around, causing chaos."

"I'd think being as high up as we are, there'd be little to worry about from beasts and the like."

"You have a keen sense, vindal," Bedimer said as he picked up his

silver lantern. He hung it from his belt, sighing as he eyed the unconscious patient on the table beside him. "I'm impressed he could sleep
through that."

"You'd be even more impressed by what other things he's slept
through." Neris shot the weary man a knowing look as she went over to
the dying lantern on the counter. Snuffing the last of the light, she
turned her gaze back to the huntsman. He was staring at her, transfixed
for a moment, a slight grin on his face. "Shall you take your leave,
charming Bedimer?"

"I think I will, vindal Neris," he said, making his way to the door.
"Have a good rest of your evening, and . . ." Bedimer stopped and
turned to his side, lowering his gaze into the darkness. Following his
eyes, Neris saw that the left hand of her slumbering love was caught
upon Bedimer's leggings. He laughed and went to remove the man's
hand, shooting Neris a confused smile. But as he went to disentangle
the sleeper's claw, the gnarled black nails dug into Bedimer's leather
leggings.

"What in . . ." Bedimer was caught mid-word as the sleeper arched
his back on the table. Without a thought, Neris fetched a sleeping aid
from the counter and then sprang back to the table.

"He's convulsing again," she said, her right hand coming down hard
on the Virage's chest. With a little force, he collapsed back against the
table. She took a breath, waiting to see what would happen next. For
several moments she waited as the man panted, preparing to bring the
potion to his lips when the fit diminished. Feeling his heartrate drop,
she exhaled.

"Is he alright?" Bedimer asked, freeing himself from the man's grip.

"Just a night fit. He has them every now and then, but it's nothing
to—"

In an instant, Virage's right hand was upon hers, squeezing her
wrist. Looking down, Neris stared at the man's face, watching as it
twisted in pain. Then his eyes opened. Her shoulders locked up as ice
flowed down her spine. In his sockets, two black orbs stared into her
rusty eyes. She thought to move her left hand and administer the

potion, but in the instant it took her muscles to receive the signal, his mouth opened. Fear overcame her stoicism as the man began to scream.

Neris tried to block out the wailing tempest echoing from his gaping maw. She drew her left hand close to the tortured man's face, but as her fingers inched toward him, his demonic gaze fixed upon her. His pitch-black orbs and sagging jaw were like pits into the deepest darkness of the void, and from it the wail of a dying god shook her to the bone. As she started down, she saw his demonic appendage crawl toward her hand. His mottled members twitched and scraped at her perfect skin.

"Move away!" Bedimer shouted over the gale as he reached for his sword. "I'll—"

"No, no weapons!" Neris said. "Just help me hold him still!"

"He has your arm! He's going to—"

"Just keep him down!"

Bedimer nodded, his ears twitching at the unholy noise. With a haggard gaze, he leaned over the terrified screamer and planted one hand on his shoulder. Then Bedimer grabbed Virage's right hand and drew it away from Neris. Seeing an opening, she pushed herself down against her patient and poured the potion into his open mouth. Through the moisture, the scream continued. Soggy cries and wet grunts sputtered as the substance worked down his throat. Then he began to cough, his muscles giving way. Closing his eyes, he gasped and curled on the tabletop, the hiss of air on every beleaguered breath.

"I've got him now," Neris said as she motioned Bedimer away with her head. The man growled in protest but backed away. The sleeper's right hand crept over the linens and found her arm, gripping it tight. On her other side, his claw fumbled around her arm. His nails dug into her flesh in desperation. She bit through the pain and kept him pinned. "I need you to go get Elis. I'm afraid I can't do the rest of the evening."

"But vindal, he still has your arm."

"I'll be fine." She shot Bedimer a placid smile. His grey eyes showed worry and disbelief. Without a word, he nodded and turned for the door. "Thank you, Bedimer." As he left, she buried her face in the trau-matized dreamer's belly and let out a deep breath.

"Calm yourself, ne vahr," Neris whispered as she drew herself to him. She thought back to their last time together and found what words she could to comfort him. Her heart raced as he shook beneath her. "Be calm, Davnian. Be calm."

13

ELIS

Elis had lost track of time as she awoke from dreams of the past and flights of fancy. Childhood dreams danced in her head as she rose from the table, wiping drool from her mouth after her restless slumber. She lumbered through the dark room to the door to their shared bedroom, smiling as she watched her little one curled up beneath a quilt. The girl slept like a babe as she clung to the blanket. Elis wanted to lie down but dreaded waking the girl from whatever benevolent place her dreams had taken her.

Still fixated on Rais, Elis felt guilty for all the times she had scolded her for daring to call her the one thing she wanted to be more than anything: mother. In her heart, Elis knew that to Rais she was, in everything but blood, her mother. Elis had cared for the girl and raised her. Deep down, Elis wanted to return that favor and welcome the small, hazel-headed bundle of energy as her daughter. But beneath the layers of yearning and superficial regret was a deep sense of shame. If she opened that door, then the woman who had died to bring the girl into the world might be forgotten. It would deny her the birthright that she had earned in life. For all of that, Elis could not bear to let those things pass. She would tell Rais about her brave mother and ensure that the woman's life lived on in her daughter's memory.

But maybe that was all just fearful justifications. Elis did not see herself as a mother and hadn't in countless years. She had only held a child in her belly once but had lost it to the dreaded Hyunisti curse, or so she was told. Hyun had said it wasn't her fault and that if the father had been anyone but one of the forest folk, then fate would have done otherwise. Elis had taken the loss in stride. Compared to the chaos and hurt from times far darker, the event seemed nondescript. Her lover at the time was so disheartened he tried to take his own life, but as luck would have it, another woman earned his love. And as implausible as it was, he had a child with her. All the better for them, Elis had thought. She could only move forward.

Closing the bedroom door, she returned to her things. She cleared the old tome and loose pages from the table, promising herself that she would put them back in their proper spot in the morning. Elis furrowed her brow at the sight of loose wax spilled upon the table. It was bad enough having every crushed thing imaginable spread out, so Rais could find a color that she liked. Scraping it up, Elis tossed it in a tiny jar to be melted again for reuse. Satisfied with the state of the room, she sat in her chair, laid her head down, and prepared to return to blissful sleep. However, as she closed her eyes, her speckled ears perked to the sound of a sharp rapping at her door.

"Vindal Elis," a muffled voice called from beyond the house's portal. Rising from the table, she walked to the entryway and unlatched the door, fixing her lavender eyes on the haggard silhouette of an older talvuo man, silver sword at his side, brilliant lantern in hand with the light directed at their feet. "Evening, vindal."

"Bedimer, why are you here at this hour?"

"Trouble with vindal Neris's project. Your sleeper is having a howling fit, and it's wracked the woman's nerve. She needs help this evening. If you would oblige, vindal."

"Yes, of course," Elis said, snapping to and looking around for her cloak and sandals. Something that could upset Neris enough to call for help was unthinkable, but she couldn't leave the other woman to fend for herself. Grave images danced through her head. She found her garments and donned them. Yet as she strayed outside, she was filled with guilt. "Bedimer, can you do something for me?"

"What is it, vindal?"

"I need you to stay here in case Rais wakes up."

"I'm sure she'll be fine either way, ne vindal." Hesitation clung to the man's voice as he shifted in place.

"No, I mean it," Elis said, shooting the old talvuo a glare. "She often wakes up at night from terrible dreams, and I told her someone would be here if that happened. I'll not be a liar to my—"

"Alright, vindal. I'll stay and keep a vigil over her," the old hunter said, waving her on. "I'll just take a seat and dose then if that's fine by you."

"Thank you, Bedimer," Elis said. With a grizzled grin, the man bowed his head.

Secure in the knowledge that someone would be there for Rais, Elis left her treetop home and made way to the old healer's quarters. As she followed the lights of paper lanterns, crossing bridge after bridge, her mind filled with worry. The fit he had earlier that day was usual for the time, coming and going like clockwork on the specified hour. His night-time fits were often just as bad but typical and predictable. Shaking and contorting were normal. Sometimes he called out in slurred speech. But she remembered one time when he was first taken in that the hysterics were anything but ordinary.

That day they brought him to the healer's quarters by Neris's command. His skin was like dried, flayed leather, and she could only imagine how every touch burned like fire upon his skin. When only a few were nearby, she and Neris administered a sedative to calm him. Thinking their task done, the two confused women shooed everyone from the room, so they could talk in private. As they began their chat, the withered husk that he was had sat up and, with a look of absolute terror, began wailing at the top of his lungs. She remembered how impossible the sound seemed for someone so beaten and disheveled.

Bewildered, she stared as his unholy rancor made her ears twitch and curl. She was sure the whole village had heard the scream but later discovered that somehow only she and Neris had been privy to the unnatural display. Crossing the final bridge, she prepared herself for the worst.

Without hesitation, she burst into the shrouded room, throwing the door open as she scanned for whatever madness lurked within. She spied the dark, moonlit body of Neris Delvori pressed against their sleeping friend, whispering soothing words as the man beneath her trembled. The air in the room was heavy with the dissonant aroma of whiskey, musk, sweat, and fear. She closed the door behind her, shedding her cloak as she approached the table.

"How is he?" Elis asked, bringing her hands to Neris's bare back.

"Worse than I thought he'd be," Neris said as she raised herself from the sleeper. Elis watched Neris's chest fall to fill the space between her and the sleeper. Her right hand was held in his. Looking to the other side, Elis spied his claw's nails digging and scraping at the woman's coal-black arms. "Gods Neris, your arm."

"Just get me some bandages and something to clean it with," Neris commanded, trying to keep composed.

Elis went to the counter. From beneath it, she fetched dry linen scraps and a jar of cleaning salve from above. Grabbing the almost-empty bottle of whiskey, Elis approached Neris's other side and used her foot to scoot over the stool they had used earlier that day. Pouring the whiskey over Neris's injured arm, she watched the claw slip away. Elis used the opening to clean the jagged scrapes with a cloth. Neris had small gouges in a few places, but nothing that would leave a scar if treated correctly. Watching as Neris pinned the claw beneath her arm, Elis applied the salve to the wounds and then tied three layers of bandages around the bleeding holes. Neris let out a sigh of relief and then turned to Elis, her red eyes heavy from the evening.

"Thank you, ne vindal," Neris said, planting herself more firmly over the sleeper's shivering, twitching body. His claws were pinned away so as not to be any further nuisance while the Delvori woman's weight kept his body in check. His head turned to and fro as sweat glistened on his brow. "Do you think you can tend to that?"

Elis nodded and then got up. A pour of water and a wet cloth later, she slumped over the sleeper's head, looking at Neris's naked frame astride the tortured man. The smell of lust clung to her, making Elis's impish mind race to curious places. She had wondered why Bedimer, of all people, was the one who had fetched her. Putting it all together, she was amused at the thought of her sultry lover having a tussle with the old huntsman. The notion was a pleasant distraction as their shared burden quaked and groaned between them.

"Well, this isn't the most romantic end to an evening, my dear," Neris said, her eyes growing heavier as she tried to keep her weight set.

"Not exactly a midnight escape or a quick release, was it?" Elis chided, replacing the sweaty, damp cloth with a new one.

"I had hoped for something a bit less dramatic, if that's what you're alluding to, ne vindal."

"Well, Bedimer isn't one for making a scene; that much is certain."

"That easy, am I?" Neris feigned playfulness, exhaustion clinging to her words.

"You couldn't do much better here. He's a good man, if a little worse for wear," Elis replied. The old hunter had seen a lot and been through more, though that was a subject for another time.

"I hate to be a burden, but I don't think I can make it the rest of the night," Neris said with a chuckle, yawning from her perch. Beneath her, the man shivered and quaked. Yet the spasms in his hands and the franticness of his grip began to dissipate.

"I think I can manage," Elis said. "You should get some rest."

She offered the woman her arm. Laughing, the shadow-like woman eased herself off their patient. Leaning against Elis, Neris turned to her, wearing a weary grin. Trying to help her upright, Elis froze as the dark woman planted a firm kiss upon her lips. Overcome, Elis held her there, steadying Elis in her arms. Then Neris righted herself, pulling her head back and stretching in place.

"I think that'll help me sleep better," Neris said.

Turning to the counter, Neris walked over and picked up her few garments and accessories. Slumping away, she turned her head, her dark ears sagging with her droopy eyes. In the darkness, the black silhouette of the other woman waved to her before she left the room. Elis waved back, still stunned by the unabashed gesture. A small, worried grin stretched across Elis's face as she sat beside the table. Looking back at the dreamer, she picked up his claw in her hands, rubbing the drying wetness and iron from his nail tips.

"Ge rolm, ne vahr," Elis whispered to the trembling man beneath her.

With her free hand, she flipped the damp cloth upon his brow. There would be another evening to curl up with her little one, one to share her dark lover's embrace, and yet another for dreams filled with childhood fancies. And in between, there would be nights like this, full of change and tumult, which she would see through. Of that much, she was certain.

14
____

UNKNOWN

Floating in the darkness of his mind, the man let go again as the cycle of love, pain, and regret began to assemble the horrors once more.

[This is my penance.] His thoughts flowed this way and that as the set pieces retook shape. [This is my punishment for failing her. For failing them.]

In the distance, he could already see the fractal of a red desert beginning to manifest, stretching into infinity as the rectangular geometry of a window formed to frame his gaze. Cold, ghostly stone sapped the phantom warmth from his invisible feet as he continued to be enraptured by self-loathing.

[Don't you grow tired of this story, young one?] a voice asked from the shifting dark as fake walls and innocuous props filled the would-be bedroom. [How many times must you live it before you've had your fill?]

[This is my—]

[Penance?] the strange voice asked, becoming clearer as his embattled brain focused on the peculiar interloper. With an animal-like growl, the odd entity chuckled. [Tell me, young one, what atonement is there in your eternal suffering? Because all I see is masochistic admonishment to assuage your broken ego.]

[How dare you!] A wave of anger swept over his being as he turned his attention to the darkness. The scene froze in place as his vengeful stare pierced the infinite blackness in the recesses of his mind. [Do you think I take pleasure in this?]

[To repeat this grisly scene so many times,] the other said, the harsh words seeming to ripple from the farthest reaches of the black abyss, [it does indeed make me question your pleasures. After all, what man would suffer such loss over and over and over again if he did not reap some kind of gain? What man would prescribe such a treatment to himself if it did not satiate some latent desire?]

[Why would I want this?] he asked, gesturing with incorporeal hands as he molded the scene to reinforce his question. His ashen lover, the bodies of the dead, and Senna's frozen form took center stage as he demanded an answer from the intruder. [Who would want to relive these horrors?]

[I did not ask if you wanted to relive them,] the entity hissed in its gravel-filled voice. [However, who else would this endless suffering serve? Tell me, what punishment would compensate for the atrocities of that day? What are you giving up, and what are you changing by trapping yourself in this self-serving prison?]

[This is not self-serving,] he protested, his wrath growing.

[How is it not?] the other demanded. [Peaks and valleys of emotion: bliss and pain, joy and sorrow, love and hatred. These are the things you recreate with every step you take in this abyss, this web of delusion that you weave for yourself to cradle and protect what remains of your pathetic soul. To stave off the beast that is feeling and living, just to enshrine your wounded pride.]

[Take that back, you monster!] His anger had pushed the limits of his emotional stamina. Looking into the endless pit, he summoned what strength he could, the glowing red gaze of the demons that lurked deep within his soul manifesting all around them. [Take it all back.]

[Is this how you would treat her memory?] the entity asked. Within the darkness, a glowing white light manifested itself. The different spectrums wound together, forming the glowing, ghostly visage of the silver-haired woman from his unending nightmares. Wearing a soft smile, Senna's transparent figure opened her yellow eyes. As she looked upon him, tears filled her eyes, her expression changing from joy to concern. [Is this how you would degrade the time you spent together?]

[Don't toy with me,] he countered as he willed forth duplicates of the dark claw that he envisioned was his left hand. Full of vehemence, he charged the glowing manifestation of his dead lover. Through the unreality, the miasmatic prongs thrust into the light.

"Davnian . . ." the illusion whispered in Senna's voice.

[Stop it!] He did not abate his assault as he tore into the luminous being. With the sound of a thousand sickening rips and tears, his monstrous manifestations tore into her ghostly body. The woman's form lurched and tossed as each new spear pierced her frame, a tinge of disgust and shock dropping into the pit of his ephemeral stomach as each hit its mark. [Just stop. Stop!]

As the last of the conjured weapons struck, the woman's body slumped over. The light faded from her impaled form as it took on an all-too-real hue and solidity. His heart raced as he contemplated what he had just done. His body crumpled over as he stared at Senna's ravished form.

[I see,] the entity said, its flat voice echoing through the darkness. [So this is how you really feel about her.]

[No.] His thoughts seemed to drip from his being as he crawled toward the brutalized figure. [No, it isn't. I swear.]

[Isn't it?] the other prodded. [You've condensed everything about her into this muddled aggrandizement of lost love and pain. It's quite clear.]

[Stop it,] he replied as he continued toward the woman's slumped body. Space seemed to shorten between them as he approached, trying to fight back his revulsion.

[Tell me again, young one, why do you do this to yourself? For penance or to forget?]

[Please, just stop,] he begged as he knelt beside Senna's body. Without thinking, he took her in his arms as the shadowy spears melted away. Looking at her face, he trembled again as he drew her close. As he bowed his head in grief, the ghastly figure brought its slender hand to his face. An unearthly cold spread throughout his cheek as she caressed him.

"Davnian," Senna's emotionless voice whispered from below.

"Yes, Senna?"

"Don't regret those days," she said, her voice faint. "Don't regret me."

"I won't, Senna. I won't." Tears built in his eyes as he clutched her in his arms.

[Really?] the other asked. [Isn't that what this is all about? Drowning your sorrow in pain? Burying the past in these brutal moments? All in an effort to condemn yourself? To denounce the time you spent with Senna? To wish it never happened?]

"No, no, Senna. I won't. I promise I won't," he repeated over and over as the other's harsh projections weighed upon his thoughts.

"Don't regret . . ." the olive-skinned figure whispered as she faded away.

"I won't, Senna. Please, just please . . ." His voice trailed off as the woman he loved disappeared, her lingering touch upon his cheek the only remnant of her existence. He felt the world tremble as warm tears streamed down his cheeks.

[Do you understand now, young one? Do you know what all of this is?]

[Yes,] he replied as he curled into a ball.

[Is this how you wish to remember her for the rest of your unfortunately long life?]

[No!] He lashed out into the darkness, his mind racing as he tried to put the pieces of the world back together. Closing his immaterial eyes, he imagined a time before everything had gone wrong. In his mind's eye, he focused on imagery from the past, years before those terrible events, dredging his spirit for better times.

"Stop trying so hard," Senna said, unshackling him from the machinations of his impairment. She wrapped her arms around him, their warmth permeating his disheveled figure. Her ghost nuzzled the nape of his neck as he closed his eyes, his mind starting to disentangle the knots of his self-impairment. "Everything is going to be alright."

"Yes," he replied, keeping his eyes closed. In the surrounding darkness, something great stirred as it made its way to him. With a deep, massive breath, the entity let out a long, turbulent exhale. The hot air tussled Davnian's imaginary hair as he sat on his knees, taking in the sensation of his lover's cradling arms.

"Goodbye for now, Davnian," Senna whispered as she let go, the warmth of her embrace disappearing as her phantom retreated to the darkness.

[So, are you ready then, Davnian?] a towering force asked from the darkness. Taking a deep breath, Davnian opened his eyes, looking at the entity that awaited him. He could tell the being was massive despite the shroud that clung to its body. Peering at him from the gloom, two huge red eyes glowed like blazing suns. Cross-shaped pupils analyzed him from the darkness as their owner drew and released another scorching breath.

[Yes,] Davnian replied. [I'm ready to leave this place.]

[Very well,] the massive being growled. Within the darkness, Davnian saw what he believed was the unfurling of the creature's massive legs, followed by a ripple of several large, unfolding structures as it stood for the occasion. [Close your eyes then, young one, and I will dispel this curse.]

[Alright,] he replied, following its instruction. As he closed his eyes, the creature took a massive breath, preparing to do whatever would cleanse his mind of the nightmare. As he knelt there, he thought back once more to the silver-haired maiden who had haunted his dreams while simultaneously setting him free. Without any further delay, the massive entity bellowed. Scorching heat and blinding light filled the void within his mind.

[Goodbye for now, Senna.] His thoughts echoed into the darkness as he let go of the dream.

15

DAVNIAN

Davnian laid there for what seemed like an eternity. His body was numb. At first he appeared to be still trapped within the dream. However, as he meditated on the moment, he felt a distinct attachment to his physical limitations, becoming sure of his corporeal form. Shifting within his head, his mind wandered as he attempted to obtain a firmer grasp on reality. He felt the shallow in and out of his breathing. As he focused, he picked up on the faint crispness of the air as it penetrated his nostrils and flowed down his throat. The coolness seeped into his lungs. From there, he could extrapolate the expansion and compression of his torso with each breath. Like a faint drum, his heart beat deep within.

As he let go of the simple harmony of his breathing, his mind adjusted to oncoming sensations. Though his eyes were closed, he sensed a soft glow emanating from near his feet. A trickle of warmth crept along his exposed skin. As the bright rays inched up his covered body and reached his head, a damp coldness on his face contrasted with his warming flesh. Something in the back of his mind nagged him. The reason for his drying tears was there, but try as he might, the visages that caused him such grief were unreachable by his waking mind.

[Focus,] a voice hissed inside, snapping him back to reality. [Now is not the time.]

Unsatisfied with his current accomplishments, he concentrated. With all his might, he inhaled as deeply as he could. As he took in the fresh air, he paid careful attention to what aromas and smells he could pick up on. First there was nothing worth mentioning as his sense of smell was overtaken by the coldness of the air. He held it in for a moment and then let go to try again. This time he took a deep, measured breath, making sure to catch even the faintest of odors. The light fragrance of wildflowers was the first to assail his sense-deprived brain, followed by the distinct smell of bark and leaves. As he continued his intake, he picked up on more distinct aromas: smoke and ash, nuts, and cooked meat. The menagerie was enough to make his dry mouth water as he took a moment to savor it.

Several minutes passed as Davnian sampled every new bouquet and stench that entered his curious nose. However, odors, temperature, and an internal sense of being were losing their appeal. He was growing increasingly impatient. He wanted to break free of his paralysis and begin using the rest of his capabilities. As he wracked his brain, his hearing homed in on the whispers of people and the forest outside. Unappreciative of his newest gift, he struggled to pry off the chains binding his other senses. He wanted to use his eyes, but they remained shut despite his protests. He wanted to taste, but despite the faint trickle of saliva within, his tongue and throat were dry and unresponsive. Furthermore, his extremities were unaccepting of any command he could postulate.

Frustrated, he let out an angry hiss of air while contemplating how he was going to make his body obey. If it didn't wake up soon, he feared he'd be tempted to fall back asleep.

[We wouldn't want that.] The faintest whisper of the other's voice echoed in his head as he struggled with his incapability. The words made his insides tremble, a nervous shiver of muscular tension rippling throughout his frame. The faintest trembling of his muscles was itself exhausting, causing him to break into a cold sweat.

Then, there it was. More than the soft glow of what he could only assume was the morning sun, Davnian felt the warm touch of another's skin upon him, caressing his left hand. Something about the sensation was calming as recollections of familiar archaic words worked through his thoughts. It dawned upon him that somewhere beside him was another person. With that idea in mind, he gained renewed strength to attempt to open his eyes.

As he struggled, he found the dim ambience of the room too much for eyes that had just adjusted to seeing the filtered redness of his eyelids. The building brightness of the rising sun was becoming increasingly uncomfortable. Fighting against every protective reflex he possessed, he forced his squinting eyes open just enough to see.

Through the oppressive ambience, he could tell that the room was a carefully assembled wooden structure. Boards and beams had been refined to make a curved, organic interior for the enclosed space. The ceiling was not high but large enough for a grown man to stand without having to stoop, though taller specimens would have difficulty. As his eyes adjusted their focus, he could make out finer details. The interior was plastered with a smooth clay-like finish that covered the walls, floors, and countertops. Shelves and cupboards lined the sides of the room, on which were stacked various glass receptacles and jars containing all manner of herbs and miscellany. At his feet were three large windows on which wooden slats had been notched as makeshift blinds. Plain curtains covered them. Contrasted to his earlier memories, the scene was far lighter in hue and tone.

Taking a shallow breath, Davnian opted to make a slow pass over his left side. Rallying the muscles within and around his neck, he turned his head to appraise the figure next to him. For several moments he waited for his strained eyes to adjust as the nearby blur of yellow and purple came into focus. Through the haze, he made out the figure of a woman with long, dark, golden hair perched on a chair beside him. Adorning her dark, bronze skin was a loose lavender dress that clung to her shoulders and swollen bust. Her head hung forward, her eyes closed as she dozed. Urging his head to tilt a little more, he saw his black, mottled hand, cradled between her own in her lap. Turning his gaze back to the sleeping woman's face, he searched her for recognizable features.

A young blond girl's words rang through his head as something absurd came to mind. Without further hesitation, he focused on taking a deep breath. As it filled his lungs, he took a moment to concentrate. He formulated the instructions required to follow through with his audacious scheme. Without another thought, he enacted his cunning plan.

"Ge . . ." Davnian's voice creaked as he strained to form the simple syllable. His tongue was limp and immobile, every signal to the muscle seeming to disappear into the ether. His jaw was more cooperative, as were his facial muscles. However, his lips ached as they drew back slightly. His throat became enraged as his vocal cords attuned to the desired frequencies. In the end, what came out of his mouth was less a word and more a guttural croak as he finished exhaling.

The figure beside him shivered for a moment as his utterance carried. The pain in his throat and mouth threatened to gag him, but he would not be deterred by physical discomfort. That singular reaction, no matter how brief or slight, fueled his desire to communicate. He took another deep breath, this time preparing his lips and gullet for the specific task. Concentrating, he forced the monosyllabic word out once more, this time as loud as he could, "Ge . . ."

Warm fingers gripped him as the drowsy female stirred. She shook her head as his mangled verbiage filled the room, tufts of her golden hair falling around her tan face. With a prolonged sigh, his caretaker sat upright, tilting her head back to let her voluminous golden hair drift away from her face. She released his hand and leaned away, stretching over the back of her chair as she yawned. Having roused her from slumber, he decided to try and gain her attention.

"Ge . . .. rollll . . ." Davnian forced out the words, an overwhelming sense of excitement building within his chest. His heart was pounding. His vocalizations still left much to be desired, but he couldn't help himself. Waking and finding himself so close to another living being, a familiar one at that, overwhelmed his sense of restraint. It was as if all the joy and jubilance that he been denied during his prolonged nightmare needed a release.

[Calm yourself,] a small, stern voice said, echoing far off within his head.

[I can be calm later,] he replied, dismissing the stranger without a second thought.

The woman beside him brought herself forward as he screeched. Opening her eyes, she peered at him, her restful lavender irises trying to focus as a look of curiosity crept across her relaxed features. Then her eyes widened as a wave of realization swept away her remaining lethargy. Just out of focus, he could make out the faintest of rustling amid her golden locks as small shadows seemed to protrude from the sides of her head.

"Neeee . . ." the third of the scripted words trailed off as Davnian's vision became acute enough to home in on finer details. He found himself locked in her gaze as her lavender orbs peering into his own. He scanned her attractive face and the strange protrusions alongside her otherwise normal human head. Each was a small, fleshy apparatus, triangular in shape in a way that reminded him of the ears of a large canine or fox, on which dangled an extended, cupped membrane, homing in on him. Small gold and red fur-like hairs coated the outside of the organ. As for the interior, it was much like a small vascular funnel, down which he could only guess his amplified wails were carried into the observer's head.

"Oh gods," his bronze acquaintance whispered as her fingers tightened around his.

"Vaaaaaaah . . . . . r . . ." He ended the sentence he had started.

"Ge rolm ne vahr?" the woman asked, her eyes darting around the room. "Oh gods, what do I do? Oh gods, he's awake. What do I . . . what . . ." She turned back to him. "A moment. Just give me a moment. I need to . . . I need to . . ." Rising from her seat, the strange maiden released his hand as she scrambled away. Trying to keep her in his field of view, he watched with building amusement as she searched the room.

"Ge rolm . . . neeeeee," Davnian said, focusing on each syllable. His grating voice was beginning to wear on his nerves, but the more he spoke, the simpler the exercise became. Despite their previous weakness, with every word, his tongue and throat were becoming more obedient. Deep inside, his body filled with energy as adrenaline and strength returned to his limbs. Through sheer force of will, everything within him was routed to the task of recovery and action.

"Gods, a moment. Just one," his acquaintance said as she stumbled out of view. To his left, he heard her moving around ceramics and glass while mumbling to herself. "This will have to do." Then the woman approached him from his left side as he turned his head toward her. In her hands, she held a large clay cup.

"Stop. Stop with the screeching," she said. He obeyed as she brought her right hand behind his head and raised him from his bed. "Your mouth is horribly dry. Take this. It's not fresh, but at least it's something." As she brought the clay vessel to his lips, he parted them. Closing his eyes, he gulped down what he could of the cool, stagnant water. The liquid tasted like the clay of the pot combined with the faintest tinge of dust and pollen, but that did not stop him from enjoying it for what it was. He opened his eyes as the last droplets fell into his throat. Taking several moments to let the moisture sink in, he flicked his tongue about within his mouth. "There now," she said. "Feel better?"

"Yessss . . ." he hissed. His voice was still hoarse, but the miraculous liquid was already having a restorative effect on his dry innards. He felt his organs turn upon each other as the moisture permeated him. He wouldn't show weakness now but could only imagine what they would try to do if he didn't remain in control.

[Try less,] the reptilian beast grunted from his mind's shadows. [Ease yourself and focus, young one.]

"Good." She smiled at him. Lowering his head, the woman sat back in the small wooden chair. "Now, just try to relax, alright?"

Taking a deep breath, Davnian concentrated on his extremities, feeling his way along each. Starting with his toes, he tensed and relaxed his muscles before working his way up to his feet, followed by his ankles and then his calves. Each pairing of flexile tissue acknowledged his command as he made ready to employ them in yet another test of his abilities. Curling and uncurling his fingers, he finished his evaluation as a shiver of anticipation ran through his frame.

"I can see that look on your face." Turning his head, he saw the bronze-skinned female's eyes, full of concern. "Just take it slow. There's no need to rush things."

[Your caregiver has a good point,] the voice inside said, its smoky tendrils working through his thoughts. [You've just woken up. Do you honestly expect to—]

[Yes, I do,] he said.

Exhaling, he brought all his muscles into play. Turning his palms outward, he pressed his hands against the table as he drew himself up. In one motion, he raised himself from the table and was sitting upright before the golden-haired maiden. A brief feeling of accomplishment settled over him as he turned toward his keeper. Before he could relish overcoming his physical limitations, a sharp pain emanated from his middle back, causing his entire body to arch.

"Dear gods, can't you ever just slow down for a moment?" she said while drawing closer.

"No, it's OK," Davnian replied, raising his left hand to stay her. Without the added support of the appendage, however, his back started to give way. Before he could return it to its place, his body curved to the left, displacing his center of gravity. Unable to stop himself, he fell to the floor. Just before he reached the hard wooden surface, he curled his legs beneath his frame and drew his arms up to brace against the impact. The force of the blow pained his forearms and elbows, knees and feet. However, the feeling of weakness disappeared as each muscle moved on its own to realign his body.

"Are you alright?" the woman asked, kneeling beside him.

"I'm . . . . . fine," Davnian said, using his arms to roll back into a squatting position.

"Don't scare me like that!" she exclaimed, her lavender eyes full of admonishment.

"My . . . apologies."

"Don't resist this time. Give me your arm." He obeyed, and let the woman take his left arm and wrap it around her shoulders. "We're going to stand up together. Lean on me for support, alright?"

"As you wish . . . good woman," he stuttered, a tinge of embarrassment overcoming him.

"Right. Now then, up!" Together they rose to their feet. Following her lead, he sat on the bed that he had just escaped. She let out an exasperated sigh. "Let's go a little slower next time, OK?"

"My apologies, good woman," he said, sighing in resignation. The woman stretched as she sauntered to the windows. "I just . . . don't want to lie around."

"I can't blame you for that," she said, turning to lean back against the countertop. "You haven't been the easiest patient these last few days. You had us all quite worried."

"Where am I?" he asked.

"In the village of the humble Hyunisti," she said, staring down at him with her radiant lavender eyes.

"Forgive me, good woman, but where is that?" he asked, raising his blue orbs to meet her gaze.

"I have often wondered that myself. We're somewhere just on the northern edge of the Grann-voren, and the few traders we get seem to confirm that. Though who's to say for sure."

[We're in Grannas territory,] the other's guttural voice interjected. [If we're in the Grann-voren, we can't be more than a few weeks from the capital.]

[Is there a reason that's important?]

[I'm unsure, young one. Nevertheless, it's always good to have one's bearings.] With that, Davnian could agree.

"Forgive me, good woman. I've been sitting here addressing you . . . without knowing your name. If you would—"

"My name is Elis," she replied, a small grin working its way across her lips. "Elis Renai."

"A Renai talvuo," he thought out aloud, memories of the specie's cultures and customs coming back to him. It was commonplace for talvuo to use their racial or tribal names as their surnames. Likewise, the strange ears seemed to fit the description that was bubbling up within him. "I'm getting ahead of myself again. My name is—"

"Davnian," Elis said, her mezzo voice carrying the name as she pushed herself away from the countertop.

"I knew it!" Davnian almost cheered, his vocal cords catching up with his eagerness as a wave of relief washed over him. Elis chuckled at his outburst, which increased his enthusiasm. His thoughts raced with how to proceed. There was an endless number of questions he could ask her, and though his body was still mending itself, his mind had already regained much of its edge. If the rest of his body followed through as quickly as his voice, he'd be in good shape. "Gods, you know me. There's so much I—"

"Calm down," she said through stifled giggles. "We can get around to all of those things once you're up and on your feet."

"I guess you're right," Davnian replied, trying to still his thoughts. The muscles in his back and legs still ached from his earlier misstep, hinting that he still needed assistance with walking. Given his apparent rate of regeneration, he was sure it would not be long before he could move himself.

"Well, while I'm here, is there anything I can get you? Are you hungry? Thirsty?" Elis asked. Before he could speak a word, his stomach answered for him with a hollow growl. "Oh gods," she said, "that sounds worrisome."

"Water and rest for now," Davnian said, his head light from the brief excitement. Noticing his breath becoming more interspersed, he forced himself to lie down. Waving to her with his right hand, he chuckled. "Though conversation is welcome, good woman."

"Overdid it, did we?" Elis asked. He closed his eyes, taking a deep breath as his aching muscles trembled. He heard her walking over as he calmed his nerves. "You're always making my life difficult. Do you know that?"

"If I knew that . . . it'd be wonderful," Davnian said, trying to imagine what troubles he had sewn in past forgotten lives.

"You've been talking strange since you awoke," Elis said as she perched on the seat beside him. He felt her weight shift and opened his eyes to see her leaning on the tabletop behind her. "I had wondered what you'd be like when you woke up but didn't once think you'd be so . . ."

"Unknowing?"

"Oddly formal," Elis said, staring at the ceiling. Her chest swelled before she let out a deep sigh. Shaking her head, she looked back at him, her expression considerate yet troubled. "It's endearing, but please, just call me Elis."

"Very well, Elis." Davnian smiled back at her. "Thank you for taking care of me."

"It almost feels like it was yesterday that . . ." she stopped midsentence as her eyes softened. "Talvuo minds are strange, Davnian. We remember everything important but forget all the banalities with the changing of the seasons."

"I'm unclear where this is going, but I sympathize," Davnian said, trying to grasp the last thing he could remember. Dreams of the golden-haired girl were the only things he could recall, along with a terrifying existence lurking somewhere in the depths of his head. He had remembered what a talvuo was with immediacy, and the other voice in his head could remember locations, it seemed. He thought about asking the other to divulge everything it knew about him. He decided that would be an exercise for when company was not present. A word clung to his mind that chilled him. A name he knew was closely associated with himself.

"Do you know what they've called you over the past years?" Elis whispered as she bent over him. Looking at her, he could tell she was as exhausted as he was. On top of that, she was dealing with complexities that he couldn't fathom.

"They call me the Virage." The word came to his mind, knowing the answer to her framed posit. "Though I don't know who that is or what it means."

"It doesn't matter," Elis said, sighing against his arm.

He reached up with his claw-like hand, feeling her elbow. Visions of a broken woman being torn apart by a demon's embrace flashed in his mind as he leaned his head to stare at his monstrous fingers. Though he didn't understand it, he knew that whatever the Virage was, that black, demonic vessel was the key to the mystery.

"What matters now is you're awake."

"I may not be for too much longer," he whispered. "I'm feeling drained, and everything is drying up." Indeed, his tongue and throat were creaking from all the hot air he had been spewing.

"Here, have another drink," Elis said, rising to fetch the clay cup.

Together they reenacted his earlier scene, but this time he took a mouthful of the life-giving liquid. Swallowing it in three short gulps, his throat and stomach protested. Water would ease the ache in time, but he'd need energy soon. He was surprised how much he had given the lack of sustenance but wrote that off to whatever force stilled and empowered his actions.

"Vindal Elis!" an androgynous voice cried from somewhere above his head. Davnian strained, trying to crane his head to look, but Elis held him down, shushing his movements.

"Kadin, keep your voice low," Elis said.

"He's awake?" Davnian felt the steps of the other enter the room and heard the groan of latches as a door swayed shut beyond his vision. He moved his eyes to his right to see a thin, almost skeletal talvuo male carrying a small bundle of herbs and flowers. The man's dull grey-green eyes scanned him, his expression both elated and terrified. As the visitor turned toward Elis, the Virage saw an afterimage. An eyeless, nose-less face stared at him, agape, and then was gone. "Vindal, we need to—"

"I'll let the others know in time, Kadin," Elis said, easing Davnian's claw onto his belly as she leaned back. "The elders will want to hear the good news, and that I can do myself. Don't just stand there; toss your bundle."

"Yes, of course, vindal," the man said, moving toward the countertop.

[Did I see what I think I saw?] Davnian asked the other in his head.

[I'm not sure what you think you saw,] the other replied. [But everything's unclear right now. We should take everything as is until you're feeling better. Gather your strength.]

[Agreed.]

"Everything vindal Neris wished for is here. I couldn't find copious amounts of lemon balm, but one of the hunters found a patch of chamomile in one of the clearings. The nightshade berries are in smaller supply than she wished, but . . ."

"I'm sure she can suss these things out when she gets here, Kadin." Davnian thought he detected a hint of boredom in her voice but noted everything the male had hinted at.

[Seems this Neris is quite the herbalist.]

[She always had a penchant for tinctures and poisons,] Davnian replied, at once recognizing his internal monologue for what it was. He didn't know how he knew Neris possessed such skill, but he knew if he met her, more latent arcana would bubble up from within his addled brain.

[Maybe we should request a meeting with this woman.]

"Kadin, could you please send word to vindal Neris that our sleeper has awoken? I'm sure she'd be thrilled to hear that all her hard work has paid off."

"If that is what you wish, I will make it so, vindal."

[She has the sense to call you formal and yet is doted on so.]

[I feel she wants to be more familiar than that, shadow.]

[Am I a shadow?]

[Until you tell or show me otherwise, yes.] The other let out a gravel-filled tumult of ethereal laughter. [Does that amuse you?]

[No, young one. I'm just intrigued. You snap to like a hawk and are as coy as a pup.]

"Davnian?" Elis's voice broke his concentration.

"Yes, Elis?"

"Nothing. I just thought you said something. Oh, Kadin?"

"Yes, ne vindal?"

"Please keep this to yourself." Elis's voice was serious now. Within the score of minutes, her tone had shifted between happy, sarcastic, sullen, bored, and cold. Somewhere in the recesses of his head this was all familiar, but Davnian couldn't help but be amused. "Do you understand?"

"As you wish, ne vindal," Kadin said.

Davnian shifted his gaze back to the man as he exited, catching another glimpse of a wraith hovering behind him. Its face was pained with curiosity, its head perpendicular to a ghostly stem of a neck before it flashed out of existence once more. Then the man stepped out of view and left.

"I'm sorry for the interruption," Elis said. He snapped his gaze back to her and flashed her a grin. She smiled in response. "Do you need another drink?"

He nodded slightly. "If you could,"

"Let me get you a fresh draught. Perhaps a dash of mint or balm will make it last a bit longer on your tongue," Elis said, rising from her chair. "I'll fetch a fresh vessel and be back shortly. If anyone bothers you, tell them to get comfortable until I return."

"I'll try, if I stay awake," Davnian said, chuckling under his breath.

"Was that funny?" she asked, turning toward him. He looked at her lavender-draped frame. In the light from the shutters, he saw her puffing out her chest, her gilded skin shimmering in the sunlight dancing through the leaves. Playfully dominant was another characteristic to add to the growing list of traits that he had logged about the Renai talvuo.

"Not at all." He tried to be sarcastic, but the strain of the inflection tore at his vocal cords. He coughed, choking on the dry mucus that had broken free in his throat. Elis approached, but he held his claw up to signal her off. "I'm fine," he grunted. "I just need to . . . not try too hard."

"Good luck with that." Her voice inflected as he had tried. "I'll be right back."

"When you return, then."

As Elis left, Davnian settled himself back down on the table, his head spinning from the simple movement. His neck muscles flared with hatred toward him, and his back still trembled from his previous fall. Despite all the accomplishments that morning, it seemed his body still needed to be helped along. If need be, he'd force it along as he had done earlier. Otherwise, he'd let himself rest.

[Good luck with that,] the other in his head said.

Davnian ignored the mocking words and took a deep breath. He didn't need to be patronized, but he would allow it. Right now, the best place for him to be was with people who knew him and from whom he could learn.

16

NERIS

Neris had received word from one of the more scrupulous aides that Davnian had awoken from his slumber. Ignoring Kadin's gawking eyes and wry smile, she sent him away and closed the door to her room. Strutting around the wooden chamber, she was fixated on her next moves. She had little in her wardrobe that she considered appropriate: the provocative non-wear from her last days as a courtesan, a crimson blouse and pair of green pants she had been given by the Hyunisti, and the charred leather battle wear with a simple shirt and drawstring slacks. She had various side ornaments and replacements that she could add atop her garb and trade out for different shawls or wraps. At such moments she wished she had her brother's greed and lust to scavenge what remained in their fallen home before Nerin's hubris.

"Zaisure Neris?" a small, curious voice whispered from her doorway. Neris turned to see the small ward of her Renai lover clinging to Bedimer's weary frame. The man shot her a tired glance, motioning to the girl clutching his leg.

"Vindal Neris here will take good care of you, little one," the world-weary talvuo said to the girl. Looking up, he shot Neris a crooked grin as he ogled her exposed frame. "If you don't mind, ne vindal, I must needs depart. I lost a shift from last night and could use sleep before my rounds tonight. Happy hunting."

"Good day, gracious Bedimer." Neris wanted to hiss but left it at pleasantness. The last thing she wanted was to play mother or babysitter, though she could make time for Elis's child. Waving the man away, she looked at the girl and motioned to the door. "Close it, my dear."

"OK," the little girl said.

As she closed the door, Neris decided upon more modest attire for the day. A piece of her black silks wrapped to support herself beneath the crimson blouse. She'd tuck the shirt beneath her plain pants and leather leggings. Beneath them would be her black garters and hose. Overtop she'd draw down the remaining loose blouse with a broader piece of black silk tied in a sash across her waist. The outfit was simple but possessed the allure she wanted. With a few strings undone, her blouse could show a bit more skin and arouse temptation in her onlookers.

"My dear, can you go into that trunk there and fetch me the black silks? There are three long strips," Neris said, signaling to the little green-eyed girl with her extended pinky, ring, and middle fingers.

"OK, zaisure," the little girl said, running to the chest.

Neris grabbed her corset, jacket, and shirt from her bed and returned them to her wardrobe. As the little girl returned with the sashes, Neris pointed to the bed. "Stretch them out on that side, and let's have a look."

"Yes, zaisure."

Neris enjoyed listening to the girl's awkward honorifics, using words that she had learned from her mother versus the standard talvuo forms of greeting or address. Vindal and vivahr (sister and brother), were common throughout all the tribes. Other talvuo women during her more unfortunate years had used the same words, sometimes in earnest, other times hollow with despair or in jaded whispers.

"Let's start with the extra-thin one. It'll be perfect for the binding."

"Yes, zaisure Neris."

Sitting at the corner of her bed, Neris motioned for the child to draw behind her. She wore a crooked grin as the little girl's pale face flushed.

"I'm just a woman, dear, like you will become," Neris said as the girl climbed up behind her. "Now, I'm going to pass you the strap as I decide how I want it crossed in front. When I do, I want you to hold it snug, pulling back gently. Like this." She handed the girl the ends of the cloth. "Now, pull back snug." As the girl began pulling, Neris continued. "Tighter. Tighter. And . . . there, my dear. Don't be shy; you won't hurt me. Understand?"

"Yes, zaisure."

"As you're holding it back there, I will ask you for left or right. If I say left, pass the cloth in your left hand beneath my right shoulder. If I say right, pass from your right beneath my left shoulder. Now, for example, left." The girl flubbed it for a moment, which Neris had anticipated, but without a word, she corrected herself. The little brown-haired girl was a quick learner. "Good girl. Now right. Good."

The process of tying up her bust was simple enough that she could do it herself, but with the girl around, she could be fancy. Using the longer strip was the right choice, allowing her to make a striped cup for each of her breasts.

"Zaisure Neris," the little girl whispered beside her.

"Left. What is it, my dear?"

"Can I spend the night next time my zaisure is over?"

"Right, and let me think."

Neris had told Elis various times that she was content with having the child over. The room was more than big enough for the three of them and often served larger crowds at the Delvori woman's fancy. Thinking of Elis's child, she had even had one of the couples work on a child's bed for her. Indeed, if all things went well, Neris hoped she could move the reluctant hermit and her child into her abode. The space was twice the size of their hovel-like house at the edge of the village and could be partitioned into private sections if need be.

"I've told your mother that I would be more than happy to have you around, though I think she's a bit worried you'll pick up bad habits from our evenings together," Neris said, adjusting her chest to sit even within the fanciful brace. "Honestly, I think she's afraid to be a burden."

"A burden?" the little girl asked.

"Yes. She knows you have nightmares. I think she's trying to get you to grow out of them. Taking you around everywhere doesn't help with that, and grown men and women need their personal time." Neris contemplated her words as the girl sat quietly behind her. With her left hand, she waved to the blouse beside her, gesturing to her shoulders. "Grab that, dear, and drape it. That said, I would be more than happy to have you over more often. Though if you were to do so, I'd ask you one thing."

"Anything, zaisure!" the girl said as she shifted to grab the blouse.

"Stay close by, and avoid treading upstairs."

"Why zaisure?"

The girl's curiosity and concern at Neris's request were to be expected. The previous day, her brother had taken one of the Hyunisti women in front of Elis's daughter. That was fine in and of itself. But if she knew her brother, it had been a display of perceived authority. Her brother was a schemer and a lustful wretch. The weak and fragile ones flocked to his uncandid graces. Like his father, her brother could not be trusted to be fair or pleasant to anyone but himself.

"It's not a place for children or pleasant young women like you," she said, turned on her sultry, seductive contrivances as she spoke.

The little girl draped the crimson blouse over her shoulders. Careful to not catch on her bandaged arm, Neris snapped up the garment and pulled it over her head, letting the cloth fall over her top. Having never worn the clothing before, she was curious at how low cut it was. Choosing to string it up tight, she dismissed the strangeness. The Hyunisti were shy and somewhat daft, but they were as carnally libertine as any Delvori she knew.

"I promise I won't, zaisure. Can I come over next time then?"

"Of course, my dear. Forgive me, young one, but your name again. What is it?"

"Rais, zaisure."

"Of course, my dear Rais," Neris said, stretching into her hose.

It was cold to feign not knowing the name of her lover's child. The whole display was a waltz by design, meant to be a give and take, or at least for her to appear two beats behind. The little girl clapped behind her, seemingly elated. Sometimes Neris hated the game, but often she played it well, and no one was worse for the gestures.

"Now the leathers, and we're all set, my little Rais," she said as she slipped into her pants. "Are you ready to visit your mother?"

"Is zaisure at the healer's hut?"

"Yes, she is, my dear," Neris grunted as she bent over to strap the protective wear tight. Her legs had grown slenderer in the months since she had last worn them. Thankfully, the Hyunisti had retailored them with broader and shorter straps, allowing for better sizing for her frame. "Are you excited?"

"Zaisure hasn't taken me there since the sleeping man arrived," Rais said, dancing in place on the bed. Enthusiasm hung on Rais's every word as Neris strutted in front of her small vanity, eyeing the mirror to make sure everything was in its place. The red blouse was cut just low enough to expose her silk-covered cleavage, the luster of the material complimenting the texture of her obsidian skin. "So, he's awake?"

"That's what I've been told, my dear," Neris said, pointing to the broad length of black silk that remained on the bed. With understanding, Rais grabbed it and brought it to her. "I'm hoping he's not too ill from being asleep for so long."

"He's had really bad dreams too, zaisure told me. And he has really bad shakes, and he . . ." Neris was amused by how much Elis had told the child. "I hope zaisure will feel better now that he's woken up!"

"So do I, my dear," Neris said, though the image of Davnian's black, bottomless eyes still clung to her brain from the night before. "And maybe when everything is done, we can convince your mother to have you name her properly."

The little girl behind her fell silent. Neris had avoided the topic, using the term "mother" and knowing that Rais would respond with the correct words. It was a sensitive topic to bring up, but Neris couldn't help but prod. She wanted to make Elis realize that having the child idolize a dead woman was as perverse as stealing the admiration and respect that she wished to preserve. Content with her image in the mirror, she turned around and looked at the young girl, whose hands had crept to her face as she held back tears.

"In due time, dear. For now, call your mother as you both wish. No need for tears," Neris said, strolling across her room.

On her nightstand were two wrapped leather holsters. The first was a leg holster for a set of six small throwing knives while the second was a belt holster for a larger hunting knife. She fit the hunting knife and its holster into her sash. Then she tied the throwing knives behind her right flank, smiling at the familiar feel of the leather and metal against her quad.

"There now," Neris said as she turned back to the child. The little girl had dried her face on her small white hands, shooting her an almost defiant look with her emerald-green eyes. "Better, young one. Now cheer up, and let us not keep your mother waiting."

"OK, zaisure Neris," Rais said, her face clearing as Neris ran her black hands through her hair. Neris had enjoyed her brief time with the little girl, feeling encouraged that the little sprite had a bite in her that was worth exploring. Combining her pragmatic teachings with the tempestuous and solitary lifestyle of her blond lover would be interesting to see furthered in the little girl.

With Rais's hand in hers, Neris strolled out onto the bridge that led toward the old healer's quarter. Blinded by the sunlight, Neris shielded her eyes as she led the small Hyunisti girl. Biding her own anticipation, she stifled bemusement as they walked.

17

____

NERIN

"Neris!" a small, petulant voice cried out around him as Nerin stumbled through the darkness of a maze of stalagmites and toothy crevasses.

A child called after his sister, its voice small and annoying to his perfect black hound ears. Wherever they were, he would find them and set them straight, and then he would find his sister and escape the haunted tunnels. If only he could see properly, he would have prevailed by now. But all was not lost. In front of him, he saw a glowing green wisp, a herald of his powerful master. Through it, he would find his way and return with his sister to their kingdom.

[This way,] the hissing voice of his great adviser whispered, the green orb dancing around a corner of jagged stone.

The path was uneven and littered with rocky debris, but he did not falter. He was trained, muscular, agile, and careful. His senses were acute, his every move well planned. The damp stones and loose rubble would not trick him as he skirted the corner. With his red eagle eyes, he spied the dancing flame hovering above the ground in the distance. With spite in his breast, he pushed forward, the rocks around him rippling as if possessed.

"Neris!" the boy cried again. Nerin turned to look behind him but spied no one. Then the cry came from in front. "Neris, where are you?"

Blood pumping, he raced toward the light. No one would reach his sister before him. As he got to the flame, a tremor ripped through the cavern. Rocks rained down on his head. He shook his black mane free of debris, huddling near the bright green sprite until the rumbling stopped. Readying to stand, his eyes caught a glimpse of something strange. Beneath the soundless flame, he spied something buried in the wet dirt. Without another thought, he dug his hands around the object, pulling it free from the mud.

It was a silk-garbed poppet. Blackened wood made up its body while moldy rope strung the thing together. In one of its hands was a small wooden lance made of stained white oak. Atop its head was a mixture of dried resin and tufts of black hair not unlike his. The childish implement disgusted him, but as he went to drop it, a whiff of his sister's hair rose from it. Just then he heard scurrying down another passage, the green wisp near him transporting down the tunnel in a flash. Near it he saw small black limbs skirt the side, the light disappearing with the child.

"Neris!" the child called, the cave ringing with his tiny voice.

"Come back here!" Nerin commanded, yet the boy did not abide.

[Hurry, my young master. This way. Hurry! We're almost there.]

The air was thick with dust and mold. The tunnel walls swayed with his vision as he forced himself downward. He would not let anyone have his sister. All around him, tiny voices urged him onward. He needed to reach her before it was too late. Just a little farther, and she'd be safe.

Rounding corner after corner, dizzy from the endless winding, crawling, and slipping past rocky outcrops and slippery patches, Nerin reached the maze's end. There the boy stood, looking away as Nerin crept up behind him.

"Neris, I found you!" the boy shouted, his black talvuo ears rising from beneath his dirty black hair. Walking forward, the boy was unaware of all else.

"Nerin!" His sister's angelic voice reverberated through the halls as she cried for him.

[Stop him!] a thousand voices screamed.

He couldn't wait any longer. Rushing forward, he grabbed the boy from behind and threw him into the wall. With bloodlust in his eyes, he watched the little black frame of the talvuo boy shrink against the wall as he fell into a fetal position. The child groaned and spat blood from his bruised face. With a sharp kick, Nerin sent the boy spiraling on the floor, coughing and gasping for breath.

"Nerin!" his sister cried.

Nerin turned toward the voice. There at the back of the small hollow was none other than his sister. Clothed in a tattered black satin dress, her frail, tiny body lay against the wall as her big red eyes looked up to him, filled with horror.

"Neris, it's me. I'm here," he said, his voice filled with all the love he could muster. He bent down to her and pressed himself near. "It's alright, Neris. I've come for you, we can go now—"

"Get away from me!" Before he could move, her hand struck his cheek. Her small, thin arms could do little to his face, but the bite of her hit stung him harder than a stone to the temple.

"But why, Neris? It's me. I'm here—"

"Nerin, stop. Get out of here!" Neris cried, her eyes looking to the side. He followed her gaze to the boy huddled on the ground, watching as he tried to stand. Nerin's gut filled with bile as the little brat looked up at him, defiance filling his dirty, rust-colored eyes.

[The boy wants to take her from you.]

Nerin pulled away from his sister and got up to face the little cur. Gaunt as a ghost, the small thing was weak and pathetic, but his sister cried for the boy.

[The boy would have her fill his weakness. He would use her.]

"You would call out for this boy over me?" Nerin's voice trembled as his sister's eyes filled with tears. "You would cry for this boy when I've done so much for you?"

[Hurt him.]

Unable to control his wrath, Nerin kicked the boy's fragile chest. The worm sputtered, the air knocked from his lungs. Before the boy could recover, Nerin sent another and then another. With a sharp blow, he clipped the boy's face. Neris screamed for him to stop, but he did not abate.

[Kill him.]

In a fit of rage, he pushed the boy over and stomped on his chest, the sound of cracking ribs perking his ears. The boy coughed and wheezed, and blood sputtered from beneath his lips, dripping from the corners of his pitch-colored mouth. As his small red eyes glazed over and his lids fell heavy over his petulant little face, Nerin turned to Neris. Her sobs echoed in his ears, making him want to end the child then and there.

"Come here!" Neris called as she trembled in place. She opened her arms to him, her eyes filled with timid joy and a bashful smile drawing across her face.

[End him.]

Nerin disobeyed and followed his sister's call. His breast swelled with joy as he looked down upon her trembling form. She had recognized him. Everything was better now.

"Come here," Neris sobbed as her tiny figure reached up to him.

He couldn't contain himself as he leaned over and wrapped his muscular arms around her. She pressed her face into his bare chest, her warm tears tickling his dark skin. She nuzzled him, pressing her nose to his nape, leaving a butterfly kiss on his collarbone. He trembled with excitement and joy to be there for her, to be the one to rescue her. Tremors of frantic happiness ignited every nerve ending. His blood pulsed in a loud rhythm that drowned out her happy cries and the interloper's bloody gasps.

"Please, just . . ." Neris stammered. She guided his hands between her thighs. A shiver shot down his spine at the thought, but with a deep, longing kiss, she pulled him closer. Legs spread, her crying turned into panting as he ran his hands up her sides. In one motion, he lifted the dirty satin dress from her. She lay there bare for him, her tiny black breasts erect and heaving as she pulled him close. He did not want to celebrate in front of the ignorant child but decided to accept his sister's graces. He would let this be the final blow to the wounded intruder's ego, thinking that perhaps the little cur would die there grasping for things he could not have.

[Pure blood, the right blood,] a familiar, bitter voice said, echoing through his brain.

Ignoring it, he let Neris push his legs free of the old sack pants he wore. His manhood was in her grip as she pulled him toward her.

"Here," she panted, eyes full of the love that he craved.

"Yes, Neris. Yes." His voice was gravelly and drunk with lust as he pressed her tiny body down.

With a sharp cry, she quaked beneath him as he took her. Looking down, he saw where her body accepted him. With ravenous lips, he pressed his mouth to her chest and drew from her the sweetest nectar in the world. She grunted and cried beneath him as he stroked harder, feeling her draw ever more around him. Her little legs clenched as tight as they could, her wrists held beneath him as he pulled back to stare into her eyes.

Reflected in the blood-red pools of her soft, beautiful face, he saw himself: tall, chiseled, dark-haired, hunger filling the irises of his rust-colored orbs. Entranced by his reflected visage, he continued, being sucked deeper and deeper into the reflection of his perfect body.

"Pure blood," he whispered as his body began to ache. He looked down, watching as his body strained to keep going. Without a word, he leaned over Neris, using his strong arms to pull her to him. Close to her face, he continued to stare, looking at his reflection. Then his tongue moved, and his mouth spoke. "Pure blood."

As he watched, the figure reflected in Neris's eyes changed. His hair became thinner and more haggard, his cheeks eroding into skin stretched over bones. His mouth, his granite jawline, and his musculature disappeared, giving rise to a bony slope with unkempt hair. Then there were the eyes, the red orbs dilating and spiraling, madness filling them as a manic expression of sadistic glee warped his visage.

"Respect your blood," his wheezing voice hissed as his shrinking frame ploughed frantically at the girl beneath him. Then his face turned. In a dizzying instant, he found his view foreign, looking up at his skeletal frame forcing itself on his crying sister. "You must respect your blood, boy!"

As his sister cried beneath the bony figure, he tried to get up. He felt pain in his chest as his heart raced in desperation. His ribs creaked and cracked as he shuffled on the ground. Tears streaked down his face. He tried to fight it, but the monster continued to taunt him. This way and that it threw his sister, contorting her little body as it had its way with her. Her body became limp, and her voice became empty as the creature roared triumphantly at its conquest.

With defiance in his eyes, he watched the beast pull off his sister, looking down at him. A long, snakelike tendril slithered between its legs as it stumbled over to him. His body turned over as his face was pressed into the ground. Fear and pain surged through him as he stared at Neris's empty eyes. Her tear- and dirt-streaked face looked at him as the beast disrobed his bottom. Anticipation and terror made his body shiver, his mouth full of iron and caking grit.

"Neris," his broken child's voice whispered to her.

As a wet drip coated his bare back, Nerin watched as Neris's eyes softened toward him. For a moment he was locked in her gaze, crying tears for his sister and himself. He reached his little bruised arm toward her, his nose filled with snot and pus. As he touched her, he felt something slither along his exposed flanks, his lips pursing in dread.

[Respect your blood,] the little voices echoed in a grisly chorus.

As the sick moistness gripped and prodded him, he tried to cry out to her. Then he watched as a monstrous worm bearing her face burrowed free. Her eyes went dead. As her body decomposed before him, the thick maggot spoke.

"Respect your blood."

. . .

NERIN AWOKE IN A COLD SWEAT, musky linens surrounding him. His eyes rolled around in his head as he tumbled out of bed. His head spun as he lurched from his sheets, trying to block out the disturbing dream. He coughed, feeling tenderness in his chest as he slumped over to the remains of the previous day's wining and dining. The vegetables and fruits on their platters had become rancid, decaying with incredible speed. The woods were a harsh place to refined tastes. Drawing himself a draught of stale water, he turned back to the bed, surveying a spot where a talvuo maiden had slept beside him the previous day. He couldn't remember much from the ritual the night prior but remembered bringing her back to dull the edge of his evening lust. Given the open place and slumping space in the mattress, he assumed she had left before he awoke.

Pouring the rest of the water over himself, Nerin shook free of the clamminess from his dreams. His stomach growled angrily as he thought about the rest of the day's proceedings. He needed to talk to the elders about the new girl and finalize the arrangements for flowers and food. He wanted the eve of the event to be full of debauchery, keeping in mind his master's demand to bring him the Virage. With everyone busy, it would be easier to have him dragged down there to pay his respects and final dues to himself and the old mage, though the very thought sent chills down his spine.

Stiffening his back as he walked, Nerin strutted over to his shutters and opened them. Outside, the village was already well awake, the people going about their everyday chores and routines. Those who called themselves Hyunisti woke early to partake of the simple tasks of sustenance, and he could at least applaud their efforts. Inhaling, he smelled the dust and pollen rising off the village below, making him snuff his nose. The simple people didn't need to be concerned about anything, especially after the ceremony. He would raise them up and bring them all greatness.

His shivering assuaged, he turned around. He imagined himself before his great silver mirror, his body toned and hardened by training and effort. But as he approached the large silver piece, his mouth drew back in a sinister curl as his red orbs fell upon blood-sketched scrawl. All over the mirror, a set of words were repeated: "Respect your blood."

With his blood racing, Nerin closed his fist. Visions of his father's ghoul destroying his sister's innocence danced before him. All around, he heard his wheezing grunts and sloppy tongue. Pain tinged his rectum and stomach as the slobbering monster's visage stared into his soul with every flash of the horrors from his night terrors. Then they were replaced by another, the demonic figure of that pale monster riding his sister. He saw it, its claws tearing at her back as it violated her womb, its blue eyes turning red with blood as it mocked him.

[Pure blood.] The Virage's voice rang in his head, the buzzing of flies and ringing of bells clouding his hearing.

[Nerin! Nerin!] His sister's childhood voice echoed in his head, guttural and defeated.

The images of the two monstrosities intermingled, breaking his sister in his mind's eye. In one half she cried to be saved while in the other she supplicated unwittingly. Closing his eyes, Nerin pressed his head against the silver mirror.

"Quiet, damn you. Both of you quiet!" Nerin growled at the images in his head.

[Pure blood,] the two men echoed in unison as they desecrated all that was holy in the woman he loved. [Respect your blood,] they said, laughing with hissing tongues and bestial eyes.

"Enough!"

Gritting his teeth, Nerin slammed his fist into the glossy surface. The glass cracked under his force. Inside the laughs and groans of those terrible men evaporated, as did his sister's frantic, empty cries. Shaking, he opened his eyes.

"Vivahr Nerin," a voice called from behind him. Turning his head, Nerin looked at the gaunt figure of a lesser Hyunisti, though one who served him well.

"What is it, Kadin?" he growled, still shivering as hatred coursed through his veins.

"I thought you would like to know that the Virage has awoken," the man said, bowing.

"Return to your duties, and keep watch," Nerin said, turning his eyes away.

He watched through the shattered glass as the timid talvuo man scurried away. His eyes searched the splintered mirror for any writing, but it had disappeared. Or perhaps it had never existed. With his nerves subsiding, he turned around and looked at the entryway, staring for a time as he reaffirmed his bearings.

He needed to be ready for the elders and planning.

He needed to steel himself for the struggle ahead.

18

———

ELIS

lis wanted to believe that she was relieved he was awake. In her
heart, she knew it would have been simpler if Davnian had just
stayed asleep forever. Bringing back water had been an easy task with
so many of the preparers for the next eve's feasting running about. Too
many of them were overly humble toward her. While she would have
declined under normal circumstances, she felt the need to rush.
Spiking the cold liquid with the remaining leaves of Neris's lemon
balm, she had watched Davnian drink cup after cup of the life-giving
substance. But an hour of small chatter and libation left him unmoved,
for better or worse.

"I'm sorry," he said, groaning on the table.

"What for?" Elis replied, cleaning up after herself as she planned
what foods she would bring. When Neris got around to showing up,
she could go home and fetch Rais with some supplies. Different foodstuffs would be worth trying on him, though she was unsure what he'd
be able to stomach. His recovery was beyond remarkable, so perhaps
the Virage could deal with a bit of upset.

Tying Davnian together with the Virage made her face twitch. For
years she had heard of a monster. The strangeness of coupling him with

her long-lost friend left her unprepared. Seeing him so weak and benign was one thing, but thinking of the horrid villain as an amnesiac bed warmer was too much. This was entirely outside her expectations. Part of her had hoped he'd wake up not knowing her at all. Part of her yearned for him to wake in a fury that would leave them all gasping in horror. At least those two things could be reconciled.

"My small-talk skills leave much to be desired," Davnian said, chuckling beneath his breath. His mannerisms were so familiar yet so foreign on the adult human's frame. "I know we promised to get back to serious conversation, but it's hard for me to be much more than an ornament without my memories."

"Does that bother you?" Elis asked, tinting her voice with care. She couldn't help it with how apologetic he had become.

"If only because I feel I've been an extraordinary burden to a friend," he said.

Elis wished she could tell him how much of a burden he had been: not just for the days of caring for his impossible state but for all the history that was coloring the present. Talvuo memories were difficult to reconcile with the dramatic changes that linked the present so closely with a crystal-clear time from an age ago. Even more difficult was the transparency of the original emotions, thrown into tumult with the present confusion.

"You've never been a burden," she half lied. For most of their shared life, he had been a joy to be around, even during the more difficult years. Only the end of it was burdensome, and only for reasons beyond their control. "Though you were trouble for the last few days. We worried your fever and tremors would get worse."

"I had a fever and tremors?"

"Yes, bad ones," Elis said. "Without Neris's concoctions to bring you down, we might never have stopped your convulsions. Thankfully, you never tried to get up, or we would have been truly distraught."

"I'll have to make sure to thank you both properly when your partner arrives," he said, patient optimism hanging on his words. She picked up on how he fought back against the new addendum to his dialect, shutting his mouth before a "good woman" could escape his lips.

"If I know her, she'll be here sooner than we think," Elis said, annoyed and relieved by the thought. Inside, part of her was wondering how she would deal with Neris and the sometimes unbearable familiarity that she imposed on everyone. Though she loved how nonchalant the woman could be. "Maybe we'll take the time to get to know each other better then."

"You must have a lot of respect for her or care deeply for her," Davnian said, making her ears rise. With her wide lavender eyes, she looked at the man lying on the table, her right eye twitching at the crooked, little grin he wore.

"What makes you say that?"

"You're always sarcastic when you mention her, but at the tail end of it, I can hear the telltale signs of reverie in your voice."

Elis had never known the boy from her past to be observant about natures of the heart, much less peculiar about the hints and gestures that betrayed odd emotional graces. But she couldn't deny what he had just said, her cheeks turning from bronze to copper as his soft blue eyes gazed at her. For the first time since mingling, she spotted a difference between her past friend and the present man. In a way, he reminded her of someone else from that chaotic time.

"That easy, am I?" Elis stumbled over her words, mimicking the phrase and form of her dark-skinned lover.

"No, you're guarded, but that's alright," Davnian said, closing his eyes.

A chill crept up her spine at the notion. He thought she was defensive. Where had he gotten that notion? What had she said that betrayed it? Then she recollected the ways she had portrayed herself. The openness and then reluctance in her posture. The leaning back and then swings in her moods.

"I'd say less guarded, more apprehensive," Elis said, puffing out her chest in a show of dominance. She smiled as he opened his eyes and looked up at her. With his same crooked smile, he chuckled, nodding.

"No, you're right. Apprehension is the better term."

There was the agreeable little boy she knew. In the back of her mind, she wondered if it was just placation she was witnessing. Perhaps in his mind, he was smiling at how wrong she was about herself. Shaking her head, she brought her hands to her face and lightly slapped her cheeks.

"Elis, are you alright?"

"I'm fine," she sang, turning away from him. "I'm going to try to separate a few more of these bundles before Neris arrives, so she can work on her potions without the need..."

Her words trailed off as the door opened. Behind her, she heard the pitter-patter of tiny footsteps as her small, brown-haired ward stumbled into her. Neris pranced in behind her, her leather-barded legs strutting as she swayed her hips. With a black sash to match her hair, Neris's iron-touched eyes fixed on Davnian as she wore a relaxed smile. Watching her turn to the table, Elis admired the way Neris's hair seemed to float above her crimson-adorned shoulders.

"Isual, Davnian," Neris said with a formalism that Elis had never seen. Davnian turned his gaze toward her, his blue eyes dilating and then contracting as a hint of knowledge spread across his face.

"Neris Delvori," he whispered, causing a pang of vehemence to well in Elis's breast. "You're Neris, the apothecary and poisoner."

"Yes." Elis watched as Neris searched beneath her, looking for something, anything else to go on. As she bent closer, Elis saw a hint of expectation cross her visage. The woman's dark ears cupped as she loomed over the patient.

"I'm sorry, Neris," Davnian said quietly.

Elis saw a twinge of hurt in Neris's eyes as she rose, but she was surprised at how fast Davnian had reconciled the woman's desire. Her heart raced as a coolness settled on her skin, calming her pained anticipation.

"What's wrong?" Neris's deep voice was cool as she turned her gaze to Elis.

"He's lost his memories, though you could ask him yourself," Elis said, turning away to finish sorting the plant matter. She needed to focus on the task, so she could have a clean space to work with later. At least that's what she told herself.

"Zaisure . . ." Rais whispered as she tugged at Elis.

"You don't remember? Anything?" Neris's voice was empty of candor as Elis listened, her ears stretching back as she pried. There were several moments of quiet, disturbed only by Rais's wiggling frame and Davnian's soft, humming breaths.

"You make potions and poisons. You dance naked in the firelight, skin glistening in the dark of ancient caves, a smile on your face. Reckless abandon, flashing knives, cold grins, and stares. Beautiful like black glass." Davnian's words were strange, a piecemeal series of recollections. They were the same sorts of pieces that he had given to Elis when she tried to push a little. Though for her, they were all things from their earliest youth. The more passionate ones were absent.

"Those are something," Neris said, a hint of longing creeping back in. "I have those knives still, ne vahr." Neris's words seemed to mimic Elis's own. Why was she feeling so outraged over such shared joy? "Have you been able to eat yet?"

"Zaisure . . ." Rais said once more.

"His stomach still seems raw. You should give him some more water. I'm sure his throat is feeling parched from all the talking of late. I put some lemon balm in it to make it a little more palatable and less bark flavored."

"I would appreciate it," Davnian said.

"A cup of water? I will do you one better," Neris cooed.

Elis rolled her eyes, still unable to pinpoint her edginess.

"Zaisure." Rais, neglected in the back and forth, hugged Elis's waist.

"Yes, my dear, what is it?"

"Is he the . . ."

"Yes, my dear, but it's OK," Elis replied, shuffling the herbs to the side.

"Can I . . ."

"If you want," Elis said. "I'm sure he'd be happy to meet you."

"Lady Neris, it's really unnecessary—"

"I insist. You will need your strength," Neris said.

His voice was muffled, and he protested lightly, which Elis ignored as she continued the last bits of cleanup. She knew if she turned around right then, whatever was occurring may be enough to send her over the precipice of the anger that was building in her breast. Using the last of the old water from the previous day, she wet a cloth and wiped down the counter, her anxiety dissipating with each swipe. Hearing Neris humming behind her set her more at ease, though Rais's nervous dancing steps made her curious.

"My name is Rais, naisure Virage," the little girl said. Elis stiffened her shoulders as she heard Davnian's muffled attempt at a reply.

"His name is Davnian, my dear. And right now, he's a little distract-ed," Neris said. "See if your mother needs anything for a bit. He'll be done soon."

Elis turned around, her lavender eyes narrowing as she clued herself into the scene. Having moved the stool, Neris had leaned forward and unstrung her blouse, plopping one of her swollen breasts free and into Davnian's face. Like a wet nurse with a babe, the man suckled from her. The thought reddened Elis's already straining features to a rosy hue. Rais was nervous beside them, trying to get the man's attention without understanding the distraction. Despite Neris's audacity, Elis was not surprised. In some ways, she wondered why she hadn't thought of doing it herself.

"Well, nectar doesn't seem to make him retch, at least thus far," Neris said, grinning as she patted Davnian on the shoulder. His chest rose and fell, and his breath whistle from his covered nose. "And you should not protest; you need your energy."

"You know, this gives me the perfect opportunity, ne vindal," Elis said, waving Rais toward the door. "I wanted to go back home and grab some supplies, different foodstuffs to try on his stomach. Some bread, fruit, and such. If you're going to be around getting familiar, you can watch over him till I return."

"Wait just a moment, vindal," Neris said, turning toward Elis as she scurried for the door. "There's no need to rush. Between the two of us, we should be able to—"

"Don't fret." Elis felt her voice empty as she tried to convey no vehemence to her unabashed lover. Neris's face wore an inquisitive look as Elis drew Rais to the door. "We'll be back shortly. Rest well, Davnian."

"Elis!" Neris called as Elis closed the door behind her.

"Zaisure!" Rais squeaked as Elis pushed her ahead, forcing the girl to keep up with her stride.

"Let's get you some paints to work with, hmmm?" Elis said as she planned what she'd bring back.

"O-OK," Rais stuttered as Elis blazed a trail home.

Elis loved Neris not just as a talvuo sister or a bedmate but as a friend and lover. She enjoyed Neris's company and had wished the two of them could spend more time together. Elis also remembered a young man with whom she enjoyed spending time. She recalled stories of knights, pretend swordfights, long days swimming, and long night longings. The two of those figures together in her head left her puzzled and filled with anger. Until she could solve the puzzle, she needed to cool off.

She needed to be away from Neris and Davnian.

19

___

NERIS

"I could have told you she would react poorly to that," Davnian said as Neris sat near his head, replacing her breast. The task was difficult given how tight she had made the weaving, but it was nothing she couldn't handle. She attempted to ignore his suggestion that perhaps she had been too forward. Yet given recollections of how lost in romance Elis was when discussing their mutual partner, she was open to reconsider. "Did you think I was protesting out of sheer kindness?"

"Shyness perhaps, though I've only ever seen you with one other woman," Neris said, thinking back to the days when she knew more than a pair of her tribal bloodline. "Though she was much more brazen than either the Renai woman or me. Either way, it wasn't as if you denied my advance."

"I don't mean to berate. I'm sorry, Neris," Davnian said, irking her senses. Apologies were not becoming of the Virage. She knew he had a gentle side, and perhaps that part was exaggerated by his current absentmindedness. "I'll stop apologizing if that makes you feel better."

"Hmmm?" Neris conveyed a scowl in her voice as she looked down at him, her face calm and composed.

"So, I assume you will be more receptive to my prodding," he began, gesturing with his claw beside her.

"Why not skip the appetizer when you can just have the main course?" Neris asked, downplaying the quizzical look he was shooting her and watching as his eyes narrowed at her suggestion. Based on his crooked grin, her humor and charm were not lost on his sensibilities.

"We'll have plenty of time for decadent servings after I've had my fill of more pragmatic things," Davnian said. The way his mood adjusted to match hers was almost perfect, enough so to forgive his previous demeanor.

"Where do you wish to begin then?" Neris whispered, teasing his bare shoulders with her hands.

"I recognize you; that much I'm certain of. I understand there's more there than just allusions and imagery and know there's more between us than we can go into now. I need you to tell me where we are, why we're here, what you know about Elis, and anything else you think is necessary."

"That's a great demand from an invalid," Neris said mockingly, running her hand beneath the linens and over his chest. "What do I get in return?"

"Aside from my everlasting appreciation?" Davnian's voice fell flat as her furry black ears arched. She enjoyed this side of him immensely, and his sudden snap to being so pointed and direct was elating. "Humor me."

"Well then, let's begin," Neris said, standing up.

Walking over to the countertop, she grabbed a draught of water for herself and then sat on the table opposite Davnian. She watched as he leaned over, grunting as he twisted in place.

"Where we're at is hard for me to place exactly, from what I remember of maps and such somewhere firmly in the northern Granvoren. From Nerin's ramblings, he claims we're in old Emri lands from before the rise of the Grannas Demesne to the south."

"Emri?" Davnian said, his eyes shifting as thoughts raced before him. Neris nodded, taking a drink from her cup. "So, we're in the Witchwood then?"

"I've heard of it, but aside from the large beasts and trees, I've seen nothing of clinging mists or the like. The only things around otherwise are these peculiar talvuo, who lust for warm outsiders' loins." Neris played coy, seeing what she could do to spark an interest in her puissant lover.

"Knowing what I do of you, I'm sure you've taken great advantage of that," he said playfully. Neris knew he was saying what she wanted to hear, playing his part in their game. "Tell me then, is that how Elis enters into this?"

"Very perceptive," Neris said. "Though honestly, I had little to do with our initial pairings. You see, this wild woman was roaming around the village one moment, child in tow. The next, she was upon me, asking my name, gawking at my attire, giving me suggestive advances."

"By 'suggestive' I assume you mean she was curious and suspicious."

"Well, suspicious is a good word for it. In truth, I had heard tales of the hermit of the village from a bonded pair of males whom I couldn't help but pervert. What a waste, given how little vigor they have left amongst their populace, but I won't complain."

"So, she approached you then?"

"We shared a lover one evening. You see, even Elis likes to escape the bonds of parenthood from time to time, and what better way than a drunken night in the company of the finer sex?"

His ice-blue eyes searched her, his lips fighting off a smirk as he analyzed her every word. Neris knew he could tell whether she was being dramatic, suggestive, or spouting half-truths. That was the fun part of it, watching Davnian piece together the actual picture from the morass of temptation and duplicity.

"You talked lives then? One night you opened your hearts and became closer than an alcohol-fired fling, I take it? The rest just naturally fell into place then."

"Exactly. So, question for you. How did you know I would upset her?"

"That was simple. She was already flustered by my conscious presence this morning. On top of that, her emotions appeared chaotic as we spoke, shifting this way and that. Words of you betrayed a competitive yet loving demeanor."

"I should have played that part better," Neris hissed, finishing the cup in her hand. She wished it were alcohol, thinking how much more pleasant it would be to indulge instead of stew over a lover's angst. "You have the right of it, as always."

"I don't know about always," Davian said, causing her to burst out laughing. "What's so funny?"

"Your unfazed certainty in your own uncertainty. Though you have me wondering, why act so different for her? Your niceties are off-putting."

"I wasn't acting."

"Let's get back to the subject at hand then," Neris said, internalizing his message. If it wasn't acting, then perhaps there was something disjointed in his methods when it came to others that she had yet to notice. He had always been straight with her, precise, and never shirking. Then again, she had nerves of steel and skin as thick as iron from her harder years. "You wanted me to tell you why we're all here?"

"Go on," Davnian said, shifting onto his back. Neris drew the stool closer, so she could sit beside him, leaning on the table. In response, he moved his claw, sliding it against the dark skin of her exposed forearm.

"You're here because we found you some days back," Neris began, imagining the scene again. His shriveled body had been almost unrecognizable. His eyes were dried shut, as was his mouth. His nose had all but collapsed into a mass of leathery skin, his body like moldy hide stretched over bones. The only identifying mark was his claw, ever-present and uniform despite his disability. Seeing that intact, she had known he would survive his deathlike state. "You were on the verge of death, withered and nonresponsive. Somehow, you managed to wander into the woods, where a group of huntsmen found you curled up beneath one of the great trees, the carrion birds keeping their distance from you."

"As for me, I followed my brother, Nerin, here. After doing something unforgivable, we left the great Delvori fortress in the east and wandered. The whole time he was ranting and raving to shadows and the wind, going on about a great mage adviser who had come to him. You'd never believe the stories Nerin came up with regarding his illusory friend. Somehow we managed to slip past patrols, brigands, and other horrors unscathed. For a time, I believed my brother's ramblings. Though now I think they're just some part of his psyche that is innately brilliant, if not for his madness and incredulity."

"Does your brother's friend have a name?" Davnian asked, his eyes going blank for a moment before refocusing upon her. She narrowed her eyes at him and pondered what could be happening behind his cold blue irises.

"He calls the entity Lord Ohran, a great mage of legend who only communicates with him."

"Ohran?" Davnian lurched up from the table before falling back onto it, his body writhing in pain from the sudden movement. He groaned beneath her, stretching out to soothe his sore limbs.

"What's wrong? What was that about?"

"I don't know," Davnian said, a look of confusion washing over his face as he broke into a cold sweat. She tried to get up but was stayed by his left hand. "Just keep going."

"There isn't much more to the story. We eventually came to these majestic woods, found this village of forest talvuo, and then stayed. Nerin is still scheming regarding some ceremony of interest to him and his imaginary adviser. The whole village is in the spirit, which aligns with their spring festivities. Food, drink, cocks, and twats for all." Neris's composure slipped toward the end as she imagined how much her brother had talked of seeding the women of the village with his greatness. No doubt he would earn a few more conquests than usual. While it was none of her business, the very thought infuriated her sensibilities, knowing well that he would then lord them over her.

"Neris, I have a favor to ask of you," Davnian whispered, his claw clutching her elbow.

"Haven't you demanded quite enough already?"

"I need to know more about these Emri talvuo. I also need anything related to this Lord Ohran you mentioned. Your brother calls him his lord, so perhaps there's something he's kept or obtained. I can't place it, but those two things together are troubling me. I need someone who can be quick and inconspicuous when it comes to this." His voice was dark as he spoke to her. Her nerves went cold as he clenched her forearm with his claw. "Can you please do this for me?"

"If I do, you give me everything," Neris whispered.

"That and more, Neris." His claw reached up to her face, a black finger caressing her cheek. "I trust you with everything." Those words rang in her ears, sending a trickle of warmth flowing down her body. She nodded and then rose from her seat. "Until then, I'm going to try to rest. If Elis plans on returning, she'll be back before too long."

"That she will. Be kind to her for me, will you?" Neris laid his claw back down on the table, chuckling to herself.

"Perhaps you can practice that yourself when you return."

Leaning over him for the briefest moment, she planted her black lips upon his, inhaling his breath as she drew back. With a victorious smile, she looked down, Davnian's blue eyes betraying that he had been caught off guard by the gesture.

"The things I do because of your charms," Neris said as she backed away. "Keep your promise, or I'll have to force myself on you." Wearing a triumphant grin, Neris slipped out the door. They both knew how this mission would end, and she had every intention of taking everything she could get.

20

DAVNIAN

As Neris left him to his thoughts, Davnian closed his eyes and thought long and hard.

He had caught it just as his mood had shifted, noticing how different he approached Neris in their lovers' gambit over the finer details of the present. There was a direct shift in his voice, his words, his demeanor. He was awash with a familiarity that knew just the right phrases and the right cajoles to use when placating and coercing the obsidian spy. The way his personality changed had made the pit of his stomach turn as he mulled over the concepts and reasoning.

[You'd do much better just letting go,] the other said, his voice like rocks rumbling along the dreamscapes of Davnian's mental terrain. [Look not on your methods. Accept them and move forward.] The shadow tyrant had the right of it, better than Davnian could ever claim. All that was left was to see to the matters at hand: recovery and Ohran.

He had tried not to be spooked by the mere mention of the name, but the syllables that made up the namesake of Madrus Ohran echoed through his skull. Like many things of late, he could not recollect where and why he recognized the mage's calling. Yet deep in his gut, his innards revolted at the mere recollection. There was something terrible, regretful, and wrong about every utterance of those words. They were cursed and vile. Tainted like a poisoned well, dark as the endless depths of the ocean, and soulless as a corpse were but the first attempts at analogies that came to mind when trying to reconcile his hesitations.

[If it's the name of a mage, we should steer clear of it.] The other's voice was low, like the rumbling of the deepest depths of the earth. [Magic is a foul thing. Unpredictable. Unescapable. Cursed and overbearing.]

[I know not what the Virage knows of the arcane, but I know enough about that name to expect nothing good to come from a meeting,] Davnian replied. [Even then . . .]

[Even then, you're curious why this Nerin knows that name?]

[More than that, I need to know why he would come here,] Davnian replied, trying to understand the strange web in which he was caught.

The name "Hyunisti" was foreign and unheard of in his addled mind, but like "Delvori" and "Renai," he knew the name "Emri." His stores of esoteric knowledge painted the forest folk as skilled woodsmen and carvers, excellent hunters, and marvelous musicians. Dancing and singing were common in the camps of the ancient people. Yet aside from the architecture, he recognized nothing about his current residing place as wondrous. There was no music or dancing and no joy in the air. He detected a buzz of excitement. Overlaying it was a dense haze of desperation and fear that was almost palpable.

Complicating the mess, Elis Renai was a friend from his youth. That much he knew. She had feelings for him that ran deeper than friendship. He needed to know their history. He couldn't help but be on guard around her, not knowing what misstep he could make in his words or actions toward her. Adding to that, she had a child whom he could not place as hers by nature, but she nevertheless seemed enraptured with her.

Neris Delvori, on the other hand, felt all too familiar. Her banter, playfulness, sultry air, and dark machinations when she so chose were all well understood. Everything from her smell to her mannerisms was fresh in his mind. Despite his distanced words, he wanted more than to give in to her cravings. Thankfully, he was indisposed and could exercise restraint, but for how long was the question.

[Aren't you glad you're no longer dreaming?] the other said, snickering before returning to its hiding place.

[If I could remember the dream, I'd have to decide which is worse. All I see around me are twisted feelings and missing pieces. I'm not well enough to make sense of any of it.]

[Then rest, young one. You'll be roused and bothered more as the day goes on, and that's if you're lucky.]

The shadow was right. Davnian needed to rest. The morning had been eventful in more ways than one, and the day promised to provide more room for the dramatic and the strange as the sun waxed to its zenith. Relaxing his muscles, he forced himself to be still and calmed his breath. Clearing his mind, he took a deep breath, followed by another.

He needed his strength, just as Neris had said.

He also needed his sanity for the maddening road that lay ahead.

21

———

ELIS

A few hours had passed since Elis had stormed out of the infirmary. With Rais in tow, she had headed home, ignoring well-wishers and greetings in a fit of passionate anger. Her heart raced, her skin prickling with redness from incredulity and heated anticipation. In her mind's eye, she had seen Neris hanging over him, nursing the man. Davnian was obedient, just as he had been with her, but such flagrant displays of affection were infuriating. At that moment, she had almost rushed to Neris, wanting to kiss her as much as slap her. Neris would do whatever her heart or mind willed. While Elis oft enjoyed playing the same bit, she could not when it came to him.

Throwing things together, she had talked in snippy soundbites to Rais, wearing down the floor as she dragged her feet and stomped in their shared living space. Visions of the progression in her absence played over in her head: from breasts and sucking, to teasing and rubbing, to screaming and fucking. Elis couldn't get the imagery out of her mind. Part of her wanted to grab her twistblade and end them in their lovers' embrace, while the other part wanted to run naked and leap upon the pyre with them. Not that any of that was occurring.

In fact, when they had returned, Elis was appalled to find Davnian by his lonesome as he slept on the hard wooden table. The smell of lemon balm lingered in the room, only a hint of Neris's scent trailing from the sleeper. Davnian had been lazy, hinted at as Elis spied the dry, powdery residue of satin nectar on his lips. Not that she expected someone who had just woken from a terrible ordeal to care much about his appearance.

"Is this alright?" Rais asked from behind her as she set up her dyes and paint projects. She had taken an interest in indigo and viridian as her colors of choice, picking some of the more exotic materials in Elis's small collection to work with. The little girl was as excited as ever, her spirits uplifted by the promise of a more fruitful visit with the stranger.

"They look fine," Elis replied, gesturing to a free table. "You can work over there if you need more room."

Trying not to be too caught up in her thoughts, Elis unpacked what she had brought in hopes of testing Davnian's palate and constitution. Neris's nectar seemed to settle his stomach, somewhat to Elis's chagrin. If solid food didn't work, Elis could follow the same course, though she had reservations at becoming so familiar.

"Need any help, my dear?" Elis asked as she spread out the last of her goods: bread, dried meat, nuts, fruit, berries, meal, seeds, and forest vegetables. Rais hummed beside her, singing to herself as she finished lining up the last of the vials and containers for her small asides.

"I'm good," the little girl said, her brown ears lifting with joy. "I hope we can talk this time."

"I'm sure we'll get a chance, dear," Elis said, pulling over a stool to take her place beside Davnian. "I'll introduce you when he wakes. Let's be quiet until then, my little one."

"Yes, zaisure," Rais said, making a quieting gesture to herself as she danced at the counter. "I'll be really quiet."

"Good girl."

Fixing her attention on the sleeping amnesiac, Elis's nerves settled. In her adolescent dreams, she had imagined having a suitable partner who could partake in her wanderlust and debauchery. Though she was not unfamiliar with jealousy. At times she had acted with intemperance, using her wiles and emotions to embitter and manipulate. Compared to the woman who had started Elis's own torturous machinations, Neris was a saint in the way she acted and shared in the joy of closeness. But then again, the woman who had crossed Elis was much more entwined in the fate of the young Davnian, whom she had decided would be hers alone.

For over a decade, Elis and her family had taken care of the child of Deldaron rin-Siscus, a proud knight and commander in the joint forces of the Ansuman States. Under her supervision, Davnian had been raised to be humble, stoic, open, and accepting of everything he saw. But then a purple-eyed, blazing-haired woman stormed in and claimed maternal custody. Her mother and father had been happy. Together, the two returned to the small wooden cottage in which the Renai family had first received the boy. But over time, the woman commandeered more and more of Davnian's time. In response, Elis had tempted him to break his promises and flaunted her youthful vigor.

Looking at his mangled, terrible claw, Elis thought long and hard about how familiar all of this was to past events. Jealousy had consumed Ilyavan and her, years taking their toll on the boy whom they shared. Then one fateful night, all that came to a boiling point. Their shared jealousy descended into despair and, in time, remorse . . .

THAT EVENING HAD BEEN like any other in the dusty town of brick, stone, and crumbling mortar. Other than a few patrolling watchmen, the streets were empty as the young talvuo maiden made her way along the back alleys with her wealthy suitor. What had started in the stables behind Jareth's mansion had carried on through channel and passage as the young couple, drunk on passion and wine, stumbled through the dark.

"A shame about your family's barn," Jareth whispered as he walked behind Elis, his hands fumbling at a bottle as he tried his impish fingers at her back. She was unfazed, knowing that while skilled in spearplay in a sporty sense, the grey-eyed youth was beyond the ability to do more than two things at once. He could wait till they reached the spot.

"A shame your stables are so open," Elis murmured, slurring her words as she pranced about, staying just out of her lover's reach.

"Apologies, apologies," Jareth said. With a firm hand, Elis stopped him, peering around the corner to make sure no one was there. As her speckled ears extended for better perception, the drunkard closed himself behind her, unable to stay his touching and groping. A devilish grin inched across her face as she spied and listened, hearing naught but the sounds of watchers' boots making their way around the squares and arterials of the town. "Any problems?"

"Just making sure you're the only one around to pry away, you lecherous cur," Elis teased, picking the most straightforward words to taunt the younger man.

"I beg your pardon, madam," Jareth said, drawing back and attempting a clumsy bow. "I'm a nobleman with noble ears and eyes unlike any mutt you've ever met. Not to imply that—"

"Well then, you'll naught mind showing me your noble prick then?" Elis scampered around the corner, skipping backwards as she taunted the drunken philanderer. Backing into an old, abandoned stone apartment, Elis's fingers fumbled at her blouse as she further tempted the young Vandasreth. Giggling, she backed into a corner of the square hollow, lying back on the pile of straw and matting that she had prepared earlier that day. She crossed her legs and pressed herself into the stonework.

Taking another drink from the half-full bottle of wine, the young nobleman stumbled toward her, grinning wickedly. He ran his hand through his ashen hair as he approached, shaking it free of the tail he kept it bound in. Looking down at her, he chuckled under his breath. His eyes were black in the dark.

"Zaisure, will you do me the honors?" Jareth growled as he took a drunken step forward, his other hand fumbling with his belt buckle.

"The only honor I want is you to be quiet and get down here, naisure." Elis feigned exasperation as she plucked the last of her buttons free. Her chest heaved beneath her shirt, her corsetry threatening to spill her supported bust. "Hurry, or I'll have to entertain myself."

"As you wish, my lady." The coy nobleman tried to bow once more, freeing his buckle. As he stumbled, his foot caught on the ground, making him stumble forward. With one outstretched hand and a cracking knee, he hit the ground. "Damn it," he hissed.

"Gods, are you alright?" Elis's love-addled brain cleared as she leaned forward, reaching for the crouching youth.

"Fine, I'm fine," Jareth said, rolling onto his bottom. Coming to his side, Elis braced herself against his back, looking him over. His cotton pants were ripped at the knee, a scraped patch of white skin exposed through the hole. Jareth gritted his teeth as he felt the injury. Beside him the bottle of wine sat on a large dark patch, wobbling as it rolled free and clinked upon the earth and rock. Turning at the sound, the young nobleman chuckled. "Well, at least the wine is safe."

"There's that at least," Elis whispered, snatching the bottle. Without a care she took a mouthful of the tart red liquid, swallowing it in one gulp. Her nerves eased after assessing that the only thing hurt worse than his swollen knee was his pride, allowing her to return to a less severe demeanor. "A drink for your leg or ego, naisure?"

"I think yes, but no more of the red for me." Jareth laughed as he felt between the folds of her open shirt, cupping and squeezing her free breast. "Something rich and full-bodied to curb the swill."

"That can be arranged, naisure," Elis cooed into his ear, enjoying the attention.

As the rest of her brain began to refill with expectations and lust, Elis heard the faint sounds of shuffling feet and hard breaths nearby. Her heart racing and her body warming, she ignored the sounds and pressed herself backwards as Jareth rolled over. The straw pricked and prodded at the cotton against her back as the dark-suited nobleman crawled over her. Burying his face in her exposed bosom, his heavy breath warmed her bronze skin as he nuzzled her. Her own breathing synced with Jareth's, her eyes closing as she swelled her chest. The cold night air danced between his wet kisses as her shirt loosened around the top of her corset.

There it was again, bated barks and gruff voices whispered from the stones beside her.

"Jareth." Elis opened her eyes, moving her ears to amplify the strange noise. Without a word, the nobleman continued his quest, wrapping his mouth around her teat. She let out a cry as the nectar drained from her chest. Trying to get his attention, she pressed her hand against Jareth, but he persisted. Shifting his focus from one side to the next, Jareth continued to make good on his want of drink. Frustrated, Elis grabbed his face and brought it up to hers. "Jareth!"

"Alright, alright, we'll save the other for later," Jareth cooed as he tried to draw his wet lips to hers.

"No, Jareth. Listen!"

Wearing a confused expression, he looked at her, his grey orbs trying to puzzle out her demeanor. "What are we listening to?" Jareth slurred as he hung over her, nudging the inside of her legs with his.

Ignoring him, she looked about, her ears moving with her eyes as she listened. As she scanned, his eyes followed hers. From the walls came a sudden cry, followed by a yowl. Then there was a pounding sound and several whimpering draws followed by a single gulp of air and then silence.

"Did you hear that?"

Moments passed.

"Probably just another couple trying to—" A young man screeched in pain, interrupting Jareth midsentence. The sound of cracking stone echoed through the chamber. Jareth's eyes snapped to the stonework beside them, his expression changing as he tried to make sense of the noise.

"Someone's in trouble out there," Elis whispered, looking to the wall at her right.

"That much is obvious," Jareth said, drawing back onto his haunches. With fumbling hands, he snatched up the wine bottle, turning it over. With his free hand, he twisted up his belt.

"What are you doing?" Elis whispered as Jareth struggled to his feet.

"You know how some people can be around here," he grunted, pulling up his loose pants as he turned to the entrance. "Can never be too careful."

"You needn't tell me," Elis said, rising to her feet. Jareth motioned for to her to stay back as he tilted his head outside the door. "Oh, by yourself then?"

"If they're belligerents, they're more likely to—"

"Give it a rest, oh noble heart." Elis pressed past him. Jareth put his hand on her shoulder, attempting to hold her back. She let her shoulder fall limp, shrugging off his defensive grasp as she eased along the stone wall. She knew the forgotten hovels well. The homeless often gathered in them, though she knew which ones were open for her midnight forays. If a belligerent or a pious rakehell were looking for trouble, she wouldn't be the first to hold back.

"I'm behind you then," Jareth whispered, creeping along the wall. They were both still inebriated, though she thanked her tolerance and fortitude that she could hold it better than her lover.

Passing the collapsed ruin to her right, she continued up the wall, reaching the corner of the duplex building. Elis motioned for the bottle. As her right hand gripped the glass cudgel, she scanned the moonlit space around the corner.

The building's northern wall served as one side of a small square, which surrounded a well and a shade tree. The brick garden walls gave way, leaving a disheveled mound of mortar and stone standing in the far corner. The rest of the debris had either been scattered or carried off. In the far corner was the shade tree, just on the other side of the small well. Three tall figures surrounded it, one stamping the ground while another picked up a large brick. The third one was crouching, struggling in the dark.

"Do it again, and really slam it this time," a low voice whispered.

"Keep him quiet this time!" the one holding the brick said.

At the base of the three figures, a dark shadow was spread across the ground. On either side of it, stripes of moonlight stretched across moist stones. A smell of rust mixed with a stench hung in the air. Edging next to her, Jareth peered at the menacing circle.

"What are they . . ." before he could finish, the far shadow brought the brick down. It made a popping, grinding sound as it slammed against something wet. A muffled scream filled the square. The cry of a young man.

Elis's maternal instincts overtook her as the sound of the injured figure resonated with her. Without a moment's hesitation, she rounded the corner. Before the men knew what was happening, she brought the glass bottle, still half full, crashing down upon the head of the closest shade. The tall man stumbled forward over their victim. As the brick bearer looked up at her, she moved with ferocious intent, stabbing the broken end of the glass into the man's side, gritting her teeth as he dropped the brick and clutched the wound. The man to her left looked up, his arms preparing to reach out, but Jareth barreled in and rammed his braced elbow into the rake's head.

The three shadows drew back, crawling away as they regained focus on their assailants. Picking up a rock, Elis hurled it at the bleeding man. As the rock crashed into his temple, the fiend spun backwards. Joining in, Jareth threw a large brick, the weight of it smashing into the leg of a crouching hooligan. Screaming, the man dragged himself backwards.

"Run! Get out of here!" the stumbling organizer of the trio said, sprinting into the dark. His comrades crawled and scampered after him, gasping and groaning as they retreated. For a second, all Elis felt was rage and bloodlust.

"Elis," Jareth whispered, a deathly chill hanging on his words. Her wrath abated as she remembered what had brought it on. Looking down at her feet, she scanned the battered, broken figure of a young man, a pool of blood welling up beside his face and left hand. "Gods, is that . . . It couldn't be, could it?"

"Elis . . ." a broken voice whispered as she bent down, her lavender eyes growing wide. Listening carefully, she fixed on the word, her heart skipping a beat. The shallow breaths of a young boy crept along the edges of her outstretched membranes. The grunting of a wounded child bit deep into her gut as she collapsed to her knees, her eyes filling with the grotesque scene.

Elis scanned the hunched, shivering frame of the young man whom she had raised for onwards of a decade. The little boy just in the years of changing breathed frantic, hard breaths between swollen blood-spattered lips. His brow was smeared with drying blood, his dirty yellow hair clinging to his face. His right eye was closed, bruises and caked dirt sealing the injured orb. His left eye looked at her, an eye colder than any child's should be, its blue reflecting her shocked visage. His right hand was dug into the earth, gripping rock and dirt out of pain and desperation. Beneath a stone was his left. Without thinking, she lifted the heavy stone and gasped, staring at a mess of broken bones, blood, and sagging flesh.

"Davnian." Her voice was hollow, her lavender orbs wide as tears welled at the corners of her eyes. The smell of dirt, meat, urine, and blood was congealed and thick around the beaten, broken little boy. Her heartbeat was slow and stilted, her skin growing cold as the night air clung to her while terror ate away at her from the inside.

"Davnian?" Jareth's heavy feet dragged as he brought himself beside her. His own breathing stopped as his muscles tensed in place. A shiver overcame the young nobleman as he too bent to his knee. Without a breath, his hand extended forward. "Dear gods. Davnian, is that . . ." Jareth stopped himself as another jolt coursed down his frame. Elis's body echoed the morbid sentiment.

"Elisssssssssssss . . ." Davnian whispered through his swollen face, raising his left arm. His little voice strained against unbearable pain, making Elis's heart leap. She grabbed his swollen wrist, staring at the mangled mess of a hand at the stump of his forearm. She wanted to sob, to break down, to wail.

"Ja . . . Ja . . . Jareth . . ."

"Don't speak," Jareth commanded, putting his hand on Davnian's stomach and turning to her. "Elis, we need to get him out of here. He needs someone to tend to his wounds. He needs help."

"I know," Elis replied, her broken heart pulsing with irregular beats as she tried to focus. They could take him to her parents and wrap his wounds. They could try to set his hand. They could wipe off all the blood and put salve on his bruises and scrapes. "We should take him—"

"We'll take him back to the manor," Jareth said, lifting Davnian from the ground. Elis watched as he took charge, raising Davnian's right arm over his shoulder while motioning for Elis to give him the left. "My mother and sister know some minor magic. Help me get him on my back."

"OK." Elis snapped to as she gave Davnian's broken arm to Jareth. Without so much as a whisper, Davnian complied as Jareth struggled to his feet with the boy.

"Give him a boost, and help me," Jareth said, wheezing under the burden of the young man. With all her strength, she lifted Davnian's legs for the young nobleman to grab. Double-checking Davnian's grip, she walked beside the nobleman, leading Jareth out of the small space and then taking her place at his left. With her right arm, she steadied Jareth's load. "Davnian, just keep your arms wrapped around me," he said, "and we'll get you somewhere safe."

"Jareth," Davnian whispered, his left eye rolling its socket.

"Don't talk. It's OK," Elis whispered as Jareth shuffled. The three of them panted and groaned as they walked through the dark alleys. Elis's heart was filled with urgency and despair as they trudged along, trying to save her small, broken ward.

At first, it was just disrespectful blame that had been placed on Elis and her midnight lover. Then she had learned how much Davnian had been sneaking out. Then she remembered how often she had tempted him, set his mind ablaze with curiosities that he had been denied. And then it all came full circle.

.   .   .

Elis let out a regretful sigh, looking around the small healer's room with a heavy heart. There was so much to talk about, to remind Davnian of, to learn what had happened over the countless years. She would find out how he still clung to the mortal coil despite the events and distance that should have made it impossible. And with an open heart, she would not allow her own personal vexations to come between Neris, Davnian, and her.

"You OK, zaisure?" Rais asked, her little frame pressing beside her. Elis looked down to see the child's worried eyes, her pale body slumping as she assumed Elis's grievous mood.

"I'll be fine, my dear," Elis whispered, patting the young one on the head. Her tan fingers wove through the girl's hazel hair, ruffling it as the child giggled. With a soft smile, Rais went back to her paints and colors. About to relax once more, Elis was interrupted by a knock at the door. She turned to the hall beyond. "Yes, come in!"

The door slid open, revealing a verdant-robed talvuo male. Elis stared as he gestured toward her with his thin, pale hands.

"Vindal Elis, the elders have summoned you for a meeting."

"Summoned me?" Elis said as she stared at the shrinking Hyunisti. She had not been summoned in years. "May I ask what about, vivahr?"

"Vivahr Nerin has raised many questions and made many claims about certain histories related to his upcoming ceremony. The elders wish to consult you about the specifics and would also like to know how the newcomer is holding up." The nervous talvuo's eyes shifted, fixating for a moment on Davnian as he slept. Obviously, someone had let it slip that he had awakened. Along with Nerin's oft-baseless claims and rumbling, she saw a whole slew of reasons they would prod and chant over.

"I will leave shortly. Let them know I'm on my way."

"I will wait for you out here and escort you, vindal."

"Close the door and wait then." Elis was annoyed. The thought of being escorted in broad daylight seemed egregious and unnecessary. As the door closed, Elis laid Davnian's blackened hand back on the tabletop and beckoned for Rais. Without a word, the little girl tiptoed over. Her pallid, little face scrunched to match Elis's own frustrated look. "Now, my dear, I'm going to need you to see to him while I'm gone. If he wakes up, there's some food on the counter and a pitcher of water. A small mug should do. If he wants to try to eat, give him a little bit but not too much. His stomach is likely irritable, and if you let him eat too much . . ."

"He'll throw it up everywhere!" Rais whispered.

"Yes. Have a towel on hand just in case." Elis had not considered that she would be leaving her little one in charge of handling Davnian but was amused to see how fast the girl seemed to be taking an interest.

"I'll keep him company, zaisure. Don't worry!" Rais was enthusiastic, a big, toothy grin unfurling on her face.

"That's a good girl," Elis said, standing up. "I shouldn't be too long. If something happens, you can run across the way to the big tree. Neris's quarters are to the left, around the bend, the first door on the right side. I expect she'll be in her room, tidying or hosting company. The nerve of that woman to abandon him while he slept."

"OK, zaisure. I'll fetch the abandoner!"

"Leave that part out, my dear. I'll be back soon," Elis said, walking to the door. She glanced over Davnian with her lavender eyes, a faint smile crossing her face. Waving behind her, she turned and shot Rais a smile before opening the door.

"Are you ready, vindal Elis?"

"As ready as I'll ever be," Elis replied, taking the lead. The talvuo male closed the door and then fell in step behind her. She couldn't wait to hear the elders' questions, much less what nonsense Nerin had put into their heads this time.

22

DAVNIAN

Dreams had been fast and frantic of late. Opening his eyes, Davnian grunted. The light was bright, searing his retinas as he tried to force himself awake. Scenes of an ashen-haired young man and golden-headed woman danced through his head along with a steely, blue-eyed stranger whispering to him of faults and fancies. The images were blurry but also familiar. If only he could hold them in place.

[Give it a rest, and try again later, young one,] the snarling, old black thing in his skull said.

[If I could remember something, anything more, I'd be less apt to try,] Davnian countered as his eyes adjusted. Despite his morning victories, his eyes had returned to being fettered by darkness and sleep. What should have taken an instant was taking seconds, the hazy pastels of brown, yellow, and coal shifting in his vision. He had hoped to catch a glimpse of black by his side as the thought of nursing like a babe once more intruded upon him.

[Perhaps you should accept more inner anguish. Getting used to being served is the last thing you need,] the other said, its voice like tendrils of smoke as he tried to adjust his position. His hands and arms were weak, but he could move them. Holding them in place was another story. He felt his feet and curled his toes. With enough effort, he could wiggle his legs and lurch his calves. He could lift his head and turn it from side to side, and he could contract and relax his back. He was still sore, but with ample effort, he could lift or shift himself. However, even after a morning of wakefulness, he could not yet travel of his accord. [Then again, maybe what you need is better service. A lineup of people to throw themselves at you.]

[It might be better if they just threw me instead,] Davnian thought, wondering if being forced to use his strength might be better. His muscles were beyond atrophied. However, even with the light nourishment, he had regained an incredible amount of strength. The premise was impossible, innate stores of knowledge and an intuitive understanding of anatomy told him. Denying what had been accomplished was not in his best interest, much less those around him. [Do you think that maybe danger would be apt to forcing my recovery?]

[Possibly, young one, but at what cost? Likewise, would your response be correct for whoever induced it?] The other's words were foreboding. Other than knowing his name and having some sense of ownership to the title "Virage," Davnian knew little about his physiological or mental workings. The nightmare he had awoken from, along with its imagery, had been purged from his brain. The only thing that lingered was a leeriness over his dread title. [Besides that, you should enjoy what reprieve you can get.]

A smile crossed his face as he thought of relaxing. He had been happy to see Elis Renai, someone whom he could tell was dearer to him than he could recollect. Her energy, concern, and chaotic moods were a joy to watch, if not a bit unsettling for conversation's sake. Neris was another story. Elegant and precise, cold but burning with a fire that threatened to consume everything around her. Given the circumstances, he should have felt lucky to be so doted upon, though tremors of reluctance and hesitation clung to his conscience. Bones were cast all around him, but he couldn't divine their meaning.

[You should fixate less,] the other prodded, pulling him from his thoughts.

[Agreed,] Davnian replied as the illusions of his tenacious mind faded, giving way to the clarity of his vision. [Though we still have a chief concern.]

[Ohran will wait for Neris to return,] the other said.

Raising his head, he looked down past his covered feet at the open wooden slats of the small room. Sunlight slid through the cracks. From his angle, he guessed the sun was high, leaning towards early afternoon. Outside he spotted movement. Focusing, he made out a wooden bridge in the distance. Shifting his gaze, he eyed a basket, several jars, and wrapped parcels as the fragrance of bread and berries teased his nostrils.

As his stomach growled from the perceived morsels. Davnian averted his gaze to the side. On the table beside him, a small bloom of hazel hair and floppy talvuo ears bobbed about. Scattered on the tabletop were various little glass and clay jars, along with a slew of plant matter and the like. Pieces of loose cloth were strewn about with wet stains. Watching closely, he followed the buzzing figure about, hearing the distinct hum of a little voice. With a heave and a plop, the small frame of a tiny talvuo girl pulled itself onto some unseen seat, looking over the complex project before her. Without a word, she looked up, her viridian eyes meeting his azure orbs. The child's white face looked confused, but as the moments passed, it filled with wonder. Frozen, she stared at him in awe as he quietly returned her gaze.

Seconds turned to minutes as Davnian stared at the little girl, unblinking as he scanned her face. In return, her curious face began to show signs of stress as she tried to keep her eyes fixed on his. Another minute passed, and her eyes began to water, but he did not waver. He heard her little legs kicking at the table in front of her, watching as her small hands danced and clenched on the tabletop. He was sure he had seen her earlier, noting the girl who had entered with the sultry, obsidian Delvori.

[Playing a game, are you?] the other asked.

[Just observing,] Davnian replied, a grin cracking his face.

"What?" the little girl's high voice broke the silence as she tottered in her seat. She blinked as she steadied herself, looking back at him.

"Looks like you lost," Davnian said, his throat dry and airy. His chest itched angrily as he spoke, but it did not stifle him from laughing at the display.

"I wasn't playing," the little girl replied, red-faced as she furrowed her unwrinkled brow.

"Is that right?"

"I was watching over you in case you woke up!" she said, prideful yet bashful, her pale face growing red. "I'm supposed to watch you, and then you were watching me, and then . . ."

"Well, then—" Davnian almost coughed as he spoke. His lungs hissed at the dryness of his throat and mouth. The herb water and satin nectar from earlier had worn off, leaving him hoarse. He motioned to her with his left hand, his vocal cords grinding as he tried to clear his throat. Watching the little one get up from her seat, he tried to wet his tongue. His saliva was the consistency of porridge, serving to make his gut spin. He maintained his composure, following the brown-haired girl with his eyes as she climbed onto the stool next to him.

"Are you hungry? Zaisure brought all kinds of food for you to try if you want."

"Water would be good for right now."

"OK," the little girl said, spinning in place. She leaned over the other table, her scrawny arms grabbing a large clay pitcher. With a couple of heaves, she pulled the container back. She leaned back once more, fetching a small clay mug. Unable to resist smiling, he watched her raise the pitcher, wobbling in place as she poured the little cup overfull, spilling some of the contents. Without a care, she cradled the cup in her hands and brought it over. "Here!"

Wide-eyed, the little girl stared at his blackened claw-like fingers as he took the cup from her. Davnian braced his right arm and, with a heave, pulled himself upwards. His back muscles were tense and shaking as he brought the mug to his lips. His left bicep trembled, making the water spill all about his linens and frame. Leaning his head forward, he sipped its contents, the liquid permeating his aching tongue and throat. Closing his eyes, he calmed his muscles as he drank down trickle after trickle. Unable to keep his composure, he handed the mug back and let himself back down.

"You have my thanks," Davnian said, taking a deep breath down his newly coated throat. His stomach lurched at the transgression, but he kept it down. The little talvuo set the cup aside and then returned her attention to him. She scanned him with pensive eyes, her wonder replaced with fervent curiosity. He waited for her to speak, but after several moments passed, he couldn't resist prying. "Alright, what is it, young one?"

"Are you really the Virage?" she asked, her voice full of childish morbidity.

"That's what they tell me," he replied, looking at his claw, on which her eyes were fixed. Neris and Elis had refused to use the title, using only his name. Lacking the necessary understanding, he feigned playfulness to the little girl. "So tell me, are you just a little talvuo girl, or do you have a name?"

"I'm Rais Hyunisti!" The force of the girl's enthusiasm made him chuckle.

[Hyunisti village, Hyunisti talvuo.] He rolled the name over in his head.

[But "Emri" is the term the dark-skinned one relayed.] The other's immediacy was apt, as expected.

"Just like that!" Rais broke his concentration, her thin white fingers directed at his face.

"Like what now?"

"When we were staring." She rocked in place, her arm still straight out. "You mumbled something, and I didn't know what you said. Your lips moved all funny, and you just did it again!"

"I did?"

"And your eyes went all funny like you were looking somewhere else. Are you talking to someone? Or are you just trying to scare me?" Assertiveness was not something he expected from a young talvuo girl who had to be half his height, much less accusations of foul play. Stifling a laugh, he thought about what she had said and realized he must have been moving his lips while chatting with the other. He'd have to make sure that didn't happen again.

[Or you could just admit you're insane and get it over with,] the other said.

Davnian smiled. "My head is still quite fuzzy. I get lost in thoughts and dreams a lot right now."

"Like daydreams?" Rais's voice returned to the inquisitive tone it had carried before.

"Kind of like daydreams, yes." Talking to an imaginary being in his head might be relatable to a young girl but would not help him if she went gossiping to Elis or others. "Do you daydream?"

"All the time!" Dancing in place on the chair, the little girl was a bundle of nervous, frenetic energy. "Sometimes I dream about my old mama, and then I talk to her, and then I think about Mama Eli—" She halted, then corrected herself. "Zaisure Elis."

"Your old mama?"

"Yeah, my old mama. She died a long time ago. She ran away from the village to save me but died in the woods. Zaisure tells me that she was brave and that I should always remember her. But I don't even know what she looked like or how she sounded, and when I ask my new mama, she tells me I shouldn't be shy and . . ." The little girl's ramblings were all post-rationalizations. Daydreams of an imaginary woman who she could only visualize through flights of fancy. A woman who was supposed to be the ideal for her to look up to. That was all Rais seemed to have of the woman she had been told to call mother. "Zaisure Elis is the best though. We live together and go out gathering berries and herbs and plants, and sometimes she takes me hunting with her, and sometimes I get to read her journal, and sometimes—"

"Sounds like the woman who saved you was a great person." Davnian smiled and raised his claw to pat the girl on the head. "And it sounds like you have a great mother."

"Yeah," Rais whispered, lowering her eyes to her lap. He patted her head again and then dropped his claw as her little green eyes became hazy with tears. He could imagine what it must feel like to hold back, to be told to respect someone whom she could never know, to be denied an undeniable reality in front of her in favor of a tribute to the past. Repressing a positive could be just as detrimental as hiding a negative.

[That must be what Elis feels like as well,] Davnian remarked to the other, thinking about how she looked at him, the words she used to dismiss his neediness or non-surprise.

"What are you doing over there?" Davnian asked, gesturing to the table beside him. At once the girl's attention refocused, renewed enthusiasm replacing her melancholy. As a single tear worked its way down her cheek, Rais wiped it away and, with a giant, toothy grin, gestured to the table.

"These are colors for paints!" As she broke into a spiel about the colors and how she was learning from Elis to make the various hues, Davnian retreated into the back of his head for comfort. He couldn't help but analyze everything since he had awoken as he tried to piece the infinitesimal together into a grand tapestry of the present. Every new inkling of information was fit into the picture, sporadic and deformed wooden blocks woven through a puzzle board of impossible length and width. But with every piece, he could infer orientations and dimensions in the visage of the current reality.

"I'm not really good at extracts yet, but I really like testing colors!" Rais was full of joy, pointing to the sheets of cloth with the stretches of color stained into them. Crushed bugs and berries with their stems, leaves, and moss rubbings adorned the fabric.

"Are you extracting colors or painting?" he asked with a chuckle, not seeing a mordant or batch of distilling chemicals anywhere on the table.

"I'm getting colors, so zaisure can mix them with sentae!"

Davnian nodded at the notion, recognizing the bizarre talvuo word. A form of face painting and perfuming, tied with a pheromone-based additive and an opiate-like mood adjuster, the substance was used in rituals by older talvuo lines. Based on the pheromones, they could elicit different reactions for their purposes, whether it be posturing, religious rites, or romance.

[At the very least, it seems your inexhaustible well of arcana is intact.]

[Useless trivia is not helpful,] Davnian replied.

"So, who do you make all the face paints for? Surely not just Elis and you?"

"I can't paint my face until I start the changes," Rais said matter-of-factly. "Zaisure offers to paint the faces of other girls in the village, and sometimes she wears them when she goes to visit zaisure Neris or someone she likes."

"Is that right?"

"I want to make blue and green! Zaisure never makes blues or greens, but I think they'd be really pretty on her," Rais continued, swerving in place as she motioned to the mess. Davnian was enjoying the conversation, but even the short exposure was wearing on his ailing body. Exhaustion crept over him as hunger pangs stung his stomach.

"Rais, is there something soft I can eat?"

"Are you hungry?" she exclaimed as she snapped back toward him.

"Yes, and I would appreciate something that doesn't need much chewing." He chuckled. "My jaw is getting sore just from talking."

"I'll get some berries!" she sang, breaking into a song about sweets and tarts as he jumped off her stool.

Overcome with a wave of nausea from the lack of energy, he watched the girl stride toward the window. She was an amusing, furious, little bundle of limbs and force with the attention span of a happy puppy and the willfulness of a bull. Trying to calm his gut, he fixated on the little girl moving across the floor, her white linen dress swaying like a sheet over her bony frame. As he watched, he felt a twitch in his left eye as a shade blurred his vision. The girl's steps started to slow down, the sound of the surrounding forest dulling as her movements played in slow motion. The shadowy figure, a person-shaped gas, trailed behind the girl and then enclosed her. Rais's song became a bass-filled growl as time seemed to stretch onward, the hazy visage engulfing her body as she continued forward. The scene stretched into eternity as the girl's limbs reached out toward the counter, her fingers' movements mechanical and meticulous in the expanse of the short eternity he was witnessing.

The miasma around her took form as a cloudy head stretched above the little girl's. Reaching downward, tendril-like fingers clung to the child's shoulders as the ghoul's face manifested. Hollow eyes and a hole for a nose combined with an ever-expanding, gaping, empty maw. His blue eyes were wide with terror. Just as the little girl's fingers touched a parcel on the counter, the malevolent shadow let out an ear-rending wail. His ears filling with the horrible sound, he gritted his teeth as he watched Rais stumble at the counter, knocking her chin as she hit the ground. Time collapsed upon itself, and the ghost was gone.

"Rais!" Davnian cried, reaching his black claw toward her as he strained to sit upright.

"Ow," she moaned, rubbing her chin as she sat on the floor. Her other hand rubbed her ankle, feeling it with her tiny, bony fingers.

"Are you alright?" His breathing was erratic as he tried to fit what had just happened into the scene. The shade was gone, and everything was back to normal.

"I'm OK," Rais said, standing up. "I just tripped." Without another word, she reached up and grabbed the parcel. She turned back, a big red welt on her chin as she approached. One hand still fingered the delicate spot. "Here you go."

"OK," Davnian said, taking the small parcel from her. With a glum look, she climbed back up on the stool. Leaning forward, he unwrapped the package, revealing a humble bundle of raspberries. "Thank you, Rais."

"You're welcome," she replied, still feeling her chin.

"Trip often?"

"Sometimes my legs get weak, but it doesn't happen too much," Rais said, turning her gaze back up to him. "I just run funny sometimes."

With a shy smile, she kicked her legs, watching as he fingered the berries in his lap. As he plopped one of the soft red morsels into his mouth, out of the corner of his eye he saw a second face staring at him. Its head spun on a plane beside the small talvuo child. With a gaping, empty maw, it watched him, an expression of anger and sorrow stretched over a sagging mockery of Rais's own visage. Ignoring the sight, he leaned over and shoved another berry into his mouth. Shutting his eyes, he let the red, tart juices coat his inner cheeks and tongue, swishing them around until he was satisfied enough to swallow. Opening his eyes, he looked back at the girl. The ghastly visage was gone.

"Are they good?" Rais asked nervously as she stared at his hunched figure. He let out a deep sigh before shooting her a smile.

"Very. Thank you, Rais," he whispered before taking several more and downing them.

"Do you want some more?" Rais asked, donning a feeble grin.

"These will do," he replied, patting her on the shoulder.

After finishing with the berries and downing the rest of the water from his tiny cup, Davnian laid back down. He thanked Rais again. Then, with his head tilted to one side, he watched as she got up and started to mess around with hulls and shells in drawing out her favorite colors. He tried to block out the imagery from earlier, unsettled by the sullen husk that had wrapped itself around Rais's skinny arms and neck. Reaching inward, he tried to prod for advice, but the other was absent from his thoughts.

Dismayed, Davnian turned his soft gaze to the child. With a shiver running down his spine, he watched her, ignoring the flickers of a tormented face hovering just beside her.

23

NERIS

Neris had half anticipated Nerin to be busy ploughing another young Hyunisti maiden, talking up Delvori luxuries and decadence. But to her benefit, the room had been clear of all but her brother's most treacherous lackey, the eagle-eyed Kadin. Despite what cleverness he feigned, Neris had discovered he was like any other deprived, servile man. His lusts ran deep, and so did his kinks. No doubt, she had spied him working over one of the drunk girls in a closet one evening, the poor, stumbling maiden dazed from whatever her brother had done to her. The things he would do to the girls were outrageous, but those same tastes would make him putty in her hands.

"Vindal Neris," Kadin said quietly, shifting from his perch in front of Nerin's vanity. Putting down a small leather-bound volume, he bowed to her. "To what do I owe the pleasure this afternoon?"

"Pleasantries as always, vivahr Kadin," Neris said, stepping into the large, circular room. Without shifting her eyes, she surveyed the room and plotted her next steps with care. "I see Nerin has left you to your own devices. To think you'd wait after the man in his bedchamber. Such loyalty is sure to be rewarded, eh, my dear?"

"Vivahr Nerin has come up with more ideas for the feast tomorrow and the ceremonies and festivities. The man is a well of enthusiasm for archaic practices," Kadin said while making a wide arc. He passed her front and moved to the left, positioning himself in the center of the room. As he spoke, Neris took several steps into the room, fingering her sash while keeping the talvuo in her sights. "As always, he leaves the chore of tidying and watching to me, ne vindal."

"So familiar, Kadin. Of course, I would expect nothing less of a man who spies on me through cracks late at night," Neris said nonchalantly as she eased next to the vanity and lifted a bottle from it. "Seems my brother has been indulging a bit much of late, though his used rags seem to be unable to quench your insatiable appetite."

"I beg you to speak softer, vindal. Your brother isn't known to be kind to his sister's lovers."

Neris shifted her gaze as she tipped her head back, downing a heavy draught of the leftover vintage. The flavor was stale but sufficient as she brought her gaze back down. The thin man eyed her, his fake grin twitching at her minor display. "So, what pleasantries have tempted you here today, ne vindal?"

"You know, my dear Kadin, I've been wondering. How long have you been haunting our halls now?" Neris asked, lowering the bottle as she walked toward him.

"For as long as you've resided in the great tree, vindal. Though we both know I've been at your side far longer." Kadin gestured to the space between them. "Your brother has kept busy since he arrived, and I've always had an interest in watching your art."

"My art?" Neris chuckled as she drew closer, bringing the bottle beside his face.

"The way you seduce, ne vindal. The way you ingratiate yourself to men and women and how they fawn over you in return. The way you open tender hearts and splay even more sensitive bodies with your enchanting touch."

"I'm flattered, vivahr Kadin," Neris said as he took the bottle from her hands. She grinned as he followed her lead, taking a hefty swig to match her own. Impulse would be his undoing. "Though there is something else I wish to ask."

"Yes, ne vindal?"

Neris rounded Kadin, her nimble fingers freeing her sash as she circled him. Drawing behind him, she unstrung the silk cloth. With both hands twisted the strand around the man's neck. With a gentle tug, she pulled him back toward her.

"How long have you dreamed of this moment, sweet Kadin?" Neris whispered as she stretched her crimson tongue out, licking the folds behind his brown, fuzzy ears. The man shivered as she teased. "Tell me, ne vivahr, have you ever felt the grace of a lover holding your breath, stroking you to release?"

"I can't say I have, ne vindal," Kadin said, gasping as she drew the silk back. Step by step, she pulled him with her, leading him into her lap as she sat upon Nerin's downed mattress. "I fear I've always been on the giving end."

"Perhaps your loyalty should be rewarded with a present then," she whispered, twisting the strap behind his neck. "Let us indulge, for receiving can be just as pleasant, ne vivahr."

With a firm grip, Neris yanked him back. As he grunted and squirmed in her lap, she leaned back. With one of his hands in her own, she brought his pale fingers to her face. Kadin turned his head as she beckoned him closer. Licking her coal lips, she tugged him close, letting his thin, pink mouth caress her own. She wrapped the other end of the cloth in front of him, bringing her hand down to his pudgy, swelling groin. As he moved his hand down toward hers, she abandoned the strap and led his arm behind him. Tilting herself back, she slipped his free hand between the leather and cloth of her legwear. As his skeletal digits fumbled around her loins, she reached her hand back around and slipped it into his trousers. Drawing his dripping prick free, she stroked it with her hand, leaning forward to plant a love bite upon the nape of his neck.

"Gods, vindal," Kadin stammered, his free hand clutching at her raven hair.

Pulling the binding around his neck even tighter, sadistic glee filled her as she watched his face redden. His breath was strained as her firm grip choked him, his body unable to resist her tilting motion. As he tried to lean back toward her, she planted her head against the back of his neck, nuzzling his pale skin. Over and over, she continued the game, feeling his body stiffen. As his head filled with blood, turning from a winded rose to grape red, she tightened her hold on his leash and his member. With wild abandon and lacking grace, his jutting fingers flicked and probed her body. Swelling her chest, she matched his frantic breathing.

"Vin . . . Neri . . . is . . ." Kadin's words tumbled out of his mouth as he began to shake.

Neris bit his ear, pumping her body toward his hungry fingers as she drew the cloth in both her hands, gripping it as tight as she could. In her right hand, his groin swelled With a grunt, her fingers were smeared with the smooth, wet coating of his seed. Gasping for breath, Kadin convulsed in her arms, his bony fingers clawing as his purple face tightened in an expression of ecstasy. Before another moment could pass, she pulled the silk to its limit. His body lurched at once as the last bit of blood and air was cut off. His frame shivered in shock. Undeterred, she held it in place. His body convulsed from pleasure and paralysis. Neris watched as a hint of realization crossed his beleaguered features. Kadin's fingertips dug into her flesh as he spasmed before falling limp in her arms.

Without a second to spare, she flung the body to her side, his sopping cock staining Nerin's sheets. Sparing no time, she wiped her hand off on Kadin's tunic. As one final touch, she picked up the discarded wine bottle and spilled it beside the incapacitated man, then tucked it neatly near his shrinking member.

"Enjoy your nap, vivahr Kadin," Neris whispered, taking a moment to tuck in her blouse and adjust her leggings. Her clit and folds were sore from the thin man's frantic rubbing and grinding nails. She would make sure Davnian paid a heavy price for her noble sacrifice.

Without another moment to spare, Neris began her search through her brother's belongings, looking for anything that might be of use to her disabled lover.

24

ERROR

[B]e empty, be free.] The words echoed in Thaimi's head as she sat with her back against the wall of the elders' hut. Across from her was the venerable, old talvuo who made up the council that presided over the village. Ever since her night with the dark-skinned Delvori, she had been pained by visions and hallucinations. But the more she gave in, the brighter the world seemed to be. She felt thinner and lighter, faster and cleaner.

At first, Thaimi felt disgusted with how she had been seemingly violated and abused. The things she allowed the Delvori man to do were unbeknownst to her, but her virgin frame was defiled when she awoke the next day. But the other nectar maidens soothed away her worry. They told her how happy they had come to be and how much better things would get in time.

"Vivahr Nerin, we are not comfortable with making such a display of Hyun's legacy at the ceremony. Her mark touched all who hold the term 'Hyunisti' dear. Our namesake cannot be ignored," Thelais, the eldest of the council leaders, said. Her frail hand shook as she motioned across the room from her pillowed seat. Crossed-legged, she shook her head, pointing to the artifacts that Nerin had presented. "These journals and mementos are sacred to our people."

"With all due respect, my gracious elders, this ceremony means no disrespect to you and your founder, but is meant to cleanse us of the shackles of the past," Nerin said. "The burning of these articles is to represent the cleansing of your most humble matriarch's worries and grief. Through this journal, it is evident that she suffered many woes from the burden carried by her people. I wish only to put her spirit at ease."

Looking at the silk-clad rogue, Thaimi felt overcome with mixed emotions. Through the aid of her sister maidens, she knew that though the path she took was hard, one so young and inexperienced was more apt to find love and lust confusing and terrifying. But her disgust was dissipating. With every word, she saw the light burning through the darkness of her lord's skin. She thought it should feel strange, frightening, but her sisters and the voices hollowed out her apprehension.

[Be empty, be free.]

"I know better than anyone how Hyun was troubled," their record keeper said from beside her glowing lord. She was voluptuous, with skin the color of the distant sands as the sun turned the sky yellow and crimson. Her hair was spun like woven gold, and her talvuo ears adorned unlike any others in the village, covered with gilded ruby hairs. With amethystine eyes, she stood in defiance of her lord's wishes. Though her sisters bemoaned suspicion of the enigmatic talvuo, Thaimi could not help but revere Elis Renai, who had lived in the time of Hyun.

"Hyun never forgot the plight of her people, and through her years wished for a peace that she could never see. If she were alive today, she would be overcome with the joy of seeing her people still moving forward. The fact we meet traders from the north and south would bring happiness to her heart, and with how we have kept our air of tolerance, Hyun would pray blessings upon us—"

"Vindal Elis, what is the . . ." Lord Nerin asked, breaking into Elis's speech, a mocking grin on his devilish face.

[Be empty, be free.]

"Be empty, be free, sister," Mais whispered into Thaimi's ear, leaning over her shoulder.

"The point, vivahr Nerin," Elis said. Her words carried a righteous heat that filled Thaimi's heart with admiration, but something deep within gnawed at that feeling. Her heart skipped a beat as she continued to listen. "One thing Hyun prized above all else was us retaining our knowledge and history. To discard them, as our Delvori brother suggests, is an affront to the ideals she held dear, to her hope that her people would never forget the good and the ill that had befallen them. From our strife, we would emerge richer, knowing what paths to tread when the storm clears."

"Well put, vindal Elis," Camrin, the third of the eldest, said. His ears had just started to grey, only decades old yet wearing the mask of Hyunisti wisdom. "We should not forget the path we have walked in hopes of not losing our way and repeating past mistakes." There was a small period of praise as other villagers acknowledged the same sentiment.

[Be empty, be free.]

"Vindal, you speak as if your acquaintance held no regrets," Nerin said, interrupting the cheering. He rose from his seat while picking up one of the leather-bound articles of his argument. "All of you! Allow me to read you a passage of your troubled well-wisher's words!"

The room fell silent. Thaimi looked over to see Elis's lavender eyes narrowing, her hand clenched into a fist at her side. As she stared, Thaimi's vision was overcome with small black lines of bile and hatred coursing over the Renai woman's features, painting her as a frenzied beast. In her chest, she felt despair for the woman she so respected.

"On this day, I look out at my people and am pained," Nerin began. "My heart breaks to see them suffer the hurried decisions of a woman gripped by fear and rage. Every day I look out to my people, smiling and hoping for better days to come. But as I watch them give birth to stillborn children, as I see them age beyond their years, as I hear their lamentations echo the weakness that seeks to overtake me, I find myself weeping every night. With all my heart, I wish I could undo the things I have done. With all my being, I wish I could hear the dancing and singing of my people once more. I long to hear their merriment and music, to gaze not upon squalor but upon the majesty of our forestry and art. Every night I pray to the gods to let me bear it all and spare my people."

As an aura of dismay permeated the room, everyone's hearts grew heavy with their namesake's sullen words. Thaimi felt elated. Her insides bustled with a manic joy as she saw pain cling to the faces of the villagers and elders as her noble lord closed the ancient journal. Tears of adoration filled her eyes as the light around Nerin grew, his skin like luminous marble before her eyes.

But the feeling of happiness disappeared as her green eyes narrowed on the Renai woman's figure. Without a word, the bronze figure stood. She saw her master turn, his beautiful lips growing into a godlike smile. But as his clay-red eyes looked down with succor, Elis's fist slammed into his perfect features. The room erupted in shock as the Delvori man spun to the floor, the journal landing with a thud.

[Vile, cursed, tainted, poisonous.] The whispers in her head entrenched themselves in her heart. Bile clung to Elis's features, seeping from wounds and blackened scrawl that etched over her. Thaimi's heart grew even heavier as she watched the woman whom she held in such high regard succumbing to darkness.

"I will not have you use a dead woman's inner anguish for your own ends, Nerin Delvori!" Elis roared to the crowd of onlookers. As he struggled on the ground, Thaimi and her sisters moved to their master's side and helped him to his knees. "You read those words proudly but do not understand their intention. Yes, Hyun had her regrets, but every day she suppressed those from her speech and manner, and do you know why you snake-tongued bastard? Do you?"

"Vindal Elis." Thaimi raised her emerald eyes to look at their embittered historian. She saw it all now, how the fires of age and anguish had stolen her dignity and love. Why else would she leave them for so long? Why else could she bear such hateful words to her lord? "Have you no heart?"

"I will tell you, Delvori, for it is something your simple mind cannot comprehend." Elis's vengeful remarks made Thaimi's stomach turn as she gripped her master's side.

"Be empty, be free," her sisters whispered around her, clinging together with their lord.

Thaimi felt the warm, radiating hand of the prideful man grip her own. In response, the whispers rushed to her ears, calming her nerves. [Be empty, be free.]

"She carried that burden because she knew she must. Her people needed her strength, so she lifted them. Her people needed her warmth, so she blanketed them. Her people needed her wisdom, so she consoled them. She wrote it down, so she could be free of it and so her people could depend on her without having to see her suffering. She moved forward and would let nothing, not even herself, hold them back!"

The room was still, bated breaths hanging in the air as everyone's eyes were fixed upon her fallen lord, Elis, and the elders. The tension in the air was palpable, but through it all, Thaimi was at ease. The pain and sorrow were something she had never understood but always known. It had clung to her every day of her life. She carried the grief and malaise of her people through her years. Every moment of joviality was shackled by the despair and the inner turmoil of her people, of Hyun. Never had her eyes been so opened as in this moment. She could understand it now, the whispers and the words. To let go. To be empty.

[Be free.]

"We have heard all we need hear, vindal Elis, vivahr Nerin," said Veridis, the farthest sitting elder. She was spritely for a Hyunisti of her age. The grey of her hair and the fatigue of her limbs held her down less than her peers. "I accept vivahr Nerin's proposal. Our fair founder deserves a proper place amongst us. I see no harm in the burning of some of her most personal effects."

"I agree, vindal," Thalais, the eldest, replied, raising her hand to the man on the other side of her.

"I will not protest the motion because never before have my ears heard of our troubled sister's pains, though I cannot ignore the legacy that she has laid bare." Camrin motioned to the crowd, narrowing his eyes in pain as he shifted them from Nerin to Elis. "I propose that the tomes and journals of Hyun be given to our eldest, Elis Renai."

There was murmuring among the nectar maidens. Thaimi felt Nerin's chest fill as he thought to protest the audacity.

"I accept this compromise," Thalais said.

"I accept as well, vindal," Veridis concurred.

"Then it is settled," Thalais proclaimed before anyone else could protest. "We shall raise a pyre for the procession. We shall pay respects to vindal Hyun and her sacrifices, to appease her spirit and allow her penance for her inner transgressions. Her personal effects will be burned, save the books that document her struggles and our history."

"Agreed," the other two elders said in unison.

"Then let us part with the wisdom of Hyun and embrace the coming of the morrow," Thalais said, ending the meeting.

All around them, villagers spoke and whispered, murmuring in curious circles about what things should be sacrificed to the cleansing and what should be kept. Thaimi felt the worry and tension leaving her breast. There was nothing to worry about, no tear to be shed for affront or travesty, no nerves to be rattled. She was finally free.

"Well, it appears you have gotten what you wanted, vindal," Nerin said as he rose. The nectar maidens clung to him, their eyes fixed on Elis Renai's arrogant, deprived figure. "Are you happy to see Hyun's most sullen artifacts remanded into your custody?"

"You seek power and change constantly, Delvori." Elis's tongue hissed like that of a viper, her eyes pained with violence. Her skin had lost its luster, the bronze corroded by the aura of malice that overtook her. "But this step is too far. I care not what hardships or imagined victories you carry on your slumping shoulders. You're using this cere-mony to stomp out memories that should not be forgotten!"

"You should let go, ne vindal," Nerin said, kindness clinging to his words. "Anger and bile do not befit one as beautiful as you."

"Speak again, and I will teach you about anger, bile, and long years, Delvori," Elis said, storming from the room.

"Say hello to Rais for me, ne vindal. I do so hope you both visit tomorrow night. It would be terrible to see our hospitality go to waste." Nerin's pleasant words filled the room with a chorus of pleading voices. If only they could free her. Thaimi couldn't help herself, tearing away from the group and running to Elis's side.

"Thaimi, you should be free of that man before you lose yourself." Elis's voice was like raking coals as she walked, but Thaimi's heart was empty, free of the burden of self-righteousness and pain. She knew what she needed to say.

"Vindal, to you and yours, be empty, be free."

25

——

ELIS

The day had left its mark on Elis, the difficulties of dealing with her own issues along with the new onslaught of aiding her awoken friend having taken their toll. She was at a loss for words when she returned to the infirmary, watching her young one smile and plod away at her rough color rubbings. Davnian was asleep on the table, his eyes pained from some unseen dreams that Elis could only just fathom. Rais had relayed how the man had eaten and how she had hurt herself. To Elis, her little ankle seemed fine, though tender to the touch. With a kiss and a pat, she sent the girl on her way. She laid a small stack of books on the table and returned to her vigil.

She had hoped he'd be awake when she returned if only to stave off her own ravenous need to escape. At times like these, she would pack up her things and, with Rais in tow, head off into the woods to hunt game or gather for the oncoming days. The peace of being away from people was something she needed, but she knew there was little point in leaving before the festivities. Likewise, Davnian wouldn't understand her disappearance. Then again, maybe he would.

"Zaisure." Rais's little voice was cheerful. In the dim light of the waning sun, Elis turned to see the girl scurrying over, a jar in hand. "Is this OK?"

"I think it will be wonderful, Rais." Elis smiled, spying the jar full of blue insect shells and indigo. The contents were crushed into a paste, which Elis surmised was Rais's attempt at gathering the ingredients for a color of her own. "Something grey and blue then?"

"Like the bottom of a snow hole," Rais said. Elis laughed, taking the small vial and looking at its contents. Rais was busy making lines and dots in the air, mimicking the point technique of sentae.

"Maybe we should see how it'll look on you, hmm?" Elis said, watching Rais's face flush. Her cheeks were like blooming blossoms laid across a white canvas. Laughing, Elis drew the girl close, "Embarrassed, my little one?"

"I'm not—"

"Oh, you're getting plenty old enough, my dear." Elis cradled the girl as she danced in place. Rais was unable to contain her sporadic emotions. "Besides, I think blue would look better on you. But maybe we should find some green as well."

"OK, zaisure!" the little girl struggled to contain her dance, wrapping her arms around Elis.

"Find anything you like?"

"We don't have a lot of green things, zaisure," Rais said, pulling away as she leered at the table. It wasn't the lack of green things that made it a problem but a lack of matter willing to give up its pigment, not that leaves and grasses weren't abundant. Elis wasn't fond of green. She could never get the shade she wanted.

"There's not much to get that pretty bright green you want, is there?"

"Uh-uh," Rais muttered. The leaves of most trees in the Witchwood were dark, almost black when no light was hitting them. The grasses were much lighter, more yellow than green.

"Well, we'll just have to feel it out then," Elis mused, trying to think how she'd do it. Leaves and grasses with the proper binding agent could be distilled with sentae to make the paint. But getting the color glossy would be the hard part. Sentae could do a lot for making even the dullest pigments crystalline but not everything. "I don't think we'll be able to do it here."

"I'm getting hungry, zaisure."

"Well, enough then, little one. Maybe we should pack up for today." Elis beamed a smile toward Rais as she gripped her tummy through her white tunic. "Why not pack up what you have, and I'll grab the leftover scraps, hmm?"

"OK, zaisure."

As Rais gathered her color etchings and vials of mishmash, Elis let out a deep sigh. All the food she had brought was in disarray. No doubt Rais had feasted during the early afternoon as Elis argued with the council and the Delvori. She was glad Davnian had gotten something to eat other than Neris's personal brew. It still nagged at her—though, all things considered, it was laughable. It wasn't the first time he had suckled at talvuo breasts, and likely it would not be the last.

In some ways, Neris reminded her of her younger self with how confident and nonchalant her demeanor was. Deep inside, she was sure Neris would return at some hour to talk the night away with Davnian, if not more. The idea was pleasant, if not beautiful.

"Zaisure, should I—"

"Don't worry about wiping up. We can get to it in the morning, my dear."

"OK," Rais said, dancing with her basket. As Elis bundled the last of the messy foodstuffs, her lavender eyes followed Rais to Davnian's bedside. The little girl put a small bottle next to him before patting him on the head. "Have a good night, naisure Virage." Then Rais continued her dance, her jittery steps leading her to Elis's side.

"What's that, my dear?"

"Mashed berries!" Rais said, spinning in place.

"Berries, are they?" Elis grinned, mimicking Rais's gesture as she ran her chestnut-colored fingers through the girl's hair. "Well, I hope he enjoys them when he wakes."

"Mmmm hmmm."

With the last bits of fading light, Elis and Rais headed home.

26

DAVNIAN

"There has never been a prison built that could hold me, claw bearer." The words were like echoes in his mind as the image of a middle-aged man gripped his brain. "It's folly to think this will work."

"The purpose isn't the prison, mage. The purpose is giving us time to plan." Davnian felt his lips moving. "Do you think I'd come all the way here just to leave you? You thought wrong then, Lori-Arma."

As darkness faded to light, Davnian saw a vast expanse before him. All around, giant obsidian columns stood, engraved with the images of talvuo kings and queens. The fine-featured talvuo whose dark skin mimicked the hue of their stonework were driven from the ancient halls of Dal Rothein. From outside the grand hall, he heard the screams of talvuo men and women, the battle cries of Holan warriors and chieftains calling into the darkness of the great cavern fortress. Fresh bodies and blood lined the floor, the gemstones and gilded treasures of the Delvori race scattered within the warded vaults of their deep home.

"This bloodshed was unnecessary. There must have been a better way!" the old man croaked, coughing as he protested.

"There are only two other vaults of such caliber in the world,

Madras Ohran: the gilded labyrinth of Ans-Ansuman and the magic font of Lorin. Neither are places I would bring one cursed such as you, and neither are open to us."

"But this, this is . . ."

"Killing two birds with one stone, mage." Davnian's voice was cold and detached. His thoughts were a mystery even to himself as the scene replayed, making his waking body grind and bite against the harsh reality. "This is a favor to you and another. The Delvori would have bent whether or not I brought down the hammer."

"But this is . . ."

As the light within the room flickered, the space around them warped. Davnian's sense of direction snapped around. Behind him the visage of the old man stood, gesturing in protest beneath crimson robes. His face was gaunt, and his frame hollow as the expanse between him and the mage closed in an instant. Behind the red figure, the giant gates of the great vaults lay cracked open, crystal light glittering on every surface around them. The old man's breath caught in his throat. Beneath the two of them, a pool of red resin formed as the blood of the dead talvuo merged with the spreading circle to create a brilliant crimson mirror. Within it, Davnian saw his own features—expressionless, cold, and empty.

Drawing back, he watched Ohran sway as he clutched his breast. Beneath his ribs was a gaping hole. His life spilled upon the floor like a great red fountain. Looking up, Ohran's face filled with pain, then a sullen joy. Within his blackened hand, Davnian felt the beating of Ohran's final moments, the mage's heart within his jet claws. As the mage fell to his knees, he crushed the throbbing organ, feeling his monstrous appendage feast upon the Lori-Arma's lifeblood.

"Let us see if death is what you truly crave, mage," Davnian whispered.

"I just . . . I want . . ." the old man sputtered as the light left his eyes before he fell prone against the stone floor.

Davnian thought he had done the impossible. He had killed the cursed Madras Ohran. The effort of appeasing his other compatriot seemed fruitless with how easily the end had come. Imagery of fires and smoldering remains flittered within his brain. All around him, the light of the grand vault was dimming, the crystal beacons extinguishing with the life of the gate magician.

Surrounded by the shifting dark, Davnian felt the floor move beneath him. In starts and stops, the black stone lurched as he made his way from the expanse. There was nothing more to be done.

Then a scream broke through the silence as the old man's haggard voice rang throughout the giant stone room.

The scene snapped back and forth. Imagery of the vault doors flickered between frames of walls and columns, blinding crystalline light, and a dead man clutching his head. A gale of fiendish mist slipped through the tall stone doors, wrapping the room in a miasma of shrieking horrors and bloody screams. Attaching to the warded obsidian walls, the airy stuff clung like molasses, dripping with slimy blobs. Faster and faster, the frames of time skipped back and forth before settling on the rising figure of the crimson-robed mage and his bloody body.

"Not again. No. I thought . . . Not again . . ." the man's cries were like a child's whimper as his hands tore at the furled red-grey hairs adorning his crown. In anguish he ripped the mane from his head, bloody patches of skull and skin exposed in his torment. Davnian felt his mindscape warping to match the horror, his composure slipping. "Virage! Kill me! Please kill me!"

The robed man snapped around, his green eyes empty of all life as he screamed at him. Beneath the skin of his meatless body, Davnian saw them writhing. The man's flesh seemed to wriggle and curl, the shell covering his bones churning like a pit of snakes.

"It couldn't be that easy . . ." he said, his voice trailing off as visions of another danced in front of his face, a green-robed figure speaking to him about the dire situation. In their words, his voice continued. "Killing him will be no trivial matter."

Like sand slipping between his fingers, fragments of the hazy memory eluded his senses. At once he was both everywhere and nowhere in the space. Blades flashed, and portals of manifest energy opened all around the vault. Fire, lightning, thunder, ice, wind, earth, metal, and magma erupted from every surface. With every roaring gate, he saw flashes of Ohran's gaunt face in his mind. His flesh boiled away like starchy froth with every flickering blow struck against what should be a mortal man's body. The room's shadows twisted this way and that, Davnian's silhouette lined by dim blue light as Ohran's figure caved in and deformed. The mage's shade filled the space with the emptiness of something monstrous and indescribable.

Then the doors shut as a wave of red crashed upon them. From outside the vault, Davnian peered at the massive stone entrance, watching as Delvori blood spilled from the ceiling over the chamber's ancient wards. One by one, the runes lit up with an ethereal light.

Beyond the doors, the voice of the man who was once Madras Ohran screamed for death.

Again.

And again.

[EASE AWAKE NOW, young one.]

Opening his eyes, Davnian searched the quaint space of the Hyunisti infirmary for any sign of friend or foe. Darkness had fallen on the talvuo village, but the haze of lantern light from outside his quarters permeated the heavy air. In the hanging night, propped up on the countertop was none other than the black silhouette of a slender, elegant Delvori woman. Within her nimble fingers, she clutched a tome, her rust-red eyes turning to him as he lifted his head.

"I see you're awake again," Neris said, closing the book. "You look both better and worse for wear."

"Dreams are a troubling thing," Davnian replied, sitting upright. Strands of muscle throughout his body ached with a dull throb. Despite the pain, the act of sitting upright was now within his grasp. The tension in his lower back had all but disappeared. "You look as charming as ever, Neris."

"That's because I'm always charming," she replied, turning her stare to the village outside. Shadows danced in dots and flickers through the wooden slats over the windows. "Too charming perhaps, depending on the fool who's stammering over me."

"I take it you had an eventful afternoon?" Davnian asked, bending forward. It felt good to stretch as he ignored the painful visages of his nightmares.

"If only so," Neris whispered, turning away from the windows. "I've never known Nerin to write, but it seems he's been keeping notes about his imaginary friend and their secret meetings. Though it's all madman's gibbering. Just reading his journal was enough to settle the point. I doubt he even reads what he writes, given the way he talks and acts. Otherwise, he might throw himself from the top of the tree."

The air was cold as it danced across his exposed skin. He could not see Neris's eyes as she lifted herself from the counter and marched toward him, but he knew she was staring into his.

"This is what I fetched, with a little help from a would-be weasel."

Neris handed him the thin book. Davnian didn't give it more than a second glance. Although there could be a missing piece of the puzzle in Nerin's writings, deciphering such madness would be taxing. He had neither the patience nor the strength for it.

"It seems you've been busy as well." Neris nodded to his side. Davnian tilted his head, staring down at a pair of dusty tomes and a bottle of red stuff, the smell of raspberries calling to him. "Gifts from other friends of yours?"

"The bottle smells like berries, no doubt the little girl's doing." He smiled. "The books were likely left by mistake. I doubt anyone would leave such old volumes behind on purpose."

"You weren't awake for her to return then?" Neris asked, sitting beside him. He could feel her warmth through the sheets. "Though perhaps it's better that way. This afternoon has been filled with intrigues and portents, and likely our fair Elis was not the least bit enthused about them."

"Did something happen while I was asleep?"

"Nothing too dramatic," Neris said, putting her hand on his leg. As she spoke, her black fingers walked up the white sheet, her pointed nails teasing his skin. "My brother made an ass of himself and stirred up quite a commotion. It seems our tempestuous partner got into quite the heated debate with him. He's been ranting ever since he returned home. Losing these has put him in a foul mood. He had a chattering quartet of maidens clinging to him as he returned."

"Elis has given us a gift through absence, it seems," Davnian fumbled over the two books as a shallow grin worked its way across his features. His heart sank as he thought about how he had missed the opportunity to talk with her that afternoon. But no matter. They would have their time. "We shouldn't waste the opportunity."

"No, we shouldn't," Neris cooed, bringing her face next to his. Her breath was upon his cheek as she leaned over, the sound of her parting lips sending a chill down his spine as she nuzzled his ear. "Though I think it'd be best if we saw to poring over such things another time, don't you?"

"I think you have something else in mind, though I'm not in the greatest way to protest. And despite how things were earned, I did promise you something in return, did I not?" Turning his gaze to her, Davnian saw Neris's narrow eyes peering into the depths of his soul. Her face was cloaked by her silken black hair. Her expression had warmed from cold to hot.

"You know I've never been one to accept anything less." With a sigh, she kissed his cheek, her left hand sliding up his thigh, gripping his leg. "Though perhaps you should dress before I string you along, hmm?"

"I don't suppose you've brought me something to garb myself in."

"Just what you were wearing when you first arrived, my dear." She was holding herself back just enough to move him, which for all intents was calming. "Though perhaps you'd rather strut out into the night bare as a babe?"

"I'll take the clothes, my lady," Davnian said as she pulled away.

As Neris brought him his attire, his mind was a blur of thoughts. Everything that should have been settled was not. Everything that was unsettled seemed distant and unreachable.

Reality was like dancing along to a tune he could not hear, played by a madman far removed.

27

———

NERIS

Bringing him to her bedchamber had been her goal since he first awoke. Though she had plotted events with the distinct knowledge that the game would be in her field, Neris was left in a sordid mood. Davnian, the Virage, was in a dark place, detached by the looming specter of some mysterious, nameless terror. She kept up her part of the bargain both in action and play as she guided her red-and-blue-clad lover to the great tree. She teased and toyed with him as they walked, but his every step seemed weighed down, each footfall becoming more onerous than the last, though perhaps it was his need for recovery.

No, Neris knew this mood. And it wasn't pleasant.

She teased the nape of his neck as they made their way inside the first of the rounds of the Hyunisti great tree, keeping her lips moist and her demeanor enticing. She didn't want him knowing the game had been swept. Not that Neris wasn't somewhat put out as well.

The first tome she found, the one Kadin had been so nonchalant about reading, was the typical rants of a megalomaniac without a clue. Nerin's lusts and motivations were simple enough. He wanted power.

He wanted the name "Delvori" to be more than a historical footnote. And beyond all, he wanted to be served. None of that surprised her.

But always curious, she had taken a keen interest in a trunk stowed beneath his bed. It was odd how carefully her brother had stashed it and even more enticing due to how it had been locked. If not for his absentmindedness, she would have been unable to open the box, but with the key on the nightstand, she had taken to prying. And inside, she found a worn-out memoir.

Beneath scrawled runes and indecipherable symbols, Neris made out the writings of her brother. At first they were the same as those in the former book. But midway through her brother's words became overwhelmingly erratic. His personage was replaced with constant references to his unseen friend and detailed ramblings of the voices in his head. Given the way Nerin presented himself, she wondered if he could even remember the things he wrote. The worst would be if he did, the whole act a culmination of infighting insanity struggling with his obnoxious persona.

The entire thing froze her at the tail, jolts of ice water bubbling up and flowing down her spine. Ignoring the unpleasantness was but another trait that she had learned well.

"Feeling tired, are you?" Neris whispered into Davnian's ear, her hands clutching his shoulders as she pressed him forward. His motions betrayed his weakness. He had not regenerated enough for such exertion, though she had planned for that. "It's not much farther now."

"This place is grander than I expected," Davnian said, his words teasing her as his breath hung heavily in his throat. Something else was amiss with him, but she could not tell what. "Do you climb this every day?"

"Multiple times, though it's nothing compared to what you've put me through."

He chuckled as they made the last round. Urging him onward, she walked ahead. Opening the door, Neris pulled her lover into her nest.

"Welcome, ne vahr." Her heart fluttered as she shut the door behind them.

Her chamber was a large, circular room, shifted to the side of the great circle, allowing for a grand view of the old healer's tree and the central terrace. Large wooden windows filled with horizontal slats lined the outer wall. She had prepared a few larger candles. As Davnian took in the sight, Neris lit one candle, followed by the others. The soft glow of their wicks lined the room with dancing gold-and-copper flames.

In the radiance, Neris's semi-lavish feather bed stood at the end of the slatted progression. Upon it was a lavish woolen cover. Tussled upon it were satin and linen sheets of various hues. A half dozen pillows were clumped at the head of the mattress with a half dozen more lumped beside the frame. Large wooden posts, polished pieces of small oak trunks, marked the corners.

Neris's other furniture was scattered around the edges of the room. A window table with a pair of wooden chairs sat on the end of the windowed aisle, a vanity with a stool beside it. A large, dark chest hugged the right of the opening while a large wardrobe stood opposite the bed along the circle. Clothing from Neris's earlier perusing was scattered at the base of the closet, something she had decided was not worth tidying.

"I see you've been busy," Davnian said playfully as he hobbled around the room. "What were you going to do if I took much longer waking up?"

"The second plan was to mount you where you lay, my dear," Neris replied, strutting as she loosened the strings of her top. "I recall telling you that I would get my reward one way or another, did I not?"

"Keep my promise, or you'll have to force yourself upon me."

"Indeed," she said, turning toward her lover.

Davnian stood in the room, bathed in the carnal light. She had seen his red-and-blue-gilded tunic mended by a midnight lover, though the patching was adequate at best. Then again, replacing golden thread and such deep colors was no easy thing for forest dwellers. His brown pants were loose upon his sinewy frame. His dirty-blond hair was an unkempt mess of curls and frizzled strands. Despite his haggard clothing and the dourness of his demeanor, his icy eyes were wide as the surveyed her demesne, bold and perceptive but filled with wonder.

"What do you think, Virage?" Neris had decided to play a different tune, using his title to draw out his feelings. A small grin cracked his flat lips as he shifted his gaze to her.

"I was wondering if you avoided calling me that out of sentiment or sincerity. Well, vindal, I can't say I dislike the view."

"I don't think we're related, paramour. Though if that's tonight's game, allow me to at least make the scenery more pleasant, hmm?"

Neris sat upon her bed, leaning back as she filled her chest. The strings of her shirt hung near their length, leaving the cut open to the black silken lattice that supported her bosom.

"I think I prefer you to call me by my name, Neris." Davnian chuckled as he shuffled toward her. Her black hound's ears picked up the creaking in his joints as his knees bent and straightened. She could also hear his heartbeat and how the pounding in his chest grew as he stared at her. With one hand, she undid the simple knot that held her sash in place. "Now, now," he said, "you're ruining all the fun. What am I supposed to do if you do everything yourself?"

"Let's be honest, my dear. I'll be doing most of the work this evening." Neris shot him an impassioned look, curling her lips into an alluring smile. "Unless you think your weary body can keep up."

"As far as I'm aware, I've never been one to turn down a challenge. Especially not one I can come out on top of."

Neris laughed at his innuendo. His every word was heavy with whatever fog was clinging to his thoughts, but she couldn't help but be amused at how automatic his responses seemed to be. Avoiding vulgarity was part of the game, at least until the fire caught. Though she wondered how it would manifest in him in this state of being. The man she had known was as flippant with his humor as he was direct with his needs. Some days the cat-and-mouse play was long and elaborate as they teased and tempted each other. On others she'd find herself pressed against a wall, the moments a blur as whatever passion came and went like a passing storm.

Plopping onto the mattress beside her, Davnian took a deep breath, steadying himself. Leaning back, he let out a boyish laugh, gripping his stomach with hand and claw.

"You truly are going to make me do everything, aren't you?" Neris feigned displeasure as she slid on top of him. "You should have more pride than having to be waited upon by a doting patron."

"A patron of what, pray tell, Neris?"

As he caught his breath beneath her, Neris brought her face to his, looking down into his blue eyes. His warm breath wrapped around her chin, and she could taste hints of berries on her tongue. Bringing her body down to his, she made short, suggestive circles with her pelvis against his. His human hand teased her leather-clad leg as he brought his demon claw to her face. His blackened fingers tugged her raven-hair free, sheets of black falling around her face. Like dark curtains, they blocked out the flickering candlelight, small rays teasing his visage before her eyes. His left hand dug through the folds of her loose hair, the smooth, mottled flesh of his claw caressing her jet skin.

"Why are you hesitating?" Davnian asked, his eyes fixed on and through her. This was the moment she had dreamed of in the years that passed since their parting. Every cell of her being revved toward taking the man below her, but a governor held her in place. Her heart skipped a beat as he lowered his hand. It slid down her side, caressing her through the thin red fabric. As her breathing hastened, he slipped the blackened thing beneath her crimson blouse, bringing it to her front. A crooked grin crossed his face as he slid his hand between the woven silk straps of her brassiere, planting his hand just over her heart. "Weren't you just saying you were going to do all the work, my lady? Or do I need to be the first to stroke?"

"Davnian . . ." Neris's sultry tone dissipated as sentiment crept into her voice. As her heart raced, she was overcome with a sense of self-loathing.

"Yes, Neris?" Davnian asked, wearing a devilish look. His right hand inched between her leathers as he teased her. His black claw held still, feeling her heart race. Beneath her, his pulse pounded.

"I'm only going to say this once, but I love you," Neris said, pressing her lips against his.

His body tightened with hers as they embraced, his human hand gripping her while his demon hand held steady. As she drew back, she looked down into his eyes, the overwhelming sentiment leaving her.

"Neris, I . . ."

"Don't say it." Neris scowled at him, narrowing her eyes as the romance fled her system. Her skin tingled with anticipation as she focused her senses back to the present, heaving her chest as she arched her chest down toward him. "That was for things left unsaid. Now, ne vahr, let's focus on the moment."

With practiced motions, Neris drew her right hand back. Using the space between them and Davnian's caught member, she slipped it from under her red shirt. With a tug, she drew the fabric over her head as she arched her back. As her hair fluttered backwards, she pulled the shirt down and around her arms, tossing it to the side as she pulled her black hair back. With his right hand grasping her by the seat, she brought her hand to the knot tied behind her neck. Below her, Davnian watched her with wide, hungry eyes.

"Neris," he whispered, his breath catching in his throat.

Without any more hesitation, she undid the silken strap. Her breasts fell free as the fabric slid away. As his claw reached for her face, she grabbed it and pressed it to her chest.

28

DAVNIAN

Lying on his back, Davnian felt Neris nuzzling his chest, the cold air of the outdoors teasing his exposed skin. His body ached in every way possible, his mind reeling from exhaustion and endorphins pumping through every cell of his being. Neris had finished what she started, but in several of their many struggles, he had been unable to resist the temptation to exert control. He enjoyed being doted on, but seizing was just as pleasant as being forced.

[I love you, Neris.] The simple words played in his head as Neris fell asleep in his arms. Despite not hearing them, she acknowledged him as she curled about his beleaguered body. It seemed right to match her sentiment, to give her that little bit back.

[Not feeling much, are you?] Gravel shifted in his mind as the other awoke from its long slumber.

[I feel great, but thanks for asking.]

[That's not what I meant, young one.]

The fire-breather in his mind struck a nerve, though it did little more than humor him. The thing was right, Davnian couldn't articulate what he felt for the sleeping woman. He enjoyed her company, he enjoyed her body, and he enjoyed the way she flirted and schemed. The rest was somewhat trivial, though the way she had become so hesitant and sentimental was almost overwhelming. The emotions just added to the haze that surrounded him, as if that was the only thing that clung to his mind.

[At least the air is clearer up here,] he replied.

Davnian had not mentioned the strange aura and mist that clung invisibly to the trunk of the great tree, nor had he wanted to sour the mood any further than it had been. At the start of their climb, he had been shaken by it, the fetid air chipping away at his energy. He wondered if it had the same effect on Neris and the other inhabitants of the giant tree. Or perhaps he was being singled out. He felt residual traces, the eerie ether glowing and fuming in small clouds that bubbled in and out of existence near the room's doorframe.

[Perhaps it's your very presence that's triggered its appearance.]

[Doubtful,] Davnian replied, thinking about the shade that had gripped the little girl in the infirmary earlier. [Or maybe it's more like the shadow stuff from that dream—no, *memory*—of Ohran.]

[Another possibility. Let's hope it's not the latter, or the mess is a coincidence in nature.]

[Perhaps,] Davnian replied, running his demon hand through Neris's long black hair.

Though his human hand felt more natural, his claw was just as sensitive, if not more so. He caressed the sleeping Delvori woman, and through the limb, he felt deep inside her. It was as if their feelings and beings connected on and off. Spikes of thought and emotion joined in spurts, sending waves of pleasure and sentiment through him. It had become something of a gimmick as they ravished each other. He caught glimpses of how he felt inside her nad the pumping of her blood through his skull. He experienced the intensity as she climaxed dancing like an electric current across his every nerve. Reality seemed to exist in a static haze, the fields of their two beings distinct yet overlapping as they pushed each other again and again.

[I see you're recovering some of your capabilities,] the other said, his stone-cold voice echoing throughout the recesses of Davnian's mind.

[My lovemaking skills still leave much to be desired, I'm afraid,] Davnian joked.

[If you're resilient enough to be mocking, then maybe you're in a stern enough mood to try your hand at something. Who knows? It may even be worth the trouble.]

[I'll be honest; I was wondering if the feelings flowed both ways.]

[Remind me to interrupt you incessantly the next time you're plowing some tart who catches your eye.] Smoke and coals burned in Davnian's mind alongside the words. [Let me be clear: what I propose has its risks.]

[So then, what is it?]

[Just like you heard her thoughts and felt her senses, you can do much more. What you felt was a conjoining, the synchronization of your nervous system with hers. In the moments you locked yourself closest to her, not only were you sensing her senses, you were connected directly to her. In essence, you were not merely experiencing what she was; you *were* her, at least in part.]

[You're starting to lose me.]

[Focus, young one. You can do more than just experience her here and now. You can experience the things she's lived, remember the things she can remember. You can spy into her memories.]

[As appealing as that sounds, I'm not entirely convinced of the worth.]

Davnian understood how valuable such an ability could be, but he dreaded invading the intimacy of the woman's thoughts. There were no places prying eyes could not find a person if they so chose, but the space between someone's ears was sacred. Then his thoughts wandered to the last moments that she and Nerin must have spent back in Dal Rothein. He had no doubt that what happened in the vaults was intrinsic to his recent nightmare. Still, he was hesitant.

[What are the risks?]

[Losing yourself inside her, for starters.] Dark clouds played across his mindscape as the other relayed its warning. [Losing her inside you. Becoming her. Her becoming you. The dangers if you go astray are nearly limitless.]

[I could break her mind.]

[You could go mad,] the voice said, his spine like a string of taught metal as the words reverberated in his bones. [You could shatter her soul. Maybe it's as you fear; the reward is not worth the risks.]

[Failure is not an option.] Davnian bit his lip as an even colder chill crept over his frame. He thought about the mage whom he had been instrumental in sealing. Though he could not place the feeling, every fiber of his being told him that Neris and Nerin's misfortunes were related. [I have to know.]

[Then you will need to listen to me very carefully,] the other said with iron rigidity. [To join your mind with hers is simple. First, place your claw upon her as you have. The closer to her head or neck, the easier the process will be. As you feel her warmth, focus your thoughts on her. Focus on the brief moments you felt yourself overlap with her.]

Davnian did as he was instructed. Running his mottled claw through her wispy black mane, he brought his three fingers to the base of her neck and gripped her firmly. Atop him, Neris stirred, rubbing her obsidian face against his chest. She took a deep breath and sighed. His eyes closed, Davnian brought his thoughts back to the moments leading up to their copulation. He imagined her straddling him, her features betraying a moment of sincerity as she reverted to her seductive self. Her loving words echoed in his ears as he suppressed the need to speak.

Letting his thoughts wander, Davnian felt her beneath him once more. Her rear was pressed against him as she writhed. For brief moments they changed positions. Biting into a pillow, he felt himself in her skin as her breasts grazed the sheets. He could taste the linen and sweat upon his lips as his loins shook. Deep inside, he felt himself throb jolts of pleasure through her frame, from her folds to the arch of her back as his claw scraped her skin.

[Keep focusing. Feel what she felt, and think what she thought.]

Neris's breath fluttered as she dreamed atop him. Davnian was overcome by her presence. Then his mind's eye was sitting atop him, her pitch bust heaving within his field of view as he stared down into his fixated blue orbs. Their musk surrounded him, and he was overcome with a ravenous yearning. Down below, he felt his body beat with her rhythm. His nails dug into her skin, sending waves of euphoria through their shared memory. With violent abandon, he snatched his claw and brought it to her neck. Davnian felt his twisted fingers tighten around her throat, and she started to gasp. She wanted it again. He felt the blood rushing to her head as their shared body gyrated faster and faster. One more time, just once more.

She screamed in his mind as her shriek reached his ears. They gasped and shook above Davnian's body in the memory as their frame collapsed over his. With several sharp motions, they urged his thrusts beneath her, laughing as he spasmed one last time.

[Then . . .] the other injected into their shared memory.

For a moment, Davnian lingered in Neris's memory, hunched over himself as time seemed to grind to a halt. He was sore twice over, his nerve endings and hers yearning for pause. Then at the back of her thoughts, something bubbled up.

[Just like then . . .] Neris's thoughts echoed in his brain.

[Like the last time.] Davnian tried to follow her emotions, feeling them out as if they were his.

[Careful.] He felt the other trying to direct his thoughts, but elation and darkness shrouded his perception. His words started a cascade of revelry, but a mire lurked beneath as their minds raced toward the bottom.

[Like that time.] Davnian felt his thoughts bubble up within her.

[Like that time.] Neris's inner voice sank into his consciousness. Their race became a rapid descent as if a giant anchor had been tethered to their ephemeral beings.

[Wait, Davnian!]

Gravel and brimstone erupted from somewhere in the fading surroundings as his consciousness slipped away. He felt his charcoal skin shiver atop the ivory male beneath him as he and Neris became entranced. The other roared from within and without, but before Davnian could pull away, his ego gave way.

[Just like that time,] Neris and Davnian whispered to each other's souls as they drifted into the darkness.

29

NERIS

Staring into the dark, Neris crouched and listened to the groans of the twisting caverns around her. She trembled while frames of jilted shadows snapped back and forth as she inhaled and froze. Her black ears turned to face the skittering of stones somewhere in the distance.

"Neris! Neris!" a male voice called, the words echoing throughout the cavern. The words were raspy and full of exhaustion, coupled with desperation and an undertone of malice. Nearby she heard the same voice roar and watched as a faint trickle of light poured into the dark hole. All around her, the cries and beckons reverberated. The shadows of her hiding place trembled with the heartbeat syllables of her name. "Neris! Come here, Neris!"

In her vision, the scene of a gaping cavern played out, filled with dark-skinned talvuo shirking to hideaways and offshoots. White- and bronze-skinned travelers crept in, and black-skinned talvuo left with them. Sometimes free, sometimes in chains, their rust-colored eyes sometimes lit but most times dull. In the dream, a pair of angry red eyes filled her thoughts.

"Nerin!" The voice was at once full of anger and glee. Before she could act, Neris heard her brother squirming and crying. Her hiding crevice spun away from her as she snuck along a narrow tunnel. At the end farthest away from the light, she heard a little boy's muffled cries and a grown man's grunts and sputters. "Just a bit more. Just a little bit more, boy."

"Father." The word fell from her lips as she walked to the tunnel's end. Images of her brother sprawled along the ground played within her frame of view. The man's obsidian skeleton was bent over the little boy, his head down and back arched. Her nerves froze, and her stomach dropped as she watched the tall figure stand up from the failed conquest. The man eyed her with bitterness and lust. Her hands began to shake as she fumbled the drawstrings of her tunic, watching as the figure towered over her. "I'm here, fath—"

"Oh, Neris!" a smiling, depraved face said.

The scene splintered between fragments as she was pinned, strangled, propped against the wall, slapped, bit, and turned. It was as if Neris's mind were being torn apart as the mangled memories melted together. Crying, pain, bitterness, regret, and endless turmoil overflowed as a thousand gaunt black skulls laughed and cursed at her. Out of the corner of her eye, a bruised and crying little boy reached out to her, snot and blood covering his round, screaming face. Dirt clung to his sooty ears. She reached for him, but she couldn't protect him. She couldn't even defend herself.

"When will you give me another? Another Neris. One to replace that whore's offspring. Pureblooded with my blood thrice over. Mine! Mine!"

That would not be their lot.

"You will respect your blood! You will respect *my* blood!"

She couldn't take it anymore.

Pinned to the ground as the braying and laughing echoed all around them, Neris's hand stopped short of the little boy. Gripping something soft, she fingered it and found a hardened point. As she was turned over, flashes of red splashed upon her face as the man above her yowled. The walls shattered as a tiny black doll fell from her hand, its tin sword coated with red and jelly. Roaring above her, the skeleton screamed as one of its orbs gushed a monstrous torrent of red.

In moments the world fell away as he slapped her again and again. Iron chains emerged from the abyss as he beat her, shackling her ankles and wrists. Bronze and black figures surrounded her, their cloaks covering her frame as they poked and prodded her being.

As they pulled her away from the shrieking monster, her non-father bellowed. "You'll wish someday! Wish like she did. Wish to respect your blood. To respect me!"

"Nerin!" the young voice shrieked as the darkness around them was embraced by gilded hands and light. The little boy's figure shrank into blinding eternity, a shadowy silhouette standing above him as both siblings cried into the effervescence.

In as much time as it took for her to be chained, it seemed that Neris was bought twice more. Gold and compliments had freed her from a lifetime of slavery as an Aluran noblewoman paid for Neris to be her consort. Then from those gilded halls in the far northwest deserts, her body and soul were taken once more, bought with the blood of mercenaries, guards, and servants. The shaded figure of the little boy whom she had left years earlier had claimed her. He proclaimed himself her savior, never knowing the truth of how she came to those halls or the hardships of the slave palace from which she had hailed. She could still see the Aluran woman's face, her sand-colored skin pale as her brown eyes bulged from her head. Her hands were dug in around her neck but could not stave off the strangling embrace of once-little Nerin.

The notion of her savior made her laugh. What had she been saved from? Dozens dead and riches squandered, forced to live in forests and caverns to avoid being taken to the gallows or worse. Around her were other dark-skinned talvuo, many of whom said they recognized her from the squalor of their old, cavernous homes. Dozens of men and women had taken up the ancestral Delvori banner. Beneath her brother, they all shared a common goal: to loot, plunder, and run.

The aromas of their encampments permeated Neris's being. Food was scarce, funds were nonexistent, and pleasure a thing that existed out of necessity. All about them hung the odor of blood, death, and rot. Images of demoralized young talvuo men and women danced over and over across her vision. But since they had recovered their princess heir, there had been a ray of hope for them all. Or so they believed.

But belief did not keep the men and women from revolting against her brother. Deep down, she wanted Nerin to forget these plans. But his lofty voice sent a shiver down her spine that she could not shake free.

"They'll respect us, ne vindal. They'll respect our blood!" Nerin told her, his voice echoing through her head, but blood and dreams did not ease the wounds or comfort the weariness of his warriors.

To sate what Nerin ignored, Neris practiced the trade that she had mastered in the sands of the Alurs. Avoiding her brother's hurtful advances, Neris coaxed and manipulated the men and women around her. From her breasts, the bandits suckled. From her lips, they found caresses and a warm embrace. From her hands, they received tender touches. From her body, they gained succor. And with that succor, they drew inspiration to keep those who would mutiny a day longer. The whore princess would feed their passions and save her brother's dream. But she knew it was too much for Nerin to just watch and bear.

"Neris!" her brother's voice had cried into the night. Together with some dozen-odd Delvori, they turned, watching as Nerin twisted the black hound ears of a younger woman. In the flickering light of candles and torches, she felt the cohort tremble, their groping hands and loins shaking as the murderous male approached. "What have you done? What have you done? What have you done? What have you . . ."

Inside Neri's tumultuous brain, Nerin's words echoed as his figure slapped her. Mouthing the same phrase over and over, his visage went between pain and anger. Vengeance crept across his face as others stepped between them, but their vision was broken as the darkness of trees and a starless sky thickened to pitch. Nerin's body flickered back and forth, at once himself and then another. The shade of a rotten, ghoulish talvuo took his place. The bare, unmistakable frame of her father loomed over her. Then it was Nerin once more, his sleek figure glistening in the flames building around them. Then it was the monster once more.

"If this is what must sate thee, my brothers and sisters, then let us share!" Nerin's voice was both a proclamation and a hiss as his black fingers slithered through her hair. "Let us share in royal blood! Pure blood!"

"My blood," the monstrous face of their father's ghoul whispered beside her ear.

With a mouth full of meat and eyes full of bile, Neris stared up at her brother's pitch torso. All around, bodies and fingers wriggled over her frame. Limbs and nails dug and clawed at her. The dissonance was familiar yet distant. This was not the first time, nor would it be the last.

The slut princess was a whole whore once more, but instead of being paid in gold or favors, she received no remittance. She gave it all to sate the shared band's greed. All to save little Nerin from his schemes. Bile and blood welled within her reddened vision. Waste and love spilled forth from them as if from open wounds all along their skin.

She couldn't take the humiliation anymore. Time and space skipped forward as she danced from memory to memory.

At some point, everything became comfortable. Neris watched her body thrown this way and that at the whim of her brother and his ambitions. Dreams like scattered moments of twilight flickered as she was forced onto her back then knees, just to keep the world from spinning out from under her. Neris's broken mind and body were adrift in a river of hedonistic furor and regret. All along the edges were leering eyes and faces. Among the snickering and bile were spears and swords aimed at her and the broken bodies of those who gave for Nerin's greatness.

Decades of wandering and whoring in the slave pits danced through her head. Those were terrible yet simpler times. No, they were bitter and full of spite, but there she had known actual comradery. Brothers and sisters who were made to offer all but rewarded with security and a chance of freedom. Floating in the river of her brother's cruel machinations, her fortunes had come full circle. She became once more enthralled by her father's menace.

But that would only hold for so long. One by one, the men and women around her disappeared. Neris saw their corpses floating in the sea of red and green. Impaled men, eviscerated women, trampled forms, and carved-up bodies littered the river of ambition upon which their lives floated. From dozens to handfuls, their numbers dwindled. Desperation clung to her as they struggled onward, their journey leading them closer and closer to the caverns and cliffs of their ancestral home.

But something impossible was in their way. Something that neither brute force nor simple tactics could overcome. Broken wills and unskilled hands were nothing before the war-hardened veterans who occupied those halls. But in that terrible unlikelihood, they had been granted a miracle.

"My lord." Neris's deep voice trembled as she spoke. The scene solidified as they stood within some dark recess, her gaze fixed upon the floor. "I have—"

"Do not address me as a lord," another commanded her. "As I've told all of you at least a dozen times. When you address me, it is Sael. Sael Virage, if you prefer. The words are not hard for you, I take it?"

Neris's thoughts committed his title to memory. "N-n-no," she stammered as several of the men nearby chuckled.

Everything had changed so much since the demon's arrival. Beckoning on a moonless night, he had walked into their camp, demanding to see the blood of Dal Rothein. One after another, dark-skinned talvuo went to answer before her brother graced the outsider with his presence. In a spate of indignance, her brother had thought to get the better of the caller. To his dismay, his threats were met with physical violence, a smack to the head, and a warning to end his life should he try such banalities again. As Nerin's presence shrank into the background of their little bandit troupe, others became more prominent as they displayed whatever egregious prowess they could claim. Malevolence overtook them all, the fleeting peace she had sacrificed her body for dismissed by the presence of the dark-clothed wanderer.

Annoyed by their disarray and intemperance, the man known as the Virage had lined them up. Scraping together remnants of armor and the cleanest garments they could scrounge from Nerin's personal hoard, everyone was made to wear some form of armor. Neris was happy to be free of the monotony, though she was pained by the influx of malice that hovered around them.

"Up here." His voice was low as his left hand nudged her chin up. She looked at the Virage, correcting her posture while gazing into his ice-blue eyes. "Good, that's much better." From somewhere down the line, one of the men snickered, saying something derogatory, several of the other men gasping with contained laughter in response. "Excuse me?"

Neris watched as the man worked his way down the line. She tried not to break her posture. The Virage stood taller than any of them, including her brother. He had lightly tanned skin and rakish, dirty-blond hair that seemed to curl and fall whichever way it wanted. Marching to the left, his odd left claw was exposed. It was a weird thing that looked almost demonic, the fingers fused such that all that remained were three monstrous protrusions. He wore simple, black, leather-and-hide armor. From his left side hung a long sword, the hilt simple yet functional.

"What's so amusing?" the Virage asked the Delvori down the line. "Would you like to share your insight with the rest of us?" Neris turned her head, staring as the men froze with petrified glances. "Allow me to repeat them, so everyone can hear. I believe it was something about the women not standing here. They should be on their knees waiting in the back. Was that it, talvuo?"

"Yeah, that was it," one of the men replied. "And what of it? You know it's true. They're better off on their backs than being out here trying to hold a real sword." Several of the men chortled at his comment. Even Nerin half laughed, standing at the side as he inspected them and the newcomer. Beside her, the other woman amongst them shivered. "I could pin her even if she were armed."

"So, just because you've seen her on her back, she shouldn't be here, am I to understand, talvuo?" the Virage asked without a hint of emotion.

"They aren't good for anything else," the man shot back.

Neris's thoughts were bitter and sullen. To the men, she and the other woman in their midst were nothing but pieces of meat. The reality had finally sunk in. She had just been traded from one panderer to another as her brother and his twisted lot used them for what lust they could entertain.

"Very well, then. Prove it," the Virage said, turning toward her. "You'll start with the one that so amused you. You, step forward."

"Wait, what's going on?" Nerin stammered. "What are you doing?"

"Get out here, talvuo," the Virage commanded the slanderer. "You're going to fight, and you're going to prove whether the women should be out here or not."

"With pleasure, sir," the talvuo male replied.

"I will not have you—"

"Stand down, Nerin Delvori," the Virage ordered without so much as turning his head, instead focusing upon Neris. He undid the sword from his belt and tossed it toward her. The blade landed at her feet. "Let us see if what he says is true. Get out here!"

"Now wait a moment. I won't have you—"

"If your man wants to speak up, Delvori," the Virage said, turning to Nerin, "then he'd better be willing to perform."

Neris picked up the sword. She felt the other woman's eyes upon her. She whispered something, but Neris couldn't make out the words.

"Don't worry, brother," the talvuo male said with a wide grin, "I can handle our little sister."

"Then we're all in agreement. You fight her with your bare hands and nothing else. She gets a sword. You win, you can do whatever you want with her, right here if you wish. She wins, well," the Virage waved his hand in the air, "we'll make sure to put a stone down where you fell."

With shaky hands, Neris unsheathed the long sword. It was weightier than she had assumed, too heavy for her to wield one-handed. Taking a deep breath, she grabbed the hilt in both hands, widening her stance while lowering the blade. Her mind raced, her red orbs searching the faces of the other talvuo, all of whom were looking at the spectacle in shocked anticipation. Shifting her gaze, she saw Nerin watching her, his eyes full of rage and vehemence that she had never seen.

It wasn't enough that he had joined in their evening orgies and desecrated her sisterly love for him. Now he wanted to make an example of her. She was caught between two men's ambitions as her brother sought to display dominance over the Virage.

"Are you ready?" the Virage asked.

"Just give me the word." The talvuo male was haughty as he assumed a wide stance.

Neris looked at the Virage and nodded.

"Begin," he said, motioning for them to do so.

The other males roared, egging her and the other male on. Whistles and calls echoed throughout the small cavern. To no one's surprise, they were all yelling for her to be pinned. The only other woman among them stood quietly, her red eyes wide with anticipation. No one cheered in Neris's favor. Not even Nerin spoke up as he eyed her from beside the Virage.

"So, Neris, it's just going to be you and me this time. Have anything lined up for me?" the grinning Delvori asked, circling her. "I know a few things I'd love to see you—"

"Shut up," she hissed, raising the sword. "Just shut up."

"Ooh, feisty today, ne vindal," he said. "Save it for when I've put you down."

She grimaced. To see them act so unrestrained and unchained hurt her pride. How she wished she were back in the desert, serving nobles and merchants. There the pain came with succor at least. Here there was no hope. Even her would-be hero stood aside and yearned for her demise. Where was the boy from her youth?

Neris was caught off guard as the man rushed her from the side. She raised the sword to counter, but before she could swing, the man lowered himself and planted his head between her legs. With his strength and agility, he pushed her legs out from under and tossed her over his shoulders. She landed with a hard crack on her back. The sword landed with a clang next to her. All around, the men laughed.

She writhed on the ground and watched through tears and pain as her assailant pranced around, putting on a show for the other men. The Virage had his cold eyes upon her. She couldn't see Nerin but was sure he was guffawing with the rest of them. She was sick and angry, full of indignation at what she knew was going to come next if she didn't do something. She couldn't stand the thought.

Stilling herself, Neris struggled onto one knee and reached for the sword. She gripped the hilt with both hands and readied to let loose with all her might. The other men became quiet and watched as she prepared to strike the man, who was standing with his back to her.

"I'm not just a piece of meat!" she cried, pulling the blade with all her strength. The man turned, watching as she fought to bring the sword to his knees. She wanted to hurt him, to kill him. All she needed was the blade to follow through. But no matter how hard she tugged, the sword wouldn't move. The men began to laugh again, hollering and mocking her. "I don't . . . I don't . . ."

"That's enough, Neris," her brother said in bitter humor beside her. She looked up at her sibling. Her eyes opened wide when she saw his heel planted firmly on the blade's tip, pinning it to the ground. "You're done humiliating me, I hope."

"What are you—"

"Sorry, little sister. Looks like I win," her opponent said as he pinned her shoulders beneath his weight.

"Delvori, who said you could interfere?" The Virage approached her side, filling the space near her brother. The man above her did not stop, wresting her legs apart without a care as they bickered. She looked upwards, shame and acceptance spreading across her features. How typical this scene was from her perspective.

"You saw as well as I could that this was done, Sael Virage," her brother said in a mocking tone. "She can't even lift the damned sword."

"She couldn't lift the blade because you were standing on it," the Virage countered, his cold blue eyes locked on Nerin. Nerin diverted his gaze, chuckling. "Does that amuse you, Lord Nerin? Blood of Dal Rothein? Does it make you hard watching your sister taken advantage of? And here I thought the Delvori were a noble and great people."

Neris blocked out the man on top of her as he unfastened her armor and belt. Her chaps were already at her knees, her armor pulled open. Her shirt had been raised to expose her breasts, the horny talvuo trying to ease himself between her legs.

"Watch your words, Virage," Nerin said, his amusement cut short by anger.

"And your actions, Delvori," the Virage replied. With a sharp turn and a twang, the black-clothed man barked from above them. "Nishais!"

"What are you doing?" Nerin yelled as he stumbled beside her.

"Instructing," the Virage said.

The man atop her turned his head for just a moment. His groping hands lost their grip as a blur of black smacked his head from the side. As he tried to roll to his feet, the other Delvori woman leapt atop him, wielding a small knife. Neris struggled to right herself as the man and woman wrestled. It took everything he had to fight off the downward thrusts from the ashen-haired Delvori. With all her ferocity, the woman managed to nick his shoulder. But with overwhelming strength, he twisted her wrist, disarming Nishais of the small blade.

"The rest is up to you," the Virage whispered as he stepped to the side.

Nerin looked at her, at the sword, then at the squirming pair. Without another word, he leapt from his spot, meaning to topple her. Kicking the sword's hilt, Neris spun away as the smooth metal slid beneath Nerin's foot. Cursing, her brother collapsed to the ground as she rolled to the knife. Behind her the other men prepared to pounce.

"Back! All of you!" A voice unlike any she had ever heard echoed within the cavern as the roaring crowd backed away. "If anyone else interferes, they'll deal with me."

Ignoring the commotion, Neris snatched the smaller blade and rolled onto her knees. Looking up, she saw the grunting Delvori slamming his back into the stone wall as he tried to stun Nishais. Watching as his red eyes fixed upon her, Neris saw his sneer and gritting teeth lose their menace. For a split second, she saw herself in his gaze, watching as her frame rose from the ground and charged toward him. Nerin yelled after her, his words inaudible as her ears focused on her assailant. In one sickening moment, she plunged the small metal blade into the man's bowels. Gasping, he lost his composure as he tried to reach his arms forward. But with Nishais's help, Neris dragged the injured talvuo to the ground. As the other woman sat against the wall, squeezing the Delvori by the throat, Neris withdrew the dagger and flipped it in her hand.

Retribution pumped through her veins as she brought the blade down, hacking into his chest. A bloody gurgle burst from the whining man's lips as she raised the sword again. And again. And again. Her mind was full of despondent mania as she stabbed the shaking figure. Then she was stopped as Nishais plucked the knife from her hand. With a roar of triumph, Nishais plunged the metal blade into the man's throat, embedding it in the cartilage.

The cavern was quiet save for the nearly inaudible hum of whimpers and whispers in the onlooking crowd. Across from Neris, the black-skinned woman laughed. Wound up with menacing passion, Nishais reached her blood-glazed hands. Overcome with malign ecstasy, her partner leaned over and planted a kiss upon her lips. Shaking, Neris backed away, finding the knife in her hands With a confused look, Nishais stared at her. But before another word was said, Neris was on her feet.

Her breath was heavy in her throat as she stared at her brother's wide-eyed figure upon the ground. With the cold air chilling the sticky rust splattered upon her exposed breasts, Neris surveyed the other males as they inched back toward the wall. Her heart was pounding, and her hands were shaking. Turning her gaze once more, she looked at the black-clad human who had instigated it all. Standing there in the dim ambience, the Virage was glacial as he stared at her. She charged once more, screaming as she lowered the small blade, clutching it with both hands.

The blade sank into something unseen as she slammed into him. But as her body bounced across his unmoving stature, Neris was in shock as he spun her by the wrist. She toppled forward as his black claw gripped the steel blade. With another twist, he turned her till she was on her back. Sitting atop her pelvis, he immobilized her legs and stomach. Nerin whimpered as he backed away while the Virage loomed over her struggling form. She slapped and clawed at him, his steel gaze was locked upon her. In the silence that followed, he bent over her while clutching the point of the dagger.

"The next time you try to stab me," the Virage whispered. "I want you to forget your anger. Forget your injustice. Forget everything except how good it felt to murder." He drew the tip of the dagger to his breast. Neris's red eyes looked down and then back up as a trickle of warm, sticky blood spread across his claw and onto her hands. She squirmed and breathed with frantic abandon. "And only once you've sunk your blade deep in my breast, only then are you free to relish your vengeance and shame. But not before."

Releasing the weapon, she withdrew the knife point. The small trickle stopped as the tiniest spot of his hide cuirass betrayed bleeding. Without another word, the Virage rose from her, leaving her twice-blood-glazed body to lie upon the rocky ground. Her heartbeat slowed as the man turned to the rest of the group.

Her mind stumbled over itself as the Virage stepped forward. With a sharp motion, he threw his arm downward, flinging some of the already congealing mess onto the space near her head. No one made a sound, save for Nerin, whose lips were curled in a look of profound hatred and disgust.

"You . . . you dared to . . ." Nerin could not find the words to speak his case, fuming as he took several steps away from the Virage. "How could you . . ."

"Have you had your fill of mockery and hollow words, Delvori?" The Virage motioned to Nerin, then the rest of his men. "Let this be a lesson to all of you about how I intend to mold you, lest you end up like that worthless pile of refuse back there."

The Virage kneeled, picking up his sword. "Now all of you, back in line," he said without a hint of emotion. He turned and pointed to Nishais. "That includes you!"

The Virage looked down at Neris. With a motion of his head, he directed her to get back in line. She nodded in quiet agreement. Without another word, the Virage stood up. As they assembled, he gazed at the motley, pathetic crew. His eyes pierced them, the cold, blue menace staring at someplace far off and removed from that cavern. For just a moment as she limped back into place, Neris thought she saw something other than his stoic façade, something dismal and melancholic.

TIME SURGED FORWARD ONCE MORE as fields and plains and caves and camps were replaced by stone chambers. There within Neris grappled with the person she adored and admired.

"I'd love it if you'd just give up already." Neris's words trailed his, sewing seductive chords into her speech. She squeezed her legs around her partner's trunk. "Just relax and let me work," she whispered.

"Do you truly expect those tricks to work on me?" the Virage growled in his familiar voice.

Neris rode around his waist as they tussled. She didn't expect him to go down but enjoyed how he played along. It was fun to see what she could get away with as she honed her talents, trying to strike from different angles and approaches.

"But the talent runs in my blood. Years of experience and training," she shot back. "They seem to work when you've let your guard down."

"True enough," he replied. He caught her hand sneaking down his left side. With a jerk, he pinned it to the stone wall behind her. "But I was the one who revived that spark."

She feigned duress and let out a desperate gasp. With nimble fingers, she snuck a small dagger from under his leather jacket while scratching him yearningly as she withdrew. With a faint glimmer in her eye, she watched as he continued to grin at her

"You thought you could reach the blade on my belt that easily?" the Virage said, drawing close. "Honestly, I thought I trained you better." With all his weight, he pressed her to the wall. Yet she managed to sneak her left hand free. With a few simple adjustments, she gripped the blade, making ready to strike. Letting out a deep breath, she gave him a pitiful look.

"Oh, you have me," she said with a hint of eroticism and submission. "Whatever will I do?"

"You're making this much too . . ." he began as Neris pulled back the dagger. Her playful demeanor disappeared as the blade found its mark, plunging into his flesh. His eyes widened and filled with pain. He grimaced as he looked down, his right hand finding the place at his front where the dagger had emerged.

He let her go, and she fell to the stone floor, looking up in horror. She hadn't meant to be successful. That wasn't the way this was supposed to work. She always tried her hardest, but he always caught her. She had never succeeded before.

"I'm . . . I'm . . ." Neris stuttered as he took a few steps back. "I . . ."

"Don't . . . be sorry," the Virage said as he reached behind him and pulled the dagger from his back. A pained grin appeared across his hurt features. "That . . . that was very good, Neris."

"No," she said, rising to her feet. "I didn't mean to . . . I didn't . . ."

"Your intent was pure," he said, taking a few steps back to find the bed. "You struck true and without hesitation. You weren't going for the kill. Nevertheless, your work was excellent." He took deep, hurried breaths, moving his hand over a red patch forming on the white tunic beneath his jacket.

"Is there anything I can—"

"No, no . . ." he gasped, motioning to her with his claw. "I'll be fine. A little stab won't have me down for long. Just come over here."

"What do I do now that I'm here?" she asked coyly, unable to dispel the look of concern on her face. "Do you want me to clean your wound?"

"Just lie beside me, will you?" he asked as his breath began to stabilize. She sat next to him and then, with a growing sense of nervousness, leaned back as he had instructed. "There we go. That's much better."

"So, what should I be doing? Should I try to fetch another dagger?" she asked with a chuckle. "Or maybe the pain has you—"

"That's not the mood, Neris," he whispered, taking a deep breath.

"Did I do something wrong?"

"Not at all," the Virage said.

She leaned onto her side and looked him over. He wore a soft smile, his sky-blue eyes fixed at some point on the ceiling, his rakish hair clinging to his brow. As she looked at him, a quirky smile worked its way onto her face. Wearing an expression unlike any other she had seen before, Neris realized how young his features were. The thought floated in her head as the ice of his demeanor melted away. The menacing, steely figure was reduced to someone in his youth, a foreign warmth unlike any other showing across his face.

"You've done nothing wrong, Neris," he said, turning his head toward her. "You've done everything I've ever asked of you. You've been a perfect student and more . . ."

Hearing his gentle words, Neris flushed with embarrassment. The Virage had never spoken that way to her. He had complimented her various times but never without his typical stoic detachment. Now he wasn't detached. There was something personal in his words, and it touched Neris deeply.

"What are you trying to do?" she asked as she tried to shirk the strange feelings he had just stirred within her. "Is this a new trick or tactic? Or . . ."

"This is no trick, Neris," he said, putting his hand on her cheek. His touch made her shiver. He wore a look of solemn happiness, his eyes becoming misty as they gazed into hers. "I just want things to be . . . simple right now."

"What do you mean? What do you . . ." She stopped as he touched his index finger to her lips, stroking her hair with his claw. Closing his eyes, he drew close to her, planting his lips against hers. His gentle kiss, soft and dove-like, only furthered her abashment.

He pulled her close, holding her in his arms as he nuzzled her head with his. Then, with a heavy sigh, the Virage brought his lips to her ear. "I'm leaving tomorrow."

Neris's heart began to race. She jolted from the shock but stayed motionless as he caressed her shoulder.

"I . . . see," she said with diminished passion.

"Yes," he replied, his tone matching hers. "It was going to happen eventually. With the victory here, I need to get moving. If I don't . . ." He paused, trying to find the correct words. "If I don't, then it'll mean much worse things for everyone."

"Right," she teased, "as if things could be much worse than they were."

"They can always be worse."

"I've been through worse, Virage," she replied, putting her hand on his shoulder.

He laughed. "Stop with the formalities, Neris. Just call me by my name."

"Fine, Davnian. You know what I've been through."

"Yes," he said, keeping his heavy eyes upon her, "but the things I'm speaking of are so far beyond that, you could never imagine."

"I have a good imagination," she replied coolly, shooting him a smile, but her hopes of cheering him up fell flat as he shook his head dismally. "Well then, at least tell me where you're going next."

"Somewhere far, far away, Neris."

"I take it you don't want company?" she asked, mood slipping

"With all my heart, yes," the Virage said, his eyes beginning to water, "but with all my reason, no."

His words were heavy on her ears. Her lips curled into a heavy frown. She looked at him as a tear streamed down from his right eye and merged with the pools forming beneath his left. Her own eyes also became misty.

"Why?" demanded, turning onto her back. "What reason do you have?"

"Because where I'm going, no mortal can follow. And before you're stirred to ask, no, you cannot wait for me, Neris," he said, his tone sincere and resolute. "Do not wait for me."

"Why?" she asked, starting to pout.

"There are many reasons," he said. "I may never return. I may come back, but it could be years from now. I may not even be the same person. I may not be able to . . ."

"Was all of this just for its own sake, then?" Neris asked through her tears. "Was this just . . ."

"A fling? A game?" the Virage said, raising himself over her. "Is that what you're asking me?"

"Was it?" she said, clutching the bedding while anticipating his answer.

"Everything I told you," he said, easing his claw onto her clutched hand, "this wasn't all for nothing. No, this wasn't a game, not to me, and most definitely not to you."

"Really?" she asked, looking up into his watery eyes.

"Very, very much," he said, closing his eyes. "I only wish things were right."

"Why aren't they right?"

"Because it's not done yet," he said, grimacing as another tear ran down his cheek.

"What's not done?"

"The thing I must succeed at doing. The goal of all of this," he said, opening his eyes and shaking his head. "There's too much to say."

"Then, what—"

"I want you to leave this place, Neris. I know how your brother is, how his men are. You must flee. These people are nothing more than leeches upon you, and they will drag you down if you let them. If you must have company, take Nishais with you, but no one else."

"But Nerin," she said, trying to justify the time she had spent around them, "my brother—"

"He's the biggest leech of all. And you know it."

"Yes," Neris replied, acknowledging what she had known for a long time. "Yes, I know."

"You deserve much better than him and this life, Neris. And now that they have what they want, there's nothing to stop them from ruining it."

"Do you really think so? Who am I kidding; we both know they will. You're right, as always, Davnian."

"I'm not always right, but in this, I am. I know it because they're already eyeing those vaults greedily. I know it because they whisper behind my back."

"And you told them never to enter them. You should have known that would only whet their appetites."

"Hence, I'm not always right," he said frowning. "When I realized I couldn't . . . that I couldn't seal them, it was the only thing I could do."

"Why not destroy them if they're so dangerous?"

"Because destroying them, even burying them, could disrupt the seals within them. If any of it is damaged, then . . ." He held his breath, closing his eyes once more. "I can only imagine what would happen. That is why you must leave no matter what. Do you understand?"

"No, but I will take that to heart."

"As soon as I'm gone?"

"As soon as you're gone, Davnian."

"Good." His heavy frown lost its weight.

"What do you want of me then?" Neris asked, looking up at the man who had taught her how not to be used. He had revived her ability to seduce, to be deceptive. He had trained her to be more aware than she had ever been, for which she was thankful. But this last lesson was perhaps the greatest.

"I want you with me here tonight," he said softly. "I want to love you tonight, Neris. But only if you want the same in return."

Neris bit her lip, overcome once more by an unfamiliar wave of emotions and timidity. "I want to love you tonight, my Davnian," she said as she batted her eyes and wrapped her arms around him.

For the briefest moment, her memories drifted to the scenes before the great vaults of Dal Rothein. Her thoughts curled upon themselves. Visions of shadows and screams echoed within the masonry of her skull, but she fought them off. Neris couldn't let go of the moment. The feeling of pain. The sense of loss and regret. In flashes of bitterness and tenderness, she saw the crumbling doors, the crashing stones, and the red and green mists of something sinister yet and indescribable. But watching Nerin's battered shadow shift beneath her feet as she dragged him away from the unwinding bodies of their comrades, Neris's heart forced the context back. Darkness filled her vision. Abandon welled in her breast. Erasing the trepidation, fluttering gold and amethystine glimmers teased at the corners of her vision. Then the recollection came into focus.

"Neris." Another woman's voice carried to her dark furry ears. Ignoring the prompt, Neris's nimble fingers felt around her bedmate's warm skin. Seeking the round of her partner's breast, Neris smiled as she slid the tips of her fingers around the other woman's nipple. With a tiny flick, the woman beside her groaned. "Come now, Neris. It's sore."

"You're still not used to such fervent attention, ne vindal."

Neris's deep voice was answered by a none-too-familiar groan as the bronze-skinned talvuo beside her rolled to face her. With an impish grin, she played innocent. Golden tangles covered Elis's face as she huffed. With a heavy hand, the Renai talvuo swept her damp, matted mane.

"You're insatiable once you get started," Elis said, sighing as she opened her dark eyes. Neris looked her over. Dots of purple and maroon had left small sweat-smeared streaks on her partner's sentae-adorned face.

"I seem to remember being the one to draw things out due to a certain someone's indiscretions." Neris let her tone drift cold as the sensation of her blistered chest and loins echoed across her senses. "I've just been trying to repay the attention."

"Do you have to use that tone?" Elis rolled her eyes as she glanced over Neris's shoulder. Her lavender orbs glimmered in the flickering candlelight. "Given you have yet to snuff the flame, I'm guessing you're suggesting more?"

"Just trying to stave off the night, my dear," Neris cooed. Elis flashed her a grin before rolling onto her back. Beneath the silken sheets, Elis shivered. Neris teased her side, drawing a bemused hiss from Elis. She continued her tender assault, her hand drifting from the woman's chest to her waist, then to her hips, slithering like an uncoiling snake beneath the sheets. Neris felt herself getting warm and ready, but with a heavy hand, Elis stayed her motions. Neris's eyes wandered over Elis's features, watching as the minor frustration and doting light in her eyes faded. Another shiver ran up her spine as her body stiffened. "Is something wrong, vindal?"

"I need to get my house in order," Elis said as she released Neris. She slid her arm beneath the blankets and rested her hand upon her stomach, forming a bend in the hillscape of fabric. "I can't keep asking Bedimer or Thaimi to look after Rais while I'm busy tumbling here with you, and gods know who else."

"Are we just tumbling the nights away now?" Neris asked, feigning hurt. Elis chuckled as Neris continued. "I think you're too hard on yourself, ne vindal."

"I've been trying to do well by Rais for so long," Elis said with a hushed voice. "Despite how much I care, I can't help but feel weighed down by the need for it. Until she came along, I was content letting myself drift away from the people. Sure, I had my fill of friendship and love when I sought it, but I didn't need to hold on to anything. I was able to just move on from one day to another."

"That's only natural. You went from being free and unbound to having to provide."

"When I think about her mother, sometimes I find myself disgusted with how terrible I've been." Elis laughed with a hint of melancholy.

"Terrible? What terribleness have you caused?"

"It's not what I've done. It's what I haven't done." With another sigh, Elis's hand curled up upon her stomach. "I could never do the things Rais's mother did. She did everything in her power to have that little girl. She was willing to leave the village and trek to the ends of the world if it would save her from the bad blood and ill fates of the Hyunisti. She gave her life for her, Neris."

"Yes, as you've told me before." Neris sighed and donned a soft smile.

"But here I am, leaving her alone for another night. Letting her curl up terrified in that lonely, little place. Sure, Bedimer agreed to watch her again, but relying on his guilt only makes it even more terrible."

"Well, she's old enough to start learning how to stay by herself," Neris said. "Has she not been getting braver?"

"Rais always tells me she's sleeping better when I come home, but they always tell me how she murmurs and cries. I keep hoping the nightmares will break someday."

"Well, my dear, in the little time I've been here, she seems to have improved marvelously."

"Oh, really?" Elis choked a laugh.

"It wasn't that long ago when you told me how she would still scream into the night, even when she was in your arms."

"That's true."

"Perhaps you need to give her room to grow," Neris said as she brought her hand above the sheets and planted it atop Elis's covered hand. As Elis fought off a grimace, Neris squeezed her hand. "One of the lessons about being a mother is understanding when to hold or push them."

"Gods, enough with that." Elis's brow furrowed as her eyes watered. She hated it when Neris called her so, but Neris was right.

"You also haven't had quite as illustrious company as someone of my personal affection, vindal," Neris said as Elis feigned a sneer. "Now you have a reason to want to go out by yourself."

Elis huffed. "Putting myself before my child is not the kind of character I wish to foster."

"If you don't take care of yourself, no one else will, my dear. And if you're nothing but a bitter, frustrated woman, how do you think that will affect little Rais?"

"I get the point." Elis shook her head and let out a stifled grunt. "I'll try taking that to heart, Neris."

"Thank the gods. Sometimes I forget you're the older one." Neris laughed. "You have a habit of downplaying your roles, my dear."

"Do I?"

"Yes. But maybe that's just how it all works out."

"How so?" Elis asked, shuffling closer beneath the sheets.

"Well, you have a paramour who enjoys doting. Who knows? Maybe you'll even capture my heart." Elis laughed at the notion. Neris enjoyed teasing her, even if it was only half play. "My offer still stands, vindal."

"I'm still considering it."

"Good. I'd prefer not having to wander in the cold night to fetch you."

"If you wore something more fitting, you'd be less bothered by the cold."

"I just can't help the stares I get, vindal. I'm used to having all eyes on me."

"Gods, you're unbearable."

"I know, my dear." Neris let out a deep, longing sigh.

Overcome with sentiment, Neris rolled onto her back. With a crooked smile, she stared at the ceiling of the round arboreal room. The flickering flames of the candlelight created a pulsing gradient that swept back and forth across the clay-lined surface above. For several moments they lay together in the darkness, neither one speaking. Neris's ears relaxed. She heard the Elis's calm breathing along with the small puffing of the flame beside her. Her own breath adjusted until their chests rose to the same beat. In her chest, her heart pounded with heavy, calm beats.

Stirring beside her, Neris looked as Elis turned once more onto her side. She held back a laugh as Elis stretched her bronze arm beneath the blanket and wrapped it around her frame. Drawing close, Neris felt Elis's breath upon her ring-adorned ears. Nuzzling the black folds, Elis's golden curls drifted over Neris's shoulder. She was warm to the touch, sending a shiver across Neris's sweat-puckered skin.

"Shall I get the light, my dear?"

"Perhaps. But maybe we should stave off the night for a few moments longer," Elis whispered. "If I'm terrible tonight, I may as well indulge, if only for a little while longer."

Neris grinned as she went to seize her paramour, but the arm that first held her in its embrace slid back as Elis wrapped her hand around her wrist. With a deep breath, Elis exhaled and nibbled at the folds of her hound-like ears. Growling, Neris stiffened her frame as she twisted herself beside the Renai. Neris slid her other hand over Elis's thigh as the bronze-skinned woman straddled her. Neris nuzzled Elis's gilded ruby ears, clamping her teeth around the petrified ring in her left ear.

"Enough of that," Elis grunted as she brought her face close to hers. "You almost sucked it out last time." Before Neris could muster a response, Elis planted her lips on hers. Caught in the short embrace, Neris slid her free hand up her partner's back. Elis worked her way from Neris's lips, planting small, warm kisses along her chin and neck. Elis seized her other hand and planted it above her head with the other frozen member. Grinning wickedly, Elis planted a kiss on her chest. "Not tonight, vindal."

"Then perhaps tomorrow?" Neris cooed.

Motioning with her hips toward the other woman, Neris watched as Elis raised her face back to hers once more. Together they rocked their bodies in suggestion, Neris's red eyes focused upon Elis. As Elis lowered her head first to kiss and then to traverse the darkness below, Neris felt passion embracing her. Amethystine glimmers filled her mind as the scene faded.

But the feeling and the longing remained.

30

DAVNIAN

[Y ou've returned, young one.]

Moments relived had become minutes and minutes hours as Davnian lay ensorcelled within Neris's memories. He had lived through a haze of pain, abuse, victory, heartbreak, and blooming love. But the one thing that he wished to know, what had happened in the vaults of the Delvori, was limited. Frustration was his master as he cursed to himself, annoyed with his pursuits and the selfish curiosity that overlooked the profundity of his lover's feelings.

[So, there's nothing gained then?]

[Nothing more than what we started with,] Davnian replied. In his head, he remembered calling to her Delvori brothers and sisters, to Nerin to halt at the vaults. With Neris's words, he bade them to stop. But they had fallen on deaf ears as Nerin treaded upon unhallowed ground. Everything after that until they emerged from the fortress was blank. Had she dragged him from the rubble? But what happened to the others? [The only thing we can be sure of is that Nerin went into the vault. A vault I presumed dangerous but not with enough conviction to just end them all there.]

[Could Ohran have been freed then? But why would you leave all that to chance?]

[Perhaps. Whatever transgressed is beyond us.]

[What can you imagine?]

[I don't know.] Davnian thought back to the writhing skeletal form of the old mage from his earlier dreams. His body and face twisted, his skin writhing as if a thousand worms crawled underneath his skin. How his flesh and form had shifted. Was it just his foggy brain playing tricks on him? Was it just the horror of the moment? Or was there something else? [Either way, we know that Nerin and Neris emerged alone.]

[As you said, we learned nothing,] the other said, mocking Davnian from its ashen abode in his brain. [And even then, you dismiss everything else. Those feelings you berate yourself for being dismissive of?]

[You have the right of it,] Davnian replied. His body was cold beneath the silk sheets of Neris's bed. His claw rested upon the nape of Neris's neck, his other arm wrapped around her as he cupped her body with his. Her skin was both warm and cold, an inkling of clamminess on it. Murmuring in her sleep, Neris seemed both loving and frustrated. No doubt her mind had run laps as it turned from one pain to another, only to find love, lose it to emptiness, and once more give in to its temptation. [Gods, what kind of monster am I?]

[A monster who knows there are greater terrors than him,] the other said with a voice as flat as shale. [It appears we will need to keep searching. First thing in the morning, we must study those tomes. Worry no more until then, young one.]

[Agreed,] Davnian replied.

Taking a deep breath, he burrowed his face in Neris's pitch-hued hair and sighed as he kissed the nape of her neck. Bringing his claw down around her arm, he gripped her tightly as he drew himself closer to her.

31

———

NERIN

Though everything conspired to go his way, Nerin could not help but feel a throbbing sense of terror cling to his pulse as he sat in his bed. He had heard of the awakening of the Virage through his subordinates. Adding to the pyre, parts of his request had gone unheeded as the village elders chose their blond strumpet over his guidance. But almost everything was right in the world. Now he had four maidens and with them a partial success in swaying the village to remove its pitiful namesake's bindings. Though it was not the best outcome, even Lord Ohran would have to praise him. And yet he did not wish to travel into the depths of the tree, instead favoring a perch bedside.

Clutching his head in his hands, he tried to discover what he might have done to ensure his total victory. But try as he might, visions of that buxom, bronze witch clouded his mind. She was in league with the Virage; he was sure of it. Whatever her part in the monster's scheme, Nerin was confident they would leverage his sister as well. Though Neris jilted him at every turn, he was sure that if he could expose their manipulations, she would see the truth.

"Naisure, ease yourself," a dull voice beckoned from the hall.

Looking up, Nerin spied the form of the comely woman whom he had bedded and brought before his lord only an evening ago. She wore a simple cotton sheet around her frame as she gawked from the hallway, her green eyes fixated on him. She was different, sterner than the day before, and as she walked in, an aura of obedience filled the room.

"What are you doing here, um . . ." Nerin searched his memory for the woman's name.

"Thaimi, naisure," she said in a pleasant voice, her hazel ears perking up as she shot him a serene smile. "I'm here only to serve you."

"Shouldn't you be at home? Surely you'd rather be there than . . ."

Without a word, the woman placed her finger on his lips. His rust-red orbs scanned her, watching as her pallid form circled him to the bedside. As she sat beside him, a jolt of excitement shot up his legs.

"You are worried, naisure. We can all tell," the dull woman said as she gestured to the doorway. From outside, the other three nectar maidens emerged, their ugly faces and soft green eyes fixated upon him. He scorned the thought of being doted on by such an inferior breed. Yet as each woman took place around him, Nerin was overcome by a sense of elation. "You are strained, naisure. Let us bear your burdens."

"Empty them," the others said in unison. At once Nerin understood, remembering his master's summons. To obtain power was to empty oneself of slights and troubles of the heart. To maintain this was to be free of conscience and apprehension. Though he did not understand it, he knew his inhibitions had beckoned the women to his side. No doubt, it was a sign of his prowess.

"Yes, naisure. Just as the lord spoke." The woman at his right placed her hand upon his bare chest, nodding.

"Just as the lord spoke," the others said.

"Just as the lord spoke." Nerin's voice trailing theirs as one of the maidens placed her brow upon his knee. The other two cradled him in their arms, whispering their admiration as they caressed him.

"You must rest, naisure. Tomorrow begins the final trial," Thaimi said from his right side.

The women at his feet rose, their eyes fixated upon him as the maidens at his right and left coaxed him back. Waves of passion and nausea overtaking his senses, Nerin turned and followed the two to the head of his bed. Behind him, the other two maidens crept up, their faces grazing his legs as he dragged himself onwards.

As he collapsed upon his pillows, the women at his sides draped themselves around his arms and chest. The other two women curled around his legs, their soft breath tickling his skin.

BOARD INQUIRY FOR INCIDENT
#04067521

Standing in the middle of a large, dim chamber, the luminous haired android Maximillian Verudt stood. Behind him, a carbon and metal podium rose facing an amphitheater of assistant androids and bright alloy-glass displays. Above the stands, six balcony-like stations surrounded him. Each possessed two terminals and two carbon-fiber seats occupied by one of the six pairs that made up the Ientec Foundation's board.

Starting on his left-rear flank, his ruby-haired brother and sister sat. They oversaw diplomatic relations, cultural outreach, and humanities. Following clockwise were the sapphire-haired siblings, which managed sanitation, engineering, and industry. To his left-front flank sat the golden-haired pair entrusted with economics, trade, and banking. Beside them, a silver-haired duo leered. They were responsible for security, military operations, and defensive strategy. Next were his emerald-haired siblings entrusted with scientific research, historical analysis, and data management. Last was the amethyst-haired pair in charge of entertainment, service provisioning, and biologic support. At the rear podium, a lightless skinned gynoid with amorphous non-reflective hair presided as mediator. With his physical capabilities locked down, Maximillian's focus was upon the inquiry.

He had spent the better part of the last thirty-eight hours reiterating previous research reports into the analysis of the small planet of Genea, a world situated beyond the space-time anomaly known as the Genean Distortion Field. They had covered past incidents of Omega-3043's activations, including linked analysis sessions #7329, #7328, #7327, and #7265. They had surveyed imagery, analyzed gate resonances, and poured over reports. From iron age fortress vistas to Jovian red sandstorms, he presented evidence to answer their every query. Yet after two rounds of argumentation, the board was at a stalemate in deciding whether or not it should limit Maximillian's autonomy.

"Thank you, Overseer Mammon," the lightless female android called from the podium behind him. She bowed to the golden-haired android across the room. Turning her glowing rainbow eyes to the right, she pointed to the silver-haired gallery. "Thank you as well, Overseer Oda."

"Thank you, chancellor," the male of militaristic pair said. He bowed his head without taking his blazing white eyes off Maximillian.

"Second round arguments are closed, and votes are in. Five for and seven against. Lacking a two-thirds majority, we will now begin third round arguments. President Maximillian Verudt, you have the floor."

[Thank you, Cynthia,] he replied. Maximillian monitored his every thought as hundreds of thousands of threads scanned his running processes. [Cynthia, please bring summary information on Koppa-7.]

[Acknowledged.]

At once, the holographic displays across the room filled with details relating to the creature in ancient Inun legend referred to as 'the worm.'

[Foundation classification: Koppa-7. Type classification: Outer Being. Location: Unknown. Common identifiers: Fones...] the displays continued describing various physiological and supernatural aspects of the entity. Its powers included material incorporation, annihilation, anti-causation, and a capacity to learn through assimilation. Numerous redacted fields revealed its connections to over twelve-thousand objects of various classification levels. Maximillian focused their attention upon the most crucial to his stance.

"May I query chancellor?" the dagger-eyed silver-haired male stared him down as he asked for permission to speak. Following a singular synaptic acknowledgment from the chancellor, Overseer Oda prodded. "President Maximillian, what are you withholding regarding Omega-3043 and Koppa-7? All relative analysis regarding the two requires executive clearance."

"Yes, Max," Overseer Mammon spoke from her overlook, interrupting their brother. As he piped an interjection, she continued to cut him off. "Given your willingness to show your hand, I assume you wish to propose a reason for ongoing study?"

[Cynthia, open relative analysis summaries linking Omega-2901, Omega-3043, and Koppa-7.]

"As you wish, Maximillian," the chancellor vocalized.

As the details of Koppa-7 shuffled on the alloy-glass displays, new information about both Omega-2901 and Omega-3043 popped up. Each board member received clearance keys for accessing the related analysis files. As he waited, Maximillian detected hints of resignation as his siblings probing processes halted their assault on his psyche. Overseer Oda sneered as he shuttered his terminal.

"This Omega-2901, one classified as a Lori-Ama from the target planet," Overseer Mammon pondered as she gestured to the room, "of what interest is he?"

"It's obvious from the reports this extends well beyond general curiosity," the female silver-haired piped from her seat. "I see private communications between Council Grandmaster Hamora Merchante and President Verudt in the links. Overlooking the goddess of light, this Madrus Ohran is of particular concern."

"President Verudt, please share your insights on this Omega-2901 and Omega-1644," the golden-haired Mammon requested.

Preparing the next trickle of information, Maximillian watched as the ongoing rejection total wavered between seven and eight. He was close to subverting the resolution.

[Cynthia, declassify relative analysis for Omega-1644.]

32

NERIS

All along her body, Neris felt the dim haze of morning light permeate her being. Shifting beneath her silken sheets, she stretched and writhed, arching herself forward and back. An impish grin broke across her face as her back basked in the warmth of her lover. Davnian's claw gripped her breast as he stirred beside her.

Without a word, she brought his left hand to her lips. With a kiss, she let go and slipped out from beneath the sheets. The brisk morning air prickled her skin, the first rays of morning light scattering over her obsidian figure. Davnian grunted as he sprawled over her spot. Looking down at him with her rusty-red orbs, she smiled as he cracked open his left eye. The icy marble in his skull stared at her as his waking features betrayed his drowsy fixation. Chuckling, she made her way to the wooden slats of her window and, with a small effort, forced them wide open.

"Gods," Davnian said as the full glory of the morning sun pierced the room. Dust and pollen clung to the light as it drifted throughout the room.

"Too much?" Neris prodded as she pranced back toward the bed.

Blocking the sunlight, she watched as he struggled to open his eyes once more.

"My eyes are still having problems adjusting," he murmured, kicking at the sheets. As the blankets slipped away, she snickered as his thin, ivory frame fell limp atop her mattress. She saw his flesh prickle as the air gripped him. "Amused, are you?"

"Just entertaining the thought of keeping you that way," Neris teased as he buried his head in her pillows. "Maybe watch you squirm with a mouth full of pillow?"

"As entertaining as that sounds," Davnian said, lifting himself from the mattress, "I think there are other things we must tend to." She noticed his bony frame had regained some of its tone as his shoulder and upper arms forced his torso toward her.

"It's always business with you, ne vahr," Neris hissed as she half turned. Bright sunlight poured over her right side while a stream of golden rays pummeled the tossing man. He growled, jerking himself upwards and tilting his head away from the light. "Still, I suppose you have the right of it," she said.

"I'm glad you agree," Davnian replied as he blocked the light with his right hand.

"So, off to that little room with its tables and shuttered windows once more?" Neris wrapped her arms around herself, feigning tempestuous scorn as Davnian struggled to his feet.

"We left the books there. Besides . . ." He lowered himself to his knees, fetching his discarded garments with his twitching arms. "We both know it's safer there than here."

"Is that so?" Neris ignored his rationale as she strolled over to his beleaguered frame. With a heavy sigh, he looked up at her. Laughing, he took her arm as she helped him stand.

"Neris." Davnian's voice was quiet as he stood beside her. Her canine ears perked up, the blackened folds of her loose skin arching toward him.

"Yes?"

"Does something feel off here?" he asked, his claw still upon her arm as he stood at her side. "Does something feel unnatural? This tree? This village?" His eyes turned toward her, concern covering his pallid features.

"Things have always felt off for me, Davnian," she whispered.

He let out a small laugh as his eyes scanned her hardening features. The ghost of the man from last night had returned, a visage that haunted his features before she had teased free his inhibitions and worry.

"I've seen that look before." He smiled as he brought his claw to her hand. As his mottled fingers fumbled over hers, her red eyes were cold upon him.

"Where was that?" Neris's voice was hollow, feeling scorned by his haste.

"The last time I left you," he said, a sullen half-grin etching itself on his face.

Taking a deep breath, Neris cooled her breast as he plopped down upon her bed. She closed her eyes as he struggled to dress. Folding her arms across her breasts, she opened her eyes and strolled to where he sat. She narrowed her eyes as he finished wrangling his pants about his waist. She hated acting this way, but in all the years since he had disappeared, she could never quite place the feeling of loss she had felt. But with this simple gesture, his focus upon some new goal, she was able to comprehend what a younger woman could not.

"Before you begin your derision, let me say one thing," Davnian said.

"And what would that be?"

"When I left, I broke your heart. I took away a fancy that you had only begun to dream. But even then, you understood something that I know you understand even now."

"Are you trying to tell me how I felt? How I feel?"

"No, Neris. I'm telling you I felt it." He reached up and placed his claw upon her outstretched hand.

A moment flashed before her as a brief painting of their final reverie replayed across her features and sight. The moment he bade her farewell, leaving her with his final warning danced within her head. The disgust she felt was matched only by that reflected in his present being as she saw her own reflection reaching out from the bedside. Gasping, she stepped back, watching the dream fade as she slipped out of reach.

"Gods, what . . ."

"You felt it last night when we embraced each other. Those flickers of feeling the other, the touch and passions reflecting across our minds and bodies," he whispered. She shook her head, shirking the distant past as thoughts of their lustful evening filled her brain. Neris felt unnerved and betrayed, but his words echoed through her as she remembered how it felt to lose herself. This wasn't the first time he had shared her thoughts or touch, but never had it been so strong. So overwhelming.

"I know," Neris said, trying to regain her composure.

"I trust you, Neris, and I know you trust me," he said as he stood up. Garbed in a vestment of gilded red-and-blue stripes, Neris couldn't help but grimace as his blue eyes fixed upon her. That same concerned look, full of empathy and compassion. It made her sick. "You know I wouldn't be this deterred over some trifle."

"You truly vex me, Davnian." Neris chuckled to herself as she turned away from his gaze.

"Thank you, Neris," he said as he passed by her.

"It's bad form to leave a woman scorned," she said as she watched his crimson-draped frame ease toward the door.

"I'm only across the way, Neris," he called back. "Providing I make it across the bridge."

"Ugh. Just wait outside while I dress," she said as a wave of ease bathed her breast.

"Very well," Davnian said, turning toward her.

She shot him a frosty, dispassionate glare as he cracked a crooked smile. Then she commanded her demeanor once more, easing her posture as he ogled her one more time. With narrowed red eyes, her sinful nature overcame her turmoil once more.

"I believe I said outside," Neris said, turning away from him.

"I'll be waiting," Davnian replied.

As the door creaked open and closed, Neris studied the loose garments on the floor. She had no clue what to choose for the day. In the end, she knew what it would be. Something flamboyant and preposterous, risqué, and seductive. Like always, it would be something that would draw all eyes to ogle and leer. Something no one could ignore.

33

____

DAVNIAN

[That could have gone better,] the other in his head growled, awake from its slumber as Davnian struggled into the great arbor's spiral hall.

[I brought too many things to the surface last night,] Davnian replied.

[You kept your word to her.]

[I did, which only made it that much more biting,] he said as he felt at the clay covering beneath his leather soles. Small window ports had been notched into the giant tree to let light into the winding path. Only a half turn down the opening between the great tree was where his temporary quarters resided. Stumbling downward, he looked out at the treetops as they shed the dim glow of morning. The bright sunlight lit up the forest as talvuo scurried across bridges and terraces outside. [The vista is impressive.]

[Truly.]

[And the miasma is all but gone now.]

[Yes, it is,] the rocky voice said as Davnian surveyed his surroundings. The dense haze that drifted and bubbled throughout the spiral incline had all but dissipated overnight. Though he was tired, at least he could breathe at ease. [Strange, don't you think?]

[I was certain it was related to the structure,] Davnian mused as he limped toward the wall.

Propping his back against the smooth grain, he eyed the path back toward Neris's room. All night the stuff seemed to bubble within the halls. Yet it refused to swallow the space within her abode. With Neris unaware of anything off, he surmised that whatever he sensed was similar to the wraith haunting the little girl whom Elis kept by her side.

[Perhaps it's nocturnal.]

[Maybe.]

Narrowing his eyes, Davnian watched as a brown-haired talvuo male rounded the bend in the corridor. For a moment, they met each other's gaze, the pale, thin-nosed man's eyes wide with paranoia as he stopped and then ran off down the spiral. As Davnian watched him pass, he caught the afterimage of the same man lurch into frame. It turned and leered at him, its mouth screaming as a writhing blackness filled its mouth. Then its head snapped forward as it was dragged onward like an unwilling shadow.

Before he could interrogate his cohabitant about what they just witnessed, he heard faint footfalls approaching from farther up the corridor. Looking back, he expected to see Neris emerging from her room. Instead, he saw a white-garbed maiden.

The woman's pale skin was like thin milk, whiter than the thin cotton cloth that draped her frame. Nothing was hidden beneath the translucent weave, the faint spots of her chest visible as the sun illuminated her garb. Behind her, an obsidian-skinned talvuo male strutted, his black hair slicked back with grease as his hound-like ears hung limply beside his long, hawkish face. As the pair whispered to each other, Davnian's muscles tightened. His right hand motioned for a blade he did not possess while his claw curved like a jagged hook.

The pale woman's head turned from the dark-skinned talvuo, her green eyes fixing on Davnian. Following her gaze, the rusty-eyed male stared at him. Together, the pair froze in the hallway.

"Nerin Delvori." The name rolled off Davnian's tongue as he studied the two of them. Standing there near the gaping causeway, every fiber of his being told him to run, but he stood his ground.

"Sael Virage." Nerin's voice caught in his throat as he stammered out the demonic title. Beside him, the pale talvuo woman clenched his arm. Farther behind the duo, Davnian saw three other white-clothed maidens pause along the spiral. "It's been a long time."

"Indeed." Davnian's voice was still as his blue eyes danced over each figure.

A gaunt, eyeless shade clawed relentlessly at the exposed flesh of the nearby talvuo woman, its hazel hair fluttering in and out of time as its own existence seemed strained. Parts of it were broken and missing, writhing, black emptiness replacing much of its form. As it flailed, its visage turned to him. Remorseful, pleading eye sockets stared deep into his soul as the shade crawled toward him.

[It's emptying me . . .] a voice whispered from every side.

Turning his gaze from the dismal shade, Davnian spotted three other ghosts writhing toward him. The ephemeral clones of the three other maidens were gelatinous as they slid upon the ground, their faces stretched across a contorted blob of emptiness. Worms and slugs were made of sterner stuff.

"And to whom do I owe the pleasure, naisure Nerin?" Davnian gestured his hooked claw toward the nearest talvuo maiden. His heart pounded as adrenaline flooded his blood. In the back of his brain, an overwhelming sense of malice overtook his sensibilities.

"Thaimi Hyunisti, good man," the talvuo woman said with perfect placidity.

"Naisure," the other maidens behind Nerin whispered in unison.

[Betrayer.] The word worked its way across his brain as Davnian felt his eyes dilate.

He refocused, shaking his head as his senses gave way to dizziness. Reality seemed to bend and warp for a second, and in that brief moment, he glimpsed another world. Where Nerin stood, uncountable green embers burned as emptiness boiled in space. Stretching from the void, tendrils of erasure filled the places of each maiden as their ghouls were gnawed away by the vulgar shroud. Buried deep within the embers, the dissolving skeleton of a child tore at the floor. Then, just as fast as it started, reality solidified around him once more.

Burning hatred and disgust erupted within his breast, straining his resolve as he stood and stared at the procession. He didn't need a weapon. His claw would do. Five strikes to tear down the profane things before him. Five blows to feed his bloodlust.

[Not here, Davnian. Not now,] the other said, its voice breaking through his frantic analysis. Flames of renewal erupted throughout his mindscape, searing away his vengeance.

"A pleasure to meet you, Thaimi," he said, offering his hand to the talvuo woman.

Without a word, she reached out and accepted his gesture. His blue eyes fixed upon her, Davnian bent over and touched his forehead to the back of her hand. Pulling back, he looked into her empty green orbs.

"If you'll excuse us." Nerin shifted in place, his dark hand closing around the maiden's other arm. A grimace worked over Nerin's features as he tugged at the Hyunisti woman.

"Certainly, naisure. A good day to you," Davnian said as the man stormed past.

The other maidens hurried behind the departing pair. Just as the other pale talvuo's shade had done, the pleading shadows tried to claw free but were dragged down against their will.

[What was that just now?] The other's voice was empty of earth and fire as it spoke.

[I don't know,] Davnian replied.

It was clear to him that what he had mistaken for an oddity with one little girl was instead a plague that touched many, perhaps the entire village. But what possessed Nerin and his cohort, Davnian could only begin to imagine. His gut twisted into knots as he pressed himself back against the wall. It had taken everything he had to quell the anger and vengeance welling up within.

"Neris needs to get here soon," he said under his breath, holding his claw against his chest.

Closing his eyes, he slid down to the floor. With a deep breath, he cooled himself and waited.

34

———

ELIS

Elis had been up since before sunrise, stirred from her sleep by wistful dreams and unrequited frustration. Neris had danced in her head all night, luring her into deeper depravities as she whispered tantalizing secrets in her golden-red ears. Needing fresh air, Elis had left Rais bundled up and climbed the small wooden staircase built into the trunk of her tree. Atop the highest platform, she sat and watched as the pink-and-gold morning light overtook the dark blue and purple of dawn. Her lavender eyes scanned the treetops as she shivered with only her thin lavender gown to cover her.

In every direction, the forest seemed to stretch forever, the impossibly tall trees blocking out the horizon. But with only a day's walk north, she would find herself emerging onto the human highroad nestled between the woods and the dying grasslands. South was a farther trek, but in a day or two, she could be in the rolling plains of the Grannas.

Her mind full of the possibilities, Elis wondered when she had last contemplated how easy it would be to leave. In the pit of her stomach, she understood it was not that trivial. The beasts and thickets of brush and thorns that lined many paths made traversing either way dangerous. Diverting around those obstacles added hours, if not days, to the effort. East was a clearing that the Grannas smugglers used to trade goods, but even that had its perils. A long fork of clearance was bounded by the woods on either side for days. At least it was safe, relative to any other misadventure.

It had been a long time since Elis had fallen in love, but she found herself swooning for Neris like a younger woman. Infatuation was a dangerous thing, as was newfound love. Either way, the feelings worried her. So much of her current life had been built upon a patient, precise give-and-take with the people around her. The Hyunisti were kind but stuck in their cycle. Nothing short of a miracle could break them from it, and Elis did not have the heart to be part of their constant suffering.

"You look lost in thought." A hoarse male voice caught her attention. Unshaken, Elis turned her head, watching as Bedimer ascended the steps of her retreat. "I'm not disturbing you, I pray, vindal Elis?"

"Not at all, Bedimer. I would enjoy the company," Elis motioned to the bare wood beside her.

The haggard, grey-eyed talvuo laughed, his rough, brown ears flexing as he sat beside her. "You have a wonderful view, vindal." Bedimer coughed as he cleared his throat. "Forgive me. The evening has been long."

"Still leading the watch?"

"Trying to, when I'm not directed by other's whims." He gestured down below.

"I never apologized for rushing off that night," Elis said, blushing as she remembered how she had abandoned the man with Rais. "I hope she gave you no trouble."

"Nothing she wrought," Bedimer said, taking a deep breath.

For several moments the two of them sat quietly, watching as a cloud of blackbirds swarmed in the distance. At their front, an awkward fowl coaxed and bobbed as the flock mimicked its chicanery. One more twisted breed trying to fit in among its peers.

"How is she?" Bedimer asked, his grey eyes fixed on the scene in the distance.

Elis turned her head toward him and smiled. "You saw her. She's as healthy and bright as a child should be."

"Still have nightmares?"

"Every now and then. She's getting better, but if I'm not at home, she can be restless."

"Have you left her often?"

"Only a handful of times of late." Elis felt admonished, pondering how selfish she had been.

"I can take my post here next time, if it pleases you."

"You don't have to, Bedimer," Elis said as Bedimer shifted his gaze toward her. "I need to be better about my own habits."

"They're not your habits to mind, vindal."

"Bedimer . . ."

"No, please, vindal, do not coddle me. These faults lie with me."

"You were not the one who agreed to raise her."

"But I'm the one who abandoned her."

Bedimer let out a long, deep sigh, his grey, cloudy eyes returning to the flocking birds. She sat quietly beside him, unsure what more to say as she watched his fists clench. The man was a proud hunter, perhaps the best in the village. But with time and heartache, he had taken to isolating himself from his brethren. The night watch was a solitary position that was traditionally held by youths. Yet, Bedimer had opted to lead them. Each post was quiet and lonely.

"How many evenings do you hound yourself with those painful memories, Bedimer?"

"Every night, now and forever," the grizzled hunter said, chuckling to himself.

"You did nothing wrong. There was nothing you could have done," Elis replied, trying to soothe him. The woman who had been Rais's mother was the hunter's burden to bear, or so he had convinced himself. "She made her choice. She was brave and never wanted to burden you."

"Indeed," the world-weary talvuo said, mist clinging to the corners of his eyes. "But I was never brave. She took a chance, and I thought she was mad. If I had only heeded her the first time . . ."

"Things would be different?" Elis asked. Bedimer turned back to her, his haggard face betraying the pain he was staving off. She shook her head. "You don't know that to be true."

"Whether fate or madness, I was given a chance to try. Instead I bided my time, waiting for the pain in my gut either to be assuaged or proven right. I had given up even before the madness. I just couldn't admit it to myself."

Standing up, Bedimer looked toward the ground and then closed his eyes. Elis followed his form, watching a trickle escaped the corner of his eye.

"And though Sarais was lost to us, she succeeded where she was sure she would fail. She bore your daughter, Bedimer."

"I'm no father, vindal Elis."

Bedimer's words were those of a tired, old man who had seen more than his share of loss and pain. Elis knew the phrasing and the cycle well, having lived it in a previous life. It was times like these when she cursed her own vitality.

"But you still can be," Elis said. Bedimer scoffed as she continued. "And until you're ready, everything will continue. Nothing is broken forever."

"In my head, I understand it, but with all my heart, I cannot bear it."

"Then don't force yourself to. Your brothers and sisters are here for you, Bedimer."

"I'm not a man of social graces, vindal."

"Most Hyunisti are not," Elis chided.

Bedimer laughed, bringing a smile to her face. Groaning from his outburst, the haggard talvuo wiped his face clear of dampness as he returned his gaze to the woods. "Thank you, vindal."

"Any time, vivahr." Elis reached out and patted his leg.

"Look out over there," Bedimer said, turning to the village lofts. "It looks like they're building the stages."

"Truly." Elis turned to look at the forest. Dozens of talvuo were erecting small enclaves of bricks and mud. Other villagers cleared branches overhanging the platforms and bridges. Others stirred to the tasks of stocking preparations for the following day's ceremony. Down below, workers used large rakes to clear leaves and debris. "Spring comes, as do many changes."

"There's not much time for that Delvori's whims to be answered in tow with the rites." Bedimer gritted his teeth as a cool breeze swept through the trees. "They're like giant clay ovens nestled on the trunk tops. Food, merriment, and abandonment. It seems everyone wishes to be rid of something."

"Is there anything you'd discard, vivahr?"

"I will always carry my burdens." The old talvuo chuckled, feeling for his lantern and his blade. "And I will carry those of the ones who came before me."

Elis thought about how only moments prior, she had tried to convince the haggard man to let go of his failures, to be free of his burden. Nerin's scheming, which she was sure came from a place of wickedness, carried much the same sentiment. The Hyunisti carried a weight that had been laid upon them by generations they would never remember. It was not just enticing to let go of the past; for many, it was necessary.

"I've lived for so long, but I constantly find myself forgetting common wisdom that a younger me understood so very well." Elis sighed as they looked at the busy villagers.

"Vindal?"

Elis shook her head. "Nothing, Bedimer. Just realizing I'd be better off being less heated."

"I doubt many would begrudge you your ways, vindal."

"But I do," Elis said. "Let us leave the rest for another time. I should see to Rais. She'll be waking soon."

"And I should see to my last rounds," Bedimer said.

"It was a pleasure, vivahr. You should come by more often."

"Maybe I will," Bedimer said, easing his way onto the loft's narrow steps. "Farewell, vindal."

As Elis watched him disappear down the steps, she turned one last time to the toiling villagers. Like ants, they scoured the village for labor, each toiling about a task they had assigned for themselves, each moving as one toward a higher goal. There was something majestic about how enthused everyone had become in such short a time. And yet, there was something altogether troubling.

Turning back to the north, Elis pondered her motivations.

Perhaps it was time she sought something to be part of.

35

DAVNIAN

Davnian was weary from exertion and study. After the encounter with Nerin and his cohort, Neris had found him with his eyes shut, drawing heavy breaths against the walls of the great tree. Wearing her black corsetry and hose, she had urged him upwards. In those short moments, he had relayed what he had seen and felt, leaving her at a loss. Their time back at the infirmary had been quiet. He spent the rest of the morning poring over the diaries and manuscripts of Hyun Emri, followed by an attempt to understand the near-illegible scrawl of Nerin Delvori. All of it was a lot to take in and had left him with a bitter taste in his mouth, coupled with a gloomy outlook on life.

The emotional baggage, pleading, and resolution expressed by the former was a story as old as time. Violence begat violence. Eventually, it culminated in a gambit that had cost Hyun and her followers their lives, joy, and what little happiness they could muster. Not that her actions were without reason. The Grannas had sought not only to push them from their lands but also to eradicate the forest talvuo. They could have left, but it would have cost them their heritage.

[Despite that, their culture is all but broken,] Davnian mused as he leaned over his onetime bed. Massaging the place between his eyes, he let out a long sigh. Neris hummed in question of his exasperation, but he waved her off. Adding to the congestion of thoughts was Elis's arrival at the strange village. The dates, the amount of time, the very nature of the place bothered him. [I'm getting nowhere.]

[There's not much to glean,] the other whispered, sounding like the crackling of embers throughout his mind. [Even the specific details leave things amiss.]

Nerin's words had given him the faintest of insights, but only if he combined them with what he had gathered of the Emri's last rite before abandoning their ancient name. In his journals were ranting and ravings about the number four. Four women. Four vessels of nectar. Four seals upon which the sealed magic of the forest could be released. Four cries for salvation. Four calamities to answer the call.

Shifting in his seat, Davnian stretched his back right then left. His recovery since his tryst with Neris had been phenomenal. Even the meager scraps left within the infirmary had been enough to satiate and regenerate him. A single cup of water was all he needed to rehydrate.

Turning his gaze from the last journal, he looked past Neris and into the daylight of the village. With his blue eyes fixed on the passersby in the distance, he focused his attention on any irregularities. On the great terrace across from his quarters, he spied many talvuo setting up tables and seating. As Neris had relayed, there was to be a grand ceremony tomorrow, and everyone was abuzz with excitement. Clay ovens had been erected on smaller nearby terraces, on which small, smoldering pyres were being stoked. The evening would be a feast of merriment and fervent desires, and the next day would be the solace culminated of flames spent.

"Your frustration is showing," Neris said from her perch as she stoppered a bottle of nightshade.

"Madness, broken hearts, and whimsy are all I've gathered. Ceremonies, rites, and tragedy. It's all quite trite, lacking the detail I need to understand what we could be facing." Davnian was cold and dismissive as he spoke of the many words that he had just surveyed.

"Is there anything of interest? Anything that stands out?"

"Nothing I haven't mentioned. The woman's journals are full of regret, longing, passion, and loss."

"I see," Neris turned toward him, wiping her hands with a damp cloth. "Women can be boorish about their feelings, can't they?"

"Pain and tragedy are not boorish, but they can be overwhelming."

"Now imagine being the one burdened by them."

Neris was right in that. Davnian did not understand taking those feelings out of context. Without bearing her tragedies himself, he would not have understood Neris's either.

"I'm not going to apologize, but at least you know I'll make it up to you, good woman."

"Ugh, spare me the pleasantries," Neris said, laughing off his formalism. "I expect you to make up for it, and if not . . ."

"You'll take it anyway?" Davnian asked. Neris swayed her hips, shooting him a dispassionate glare. With a simple nod, she pranced to the opposite end of the table. "Going to look them over yourself?"

"Perhaps," Neris said as she stood opposite him. "As you were saying, dear."

"As I was about to say, the number four appears everywhere in your brother's writing," Davnian replied, his gaze still fixed on the distance beyond the infirmary. "It also appears once and only once in conjunction with Hyun's writings. If I had to guess, your brother is somehow reenacting her greatest sorrow."

"How so?"

"The details are fuzzy," Davnian said with a yawn. Shaking himself, he turned to face her. "The gist is she weakened four seals with four vessels of nectar, over which the sacrifice was spread among everyone in the village. All partook of the nectar and, in doing so, offered part of themselves to undo the binding. Following four calamities took place, which would stave off the Grannas' invasion of the Emri homelands."

"Nerin has four maidens he's taken to bedding and drooling over. No doubt the quartet you encountered this morning has piqued your interest?" Neris danced her fingers atop the table, signaling the number as she waved onwards. "So, we can assume he means to get everyone to partake of some young women's swill. But what will be the outcome?"

"The birth of the Lorinian Witchwood happened when four great forces were unleashed. First and foremost came the dreaded fog spoke of in ages past. That seems all but gone at present."

"I have yet to see anything abnormal other than a foggy mist sometimes in the early morning."

"Yes. The second was the forest itself. The trees and plants became monstrous, gigantic, and nigh impassable for those lacking knowledge of the terrain. The third was the emergence of the great beasts. Twisted and terrifying forms of the animals that once dwelled within the wood."

"Both of those things are self-evident," Neris said, yawning as his dispassion swept over her. Indeed, there was little reason to speak of that which they could easily verify. "What of the last?"

"The last Hyun called her great sorrow." Davnian let out a deep sigh as he spoke the words. Remembering what he could of the hastily scanned scrawl, he understood that the final act represented the sacrifice that had to be made to summon the other three powers. Thinking about its meaning, he was almost amused. If only such an act had ended in the victory and freedom that the ancient talvuo matron so craved.

"Back to boorish feelings?" Neris was both hot and cold as she spoke, her rust-red orbs fixed on his tired features.

"Magic is a force born of imbalance. To summon a great power, you must offer something great, or the force itself will exact its own toll. The scales must be balanced. What they called forth was dreadful, powerful arcana, the origins of which I can only guess at," Davnian said. "The enchantment required to twist the near entirety of the Gran Voren would require preparation beyond measure and a magician whose power was equal to the greatest. The only other possibility would be some source of power already attuned and waiting to be disturbed."

"I think I understand then." Neris leaned over the table, her black hand dancing over the pages. With her gaze fixed on the space between them, she sighed.

"You've got it then?"

"So much for freedom when your blood runs thin." She withdrew from the table, returning to the countertop. "For the answer to their sorrow, they had to sacrifice their future."

"And the future of their descendants, ever onward. Until the toll is paid."

"You're right. The whole thing is trite." Neris laughed, but her voice was cold, without a hint of levity. "Boorish, even."

"Your words, not mine," Davnian replied as he returned his gaze to the notes before him.

"Is Nerin capable of something that deluded?" Neris asked, directing the question to herself as much as to him.

"Your guess is as good as mine. Just because a bunch of talvuo drink nectar doesn't mean they've accepted whatever rite Nerin wishes to enact."

"What about his friend? The man he calls . . ."

"Ohran?" Davnian shivered as he spoke the name. "That I'm not sure of."

"Could he do something that compels them to accept his wishes? Could they both bewitch everyone?"

"For all the expertise I possess, I lack too many of the intricacies of my older self," Davnian reminded her. "I believe it's possible, but it would be beyond difficult. Magic can alter the mind, but to maintain such a hold requires an immense enchantment or continued straining of the will."

"What do we do then?" Neris asked. In the rays scattered from beyond, Davnian could almost see her composure slip as a shiver worked its way up her body.

"At this point, I need more information," Davnian said. With both hands on the tabletop, he pushed himself upright. "I need to see the machinations in motion. I also need a change of scenery."

"That's all well and good, ne vahr, but have you contemplated your own condition?" Neris asked mockingly as she strolled along the table's edge toward him. "I don't think you'd make it too far on your own yet."

"Good point. I concede I'm not in the best place to go wandering on my own."

"Then how about we take the opportunity for a little excursion, hmm?" Neris's placid demeanor was replaced by impish joviality. Looking at her as she came to his side, he saw a hint of reverie in her eyes. She was contemplating how they would look as they strolled hand in hand throughout the village. "Who knows? We may even run into Elis. No doubt she's on some errand. Otherwise, she'd be here by now."

"I hadn't considered that." Davnian thought for a moment. He would welcome the opportunity to spend time with her, but he needed to focus. "If the option presents itself, then let's do it. For now, I need to be about."

"Then allow me, ne vahr," Neris whispered as she offered him her arm. He took it, letting his weight distribute over his legs. "Shall we?"

"Surely, good woman."

"Say that again, and I'll let you fall off the side of the nearest terrace," Neris hissed as she guided him from the room.

Davnian readied himself for the search. The goal was to see the village and how the actors played their parts. He needed to understand the price that the Hyunisti had and continued to pay. He needed to be around them to make his final verdict.

36

NERIS

Neris took her time walking Davnian from the infirmary and up the high ramp to the village's grand terrace. As they strolled together, gawking talvuo bore witness to her struggling lover. They whispered and cajoled. Familiar faces and bedtime partners shot glances at her while scrutinizing the pale man by her side. Others were stopped dead in their tracks, their green and grey eyes filled with fear and curiosity. But no matter the age, state, or familiarity of the passersby, all eyes were drawn first to her gorgeous figure, then to the claw that hung at his left side.

[They can't tell what to think about me.] Davnian's words were fresh in her mind.

A first they took in the sights near the elders' overlook. All around the quaint huts and branches, small tables had fitted with places for food and drink. A small clay oven had been moved to the middle of the platform, where talvuo came to drop off time-worn mementos and trinkets. Calling to those who wandered was one of her brother's apostles, joined by a fire keeper and a mason to ensure nothing went amiss.

For the better part of an hour, they were content to watch while exchanging flippant pleasantries. As she flirted and gawked with the crowds, Davnian scanned and analyzed the village. He wore a gaze of deep meditation as he focused on each area within their view. Never once did he betray that something was amiss, but Neris knew better. Had everything been pleasant, he would have played his part better.

After moving on from the perch, Neris was content to stand by him. As he surveyed the world around them, she studied him in turn. Every bit of the man she had known as the Virage was on display while they moved from terrace to terrace and took in the sights.

At one point, a pair approached the two of them. In one breath, they introduced themselves to the feared visitor, and with his hollow response had abated in the very same exhalation. He did not have time for others. A colossal weight sat upon some unseen scale, and like the arcane forces from his lecture, he was trying to reason how to even them.

"Is there a reason why you're fidgeting with that?" Davnian asked as they stood in the shade beneath the bows of a great tree along the village's outer rim.

"It's been quite a while since I've spent so much time outside," Neris confessed as she fanned herself with her small silken shawl. She had been lazy and preoccupied with decadence and avoidance since she had arrived in the village. So much time spent out in the sun was wearing on her pitch skin. Her similarly hued attire was not helping, serving only to gather sweat and heat. "Thank the gods for the shade."

He laughed. "I seem to recall you being much more resilient."

"I have plenty of stamina, if that's your meaning." Neris shot him a heated glare. He donned a crooked grin as she feigned annoyance. It was true. She had always been somewhat athletic and toned, even after months of lounging before they retreated from the ancient Delvori fortress. Months of lying on her laurels--or back, as it were—had done her a disservice. "Perhaps I should coax our blond paramour to take me on her adventures."

"You should," he said matter-of-factly. "I feel like you'd enjoy the hunt."

"And the filth," she said, sneering.

"Like that ever stopped you."

Neris was both hurt and heated. His words stung, but they weren't wholly untrue. Still, with visages of her previous life's tormentors fresh in her mind's eye, it did enough to unnerve her.

"I didn't mean it that way," Davnian said, one step ahead of her comeback.

"No, what you said was fair. And I do have my moments," Neris said as she shook off the displeasure.

"I'll divest the two for you. Erotic and all pleasing."

"I'm not sure I completely agree with those words either, but I'll accept them." She feigned annoyance once more as she turned her gaze toward the village center. The bridges and terraces were abuzz with talvuo preparing for the evening's festivities. Between strands of sunlight and sweeping waves of moving branches, they gathered around the increasing number of clay ovens. Purging and renewal, so sang the song of spring. "The whole place is overtaken."

"They're hopeful and excited," Davnian replied.

"I'm sure the promise of intoxicants and shrouded lovemaking add to the energy."

"No doubt. Tonight will see all forms of debauchery, and tomorrow they will gather to accept and celebrate."

Indeed. The whole display was a fight against their own helplessness. What better way to lose their sorrows than in lust and love, the confusion and the haze of a night well spent? If everything went just right, perhaps they'd all have something more to live for. Something to make their lives a little less quiet. It was a beautiful script: plain, simple, dirty, and then clean. Too bad life was anything but.

"My morbid mood must be rubbing off on you," Davnian said as he gripped her hand. She flushed at the gesture but shook herself free from the emotion.

"Not at all," Neris said, taking a deep breath. "Gods it's hard to keep my composure with you constantly . . ."

"I know," he said. "I'm not quite myself to you."

"It's like you're at your extremes," she said as her red orbs traced a line from branch to branch, bridge to bridge, then finally to her feet. "You're as cold as I've come to expect but warm like the last time we embraced. It's like being held by fire and ice."

"Both ways burn," Davnian said, to which she nodded.

"Scalding, if you will." She put on a sweet, seductive grin as she dismissed his hand. Circling his box perch, she ran her fingers down his shoulder, letting her hand slip beneath the nape of his tunic. She caressed his chest. "So, are we done with this spot?"

"I want to give it a few more moments. I'm trying to piece something together, but nothing is quite right."

"Care to elaborate, dear? Or are you just going to continue being obtuse?"

Davnian laughed as she squeezed his chest. He was still mostly bone, but some form of muscle had returned. She was distracting, perhaps even annoying his sensibilities. Still, that was part of the game. If he didn't say no, she wouldn't stop.

"I see shades everywhere, Neris," he said without a hint of his previous joy.

"Shades?" Her mind leaped to thoughts of shadows dancing at the corners of her eyes, ghost stories, and other lore used to warn weary travelers and entice the imagination. Monsters, demons, and mages existed. Yet standing in the light of day, such thoughts seemed misplaced. "Ghosts is it then."

"Not exactly. Maybe they're souls or reflections thereof. But I can tell you with certainty, every one of these Hyunisti has one," he said, pointing at the shuffling masses.

"Everyone?" Neris's voice betrayed her incredulity.

"I have yet to spot a man, woman, or child without an accompanying visage," Davnian said.

"What does that mean?"

"Most likely this is the way the spell exacts its toll." Davnian drew a deep breath. "These shades are likely the residual traces of the magic that was stirred. Each is attached to its host, draining them of their part of the grand bargain."

Neris contemplated his words for a moment. Were the sicknesses, stillbirths, and other manner of weakness the result of this phenomenon? Neris stretched her shoulders back as she gripped Davnian, the weight of realization increasing its burden. In the pit of her stomach, she felt a pang of disgust. It wasn't a question of whether the world could be so cruel and twisted. She knew for a fact that the world merely was.

"Well, you sure know how to bring one's mood down low," Neris said as she withdrew her hand from his shirt. How many of the men and women she had bedded had decaying shades leering at her? Among those she had yet to know, how many were accompanied by festering ghouls betraying their weakness? No, not their own faults. The penance they bore for their ancestors. Her skin tingling with dread, she stepped sideways into the sunlight. Despite the golden rays of warmth, a bitter chill crept up her spine. "Gods, it's not even night, and I'm covered in bumps."

"Would that I could keep it more elated." Davnian laughed, though his tone was dark.

"If you've gathered that much already, what piece still stands out to you?"

"That tree," Davnian said, pointing to it.

Neris followed his gaze, her rust-red eyes focused on the giant tree standing at the village center. The ancient tree, former home of their namesake, the giant fortress-like wood that she and her brother now inhabited, was the counterpoint to his newfound knowledge.

"Remember when I asked you if anything felt strange?"

"Yes," Neris replied, a faint hint of annoyance creeping through her voice.

"Something was there last night. At first I thought it was just something residual. Something lurking. All through the night, it stood outside your bedroom door. But then this morning, it was gone."

"You're not helping with the theatrics," Neris said as she tried to coax the warmth on her skin to ease the chill inside.

"I can now say without a doubt, it's not gone. But what it is, I can't tell yet," he said.

"Can you describe it?" Neris asked. Any form of assurance or certainty would be better than imagining what things only Davnian saw.

"It's like looking at something that's there but in the wrong place," Davnian said. "Like how the air shimmers in the heat but more pronounced. Almost like it shouldn't be, or something else should be there. I'm sorry; I'm failing at this."

Neris laughed. "Well, I'll be spending the rest of my nights in my lab."

Davnian chuckled in return, lightening her disposition. "Shall we make for a warmer spot, ne vahr?" Neris said, trying to shake off the dark mood. She was about to cajole him further but was halted as his human hand snared hers.

"Sit here with me for a bit longer," Davnian said quietly.

"Feeling sentimental?" Neris asked, chuckling as she regained her composure.

"Yes. And this is pleasant."

Neris flushed once more. Without a word, she nodded and then took a seat beside him. For a few moments, they could embrace a bit of time together, continuing the pleasant fiction that they had started the previous evening.

If only for a short while longer, they could pretend it was real.

"Zaisure!" Rais called as she skipped among the tall grasses and clover of a secluded clearing near the Hyunisti village. Elis looked up and shot the little girl a smile as she sat among old hewn stones and wooden posts. All around them were the small plots and mounds of those come and gone: lovers, singers, foragers, huntsman, warriors, and children. No one was spared the long-lived curse of the Hyunisti bloodline, but together there was a place of peace to call their own, nestled near the grave of their namesake. Elis laughed as Rais ducked behind a grave, her little brown ears giving away her location. "Come find me, zaisure!"

"But I've been watching you the whole while, my little one."

"But I'm hiding!" Rais's ears twitched as she protested.

Elis did not want to get up. All around her were baskets of wild berries and plant matter. They had spent the better part of the morning down in the dirt picking them. The day was already half gone, and the evening would be long and tiring whether she engaged or not. She just wanted to sit and think a while longer. If she got up, what excuse would she have to stay put?

Laughing at herself, Elis stepped off her boulder and crept toward

Rais, avoiding sticks and stones that might give her away. Behind the grave, the little girl giggled and then quieted herself. Her floppy brown ears went to full attention as she took a deep breath. Elis's own red-and-gold cups homed in on her as she listened to her little one's tension. With patience, Elis filled her lungs.

"There you are!" she exclaimed, springing over the grave and wrapping her arms around the little girl. Beneath her, Rais struggled, frantic and laughing as Elis's fingers teased her sides. In a bold move, the little girl rolled away, but her freedom was short-lived as Elis rounded the stone and pulled her close. The writhing mass of limbs and giggles shuffled and protested, but Elis did not abate her assault.

"Zaisure. Zaisure! Please, zaisure. You found me. Please, zaisure. Please . . ." the little girl stammered out plea after plea.

Elis ceased her attack, confident in her victory. In one motion, she wrapped her arms around Rias and hugged her tight. Within her arms, the little girl gasped for air, still laughing between her breaths.

"I told you," Elis said as she nuzzled the little girl's head. "You can't hide from me."

Rais quieted down. Leaning back, she nestled herself in Elis's grasp, her dark hair and yellow day dress wrapped around her as Elis's body enveloped her frame. Elis planted a kiss on the girl's forehead. "Alright, up you go," she said, releasing Rais.

"Chase me!" Rais called as she tumbled forward onto her feet.

"You better run."

Elis chuckled as the girl stumbled and weaved between stones, posts, and stumps as she tried to put distance between them. Elis waited, counting beneath her breath. As the numbers rolled off her tongue, Rais continued onwards while shooting back excited glances. Elis began to walk forward, readying herself to follow.

"Chase me!" the little girl called back to her.

"Are you ready?"

Just as Rais reached the edge of the clearing, Elis shot off. With careful, powerful steps, she gained speed, weaving a path free of debris and obstacles as she accelerated. In seconds she had worked up enough speed to more than triple Rais's pace. Watching as Elis gained on her, the little girl shrieked. Instinctively, the hazel-headed talvuo started to make a curved path. Elis began ignoring obstacles, choosing instead to leap over them or use them as footholds for more powerful strides. Chasing Rais was like hunting game, minus the sharp brambles she'd be carrying.

"No! No!" the little girl shouted between panting laughs.

From a hundred paces down to a dozen, Elis went to cut Rais off. But despite her skill and efforts, she miscalculated as her split white tunic caught upon an ignoble plank of wood. Gritting her teeth, Elis went into a spin as she rolled to the ground. Barring a few bumps, she regained her composure just in time to spring up in front of Rais and grab her.

"No! No, zaisure!" the little girl cried as Elis rolled with her. Tickling Rais, Elis's eyes betrayed her own haphazard joy as the bundle of yellow and white squirmed with all her might. Rais reached for Elis's sides as she attempted to fend her matron off, but Elis was too fast and hawkish to let a single probing finger through. "Please! Oh, please! It's too much. Zaisure . . . zaisure!"

Elis laughed with her as she pushed Rais to the brink. The little girl gasped, unable to speak another word between her raucous laughter. As the little girl's pale face went cherry red, Elis abated her assault.

"No . . . no more, zaisure," Rais said, sweaty and trembling in her arms.

"No more?" Elis whispered into the little girl's ear as she hugged her close. "Are you sure?"

"I'm . . . I'm sure, zaisure . . ." Rais's words trailed off as she coughed and then giggled. Covered in leaves, dust, and dirt, her yellow dress was a little worse for wear. Elis would have to get that out later. She looked over her own white-draped frame. Her tunic was covered in dirt and plant stains. Motioning for the girl, Elis helped her up. Together they walked back over to the old stone monuments and the circle of baskets.

"We'll have to get all cleaned up," Elis said.

"Are we going home already?" Rais's red face was overcome with sudden shock as she pranced beside Elis. "We haven't picked the blue ones yet!"

"Ah, the little blue ones. Well, why don't you grab one of the small baskets and pick some, so we can boil them later, hmm?" Without a second's hesitation, the girl spun to action.

"Oh! OK, zaisure!" she cried as she fetched a small basket.

Elis watched as Rais buzzed about the stones and posts, distracted by her task. Elis sighed, relieved to have time to herself once more. Settling back on the ancient boulder, she watched as the girl bobbed from gravestone to grave post as she scanned for the tiny little things.

With careful fingers, Elis tugged at the twistblade at her side, feeling its simple handle and tangled barbs and blades. When she had set out, she had contemplated staying away for the length of the festivities and ceremonies. She and Rais could hunt, forage, and hide away until everything had cooled. The tensions that threatened to drive her mad would be done with for the time being. But as she thought about such an idea, Elis realized that returning would only lead to more headaches later. It would be better to just run away and leave everything behind, but doing so would mean destroying a beautiful relationship that had potential. It would also suggest turning her back on a long-lost friend and lover, one whom everything in her said to accept, but trauma beckoned her to run.

At the end of it, Elis knew she wouldn't leave, but she also knew she could no longer be a hermit. She couldn't bear to be part of the village yet disavowed of it. There were two roads ahead for the others. Without a doubt, she knew Davnian would leave. Whether through recovering his memories or in search of them, that moment would come. Neris would either choose to stay with her brother among the talvuo or leave and follow her star-crossed lover. For Elis, she had to accept her place among the people whose stories were deep within her. They needed a shepherd to care for them, a matron to lead them. Only after that would they know peace and prosperity once more.

"Zaisure!" the little girl called.

Elis turned her head, watching as Rais charged forward with a bundle of flowers and debris. There was that matter as well. Rais needed to be cared for. She needed a place to grow, to cherish, to call her own.

"Ah, look at that harvest!" Elis said, chuckling as the little girl rammed into her. Flower petals and dust scattered over her plain white tunic. Green bits and leaves got lost in their hair as she calmed her little one down. "Careful now. Careful. We don't want to lose it all."

"I'm sorry, zaisure," Rais said, huffing as Elis picked through lost fragments.

"It's alright, my dear," Elis said. Rais set the basket down as she tried to help, giggling as she picked flower petals and debris from spots of dirt and foliage. "There, there. Now let's fetch the rest up, shall we?"

"Yes, zaisure!" Rias said as she picked around Elis's feet.

More than a village, the little girl needed to be loved. She needed lessons and confidence.

"What do you say to one more tussle?" Elis asked as she loomed over her.

Without another word of warning, Elis descended, undoing their hard work as they wrestled around. As Elis released Rais to let her run, she knew there was so much more to it. Rais needed the mother that Elis could be, if not the one she already was.

38

DAVNIAN

"So then, you're an amnesiac?" a world-weary talvuo man inquired as Neris plied her wiles while doting on the grey-haired huntsman. Bedimer was his name, as Davnian recalled. Adorned with a blade and a silver lantern, the old man was outfitted with unsurpassed finery compared to most of his kin. Looking at his green-clad frame garbed in a harness of hardened leather, Davnian would have mistaken him for any of the other would-be soldiers or hunters. But even without the ornaments, Davnian could tell the man was seasoned, if not jaded. "Many have feared your awakening, but if they had the chance to speak, I think they'd be as befuddled as I am."

"Even then I doubt most would forget their worries." Davnian laughed, tapping his claw along the wooden railing of their current vista. They had made rounds and begun their trek to the outer reaches of the village, taking a solitary, far-off path at the farthest reaches of the Hyunisti's home.

"I must admit, naisure Davnian," Bedimer began, gesturing to Davnian's claw, "even I'm somewhat put off standing so close. You're well within reach. I doubt I'd have time to react."

"Is that suspicion, brave Bedimer?" Neris cooed from beside the old man. She ran her hands along his shoulders, but the huntsman was unfazed.

Bedimer laughed. "Your wiles are put to ill use in public, vindal." The old man wasn't used to the attention, much less in the company of others.

"But there's only the three of us here. Think what mischief a trio could do hidden beneath the branches, vivahr." Davnian almost laughed as Neris overplayed the part. She was less than serious, though he knew if the man gave her even a sliver of interest, she would take him for everything he had. As she danced her other hand across his hanging arm, Bedimer staved off a shiver. "Besides, your duty comes later, and surely you're well-rested this late in the day."

"A younger me would be ripe for the task. But even now, I should get to my rounds," Bedimer said, brushing her off.

As Neris continued to ply at the man's morale, Davnian glanced every now and then to the Hyunisti's shades. He was a rarity, something Davnian had only glimpsed among the other villagers. The talvuo was gripped by two figures: the ephemeral husk of himself and a talvuo woman attached to the other. As Bedimer played Neris off, his shade betrayed a weary demeanor. Sagging, bubbling shoulders and hanging, gaping eyes gripped its visage. Its body was stoic and static, unwavering as the female shade beside it tugged and tried to drag it off. The feminine one wore a face mixed with joy and worry, like a jester's mask flipping between moments of applause and scorn. Unlike the other, it was animated and alive. Every now and then, it turned to Davnian with a look of wonder and supplication. It gestured for help to move the shade so stuck in its place, but Davnian could not do anything about it.

"Very well, though I expect to hear your call again one of these nights." Neris wore a playful smirk as she pranced away from him.

"You know no shame, do you vindal?" Bedimer said, laughing off the remark, embarrassed as his personal tryst was laid to bare at Davnian's feet.

"There's no shame in self-indulgence, especially that which is reciprocated," Neris teased as she ran her hand along Davnian's shoulders.

He wondered how long she could keep up this act before either dismissing the idea or forcing the outcome.

[There's no worry. You're here to distract her, after all,] the other within his brain replied to his query as if it were certain.

[I'm sure there are plenty of distractions around,] Davnian said.

"My apologies for not staying longer," Bedimer said, bowing his head. "Naisure, vindal."

"You may have leave, gracious Bedimer, but please, don't be shy." Neris ran her free hand along Davnian's chest as she bowed. Davnian echoed the gesture.

"One thing, good man," Davnian said, stopping Bedimer just as he went to turn.

"Aye?" Bedimer said, his grey eyes fixed on him.

Davnian contemplated some words, watching as the feminine shade was dragged along by her host's mass. The male shadow moved like a statue, its form disfigured by the haze of light around it.

"Take to heart what Neris aims for, not what she hints at," Davnian said as he watched the old male shade tremble in unison with his host. "It'll do you good, vivahr."

A curious look overtook the old talvuo. Bedimer replied with a simple nod. Turning from them, the grizzled huntsman took the opportunity to escape. They watched for several moments as he worked his way along the bridge network. The shades behind him followed, but the male one's features betrayed a glint of change. As he disappeared around a shadowy bend, Davnian couldn't help but laugh under his breath.

"What was that about?" Neris asked, her black hound ears raised toward him.

"Just amused, Neris."

"Amused, are you?" She brought her face close. "Anything you'd like to share?"

"I think you've become more ambitious since our last meeting," Davnian said, changing the focus of their conversation. He caught himself and pondered the statement. Had she been less ambitious back then? What brought that forward? In the end, it mattered little.

"It's easier to be ambitious when almost everyone is receptive in their own way." Neris chuckled as she gripped his arm and chest. She prodded him a bit, causing his nerves to tense ever so much.

"So, you were serious?' Davnian brought his claw to her teasing hand upon his chest. Squeezing her obsidian fingers, he shook his head. "I should have known better."

"Less serious but in need of a good distraction," Neris said. He was about to laugh when she brought her right hand to the back of his head. Gripping his mane, she turned him and planted a kiss upon his lips. "And you are so very distracting."

"Give it some time, and I'm sure others will pique your interest," Davnian said. Before she could scoff, Davnian returned the kiss with another. A moment later, he pulled back. "Though if I know you," he whispered, "you'll undoubtedly use me for an escalating level of mischief or mayhem."

"I've never been the one to cause trouble," she said, grinning, "just the one to lure."

Neris's red eyes scanned him as he looked over her beautiful black features. Wisps of her hair had come undone, the black strands tugging at her skin as a light breeze caressed them. Davnian was unsure how much trouble he had ever caused, but Neris's sultry, matter-of-fact disposition cemented one thing. It was more than he assumed or imagined.

[Now's as good a time as any then,] Davnian thought.

[For what?] the other in his head replied.

[You know very well what.]

Indeed, the other knew exactly what had been bothering Davnian. The day that was about research and investigation had been overtaken by light and amusement. The pieces of the puzzle that he had gathered since they left the healer's hovel were small and left too many gaps to surmise the rest on his own. The time they had was limited: the evening and the morning to come. However, as luck would have it, only one place was left to search: the great tree itself. It was wholly distorted from the outside, marking it as the center of strangeness around them. But he also knew that whatever lurked within was neither reasonable nor benign. Only one question lingered: would he go it alone, or would he drag everyone and everything down with him?

[You're as predictable as ever,] the other snarled from the recesses of his brain.

[How so?]

[Why charge into hell when you can get away from it? Didn't we conclude that mages and magic are terrible things to be involved with?]

If the source was a mage or some ancient magic, then the other had the right of it. But if the mage was what they both feared, Davnian knew there was only one way to stop whatever was coming. He had to confront it directly and without reservation.

[If it's Ohran, then we both know I must,] Davnian replied. He closed his eyes and let out a deep sigh. The other was aflame within his brain. Fire, brimstone, and tempests of ash clouded his thoughts, but Davnian dismissed them. [I did terrible things to seal that man. If I was willing to commit atrocities to that end, then what disservice do I do to those around me by letting this thread be sewn? No, it must be cut before it can be woven any further.]

[Wholly predictable,] the other said. [Don't call on me when the world comes crashing down around you.]

[Thank you,] Davnian said.

Opening his eyes, he pulled Neris close once more. Her red orbs remained open as she scanned his features. A nervous tension had washed over the edges of her otherwise willful guise. His kiss did nothing to alleviate it.

"I've seen that look before," Neris said.

"No doubt at least once." Davnian chuckled as images of his sincere, concerned face flashed before his eyes. Tension and heartbreak flooded his senses, causing his eyes to water. Laughing it off, Davnian released Neris and wiped his eyes. She remained close, her eyes fixed upon him. "We've let the day get away from us."

"I see," Neris said. "The afternoon is already upon us, but we set out to scheme and plot, did we not? Perhaps I'm the distracting one, hmmm?"

"Only in good ways," Davnian said, squeezing her captive hand once more. Looking her over, he observed how the sun illuminated her figure. The rays adorned her with an outline of gold and bronze. For a moment, he let temptation sway him from the path. He raised his hand and stroked her side, watching as her calm, placid face betrayed a nervous smile. Looking at her, he reached the answer to his question. "Gods, if I had all the time in the world."

"And you don't?" Neris joked. There was something profound and terrible in the way she mocked his words. Something that nagged him, but he had to leave it. Now was not the time for more uncertainty. He could only let the enchantment last so long.

"Tonight, I want you to indulge yourself. Be free and merry. Be enraptured. Love. Lust," Davnian began. "But when first light breaks, I want you to be rid of this place. Take Elis and Rais with you. Let no one else follow. Should they, I want you to put them to the sword. Do you understand?"

Davnian watched as Neris's nervous smile trembled for a moment. Her red eyes looked toward him, his blue orbs reflected in the hazy mist clinging to them. A moment of silence lingered between the pair as Neris's breath stopped in her throat. Moving his hand to her chest, he placed his fingers over her heart. The blood within her pounded with heavy beats.

"I-I don't understand," Neris stammered, her composure slipping as she shook her head. "Why? Where is this coming from?"

"Tonight, I intend to see to two things that I must do," Davnian said. "First, I need to make amends with Elis. I need to tell her how much I've appreciated your combined aid. I need to show her my commitment. I must also tell her the very thing I'm telling you right now."

"That's fine," Neris said, ignoring the implications. Her voice was fighting between nervous tones and the sultry disposition she would prefer to keep. "I understand that. Oh, how much fun it will be to doze and contemplate how the two of you—"

"One second. I need to find Ohran," Davnian said. Neris shut her mouth and disentangled her groping hand from his hair, sliding it down his back as her fingers grabbed at him. "I need to find your brother's imaginary friend. I need to ensure that whatever your brother is plotting is halted before tomorrow or at best confirmed as simple madness."

"Wouldn't it be easier if I spied a bit more for you?" Neris's tone shifted from trimerous to cajoling as she worked to reason with him. "It'd be simpler if I helped; you know that. I could keep an eye on him. We could easily put an end to his petty scheming."

Davnian didn't want to have this debate. He knew with all his heart that, yes, it would be easier. With all his reasoning, yes, it would be simpler to have aid. But with that same heart and reason, he also knew the dangers were anything but easy. The arrangements would be anything but simple. And the possible end was something that would be hard for him to bear, much less anyone else. She said she could help, but did she have the resolve if worse came to worst?

"Can you kill Nerin?" Davnian asked, his voice cold.

Neris froze as a chill sweep across her features, her eyes fixed on him.

"Could you kill those girls? The maidens he keeps at his side?" Davnian's ice-blue eyes focused on hers, watching as the iron-red irises shifted to the side. Her face had bouts of clarity mixed with hints of hesitation. He needed her to understand the path on which he was set. In his heart, Davnian didn't want to hurt anyone, but should the time come, he couldn't afford to let any of them stand in his way. As he and Neris sat there for several moments, he loosed his final question. "Would you kill them all for me?"

"Davnian, you know if you commanded me, I would—"

"No, Neris. I will not command you to kill your brother. If you want to run him through, then I will welcome your aid, but I need your conviction in this. There can be no doubts."

Davnian knew what the answer was. Despite how much Neris had given for Nerin, despite the torments and personal grievances she possessed, and despite the pain he had caused her, Neris still cared for him. He had seen it in her heart. In the deepest recesses of her soul, Nerin was still the little boy she wanted to protect from the vile man who had robbed them of decency and childhood. Even if Nerin had become that same type of monster, Neris would try her best to protect him from himself. One temptation, one slap, one scolding at a time until it went through.

"You want to be free of him, but you don't want to murder him," Davnian said.

"What do you know about what I want?" Neris demanded, her red eyes watering.

"You still want to save him," Davnian said.

"Gods damn you." Neris inhaled deeply, the murmurs and tension clearing from her voice. She steeled herself as heat and anger lingered on her words. With a menacing glare, she drew back her free hand and let it fly across his face. Davnian dropped her other hand as she withdrew. In the leaning afternoon glare, he thought how reddened she had become. He had unleashed her wrath in all its form. Stamping her foot, she gritted her teeth as she let her hand fly back once more. Her knuckles bit into his face, the force of her blow turning his head. "Damn it, Davnian! Gods damn all of this!"

"What's wrong here?" a deep, frantic voice called from several paces away. Out of the corner of his eye, Davnian caught a glimpse of a shy, hazel-headed girl wrapped around a woman's rope-sashed waste. Small, gilded locks fluttered on either side of Neris's frame. "Is everything alright?"

"Zaisure . . ." Rais murmured from behind the tall, foreboding Delvori woman.

Neris continued to stare at him with vengeful eyes. As her breathing slowed, she started to regain her composure. Behind her, Elis carried baskets of plant matter and flowers. Worry spread across Elis's bronze face, she turned her lavender gaze first to Davnian, then back to Neris. Davnian felt a bruise starting to form on his cheek.

"Davnian? Neris? What's going on here?" Elis asked as they both sat silently.

As he searched for words, Davnian watched as Neris cooled her features. "Nothing, vindal Elis. We were just having a lover's spat." Neris shot him a glare. Davnian refrained from speaking as he sighed and nodded. "One moment he's doing everything right, the next he's trying to tear it all down," Neris said. "Gods, he's always been a vexing man."

"That he has been," Elis said, still in a stupor from the commotion. "Are you both sure you're alright? You both still seem . . ."

"Everything is fine, ne vindal," Neris said as she wiped remnants of tears from her face. "It seems even I get taken aback by some things." Neris went to spin up another of her propositions, but before she could, Elis lowering her baskets to the ground and wrapped her tan arms around the obsidian-skinned woman.

"Whatever it is, it'll be alright," Elis said. Davnian watched as shock crossed Neris's features, warmth and empathy illuminating her face for an instant. Then Elis withdrew, planting a quick peck on Neris's cheek. Davnian chuckled as Elis turned to face him. "Why are you laughing? You need to stop worrying her so much."

"Yes, good—" Davnian caught himself, watching Elis's lavender eyes narrow upon him. "Yes, Elis."

[All of that drama, and yet you allow yourself to be derided and scolded.]

[I'll have plenty of time to clear things up later.]

"Where have you two been?" Neris asked, breaking the tension. "Picking flowers?"

"Spending some time fetching petals for Rais," Elis said.

[No, she was spending time not thinking,] Davnian thought as he caught her stumble over her words for a moment. No doubt, she had been off trying to gather her wits. It was good she had the better part of a day to contemplate and stave off decisions. [If only there was more time for meditation.]

[This really is the path you're set on,] the other remarked with glass-like placidity.

[There's only one way through this, and all else leads astray,] he replied.

"I know this may be abrupt, but would the two of you like to come for dinner?" Elis asked. "I know there will be feasting and merriment, but I was thinking we'd spend a quiet night before the ceremony tomorrow. We'd love to have you," Elis said, half to Davnian and wholly to Neris.

"My dear, I think, for now, I'm going to retire and prepare for the evening."

"I'd love to, Elis," Davnian said. "And I'd love it if you came with us, Neris."

Neris shot him another heated glare. She scanned him for several moments, trying to understand why he had asked her along. Davnian donned a calm smile. A small twitch erupted near her cheek as she contemplated his words.

"Neris doesn't have to—"

"On second thought, I will come along," Neris said, turning back to Elis. Her posture softened as she shot the blond-haired talvuo woman a soft smile. "After all, it may be a while before we can all gather in the same place again. What with how erratic we tend to be."

"Truer words," Elis said. "Alright then. Come, Rais!"

"Yes, zaisure," the quiet little girl said, aware of the tensions.

Davnian waited behind. Neris stood behind him as they marched onward.

"Hey!" Rais turned and called back as they made their way over the following bridge.

"We'll be right there!" Neris said.

"Yes, we'll follow right behind," Davnian reassured them.

Elis turned her gaze back to them, then to the little girl. With muffled words, she hurried Rais along. Only one treehouse was at the end of the chain of bridges, which Davnian surmised must be their abode.

"I'm sorry, Neris," he said without turning toward her.

"You're not forgiven," Neris replied with her telltale calm and composed voice.

"I don't expect to be," he said. "I just don't want to give you hope for something that may not be possible."

"Don't get me wrong," Neris said as she paced a few steps ahead. She turned back toward him, her red eyes filled with certainty. "I don't plan on leaving and waiting, never knowing."

"Neris . . ."

"I'll take leave of this place, along with Elis and Rais. But when all that must happen is done, I will be here to drag you along. I'm tired of waiting, but I'm not going to let you get away. I'm taking everything, whether you give it or not."

Davnian sat transfixed by her, his blue eyes wide as she set the terms of her claim over him. He was close to laughing when she narrowed her eyes, the sun gilding her black lashes as she stared him down. There was no argument to be had. Neris had spoken her peace and decided what she would do.

"If it comes to that, I expect you to drag me kicking and screaming if you must," Davnian said as he stepped toward her. "But not until all is said and done, Neris."

"I won't interfere." She turned around and began walking. "But I do not promise to withhold my ambitions."

Davnian let her walk on ahead of him, thinking about her final statement. Perhaps he had judged her wrong. Maybe she could do the deed, and perhaps she even wanted to. Needed to. But even if her desire overflowed, Davnian feared it would not be enough. Deep in his gut, he knew whatever profane thing sat at the heart of all of this was beyond the reach of mortal hands. Something ominous and monstrous, ancient and terrible, was waiting for them all. The only thing that could stop such horror was a far greater terror.

As he followed Neris, he hoped the Virage was all that and more.

39

———

NERIN

[Vivahr Nerin.] One voice played in his head after another as he spoke with a lowborn Hyunisti about their woes and melodrama.

The flock took to his wishes in ridding themselves of objects sanctifying their feeble past and culture. He should have been happy about their acceptance; it was a victory above all else. But as he conducted the day, the endless greetings had wormed their way into his psyche. Each face and syllable filled him with duress and reprehension. He was no brother in blood or race to these weak men and women but played the part nonetheless. He was so close to the promised day. He just needed to suffer it all a little longer.

"Vivahr Nerin," an old grey-eyed talvuo said as he passed by Nerin's rigid frame.

"Vivahr." Nerin feigned pleasure as he greeted the leather-garbed talvuo. The day had worn on him. His hospitality was at its end. He was exhausted, and some unspoken cruelty in the back of his mind made him want to run screaming from the treetops.

Was it the Virage's lingering presence somewhere about? He had seen him wandering with Neris in the afternoon. He watched as she hung about him, flirting and pandering to onlookers. The circles they made seemed sinister as Nerin had worked on his projects.

Or perhaps it was the missing Kadin, whom he had tried to summon for the better part of the late morning. The sniveling weasel had run from the boughs of the tree after a night stewing over his transgressions. But shame was no excuse for lack of diligence. When Nerin called, he was expected to come. Nerin could send one of the fire keepers or grunts, but none of them had the instincts not to give away their intent. Maybe it was the lack of eyes and ears to spy upon the monster and his sister.

"Vivahr Nerin. Vindal Thaimi." A pair of dusty-headed women approached and bowed.

Nerin shot them a smile while the Hyunisti woman beside him bowed. The villagers had started to make their rounds as the afternoon grew long, with the sunlight growing gold and hazy in the distance. Festivities had begun as food and drink were served about the terraces. The Hyunisti laid out all their finery, though it was tepid for even the most backward of peoples. Still, Nerin felt compelled to acknowledge them despite their lack of sophistication or tangible bounty.

"Good evening, and enjoy yourselves, vindals." Thaimi's plain voice was pleasant as the two departed. Nerin shot her a glance and watched her dull green eyes survey the couple's path before returning to the nearby oven. "Isn't this pleasant, vivahr?"

"I care not if it's pleasant. I care only that the evening comes and is done with," Nerin said spitefully beneath heavy breaths. Every time the woman talked, it was like a weight was placed upon his chest. He had spent too much time with such company. "I should leave you to this rabble."

"Still yourself, my lord," Thaimi said. A confluence of reassurance washed over his gilded figure as he stood with his purple robes on the grand terrace before his tree-like fortress. Yet the placation could not breach his ego.

"I'll be stilled once all this is over," he said. The woman was a perfect supplicant, but she had an infuriating way of seeming to command his senses. The thought he may be taking a liking to her was frustrating in and of itself. She was bent to supplicate and serve his whims and needs, ordained to join her fellow maidens in serving her bland nectar. She was and should be nothing more. "You would do well to remember who speaks and commands, Thaimi."

"As you will it, vivahr," she said in a voice of perfect servitude. Yet in his head, she mocked him. No, she was just wearing on his nerves.

"I'm going to retire for a bit," Nerin said as he made to retreat. The woman shuffled her feet, but he waved her away. "No, stay for now. Leave me be."

"I will fetch you when the time comes."

Nerin left the sheet-garbed Hyunisti woman. Her last words pummeled his senses as he crossed the high bridge of the treetop village. There was one more step to all of this, but it could wait. The light of day was nothing but gold and crimson as he shook free of her influence. The dullard did not understand how she grated on his resolve or how her actions bored him. Dismissing hollow pleasantries from some pale talvuo loafing about, Nerin entered the giant recess of the grand tree. However, as soon as he thought he had escaped, he found himself staring at the backside of his obsidian other-half.

"Neris!" Her name bubbled up faster than he could regain his composure. Without a second thought, he ran up to her. She turned her head, her blood-red eyes watching as he took his place beside her.

"Ah, vivahr. Good evening." Neris's voice was formal as she strutted toward the ramp of the great tree. Inside, the ambience was dusky shades of waning sunlight topped with crowns of long shadows and dark recesses. The lower floor was in disarray as furniture from the higher rounds stood ready for the following morning. The path to the grand spiral was a winding road of tables, chairs, benches, and the like. "I see you've been busy. Is all of this for your ceremony tomorrow?"

"This place is as much a store as it is a fortress," Nerin said as they reached the first steps. "One thing you can say about these poor folks is they are industrious when pushed to it."

"Indeed, vivahr." Neris sighed as she walked along the round.

"I see you're without your plaything," Nerin said. A shiver of acknowledgment tremored up Neris's features, letting him know he had struck the proper chord. "So, have you already grown bored of him?"

"Not at all." Neris's voice was cold as she refused to look at him, her defensiveness expected. "I'm just pacing myself, dear brother. Gorging on your favorite dish can cause discomfort and boredom. It's better to savor the taste and wash it down with something cleaner."

Nerin knew what she was trying to do. The Virage was her favorite? No, that couldn't be. Even if his hold on her was strong, he had no doubt that deep inside, she knew what she longed for.

"You're wearing that pathetic face again."

"What?"

"The one where you're assuming your privilege," Neris said as he paused on the path. He had dodged the first of her verbal blows with ease, but despite knowing her tricks well, the second nicked his sensibilities while the third cut deep into his resolve. "But I would expect nothing less from a sniveling, little brat like you."

"Neris . . ." His voice became heated as he started to trail her.

"I come here to quench myself, and now I have to face everything I've become." Her voice resounded in the wooden rampway as his hound-like ears cupped toward her. He felt the blood in his face as she continued to assault his ego. What was going on? This was his retreat. What demonic hand conspired to wreck his evening with one of his sister's foul moods? "Gods, Nerin, how long have we been doing this?"

"We do this because this is who we are, vindal. We're brother and sister. We're royalty. We're . . ."

"Ah, yes. Pure blood, brother?" She laughed out the last line. Her deep voice filled his heart and body with pain and longing. "You still can't see it, can you?"

"Ne vindal." He shifted his approach as he ran up behind her. He would play the part of the understanding brother and get under her skin. They loved each other and had suffered much in their shared times together. "You and I both know how painful life once was. But everything is different now. We're together again. We're going to make everything right. Together."

"Together?" Neris stopped halfway up the round. Nerin took his place behind her. Just as he was about to reach for her, she turned in place and shot him a heated glare. "What part of all of this have we done together? What part did we decide on? What piece of these ambitions did we both shape?"

"Neris . . ." He continued to use his placative voice as she drew forward to close the gap between them. "Didn't we come here together? Didn't we spend all the that time as bandits and raiders together? We sacked those Holan scum in our homeland together. We left that desert wasteland together. In the end we escaped that abyss of caves and darkness together."

"We were part of all those things together." Neris's voice became cool once more as her blazing stare softened. "You're right; we survived so many of those days and nights while being in the same circumstances."

"Of course I am," he said as he placed his hands upon her upper arms. She was warm to the touch. "Compared to some, I've always been there and waiting, ne vindal. Was there ever a time we weren't together that truly mattered?"

"You're right. You were there when I was being slapped, gagged, pinned, and raped back in those caves. We both knew what father liked, and you no doubt most of all when his favorite plaything was away." The ice in Neris's words sent a shiver down his spine as her vehemence sank to a level that he had tried to forget. Her fingers danced along her forearm as she continued. "You were even there when I'd get on my knees for all of your kinsfolk. When I'd bend over, forward and back, for you and yours, dear, sweet little brother."

He shivered as he sputtered out words, trembling as he tried to put on his persona once more.

"Arguably, we were in that fortress together. Though the night before, I had to fend for myself. Not that I wasn't used to being doted on so roughly. A warband of Holan men isn't the worst of what I've been through. In fact, I think I enjoyed it." Her lips curled into a cruel smile. "Just thinking about all those rough, hungry hands and loins, dear brother. At least they were there with me. They even heeded my direction between my gasps and heaving."

"Neris, stop it," he commanded as the lewd imagery flooded his brain. What was this torture? Was she taking pride in how her body had been sullied by those curs? Was she mocking what he had offered out of necessity to satiate their dumbfounded companions? No, she had started that. She had done it to pull them away from the arduous path. They had worked and suffered, but above all, he had sacrificed his desire to appease them. Where was his reward? Yes, it had been proper to offer herself to him and his. Was that not right for his service? For staying by her? For finding and saving her from those who would corrupt their blood?

Nerin's anger reached its peak as pride and confusion swelled in his breath. He felt gentle hands crawl along his body, heard whispers of benevolence scatter throughout his brain. As they stood in the dark side of the round, a nearby window showed darker hues of blue as they stretched toward the black horizon. The world was sympathizing with his burden as he stood their gripping Neris's arms.

"Alright, ne vivahr," Neris said as his grip tightened.

"There. That's a good girl." Nerin smiled through gritted teeth as he focused on her full red orbs. His fine-featured face, beleaguered by weariness and scorn, appeared twisted in her eyes. "Everything is alright now. Now we just need to—"

"Don't mock me, Nerin. I'm done trying to reach you," Neris said as she pushed him away. As he tried to regain his hold, she stepped back and smacked his hands away. "I'm done pretending this will ever be right. Good evening, vivahr!"

"Neris!" he shouted, lunging for her arm.

Neris dodged him and spun as he tumbled to the side. He tried to recover but found her foot beside his leading leg. With a twist of her hips, she swept his foot from under him, and he fell forward. He braced himself with one hand and protected his head while his opposite shoulder slammed into the wall.

"Don't you dare to touch me, Nerin Delvori," Neris warned as she turned and marched off.

"Neris! Neris, get back here!" he commanded as she made way around the tree. "Neris, get back here and fix this! Help me up!"

"Go find our father's legs and crawl back under them." Her words tore at his gut as he lay there. His shoulder was in immense pain, his knees scuffed, and his purple robes torn.

"Neris!" he called, trying to right himself. Trembling, he fell back prone, the heat and anger in his breast welling over. The pain and longing reached his face as his eyes watered. As hatred and bile over-flowed, a cacophony of voices tried to ease his pain. They whispered for his patience and stoicism, luring him to a freer, emptier place.

But he didn't want to be free or empty.

"Neris!" he screamed, his voice cracking as the name strained his voice and his heart.

40

———

ELIS

Elis's small abode could barely accommodate three, much less four of them. As Elis and Rais prepared the small bits and whatnot, Elis lured Davnian and Neris to the upper terrace in a bid to leave the housework to the inhabitants. With a couple of bottles of honey wine, the pair seemed content to wait out the setup above her abode. All the while, her ruby-haired ears listened for telltale signs of arguments and fighting. As a pleasant surprise, the turmoil had abated.

The meal itself had been simple soup, bread, and aged cheese. Neris had grunted, no doubt used to rarer fare. Elis laughed at her scoffing but knew she appreciated the hospitality. Davnian, on the other hand, was less picky, though more distracted than anything. He had laughed and commented as they talked but did not add much to their conversation. Despite his overall morose demeanor, he had worn a jovial smile as Rais tried to tell her story of sitting with him the day prior.

With the late afternoon winding away and the gilded rays of sunset encroaching, Neris took her leave. Elis listened and peeked from her window as Davnian followed the Delvori out. For several moments they whispered together before Neris let out a sad sigh. About to turn around, Neris spun Davnian in place and brought her lips to his. Without another word, she turned and strutted off into the evening.

[Remember, I'll be coming back for you.]

Neris's words unsettled Elis as they rattled through her gold-seated brain. She had expected something akin to them from Davnian but not from Neris. Why would she be coming back? Was she reading too much into them? Maybe she meant that night. But the sense she had from the tone made the hairs on her neck rise.

The rest of the early evening had drawn on. Rais had begged to take out her colors. As Davnian watched patiently from the corner, Elis obliged. For a few hours, they tested colors with sentae, prepared older mixtures for application, and steeped the blue flowers from earlier that day. As the sun's gilded reds gave way to dark blues and purples, Elis pondered a series of blue and green vials. The pigments were weak, as she had feared, but when added to the potent sentae, they seemed vibrant and alive. By the morning, they would be ready for application. Perhaps it was time she tried doing Rais's face.

With the last hour of the azure evening fading, Rais let out a deep yawn, and Davnian dozed in the corner. He was just like his boyhood self, if not a little less severe despite the morbidity.

"Alright, Rais, let's wrap up," Elis said as she pulled the girl away from her project. Rais nodded in response as she staved off another yawn. Elis fetched the lantern, then led the little girl into their small bedroom.

"We didn't get to talk a lot," Rais said as Elis closed the door behind them.

"You'll have plenty of time to talk in the days to come. Let's change back into your other dress."

In response, Rais raised her arms and struggled to free herself from the yellow sundress. Elis patted her elbows. Rais straightened her arms upwards, and Elis pulled the dress free. Elis ran her hand through the little girl's hair and then drew Rais near. She tickled her brown ears. The little girl giggled and sighed. With agility, Elis fetched one of two white dresses. Elis had Rais stand with her arms up as she placed the garment on her. After coaxing her into bed, Elis tossed off her sullied white tunic, then reached down and fetched one of her loose lavender dresses. Donning the garment, she turned to Rais, who was huddled under their quilt.

"Are you going to stay up, zaisure?" Rais asked, fighting to stay awake.

"Just for a while, my little one," Elis said as she sat beside her. She stroked Rais's hair, then bent over and kissed her forehead. "Davnian and I are going to talk for a bit. Is that OK?"

"Yes, zaisure," the little girl said, yawning once more.

"If you need anything, we'll be either in here or right outside. You can call for us."

"OK, zaisure."

Elis smiled and planted another kiss on the girl's forehead. "OK then, my little one," she whispered. "Go to sleep, and dream sweet things."

Taking the lantern with her, Elis left the room to find Davnian much more awake than she had left him. Wearing a grin and a look of curiosity, Elis stared at her long-lost friend. "I thought I was going to have to find a bed for you as well," she said, snickering as she entered the room. "Though maybe you were just pretending to be asleep?"

"I was just trying to ease myself," Davnian said. "It's been a very long day."

Of that she had no doubt. He had only awakened the day before, but he had spent an evening with Neris, and then the next day had rummaged across the village. Still, he continued to stand and speak despite the ire he had put his body through.

"Where do you want this to go?" Elis asked as she stood near the table.

"How do you mean?"

"I mean, how do you want to start this? I know you're only here to prod me about ancient history." Elis feigned bitterness as she fidgeted with a bottle atop the table.

"If only that were true. Though I'm not going to lie, Elis. I don't know where to begin."

Elis watched him in the faint lantern light. His figure was so familiar, wrapped in his gilded red-and-blue tunic and plain brown trousers. His disheveled mane was like a brown hood about his head. His blue eyes were black in the shaded room, the lantern a speck of light dancing in his orbs. His expression was warm but stoic, though Elis thought she detected a hint of bitterness in his visage.

"I want to discuss several things with you," he said, "but none of them are easy. The weight of my soul burdens me just standing here."

"The weight of your soul?" Elis almost laughed but then shushed herself before her voice became too loud. Rais was on the verge of sleep in the other room. "You always did have a plain yet dramatic way of talking."

Davnian shot her a grin. "I'll blame that on a younger me then and not my present state of mind."

"Perhaps we should talk elsewhere," Elis said.

"Why's that?"

"Your overwrought tongue is going to bring out the worst in me," Elis said, gesturing to the closed bedroom door.

"We can be quiet," Davnian whispered as she made for the door.

Elis chuckled. "Yes, but then I'll fall asleep."

Davnian let out a defeated sigh. Handing him the lantern, she exited, and he followed close behind. As they rounded the back of her house, they came to a set of wooden slats that formed a crude staircase up a branch-lined path of the tree's trunk.

"Watch your step," Elis said, looking back as they walked up alongside the massive arbor.

"I'm familiar, Elis."

"Yes, but now it's dark. I'll not have you falling from the treetops on my watch."

Up above them, the night sky had started to turn a dark purple. In the distance, cheers and murmurs echoed from the village. For many, the time of revelry was just beginning. Turning her gaze for a moment, she saw the burning ovens dispersed throughout the forest. Spots of flickering flames erupted every now and then, only to be surpassed by the dim glow of paper lanterns strewn about the canopy. Without a word, Davnian followed her as they rounded the trunk twice before emerging onto her small, private terrace.

"This is a pleasant view," Davnian said.

Elis looked over the platform, spotting the remaining honey-wine bottles. One was half empty, and the other was full. Neris must have drunk to cool her mood while Davnian abstained. She wanted to pick up the open bottle but stayed herself. "You can see the whole village from here. It's all lit up."

"As much as it will ever be." Elis smiled as she sat on a small stool. "Most nights, there's only a few lanterns to light the way."

"For the bridges?" Davnian asked. Elis nodded. "Makes sense. Almost everything is unshrouded. Moonlight suffices on most nights, I take it?"

"Indeed"

"I'm still not sure how to begin this," Davnian said as he sat on the hardwood platform. Crossing his legs, he looked up at her. "There are too many things to ask and very little time."

"You make it sound as if you'll be off tomorrow." Elis almost laughed at the notion.

"I'm getting dramatic again. Let me start once more. I wanted to apologize to you first."

"For what?" Elis asked as she continued to ignore the bottle.

"For not remembering you like I did Neris." Davnian's voice was full of remorse and intensity as he looked up at her. Elis looked down at him, her lavender eyes wide with how direct he had been. The way he delivered an apology was as she expected. The whole act played to sensibilities that made her feel more awkward. She didn't need an excuse.

"Gods, Davnian, it's fine," Elis lied as she focused her gilded ears upon him. She listened for his voice, his breath, even his heartbeat. He was so sincere it hurt. "Is that all you wanted to say?"

"I could ask you a thousand things, but . . ." Davnian paused and sighed. "First is the apology. Second is . . ." For several moments she watched him as his gaze drifted toward the small lantern set before him. Its small white light reflected in his eyes, revealing faint whispers of confusion and uncertainty. "This was so much easier with Neris."

"Oh?" Elis teased. Her mind exploded into a thousand pieces of imagery, from everything revolting and taboo to cordial discussion and blatant flattery. "I'm not as easy?"

"It's not what you're thinking, Elis," Davnian said, raising his eyes to hers.

"I'm not thinking anything." Elis feigned ignorance as she gave in and snatched up a bottle. She raised it to her mouth and began to drink.

"Good woman, you're not fooling anyone."

"Hmmm?" Elis was halfway through a second mouthful of the super-sweet vintage when she tried to interrupt his insufferable pandering. She almost spat but covered her mouth. Trickles of the sticky liquid ran down her chin. "What was that?" Davnian laughed as she nestled the bottle between her legs. "This is what Neris is talking about," Elis said as she shook her gilded mane. Annoyed, she ran her fingers through her hair and freed up some tangled locks.

"I'm sure there's much more to it than overly formal speech."

"You know what I mean. It's how familiar you are. And how familiar you aren't," Elis said. Davian stopped laughing. She took another shot.

"Neris said as much. She told me it was like seeing me at extremes. Is it the same for you?"

Elis lowered the bottle and then wiped her lips. "No, it's like seeing a ghost."

"A ghost?"

"You look so different, but gods, you're still the boy I remember."

The man in front of her was much like his father, colored with the dramatic parts of his mother. He was too thoughtful and too cold. Too simple in his statements, but also complex in his delivery. His gestures were the same, save for his left hand being more useful than in his previous life. The way he smiled, frowned, looked confused, and even how he laughed was like watching memories come alive. If not for the look of maturity that clung to his somewhat youthful features, Elis would be hard-pressed to say he was different at all, though she had seen other sides of him.

"I can only hope that's really the case," he replied. His jovial mood ended as he reached for the bottle. Elis chuckled and handed it to him. Focused on his form, her starlit eyes watched him take a draw from the vessel. As he lowered the green bottle, he gagged. Shaking his head, he passed the wine back. "Gods, it's so sweet."

"Yes, it's honey wine," Elis said. "Still can't hold a drink down, can you?" she added, trying to lighten the darkening mood

"I must not be used to it." He shook his head. "Or maybe my throat and gut still aren't ready."

"Maybe," Elis said as she took another drink. She wanted to get drunk and lower her guard, but her nerves were steeled by that which was too familiar. She couldn't be open with him, given his current mood and her own inhibitions. Her spirit was being tugged by forces pulling in opposite directions. Fleeting moments of clarity told her that honesty and truth were worth it. But from that truth could erupt actions they would both regret.

"I believe you're supposed to be getting me drunk, good woman." Davnian chuckled and gestured at the bottle as she took another gulp. "Though that's only if your endgame is the same as Neris's."

"A few swigs of honey wine won't do me in, good man," Elis teased.

"Elis, if I asked you if you'd leave tomorrow morning, would you?" Davnian said, dismissing all levity once more. He had her full attention as she tightened her grip on the bottle.

"What brought that on?" Elis shot him a look of surprise leveled out by her own platitudes from earlier that day. "Are you planning on leaving?"

"No," Davnian said, tapping his claw on the floor. "But Neris is, and I want you to go with her."

"Why is she leaving?" Elis was taken aback as she tried to process this new information.

For a few moments, he sat in silence, his eyes turned away. She went to speak but then quieted herself as he gestured to the air. A few times, she thought she saw his lips moving, faint traces of words appearing as if he were whispering to himself. He shook his head and, with a heavy sigh, looked back at her.

"Something terrible may happen tomorrow. Something not seen here in hundreds of years," Davnian said, a cautious severity in his eyes as he surveyed the night sky. "There's something arcane and terrible about this forest, specifically the spot where the great tree stands. I'm sure you know of the curse upon the Hyunisti. Well, if the ceremony tomorrow is the same as that which brought calamity here, I don't know what will happen."

"You're talking about Hyun's sorrow?" The talvuo matron's name caught in Elis's throat as she spoke. The plight of the villagers and the rites that Hyun had sealed away toiled within her brain. "Did you read through her memoirs?"

"Yes," Davnian said as he returned his gaze to her. "I skimmed through most of them, reading about her pain and suffering. But I also scanned another journal written by a mutual acquaintance of ours. His writings spoke of many peculiar things, and from that I gathered his ambitions paralleled hers."

"That's not possible, Davnian." Elis almost laughed at the audacity. "You're talking about Nerin Delvori? He may have read her journals, but there's no way he'd take them at their word. Besides, there's nothing explicit in there about what happened, save for a few symbolic mentions."

"You've read them as well then?" Davnian asked. Elis nodded. "You're correct," he said. "There's nothing any being could take at face value and gather the necessary means to fashion such a fantastic spell. And yet, his ramblings are echoes of her words."

"Do you only bring bad omens with you?" Elis shivered. The Virage was notorious for the wake of destruction that followed him, campfire stories filling her mind once more with tales of the demonic figure. She took another drink. It would be her last, or so she told herself.

"I know not, but the villagers seem to think so." Davnian gestured to the village beyond. "But they still welcomed and approached me. Curiosity defeats survival, it seems."

"I don't know whether to call that terrible or civil. And your perspective, it's almost as warped."

"So, let me ask again. If I were sure something terrible would happen here tomorrow, would you leave this place with Neris? Would you take young Rais with you and be gone from here?"

"You're asking me if I'll uproot my life for something you are unsure of," Elis said, feeling a tinge of numbness touch her lips. "I don't think you understand the weight of that, Davnian."

He nodded. "Asking anyone to leave their home is hard."

"It's more than that." She waved her hand in front of her, turning her gaze to the sparkling diamonds above. The moon was far off near the horizon, the silver crescent hovering above the tree line. "Gods, if only you remembered."

"You lost your home once, correct?" Davnian asked. She snapped her gaze back to him, her face donning an incredulous stare at his almost flippant query.

"It wasn't just my home," she said, smiling bitterly.

"I . . . see."

"Do you?"

Elis hesitated to berate him further. Her point had struck home as he realized what her loss had entailed. Maybe he was able to piece together the impact of the tragedy. Perhaps he was even able to see his place in it. Calming her nerves, she leaned back and puffed out her chest. Feeling larger than the night was all she had to ease the tension.

"Davnian, I have to stay here," Elis said. He was about to reply when she continued. "I'm all these people have left. I'm the only living memory of who they once were. I'm the only one who can tell them stories of better times. Davnian, these talvuo can't even live like talvuo.

They can barely even live like humans, and they can't just leave. To the south, the men of Grannas would hang and torture them. To the north, the wastes of Ansuman would swallow them. If I leave the woods, I will sever their last connections to their heritage. The Hyunisti would be no more."

"You're not an object of the Hyunisti, Elis," he said.

"No, but I promised Hyun that I would see her people restored."

"And you also promised her that you would keep moving and not be held back by the past."

His recollections of her last meeting with Hyun infuriated her. He had read parts that she knew well but could not honor. No, he didn't understand what he was talking about.

"Davnian, I will outlive every one of these talvuo. I will outlive their children. I will outlive their children's children." Elis glared at him as she continued. "Losing time to honor my word to her, to see these people raised, is not a loss for me. I'm moving on, away from my lack of involvement. I'm no longer shirking my responsibilities."

Davnian sat quietly for a few moments as she stared him down. Nodding to her, he raised his human hand and took the bottle of wine. With a sigh, he took a heavy draught, consuming the last of the bottle's contents. He did not sputter or cough this time as he drank the dark liquid. For several moments he paused, then gestured to the other bottle. "We should open that," he said, laughing under his breath.

"Do you need it?"

"No, but I need to find the words. Elis, I need you to go with her."

"Why? Do you think we'll all die tomorrow?"

"I can't be positive. I—"

"Do you think I'm just going to obey you, Davnian? That if I drink enough or listen to your heartfelt pleas, I'll go along with your plan?" Elis felt the numbness on her upper lip as her words betrayed her emotions.

"No, I—"

"I'm not the little girl who tended your crib anymore, Davnian. "I'm not the lovestruck young woman who cajoled and planned to have my way with you. I'm not even the young woman who learned from that mistake. I'm past all that."

He closed his eyes and placed his hands upon his head, his lips curling as whispers escaped his mouth.

"I have a life here, Davnian. I have a place here."

"If I have to see any of you lost like I did Senna, I don't know what I'll do!" Davnian blurted as he pulled at his mane in frustration. Elis leaned back and stared at him, watching as a trickle of tears escaped down his cheek. It was like a slap in the face, bringing up someone else who his mind had gone to.

"Who's Senna?"

"I . . ." as he hesitated, his features betrayed confusion over his exclamation. Scratching the terrace with his claw, Davnian continued to mumble to himself as he tried to find the words. She felt a pang of regret as he spoke. "I don't know. I'm sorry, Elis. I don't know why I said that. All I know is I can't bear that again. I don't even remember what that was, that cursed nightmare. But still . . ."

"You don't remember her either?" Elis bit her lip as she fetched the remaining bottle of wine and snapped it open. It was bitter and comical. She sighed. "So many women and times you don't remember."

"I'm sure I don't remember the men either." He choked out a dismal laugh as he took a deep breath. She sighed once more and took another drink. The waning lantern light exposed the frown on his face as he rambled on. "The only thing I know is the nightmarish arcana that seeps from my brain. You're right. I have no right to demand anything of you, Elis. I have no right to presume anything of you or your ways. Nor of Neris. Nor of anyone else in this gods-forsaken village. I can't remember anyone beyond a few vague moving pictures in my head. I have no right to make accusations. I have no ground to even support my claims other than some fanciful tales in a few books and dark memories of something sinister from a previous life. Oh, I see shades and tempests, but only I see them. If I knew who or what the Virage was, I would stake everything on that monster's title and prowess. But I don't. The only thing I can do is stake everything on the man I am now and on the person I may have been to so many. Maybe that's not even valuable. Maybe I've always been a monster. But I would wager everything I don't remember on my hunch being correct. And if it's wrong, I pray to whatever gods will hear me that I never regain another deceitful memory."

Elis did not know what to say as he ranted and gestured. His confidence in his statements of doubt and self-loathing was immense. His ambitious pursuit was cut short by his confused emotional pleas. Once more, he was the young boy from her youth, unable to discern right from wrong as he steered headlong in one direction and stuck to it. The whole thing warmed and frustrated her. How easy it was for him to disarm her with his uncertainty. Neris seemed to believe him if Elis took him at his word. But the man who turned boyish was unguided and rushing headway into things he did not understand and could not explain to anyone else.

"When will you know for sure?" Elis took another heavy drink from the bottle as his eyes lit up.

"Before tomorrow morning," Davnian said. "I should know before the ceremony."

"What happens when you find out?"

"In the best case, I return, and nothing is out of place. In the worst, I don't return at all."

"If you don't return, then that's when we should leave?" Elis asked. Her head was abuzz from the alcohol as thoughts wormed through her brain. In years long before, she had been the one guiding him along a path that she had plotted. For better or worse, everything had turned out fine. She had grown past being a manipulator, but the mischievous thought overtook her senses as an amorous look crept across her features.

"Before the ceremony begins, take Rais with you. Take whatever you hold dear and necessary—weapons, changes of clothes, a pack of food. Make your way out of these woods, and never turn back."

Elis sighed. "I don't know why I'm even entertaining this." Sliding down from her stool, she plopped herself in front of him. "You make this so hard on me, Davnian."

"Elis," Davnian began, but she shushed him. The buzz was like a roar in the back of her head. Perhaps she had overdone it, letting her yearning get the better of her. With a promise to herself, she took one last heavy draught of wine, then passed the bottle to him.

"Drink," Elis commanded as she looked over his features in the dim lantern light. The flame within teetered on and off as its life waned. Davnian looked her over, his blue eyes full of worry and remorse. He half-smiled, half-frowned as he let out a sigh and brought the bottle to his lips. A crooked grin inched across her face as he matched her display, coughing as he put the bottle between his legs. "There, that's better."

"Do you promise me you'll at least entertain the thought? Whether Neris shows up at all?" Davnian's voice was low as he extended his black, mangled claw and took her hand. She let out a groan and a snort, shaking her head at the audacity of the situation. He went to speak, but she cut him off.

"Whether or not Neris comes in the morning, I'll consider it," Elis said as she wrapped her other hand around his claw. "And if you're nowhere to be found, I'll go on a hunting trip with Rais. Just the two or three of us."

The blackened flesh was smoother than she remembered. It was almost like water, neither cold nor warm. She was lost in caressing the mottled thing as she closed her eyes. The ridges and bumps reminded her how his bones had been strung back together. Feeling it flex as he gripped her, she recognized it was full of strength and resilience that had been lost to Davnian an eternity ago.

"Elis?" Davnian's voice broke her train of thought.

"What?" Elis felt a sultry crassness at the edge of her voice as she responded.

"I have to leave soon."

"Oh?" The alcohol and her cynicism broke the spell of shyness and hesitation cast over herself. Catching him off guard, she pressed him back against the terrace and sat on top of him. "That's too bad."

"Elis, I . . ." He stopped as she shushed him once more. Picking up the bottle from between their legs, she set it aside and lowered herself to him. He mouthed an objection, but she silenced him by placing her mouth to his. Beneath her, he tensed and feigned resistance. With her bronze arms turned to grey in the dim light, she pinned his hands in place near his head. Licking his lips, she forced her tongue in. She could taste the sticky traces of honey and stewed greens upon his breath. He squirmed at first but then stopped as she withdrew her face. He looked confused and concerned, but she was fed up with waiting. If she had to change things up, then something else had to give.

"I'll entertain you, Davnian," she whispered as she pressed her body to his. "But in return, you have to entertain me."

41

—————

NERIN

For what seemed like hours, Nerin had beat on Neris's door, screaming for her to make things right. He had pleaded, threatened her with losing her place beside him, but nothing brought her out of her chamber.

Unable to calm himself, Nerin chose to seclude himself in his room. The anger and uneasiness of the evening ate away at what little resolve he had left. The whole day was appeasement of those who did not deserve to look upon him, much less call him their brother. All the appreciation was equal to that of fly spit. Only one person's admiration was worthy of his attention, but she was too far gone.

In the darkness of the tree-top chamber, Nerin heard the whispers of his master and supporters all around. They called to him. They yearned for him to fulfill his final part of the contract and take his place. There was one step left before the following day's ceremony, and yet he could not drum up the courage to make the journey to the ordained space far below. Today's affront was the final straw of a thousand hammers levied against his ego. His black hound ears hung limp while his body sat rigid and hollow. What was the point of greatness if he could not capture the thing he prized most? He had told himself he would make Neris see the light, force her to recognize her place, but the hold of others was too strong on his beloved Delvori kin.

[When the time is right, we will face him together!] his lord had proclaimed as he prepared the last of the nectar maidens. The Virage's hold was no doubt the source of the malady that had eroded his sensibilities and locked his sister in chains of bitter malice. But was that true? Was he just deluding himself into believing that sordid lie when perhaps she was just a thrall of the world? Maybe they both were only slaves to their dead father's will, forever driven by a fear of and a lust for abuse.

Nerin did not know how long the space around him seemed to stretch and distort in the near-perfect darkness of the blackening night, but he did not care. Sometimes he scanned his surroundings, his rust-hued irises wide and dilated. Everything seemed to be falling away. Still frames of non-locomotive change flashed in his brain. At times he felt as if he were sitting upon his bed contemplating the madness around him. Other times he felt aloof as if traveling a great distance in little time.

[I'll come back for you. I promise.] Nerin pursed his lips as his face curled in scorn. His eyes were drawn shut as visages of a little black-skinned girl rolled between the folds of his brain. In those dark days, neither of them knew the truth of those who disappeared in the covered black carts. Neither of them understood what end a prisoner would meet once sold to the brown- and gold-skinned traders from afar. Nerin had run in the dark of the night as his father howled for his affections. He had found the small cages used for animals and children, among them the frail Delvori that had not respected her blood. How much had he longed for the day she'd return? How many nights had he screamed for his sister, begging to be saved? And still, she never came back.

[Be empty.] A chorus of all-too-familiar voices erupted in him as Nerin stood paralyzed for several moments. Spinning within the darkness, he felt as if the floor had changed out from under him. He felt the ground. His warm feet fondled what he imagined was the smooth, damp stonework of some ancient structure. The scent of decaying wood mixed with that of dusty, rotting mortar. Silence ruled the space around him, save for echoes of a single droplet from some deep well.

[Free yourself.] The words welled up from the ether once more. Nerin watched as small green lights sprang into existence all around him. What courage and willpower had denied him, madness and fatigue had provided. Surrounded by a dome of tiny mirrors reflecting his shade-like visage, Nerin stood once more in the hallowed hall of the ancient recess deep beneath the Hyunisti great tree. In the light of the small wisps, the room seemed to be someplace out of space. At the heart of the chamber, a vortex of mist and green-hued miasma churned and frothed. To his eyes, the pulsing tempest took on fanciful shapes, everything from faces to bodies reaching from deep within the well-like sepulcher of the sacred place.

"You've finally come to, my young master," his adviser said, his ethereal voice echoing within the room. From the convulsing clouds of spite, a black-robed monstrosity emerged. Its size and shape were unlike anything Nerin had seen, but he knew the figure to be none other than the great Madrus Ohran. "Here at last to receive the final blessing I would bestow upon you."

"How did I get here?" Nerin asked, his words slurring as he stumbled in place. A wave of nausea overtook him as he bent forward. The solid stone tiles emitted a fetid odor that threatened to overturn his stomach. "Lord Ohran, what's happening?"

"Your regret and desires hold you back, my young master," the dark-robed thing replied, speaking in a voice comprised of a thousand trembling screams as it paced soundlessly behind him.

Imagery of the previous nights percolated from deep within Nerin's brain as he watched the ancient mage take one maiden after the next. Thaimi's pale, limp body bubbled up as his thoughts found her splayed and subdued by the thrashing of the ancient mage. Then his mind's eye turned inward as he saw Neris standing before him, her red eyes wide with terror and defiance. Then it was if he were upon her, the black, writhing mass of education and breaking put into effect on the woman who held the reins of his psyche. Coughing and gagging, Nerin spun back as the fever dream reached its climax. His sister choked and writhed as the endless stream of shadow filled her being to the point of bursting. Then she fell flat against the darkness, her obsidian shell subdued.

"Stop!" Nerin commanded the endless whispering things around him. What trickery was this? Did his master wish to break his sister as he had broken the weak, pathetic things of the village? Was this the answer to his emotional dilemma? No, Nerin yearned for her obedience, her supplication, but it had to come willingly. "Lord Ohran, why are you—"

"Why am I, young master?" The small, audible fragments spoke in unison as Nerin found himself bent over once more. His stomach heaved, and dark chunks of food and fluid splattered across the floor. "Do you not remember?"

"Remember what?" Nerin could barely talk as his stomach lurched again.

What came up caught in his throat several times before he could force it out. The taste was full of bile, the acrid flavors and smells surrounding him. He went to speak but found his red eyes drifting about the room. Near the giant stone doors, three women stood, garbed in pale cotton as they looked upon his hunched frame. Stumbling, Nerin approached them, his eyes filled with relief as he made his way across the cold stonework. But as he reached them, he was taken aback as their dead green eyes, which were fixated on his face. Within their pupils, he saw thousands of green, sputtering lights. Beneath their dresses, their bodies twisted and reshaped as if something unwholesome writhed beneath the cloth.

In the back of his brain, Nerin heard a small boy's voice calling for Neris once more. In response, visions of his broken sister flashed before him again and again. He felt the warmth being sucked out of her writhing black body. He could taste the fibrous, textured recesses of her gut and throat. His hands and feet were sticky with blood and mucus. He felt her muscles and bones around him as he filled her from every hole, every pore. Expanding inside her body, Nerin felt her bones cracking against his growing frame. The sound of her pumping blood and splitting muscle fibers played against his eardrums like strings and percussion. Then, in one sordid mark, everything around him popped and collapsed.

Like a lump of meat, he lay beside her and watched Neris's twisted, shattered frame seep blood and worse onto the ground. The scene flashed as each maiden's broken body replaced that of his beloved. All at once, their empty faces reshaped. Emptiness was replaced by pleasure. Pleasure was dismissed by fear. Then in a last grotesque show, each one screamed, their wails amplified by the chamber's domed recesses. Then it all stopped. In a blur of motion, each one faded out of the room, their wraiths confused and demented as they left the space. A sense of repulsion and devastation hung about his psyche as their emotions washed over his skeletal remains.

With the dreamlike visions fading, Nerin Delvori clutched his stomach as he lay upon the ground. He watched as his maiden triplets contorted nearby, and with a look of pure horror, he thought he saw each doubled. Screaming pitch-black blobs rolled near each contorting body. Scythe-like nails reached toward him as each blamed him for their torments. The green gases and dancing flames multiplied innumerably in the space of the room as he tried to roll away. The faces of the three pale things stayed fixed upon him, their eyes filled with terror as their white, toothy grins gnashed in joy at his revival.

"I didn't . . . I thought . . ." Nerin's stomach twisted into knots as he rose from the ground. The robed figure was nowhere to be seen as Nerin backed up the stairs in the middle of the chaos.

"You thought what?" a voice like thousands asked under his breath as he stumbled backwards.

He then understood the horrors around him. With a scream, he looked down upon his perfect black frame. Yelping, he scratched at his arms, watching as the sinew and muscle contorted underneath his smooth black skin. Thoughts of running from the place filled his brain. Images of his sister played before his eyes, sacrificing herself once more for whatever innocence she could spare. Then the memory disappeared as quickly as he had recalled it.

"I sacrificed for this!" Nerin screamed. "I sacrificed to attain greatness, mage! You promised me power! You promised me a way to save her!"

"Yes, you're sacrificing so much." The words crept up from his throat as he took another step back. The three white things crawled toward him. He could not bear to look as the frightening women shambled like broken dogs upon the stone steps. "But to achieve greatness, you must abandon all desire. You must be free of doubt. Be empty of all hollow ambition."

"All of this was to be mine!" Nerin shouted to the emptiness as raucous laughter escaped his lungs. The maddening squeal was like splintering glass to his black, furry ears. His eyes spun in his head as he tried to maintain control. "I won't . . . I can't . . ."

Nerin shook his head as he felt the edge of the great well at the room's center. The three white things in front of him continued their approach, cutting off any direct means of retreat. Like a small child, he shivered in the gathering miasma. His neck was stoppered as his body tried to heave once more. His loins and bowels let go as he cried out a name he could not remember. A woman was somewhere in his memories, her dark face and red-eyed features equal to his. Her name was right upon his tongue, but he could not recall it. It was the same as his but effeminate. Then the greatest horror dawned upon him as he lost the last bit of self he could muster. Every memory of himself was disappearing in the green haze around him.

"Be empty, ne vivahr." His heart leapt as a dark swirl within the gas came forward. Dark hair and black skin met his gaze as he tried to reach out. Overcome by weakness, he leaned back.

With a crash and a cold embrace, the dark waters of the sepulcher sapped what little strength remained in his body. All thoughts gave way to darkness as the sense that was Nerin Delvori dissolved into the emptiness around him.

42

___

ERROR

They had watched as Nerin descended into the dark hollow of the village's great tree Surrounded by thousands of grateful souls he was freed from the bonds of mortal complacency. Through the love of all that dwelled within him, their host had lost all feelings of sadness and joy. Reason was without purpose, as were hope and misery. All that existed was oneness, a beautiful finality to which the flesh's eyes had been exposed. They were empty and free, but one more task remained. To free the village, they must break their past. The must break the matron shackled by knowledge and history. They silence the great chaos in their midst. And without a link to the obvious, the many within her needed bait.

Wandering through the night, they heard the howls of the Hyunisti people. As the villagers danced near smoldering pyres, they felt their souls harmonizing. Looking out over the grand circle of the elders from on high, they saw the flesh shells of the talvuo look onwards as the shades of their bonded selves circled and chanted. Their wraiths cried in fear and anguish, all the while wearing expressions of bliss as their visages hollowed into perfect placidity. Soon they would all feel the glorious existence of being empty and free.

Looking up to the stars as they wandered, a tinge of horror overtook the smallest of the shell called Thaimi's thoughts. At their side was none other than her own shade as it clawed frantically at their being. The ghost of the past and present wanted back inside, to be one with them again. With its penetrating tendrils, they felt a hint of dread. A fear of unity and the morrow filled the wastes of their mind. Purpose was threatened with confusion caused by what little brain remained. But no matter how hard it tried, the many inside the girl would not be deterred.

[Be empty, be free,] they whispered in unison with the tiniest essence of her remaining soul.

Passing a mead-drunk hunter, they felt their body's heart skip a beat as images of love and dreams flashed before their many eyes. Not long ago, Thaimi had wished to love. Growing up the daughter of a gatherer and huntswoman, she had never given it much thought as to where her life would lead. At the far reaches of what was once her mind, the stories told by her parents dwelled. The tales had been passed down by their parents, others before them, and the golden-haired talvuo governing their past.

Together they remembered the story of Hyun's lover, Temer Emri. The pair had been bonded since childhood: she a forester and he a musician. For a generation, they grew and shared in their love. Temer wrote ballads and tunes about the forest folk, inspiring dance and merriment. Hyun fostered deeper cooperation with the mages to ensure her people a place in the woods of Lorin. With magic taught by human hands, the pair wove a spell of prosperity and growth through the woodlands and hills. But then the war came, and the mages needed the Emri to help them secure the woods from their vassals turned enemies. The chiefs of the Emri agreed, so Temer's songs became of war, and Hyun's trees were bent toward the making of walls and siege works.

Theirs was a sad tale of two lovers as old as the trees themselves. Thaimi's young heart couldn't stand the thought. The girl had shed tears of sadness and hope. She wished for a bright future for the pair, but the story was always the same. In the end, Temer died at the hands of Grannas assassins meant to kill his beloved, and the woman retreated into anger and desperation. Then the Hyunisti were saved by a grand act of sacrifice, protected from the outside world by the rites of the last Emri chiefs and priests. They became the Hyunisti to honor her, something their host had loved and endeared in her heart. The dreams and romance of the people's history and future had made the maiden's heart swell to the point of bursting. She had wanted to see and embrace the oncoming days.

The fading memory of a hope-filled girl's shadow gripped them by the neck. It wanted them to feel how that girl felt, to remember what happiness and despair could be like. But they had shown her the truth.

[Emptiness is freedom,] the thousand voices of called from deep within her.

Yes, as they strolled in the cold night air clad in nothing but a flowing sheet of cotton, they were unfazed. They felt the cold, but it did not make them shiver. The grain of the wood beneath them was rough and coarse, but it did not scrape their feet. The pale moonlight above, illuminating the starry sky in the purple morass of the heavens, was but an affront to the one simple truth. Though the light and stars burned in frantic abandon against the dark, they were lost to absolution. Only the dark was luminous. Indeed, the more they looked upon the sky, the more their frame's empty eyes saw the real face of chaos. Each pinprick of starlight was a well of despair, and the moon was like the harbinger of doom. Only the infinite cosmos and brightness of the nothing held the ultimate truth.

The shreds of what was once Thaimi feared the final release, but Thaimi could do nothing to stop it. They were already moving forward together. And together, they would be as one with all at last.

"Thaimi," a tiny voice whispered by her side. They looked down through pale, glazed orbs at the small, skinny frame of a tiny talvuo girl. The girl's bright green eyes were full of timidity as she clutched their deathly white hand. "Are you sure it's OK? Zaisure said she was right outside. Zaisure said I should—"

"Everything will be fine, my dear. We're just going to the great tree. Zaisure will be there, I promise," they replied in time with Thaimi's resonating vocal cords, forming a cohesive whole. "Your mother will be there too."

"Thaimi?" the little girl asked, her voice wavering.

With their slender, milk-colored arms, they bent down and hugged the little girl. At their side, the ghoulish face of Thaimi's regret screamed and scratched, tearing at them and the little girl. Black puddles of bile inched down from its empty eye sockets, dripping like phantom tears as it tried to pummel their arms.

"Now, now, Rais. It will be OK. I told you, zaisure Elis will be there!" Pitch perfect, they sang in the young talvuo woman's voice. "You'll see. Vivahr Nerin and even that scary human will be there."

"Davnian will be there too?"

"Why, yes, didn't I already tell you?" they said as they moved into position, the woman's bones shifting. With confidence and precise delivery, their body stood up while smiling at the little girl. "We don't want to keep them waiting, do we?"

"Nnnnnn-nn . . . No!" the bashful little thing exclaimed.

"Good," they said, laughing in response.

As they turned to lead the way, Thaimi's weakening spirit clung to the little girl's body. The young talvuo's ghost looked onward, empty-eyed, confused, and uncertain. The vengeful spirit tried everything it could to reach out to the little one's ghoul. Despite their similar states, they were disjointed in their realms of existence. Nothing the ghost could do could reach the little girl or her shade.

"Evening, vindal," a huntsman said as they crossed the last terrace before the great tree.

"Evening, vivahr Bedimer," they replied, flashing their dull green eyes in the moonlight.

"Evening, little Rais. Where's Elis?"

"We're going to meet her!" Rais said, her voice full of puzzled excitement. "Thai . . . Thaimi came to fetch me!"

"Is that so, vindal?" Bedimer watched them as they continued. The little girl danced as she held their right hand, stumbling as she tried to keep up with and face the onlooker.

"Come now, dear," they said in Thaimi's voice.

"Well, see you then, girls," the old huntsman said as the two of them continued on.

"Bye bbbb . . . ye," the little talvuo girl wheezed as they dragged her on.

For the briefest moment, Thaimi's wraith embraced the grizzled hunter, the black putrescence of its tears and gaping maw covering him. For the tiniest instance, they thought they detected the faintest glimmer of change in the old hunter's stance. His grey eyes flickered toward them for the briefest look before turning back. Beside him, twin shades turned their heads.

"Ttthh . . . Thaimi . . ." the little girl stammered as they crossed the bridge, entering the great tree's dark foyer.

"We're almost there, little one," they said, leading the girl to the spiral of the tree. "Just a little farther."

Excited and scared, Rais followed them as they descended into the depths of the ancient structure.

43

———

ELIS

Elis lay on her back for several moments, her heart pounding. The night air danced across every inch of her exposed, gilded skin, gooseflesh percolating across her outstretched arms and chest. With deep breaths, she stared up through the shallow branches, looking at the stars and waning moon far above. Beside her, Davnian's breath mimicked her own as his heat warmed the drops of perspiration cradled between their naked bodies.

"Gods," Elis whispered.

Looking up at the twinkling lights spread across the black velvet of endless space, every nerve in her body tingled. Her nipples stung from the roughness, and her head was abuzz with dizzying romantic queries. For moments it had seemed like they were sharing each other's bodies. During others it felt like they had switched.

Elis closed her eyes, taking a moment to gather her thoughts. Like every spring, she heard dancing and laughter, sharp cries of promiscuity coupled with cheers and song. It was the one time of year that the people could find their voices and their feet, but this time it seemed that the whole forest was joining in. The entire wood was part of their party.

"That looks much better on you," Davnian said.

Turning her head, Elis looked at him as he smiled. His eyes were like snow as he caressed her hand within his. A tuft of her golden hair fell upon her chest.

"That smile. It's like the one you wear with her. Soft, gentle."

Davnian reached out and touched the corner of her grin with his claw. Elis laughed as he traced it down around her neck, the tip of his blackened fingers tickling her skin. As he ran his dark hand through her gilded locks, Elis leaned toward him. He curled over her, planting a warm kiss upon her lips.

"You smile like you always do," Elis whispered, nuzzling his chin, "but your eyes are softer than they used to be."

"Is that right?" Drawing her close, he nuzzled her red, speckled ears, his teeth nipping at the folds.

"Stop." Elis pushed him back and watched as he collapsed beside her, laughing. "You keep playing that game, and I won't be able to let you off without recompense, young man."

"Recompense?" Davnian mocked. "You make it sound like I'm indebted."

"You will be if you keep that up." Elis curled her right arm and leg around him, burying her head in his stiff brown hair. The alcohol was still nipping at her lips and head as she sighed. "I'm not in the mood," Elis teased, twirling his hair in her fingers.

"Good idea. You climb over me, and I might make you stay up there."

"Not a chance, young man." Elis sighed once more.

They were quiet for a bit beneath the stars, chuckling at the nonsense going through their heads as they danced their fingers upon each other's frames. The night was getting on, and though the party-goers continued their debauchery, she felt the darkness tugging at her. Time was spinning round and round, and her every nerve wanted to stay in that moment forever. Sleep called to her as the chill of the night was numbed by the warmth of Davnian beside her. But he needed to go, and she had two promises to keep come morning.

"The night is going long, isn't it?" Davnian asked, his claw clutching her right hand.

"It is," she replied as he drew her hand to his face and placed a warm kiss on her palm.

"There's someone who'd love to curl up with you." Davnian rubbed his cheek against her hand, taking a deep breath.

"I shouldn't keep her waiting much longer."

Melancholy worked across Elis's features, her ruby-haired ears slouching as she buried her head into Davnian's arm. Taking a deep breath, she inhaled the smells of his skin and hair, taking in the shared ardor brewed between them.

"Don't wear that face," he whispered as he touched his claw to her cheek. Looking up, she saw him staring down, wearing the same gentle smile and soft eyes. "Your daughter needs her mother, and I want nothing less than for you to return the need. And I've been kept away too long."

"Davnian." His name was on her tongue as she planted her lips against his shoulder. He was right, and in her heart, she had a need as well. To be close to Rais and curl around her. To protect her. Brightening, Elis shot him a coy grin. "I guess you have the right of it, young man."

"You're going to keep calling me that, aren't you?"

"You'll always be a young man to me," Elis whispered.

She drew herself over him. Leaning down, her golden hair blanketed his face as she kissed his lips one last time. Pulling back, she stared into his eyes, looking at her own lavender orbs reflected in the darkness between them.

"Shall we, good woman?"

Elis and Davnian gathered up the remnants of their evening. Tucking the loose bottles away, Elis donned her evening gown. Davnian draped his loose red-and-blue striped tunic back over himself, taking the time to adjust his pants and sash. With a nod, Elis led the way while Davnian carried the basket and leftovers behind her.

Turning the last round of the narrow rung-way, Elis planted her foot on the terrace behind her home. She reached out and helped Davnian down the final step of the plank trail.

"Thank you," he said as she turned away.

"You're welcome."

Elis's feelings were hard to contain. Davnian had more than entertained her. He had let himself be swayed by her inhibitions and her longings. The severity in his mood had dissipated as they loved each other. For that, she was thankful. Behind her, she heard his body stiffening. He had to leave, and portents of a new life hung before her. No, it was just a precaution, but she had to keep the promise at this point. Otherwise, everything would be just like it was then, with her taking everything and giving up nothing.

"Elis," Davnian put his hand on her shoulder as she went to step into her home.

"Yes?" she almost shrieked.

"We didn't leave the door open, did we?"

Elis furrowed her brow as she looked at the open door. With a hiccup, she gulped down a gasp of sweet honey-flavored exasperation. Then it dawned on her. The room was dark on the other side, and through the window on the left side was not a drop of candlelight. But there sat the door, ajar. Elis's stomach dropped.

"No, we didn't," she said.

Hurrying through the portal, she dropped the bottles at the door and crossed the shrouded main room. As she reached the door of their shared bedroom, she donned a warm smile to comfort her little girl.

"Rais, I'm sorry I was out so long—" Elis's voice caught in her throat as she investigated the empty darkness of the bedroom. Where her daughter should be was a clump of crumpled quilt and kneaded pillow. A wave of nausea bubbled up through her chest and neck. Her face flushed, burning as she shuffled in the space.

"She's not here," Davnian said, coming in behind her.

"No, that's not—"

Elis turned around and pushed past Davnian. With a nervous laugh, she bent down, looking beneath the table.

"Rais, dear, why are you . . ."

The girl wasn't hiding beneath the table.

"Oh, I know where you are," Elis whispered to herself, storming for the door.

"Elis, wait!" Davnian called after her.

"Now, now, little one." Elis put on a playful act as she went behind her house. She turned to the open space just opposite the narrow plank walkway. Spying a few stacked crates and a barrel, Elis grinned to herself and marched toward the column. "Were you spying back here?"

"Elis!" Davnian called.

Elis's eyes went wide with confusion. Rais wasn't there either.

"I don't . . . I don't understand."

"Elis, she's not here. Rais isn't here." Davnian turned her about as he gripped her by the shoulders. Looking up at him, her hands began to shake. "Easy now, Elis. Easy."

"Davnian, where's Rais? Where's my . . ." Her voice was frail as her thoughts raced.

"Elis, I don't know. But she couldn't have gotten far, right?"

"Why would she . . . why . . . Davnian, where's my daughter?"

"Elis, calm yourself. We need to think clearly." Davnian gripped her arms.

"Don't tell me what to do!" Elis snapped, shaking away his hands. "Quit telling me to be calm! Where's my daughter? Where's Rais, Davnian?"

"I don't know," he said, enunciating each syllable. "But shouting isn't going to get us anywhere, Elis. We need to look for her."

She wanted to yell at him for his flat lines and low voice, but looking into his eyes, she saw his concern. Still shaking and with upset bubbling at the back of her tongue, she pushed past him once more and marched into the house.

"What are you doing, Elis?"

"Getting her blanket," she said, fetching the girl's quilt. The tiniest trace of Rais's body heat filled Elis with hope as it transferred from the cloth to her skin. Fighting back a sob, Elis stormed out of the room. "It's still warm. She can't be far."

"OK then."

"Where are we going to look?" Elis asked.

"She's probably looking for us, or maybe someone came by, and she thought to follow."

"OK, then where—"

"Elis, you're still flush in the face. I can go grab Neris, and we'll scour the—"

"You will not leave me here while she's lost, Davnian!" Elis pummeled him with her bundle. "She needs me, Davnian! I'm not staying!"

"Elis . . ."

"I'm not waiting, Davnian!" Her voice could be heard through the whole round as she screamed. In the moonlight, Davnian's face was taciturn as his eyes betrayed annoyance. Raising her quilted arms once more, she went to smack him upside the head.

"Fine!" Davnian said, sighing as he braced for the impact. As she lowered her arms, he continued. "You know these treetops better than I do. You'd be better off navigating and checking the terraces. She's likely to be near people, no? I'll check the infirmary and the few nooks beside. I'll keep my eyes open."

"Alright then," Elis said as her chest filled and fell. Her nerves were on edge as she thought about what they could do. She could navigate the dark pathways blind and drunk if need be. "If I see her," she said, shaking, "I'll bring her to the grand terrace, the one by the great tree. If you do the same, we should be able to spot each other from almost anywhere."

"Great idea," Davnian said, wrapping his arms around her. Before she could return the gesture, he backed away. "Be careful, Elis. I'm going to head the long way around just in case she wandered a weird way. I saw a small bridge running off the far edge. If I don't see anything in the infirmary or great tree, I'll weave back around the large treetop huts on the other side. If I get lost, I'll go back to the great terrace."

"OK," Elis said. She tried to visualize his path, but her head was too full of clamor to keep up. "That sounds good."

"Everything will be alright," Davnian said.

"I hope so," Elis said. She was on the verge of tears as she tried to steel herself. Davnian closed the gap between them and kissed her on the forehead. She wanted to scream at him for tempting her away, to beat him down for making her forget her path. "Davnian, I . . ."

Before she could finish, he disengaged.

"When we find her," he said, shaking his head.

Without another word, he departed to the far edge of the village. As he disappeared into the dark, Elis swallowed and then began walking down the opposite path. The distant throngs of dancing villagers beckoned her, and hopefully among them awaited her missing little girl.

44

ERROR

Outside, his brothers and sisters sang songs happy and sad for the first time in years, making what they could of a celebration meant to honor their past and pave the way for their future. They burned treasured and ancient belongings, including those of their founder. They walked barefoot and drank wine, mead, and forest teas. They ate their fill of berries and fruits, mushrooms, and vegetables. There was a sense of oncoming joy, though one he could not embrace.

[Loss and pain are worse than nothing,] a tiny voice whispered into his scruffy, timber-colored ears.

Bedimer was not one for merrymaking and parties. The spring festival itself was something he oft avoided, save for curbing his desires if only for a short while. Lovemaking was something he abstained from in his later years, feeling the burden of losing child after child, lover after lover. The forest away from the village was his rightful home. Out there, he felt at peace. Among the trees, he could lie in wait, silent and focused upon the hunt. Meditating on those ends was something he could do without a second thought, and aside from whether he brought back game or not, no one would pay for his dallying. Passion was a burden as much as a refuge.

[Don't listen, please hurry,] a different voice called in his head. This one was more familiar, but he tried not to heed it.

He did not like how things had changed around the village since the Delvori pair arrived. The male was a backstabbing fiend who wanted to change everything about their way of life. The female was a seductress, though aside from breaking a few hearts, he bore her no ill will. She was smart and unyielding. She wouldn't let him ruin her future with his needs, though in all honesty, that was beside the point.

[You must hurry,] it cried again, the shrill wail paining him.

After Thaimi and Rais had breached the entryway of the great tree, Bedimer had begun tracking the duo. Letting his thoughts wander, he feigned naturalness as he traced their footsteps. Something had been off with the way the young woman had spoken to him. Coupled with the little girl's confusion, the matter only served to heighten his suspicion. He knew Elis was nowhere near the great tree, having spied her up on the terrace above her home, entwined in the arms of the black hand. All of that, coupled with the onset of insipid voices, unnerved but drove him forward.

Thinking on the mature young woman, Bedimer considered how he had been suspicious of all the would-be nectar maidens of late. The way they clung to the Delvori when near him to the familiar yet hollow way they interacted with those around them when apart, something about it all made his gut churn. He had thought that the monster would be the more dangerous of the two beasts, but it seemed he had been proven wrong of late.

Keeping his ears perked, he walked to the spiral passage that bordered the outer round of the great tree's interior. Above, he heard the faint echoes of the clamor from outside, no hints of activity piquing his interest. Focusing on the downward end, he made out the faintest thud of steps on soft flooring, the pitter-patter of more pointed feet with it. No doubt the pair had descended, but where to he could only guess. There was no smell of wax or burning timber or heated paper. No, they had plunged into the depths in the dark with no light to guide their way.

[Yes, this way!]

[Come, come,] another voice joined in, mocking the first.

Bedimer had always wondered when his mind would go. A man could only take so much sadness and grief before breaking. He had seen men and women whom he held as sterner crumble as their loved ones passed away. Children ripped from their mother's wombs, dozing lovers' spirits departed in the dead of night, these were but a few of the travesties that were ascribed to their curse. Some of those who were left behind would just disappear into the woods, never to return. Others would be found starved to death huddled at the feet of the great trees. Others slit their own throats while still others had found their end at the horns of one of the great beasts of the wood.

He did not mourn those who fled or laid themselves to rest, for they left life on their own terms. He did not despise them because he too had lost many. In many ways, he envied them. They were free of the curse of their blood and could be reunited with those they had lost.

Pacing down the dark hall, Bedimer decided against using his silver lantern. He couldn't risk being detected just in case the young maiden had become rash or unbalanced. Keeping his right hand fixed on his scabbard, he stalked the passage with ears at full attention.

As he reached the landing of the great tree, he spied around the shrouded floor for another method of egress. A giant locked gate led out to the forest floor. The feet were still moving down below, a hint of dampness clinging to their movements as they proceeded deeper. Accompanying them was the almost inaudible hum of something deep within the earth. After a quick search, he found a hole he had never seen with a ramp that should not exist. The floor was sticky with sap and moisture, as if the entrance had just opened then and there. Following the sound, he continued onward.

There were stories of hidden depths far beneath the great tree, but no one had ever found a hint of the fabled place. Elis had told him a tale of Hyun's time and how the woman had forbidden others to seek out the ancient ruin but admitted that she had never seen the fabled depths. However, for something born out of wondrous tales, Bedimer had discovered the forgotten path. No doubt, the Delvori had opened the forbidden passage, spun by his incessant privilege claimed over everything in his demesne. How he had was yet to be seen.

[Farther, just a little farther,] the familiar voice pleaded.

[You can never forgive yourself. You can never be free,] a chorus countered, their words muddled to form a sound akin to grinding bones within his mind.

As menacing as their trickery was, they were right.

Years back, he had fallen in love with a fellow hunter, a young woman who had just come of age. Sarais Hyunisti was the daughter of a one-night stand between a porter and a forester. Raised by her porter mother and huntswoman lover, she had been taught the basics of each's craft. In short order, she had proven to be a natural when it came to trapping and scouting. Some days she would disappear on her own. When she returned, she would always bring a haul of her smaller catches and relay to the porters and fellow hunters spots where she had trapped game. She could set a blind and wait a week to spot the best prey, her patience knew no bounds.

One day he had gone on a hunt with Sarais. Together they spent a fortnight setting up a grand trap for a giant elk that marauded the eastern proximity of Hyunisti territory. Though he had loved and lost many times, he could not help but be drawn to her resourcefulness and intelligence. On that fateful trip, he had lost himself in her gaze, and before they seized their prize, he had lost himself in her embrace. The next day her traps had pinned the gigantic creature. With a steady aim, he had downed the beast with a single shot. It was the stuff of campfire tales, and when they returned, they had been celebrated for the bounty and the endearment.

Before long, Bedimer learned that she was with child. The proud and resourceful young woman had stared him down, asking him if he would be the child's father. How many times had he been asked that same question? How many times had it been fruitless? But despite all that, he said he would, and without another word, the pair returned to their routine.

Over the coming months, Bedimer and Sarais had spent a few days together at a time, sometimes on the hunt, sometimes between. Neither was bound to the idea of a household, relying on the support of the other hunters and young woman's mothers. They both loved their craft, but as Sarais's belly swelled, her warmth began to expire.

At first Sarais glowed, as all new mothers did. The joy and power of motherhood overtook her essence as it became impossible to hide her growing burden. Bedimer's heart had raced in love and hope as he watched her continue strong. She had never seemed more alive as she planned and acted out each new expedition.

Six months in, her color started to fade. It was the little things at first, unyielding drowsiness that overtook her from time to time. She would miss a detail. The others told him it was to be expected, and he abided. But then there was the morning she did not leave her home. Concerned, he visited her and found her covered in a cold sweat, her loose cotton robe clinging to her frame as she shivered from head to toe. Her hands were wrapped around her plump belly, and tears streamed down her face.

[Is it going to take mine?] The ghosts of the past scratched the inside of his skull as he snuck downward. Where in time and space this place was taking him, he did not know.

[Ignore them, Bedimer,] another answered as it ushered him onwards.

Bedimer had consoled her all he could, but a month out, the young woman whom he had grown to love started to give in to fear. Madness overtook her in its own way as she planned something he had never conceived. One night she sat him down and spoke simply. She said she was going to leave the village and make for the Holan settlements in the east. He was dumbfounded. The idea of fleeing to raise a child had never crossed his mind. The thought was madness, given her condition. At best, they were a month away from the closest border town. Though Grannas villages were closer, he hazarded they would not be as welcoming. He tried to convince her that the plan was folly, and for a short time, she agreed with him.

Another month came, and Sarais started to lose herself. She spent most of her time off her feet, doing light work at her mothers' home. Bedimer checked on her each day, asking her if she would like to walk with him or come on a short vista just outside the village proper. Some days she would agree, and they would walk hand in hand. Sometimes she would look at him, her bright green eyes full of the intelligence and pride he had fallen in love with. Other times he could not recognize her. She was close to term by then, having carried her child all the way to the gates of birth. In this he was eased, as the very act of lasting so long was a good omen.

Then one evening, as they walked, Sarais asked him if he'd bring over her old jacket and pack. Without a second thought, he brought them, and that evening talked late into the night. Sarais confided all her dreams to him, of seeing her child grow up healthy and free of their shared suffering. He cradled her in his arms, agreeing with every word she spoke, telling her that they were almost there. He told her that he couldn't wait to meet the little one and wanted nothing more than to spend the rest of his life with the two of them. Perhaps that hope, that dream and its insistence, was their folly.

When he awoke that morning, his head was spinning. Beside their tiny shared mat was a small satchel. Within it was a meticulously drawn map with a trail leading eastward. Tucked alongside it, scrawled on a sheet of lantern paper, she had written how much she loved him and how happy they would be together. With great detail she imparted her plan, the precise motions and places he needed to go to track her down. Sarais had left in the middle of the night as the pains of child-birth began to overtake her. Her last words on that crumpled note were that she would deliver their child free of the village's specter, and then they could live together, happily ever after.

[Be empty.] Something terrifying crept up his spine as fleeting words etched through his brain. The winding passage was serpentine and covered with a slippery sickness that he could not place. It was as if he marched in the corridors of his brain as the thoughts and memories bubbled forth.

In the days that followed, after tracking the young woman for nights on end, Bedimer came upon her final resting place. Out in the wilds, she had given birth to a fragile, little thing. Clutching her breast, drawing from Sarais what it could, the little baby girl clung to life by a thread. Sarais's body cradled the infant, her warm green eyes glazed with the stain of death only hours past. Against the odds, the woman had held out in the hollow of a tree and waited. Only a short distance from the intended path she had hidden. If only they had not missed the signs, they could have been there before she succumbed. But perhaps that wasn't the worst of it. No, the worst was how she looked, a warm smile upon her frozen features as she looked down at the struggling life at her bosom. There was no hint of madness or fear, just the etched finality of love and care.

Bedimer had decided to wipe his hands of it all, unable to bear the burden of caring for their child. He had known loss and seen the strength of others falter. But never had he seen such passion and strength carried out for the sake of another. Their shared dream had survived, but he couldn't bear to hold onto it for fear that his slightest touch would break it. When their long-lived matron had pledged to raise the child as her own, Bedimer asked her only two things. Firstly to tell her about her mother's strength. Secondly, to have the girl bear her namesake, for she was a survivor just like the woman who birthed her. Elis had promised to do so.

[Let it go, be free,] another voice with the same haunting tone said from every direction as he stepped onto a cold stone floor. He had traveled down a great depth, trailing Thaimi and the girl who he had given up. If it had been any other child, would he have cared to trail the glossy-eyed maiden? He didn't know, but something inside told him he had to follow. He should have stopped them before they left, but it was too late to take that back. It was too late to take any of it back. This was not the time for regrets or bereavement. It was time for action. In a sick twist, a voice wove through his left ear, mocking the tone of the woman he had lost. [Be empty, Bedimer. Be free.]

Bedimer did not reply. He had been told once that the strongest memories, passions, and feelings clung to a person, waiting for their final moment to live once more. Whether it was madness, trickery, or perhaps his finality, it did not matter. He had lived a life empty of commitments for years, trusting only his sword, his spear, his bow, and his wits. The time for second-guessing was passed. The lantern of his forefathers and foremothers in hand, he decided to illuminate the darkness.

Opening the hood of his silver box, the bright crystal within sent a beam of piercing white light through the halls of the ancient ruin. Drawing his sword, his murky grey eyes fixed on the point farthest away. In a flash, the dark stone interior radiated as if consumed by the brilliance of the sun. There at the far end of the room was the little talvuo girl in a white dress. Behind her lurked a set of giant stone doors. Looking at her, he realized her green eyes were filled with terror before she was forced to cover them.

"Rais!" Bedimer cried. He lifted the lantern with his right hand and readied his sword in his left. He stepped forward as the giant stonework at the end of the hall creaked open. The frame of some shadow emerged like smoke from its depths. "Rais, behind you!"

"Bedimer!" the little girl screamed as the unnatural darkness fell over her.

Taking another step forward, he prepared to sprint. Then above him, he heard the rumble of shifting stone. Turning his gaze for a split second, his grey eyes peered upwards just long enough to catch the sight of a small, spinning pebble.

[Be empty, Bedimer,] a monster whispered in his lover's voice as he gritted his teeth.

With a sickening crunch, he felt the weight of the world descend upon him. His bones shattered under a mass of giant stones and dirt. He had had just enough time to throw his arms forward. In the dizzying moments, as blood burst forth from his mouth and nostrils and the goo of his innards spread upon the cold gravel beneath him, Bedimer glimpsed his spared artifacts. A dismal wish clung to his heart, hoping that someone would follow his path.

With one last straining lurch, his vision reddened as his mind emptied. There in his reddened view, a cotton-garbed maiden bent down to him, her green eyes smiling.

"Be empty," she said with a thousand voices, each one mimicking Sarais Hyunisti.

[Be free.]

45

DAVNIAN

Stepping into the shadow of the great tree of the Hyunisti village had sent shivers of dread up Davnian's spine. Yet every nerve in his body directed him back to the miasma-filled trunk of the wraith-filled town. Telling himself to split up with Elis was not easy, but he knew it was for the best. A darkness lurked somewhere deep within the ancient growth, and at its heart was something monstrous.

[I think having her and that dancing briar of hers would have been a better choice,] the other in his head whispered as if trying to conceal itself from unseen forces. [We aren't even armed, and you've already exerted yourself more than enough for one day, young one.]

[If there's a mad sorcerer or worse down here, I'd rather her have a chance to flee than to die with us,] Davnian replied as he stumbled in the dark. The trail of noxious spirit gas bellowed from deep within the earth, skulking through the long spiral passage that rounded the outside of the great tree's interior. Clinging to it, the wails and ghastly faces of the dead seemed to manifest, unseen by all but him. [Gods know an even worse fate may be awaiting.]

[Let us pray for her and the little girl that you're wrong.] It was the first time he had heard an honest wish from the shadow-scaled creature in his mind. The notion that something could be so unsettling to his cohabitating companion was enough to raise the hackles on his neck. Still, he was undeterred. [You really are positive she's here, aren't you?]

[I have perfect guides.]

Three ghastly things crept along the ground in front of him. One was a bubbling, frothy mass of some indescribable black matter with the face of a young Hyunisti maiden stretched over its slug-like form. The other two were the twin wraiths that had coupled the old huntsman earlier that day. The fact all three were so disembodied spoke to desperation that he could not place. Even worse was watching as they waited at Elis's door for him, no doubt aware of a fate crueler than any he could imagine. Had they been unable to find him up top? Or was it pure circumstance? Either way, it did not matter.

[You trust these ghosts?] the other asked. [Are they not just manifestations of a curse?]

[Using my own words against me? No, you're correct. But I was somewhat wrong,] Davnian reasoned, detached from the feeling as much as from the concepts he considered. [Like Rais's wraith, they're all reacting, like souls resonating with the unknown. They've been sold, but they still want to cling to life. Some are stronger than others, more resilient. Others are not. And some are displaced.] Thinking of the shadow that gripped the woman named Thaimi, he remembered how desperate the shade had been as it dug at the empty shell to which it clung. It was trying to claw its way back inside. Deep in the bile-dark recesses of its missing eyes, he had seen a flicker of light, a glow of intelligence and wanting. [They act out because they know their lives are forfeit.]

[This miasma, these forces, we are facing something that we have no way of predicting. And in your state . . .]

The other was correct. If Davian was forced into a confrontation with anything more than a helpless rodent, he would be at a disadvantage. Walking downward with the aid of gravity was causing his knees to creak, and every step tempted his lungs to gasp. But that was not allowable. Not within these haunted recesses. Despite the measured successes of his recovery, the very nature of the place was straining his being.

Coming to the bottom floor of the great tree, Davnian watched the shades wave him onward. The slug-like thing had chosen to cling to him instead, whimpering as he paced across the barren hall. As he stepped into the unnatural round, his boots snagged in something sticky and wet. The tree had opened the way to somewhere unholy, and his entire body told him to run in the opposite direction.

Ignoring his survival instinct, he continued his descent. The air had grown stale. The wispy vapor around him stoppered his nose and curled his tongue. Every sense was overpowered by the feeling of the immaterial substance as it clawed and thrust into his eyes, nose, ears, mouth, and pores. It felt like mud slithering upon his frame, mucus and saliva dripping inside his orifices. Like being in the belly of a giant beast, the mist wanted to dissolve him, to devour his very existence.

[You're getting weaker.] The black scale's voice shook like tumbling earth in his addled brain.

[I know.]

[We should go back, get help, find others.]

[I know.]

[But you won't.]

[I can't.]

The option to retreat and return was always open, but every moment delayed at this point inched Rais closer to whatever the abyss had in store for her. They could have mustered a group to head into the bowels of the tree. The voice was also right that Elis would have been a good companion, especially with the arcane tool he saw hanging in her home. Neris would have been a welcome comfort too if he could have found her. But his instincts were that whatever dwelled in the depths was beyond whatever weapons or talents any of them possessed. It was a fool's errand, and if someone had to play the fool, he would be the only joker hung for it.

[Your stoicism is charming,] the other mocked. Davnian couldn't help but grin as he took deep, low breaths. [Well, we know what kept you alive all that time of derangement, it seems.]

[Magic? Demonic powers? The abyss's unrelenting fury?]

[Dumb ego.]

Wearing a crooked grin, Davnian almost stumbled as he planted his foot on an uneven surface. The ground had finally leveled off. Beneath his thin leather soles, he felt what seemed to be stonework. From the other side of an archway, he made out the faintest glow. The hum of some unseen machination reached his ears, the resonance like that of a distant beehive. Dragging his feet, he hobbled through the entrance, turning down a large, dim corridor.

All around him, the place seemed alive with ancient, arcane energies, the hum permeating the walls and floor. Scattering beams of gold left thin trails of illumination throughout the long hallway, emanating from the other side of a large fallen piece of stone. Painted in the gilded rays, hundreds of engravings and small, embedded statues stared down upon him. The faces of ancient talvuo men and women were transfixed upon him.

[This place, it's just like . . .]

[Focus.]

The figures around him were dressed in ceremonial garb. Leathers and furs, wooden trinkets and holy symbols, flutes and pipes, harps and lutes, drums, staves, and the like were wielded or worn by enumerable figures. Ancient writing was etched into the walls, written in a language whose symbols were shared with that in Hyun's diaries but far older. Like the words of the mage empire of Lorin, the glyphs seemed to carry a supernatural weight to them.

[Can you understand any of this?]

[I don't need to. Just look at the depictions,] the other whispered.

Indeed, there was no reason to read. The imagery all around them showed mages lined up in various rituals, inscribing wards into the stone and ground. As he walked through the hallway, the number and apparent rank of the individuals practicing the art rose. As his eyes drifted, they fixed on the stone doors at the end of the hall, the slimmest rays resting upon the split picture.

Mages and talvuo of ancient times stood hand in hand, their arms outstretched to the middle of a great circle. From them, lines of power flowed, forming a rippled and spotted series of concentric circles around the image of a twisting mass. The mass formed a face, its visage seeming to change and drift with the shimmering of the light. Rising above it was the countenance of a robed man, his head tilted upwards, and his mouth open in what he could only surmise was a scream.

[Ohran.] Davnian thought the name of the mage he was sure was depicted. Images of the screaming, pleading old man filled his head as his body twisted and contorted between his robes. He had said no prison could contain him, and no magic could hold him. He had begged Davnian to release him from its clutches, the thing that was devouring him from the inside. But Davnian had failed to destroy him, it seemed, choosing instead to seal him in the great vaults of the Delvori as a last precaution. He had hoped to find a means to end the mad sorcerer's suffering someday. [This was one of his first prisons.]

[Gods, you're right,] the other acknowledged, the sense of realization sweeping through the whole of their shared mindscape. [Does that mean the Emri and the Lorinians did this?]

[This structure must be at least as old as the Lorinian Empire, maybe even older.]

Watching the dual wraiths as they drifted beside fallen stone, Davnian followed. They stopped in front of him, beckoning him forward. As he approached, they disappeared into the dim light. He held his breath as the odor of oxidizing iron and stomach acids assailed his nostrils. Fresh death clung to the air around him as he stumbled, his foot grazing the edge of something sharp and metallic. Kneeling, he felt the small cut in his leathers as he scanned the floor. There beneath his feet and scattered upon the stonework were the remains of an old talvuo male, his squashed entrails just starting to coagulate and congeal in the putrid environment.

[Gods,] Davnian thought as he looked the man over. Turning his face upwards, he stared into the blood-filled eyes of Bedimer. [It's the old hunter from this afternoon.]

[Looks like he went looking where he shouldn't,] the other hissed. [Looks like he had his sword drawn.]

[And his lantern.] Davnian leaned over and picked up the dented silver box. Creaking the hood open, he spied the arcane stone at its center. Cracked, it spilled scattering golden rays, though with the aid of the mirror and focused opening, it still worked well enough.

[Grab the sword and light, and let's hurry.]

Picking up the old hunter's thinblade, Davnian returned his gaze to the end of the hall. Bedimer had tracked someone or something there and paid for it with his life. He had hunted the same quarry that Davnian was hunting now. With a quiet prayer, he continued, thanking the ghosts for their guidance. Upon his shoulder, the last of the ghouls gripped him. The stretched face shrank and drew itself to his ear.

[I'm sorry,] it whispered.

Steadying the sword in his right hand, Davnian paced down the hall, the miasma filling his lungs with every breath. His grip was weak as he clutched the sword. Hooking the lantern in his claw, he illuminated the space between him and the door. Dancing flickers of light sparked from the vast expanse beyond. Air hissed through the opening paces ahead, icy wind cutting through his thin garments. Shivering, he continued onwards, listening for anything more than the drip of moisture from the jutting tree roots around him.

[Davnian, that . . .]

His ears perked up, the sound of dripping water and humming disappearing into the background as the low, weak echoes of sobs reached his drums.

[Rais!]

Adrenaline coursed through Davnian's veins, releasing the restraints on his atrophied limbs. From his hobbled walk, he broke into a clumsy sprint, dodging over jutting stone and debris. Without a second thought, he slid through the open stone gate, entering the room on the other side.

Caught unaware, he was blinded as the light of his lantern scattered and refracted all around him. The golden rays bounced this way and that, reflecting off thousands of tiny mirrored surfaces that lined the room's dome-like interior. Gritting his teeth through the blinding pain, he stumbled onwards, moving to the side as he avoided a massive stone sepulcher erected in the middle of the circular room. From close by, he heard the young talvuo girl sobbing. Frail cries echoed in the chamber, paining his ears and heart as he forced himself to scan for the little girl.

At the far end, opposite the stone doors and with her shoulders up against the wall, Rais lay prone. She cried, her eyes streaming giant, dirty tears as she squinted in the radiance of the lantern. As his eyes adjusted, Davnian hobbled to her side, looking down at the little girl with a plummeting heart.

Rais's little face was covered in snot and tears, dirty from the grunge and mold of the room. Her white dress was torn and muddy. Her arms hung limp at her sides, her hands clutching her waist, her knuckles white as her little bones dug at her belly as if in great pain. Her mouth and nostrils were crusted with blood and seemed worn raw. Her brown ears drooped as if they held down by weights. Her legs had been splayed to either side, farther than they should be. Dripping from beneath her grungy skirts, a thick red puddle was forming between her thighs.

"Dear gods no!" Davnian dropped to his knees, huddling near the little girl. "Rais, Rais. Can you hear me? I'm here. I'm here to . . ."

"Maaaammmaaaaaa . . ." the little girl gargled through snot and tears as her weak hands clutched her stomach. He was frozen, the sight of the girl's broken, disemboweled body etching itself into his retinas, searing the picture into every cell in his brain. All certainty and stoicism were lost as his senses gave way to rage. His hands shook. The sword tumbling to the floor as he released it.

"Maammma!"

[Davnian!] The shadowy tyrant had grown tired of his pause, the full fury of its voice bearing down on his tumultuous psyche. [Now is not the time. You need to move. You need to get her out of here!]

[I know.]

Fighting through the rage and sadness was like fighting a tidal wave. Davnian needed every ounce of his mental resources allocated to the task of getting the little girl out of there. With shaking arms, Davnian bent down to pick her up. As he tried to replace her legs, he heard something slipping and wheezing beneath her skirts. Rais cried out in pain.

"Mama! Maaaama!" Rais screamed as he tucked her legs close. With his left arm, he gripped the little girl below her bottom. With a heave, he pulled her onto his shoulder. Steadying her with his right hand, Davnian fumbled for the lantern and sword, hoping to keep them on his person as they escaped. A thin wet, protrusion slid against his arm from beneath the girl, his gut lurching as he tried to block out the horror. With the faintest strength, the little girl wrapped her tiny arms around his frame as he rose from the ground. "I want . . . I want . . ."

"Shhhh now. I'll take you to your mother," Davnian whispered, the chill of dread clinging to his voice despite the adrenaline coursing through his veins.

[Let's hurry out of this pit. We've overstayed our welcome,] the other commanded as Davnian's muscles flexed beyond their limits, his grip and strength doubling.

Turning in place, Davnian kept the lantern low to keep from blinding himself. As he faced the doors and sepulcher, he caught sight of a young talvuo maiden standing between the split panels of the massive entryway.

"Thaimi?" Davnian called out to the young woman. His eyes went wide, and his legs began pumping as he watched her slide between the massive stone barriers. From the other side, he heard grinding stone as the massive boulders started to slide shut.

"Thaimi! Thaimi, don't . . ."

Davnian's words were harried as he struggled toward the entrance. Deep in his gut, he knew it was too late. He reached out with the thinblade and grazed the shut stone doors with the tip of the sword. Without thinking, he pressed himself against the massive rock, pushing with all his might against it in hopes of moving the enormous weight.

[Davnian . . .]

[I know . . .]

[Davnian . . .]

"I know!" Davnian shouted, his voice echoing off the walls as he pressed his back to the door. Tears streamed down his face as the horror of the situation overtook him. They were trapped.

[I'm sorry,] the little voice beside him whispered once more.

"Mama . . ." Rais whimpered in his arms. He felt her stomach turn and tighten, and as it did, the sickening prolapse wiggled against his exposed left arm. "I want my mama."

"It's going to be OK." Davnian calmed his voice, turning his gaze up toward the roof of the domed room. The mirrors all around seemed to dance with their own light, the golden splinters of the lantern shifting in hue from yellow to emerald as the light reflected. It seemed like the world was looking down upon him, hundreds of thousands of tiny green eyes staring at him and his incapability. Closing his eyes, he took a deep breath. "Everything will be OK, Rais. I promise I'll get you back to your mama. I promise."

He felt her stomach turn again, and a knot caught in his throat as a slithering sensation wrestled from under her skin as she clung to him. Now was not the time for fear or dread. Nor was it time for self-pity or self-loathing. Now was the time to act. But as he pondered how to destroy the barrier between Rais and her mother, his ears picked up on the sound of something skulking against the insides of the stone artifice at the room's center.

His eyes drawn open, Davnian looked up the stone steps that led to the center of the domed room. Large jutting blocks from all edges hung with their granite faces facing the space. Large iron chains dangled along the floor, running from the center to the jutting stone, through which the links were embedded. Catching a glimpse from the tiny mirrors strewn about, a bottomless black pit lay beneath the central space, forming a watery grave over which something once had been suspended.

Poising himself, Davnian watched as a long, muscular arm protruded from the well, followed by another as a tall, lithe humanoid drew itself from its depths. Stumbling with a child's uneven footing, it twisted its limbs in unintelligible ways. The gaunt figure lurched, crawled, sprang, and jerked as it moved from the sepulcher toward Davnian and his ward.

"Nerin?" Davnian asked, spying the dark hair and sinewy features of Neris's brother as his silhouette became bound by the dusty luminance that seemed to hang in the air.

"No!" Rais's voice was like broken glass dragged across sheet metal.

"Nerin," Davnian said, his blue eyes fixed on the erratic shade as it popped and flexed toward him. "Nerin, answer me. What did you do? What're you doing here? What happened to Rais?"

[Davnian . . .]

"Is she not . . . fee-ling we, we, welllll?" Nerin's jaw and lips moved, his vocal cords resonating with his face as his empty red eyes rolled around in his skull. His head jerked this way and that out of the lantern's rays. "I . . . I thought she was doing well wh-wh-wh-WHEN I left her. She juuuuuuuuuuust was n-n-n-not us-ed to it yet-a."

[Davnian, that's . . .]

"Nerin, what is—" Davnian's words caught as the hackles rose on his neck, his claw twitching as Nerin's awkward body shambled onto level terrain.

[Dear gods, it is. Oh, dear gods, no.]

"Little, little, little, litt-ttle girls are so small and . . . so small and . . ." Nerin stammered as his frame wormed itself upright, his head turning in place, slumped to the side as his eyes locked on Davnian. "They don't have as much room for . . ."

"Enough!" Davnian commanded, pulling himself back against the stonework. Rais's little ears were tucking in upon themselves as the fiend rambled, sputtering words and phrases. Spreading his legs to keep his balance, Davnian raised the thinblade in his right hand. "Enough with the games, Ohran!"

The shell of Nerin twisted its head, turning it once clockwise, rotating Nerin's face upside down with a crack and a grinding motion. Then the figure's hollow eyes filled with realization, its body flexing as its bones contorted. Then in one fluid motion, it relaxed. The talvuo's skull spun, settling with a click as sinew and muscle fiber tugged everything into place.

"Ohran? Oh, Oh-ran," Nerin said. His left cheek formed into an expression of surprise while the right side of his face shook and wiggled before settling on the same guise. "Ah, yes. Ohran. There is no Ohhhhh-ohhh-ohhhhhhhhhhran here among us now, Dav-nian. Just Nerin and Thaimi and Celais and Mianni and all the TALVUO dance, dance, dancing. They all want to dance, DAVE-nian."

"And you're just here to dance with them, isn't that right?" Davnian kept his back to the wall, circling the shadow-stalked figure. The gilded mirrors behind him glittered with unnatural light as the green orbs of a thousand souls looked upon his back. He had been ignoring it, but the miasma of the tree was almost like a liquid in the air. The wraith stuff howled and twisted upon itself as it was drawn from the well and sucked into the empty space within Nerin's body. "Is that why you're devouring them all? Swallowing the miasma and the life that clings to it?"

[THE ETHER BELONGS TO US!] The words thundered like the collapse of a dying star throughout Davnian's body, sending his muscles and bones into convulsions. His senses became mixed and distorted. Touch overlapped with hearing. Taste with sight. Smell with thought. His vision filled with the mangled faces and screaming maws of the living and the damned. The little girl began to shake, her body twitching like a bundle of loosely bound sticks in a heavy gale, her skin bubbling against his body. The Thaimi slug was no more as the force of the monster's words shredded what little remained of her ghost.

[Stop this at once!] The voice inside his head clutched him by the heart.

In his mind's eye, a cascade of brilliant flames poured over and throughout him. At once, the light within was sucked toward a black hole of inescapable power and truth. With the technicolor visions went the tremors and pain, diminishing into nothing as they were destroyed by the void.

[Thank you.] Davnian's thoughts reached to the other as he steadied himself.

"The sorcerer is long gone, Davnian." Nerin's voice fell on his ears once more as he stabilized. The Delvori's convulsing form eased itself, using patient, careful steps to inch closer to Davnian. The creature was almost within arm's reach.

"Stay back!"

Davnian flicked the thinblade at the being, the hungry tip nipping a finger from the man's body. The shambler stopped and with empty eyes gazed upon its dislodged, non-bleeding member. It looked at the space once inhabited by its index finger, staring with peculiar awe at the happening. Then it looked down. Following its red orbs, Davnian took a few more steps away and watched as the twitching black finger wiggled on the ground. The bones and cartilage gave way, the whole of it splintering into a mess of goo and torn flesh as it slithered back to Nerin. As it reached the naked Delvori, it punctured his foot. Taking several more steps to the side, Davnian's jaw dropped as he watched a small, writhing cyst scurry along the man's body before returning to his left hand. Like a tendril, the thing emerged, and with haste reattached itself and formed a new finger where the old one had been.

"That was not very friend-like, Davnian." The thing in Nerin's skin had grown bold in the mere moments it had been approaching. Its mastery of the Delvori's voice and speech patterns was almost complete, its skill with manipulating the musculature and framework of the body grew. Stumbling over itself, it lumbered here and there, making up the distance that Davnian had put between them with a few wooden steps. "Why harm us, fellow outsider? Why strike me, Virage?"

"Rais, it's going to be OK," Davnian whispered to the trembling girl in his arms. He couldn't tell if she had gone into shock or if fear had filled her to the brim.

"Is she bothering you? Don't worry. She'll be just like us soon," the creature whispered with Nerin's tone and articulation, the facial features softening to those of a doting brother. "Just like we softened Nerin, Rais will no longer be alone. She'll be with us and never have to be afraid again. Doesn't that make you happy?"

"What did you do to her?"

"Nerin wanted to know one last time what it would be like to love his sister. We tried to show him, over and over, but he kept seeing his father in himself. We couldn't wait anymore. We needed him to be empty, to be free," Nerin's words carried throughout the chamber as the thing within his flesh motioned around the room. "We were always going to save the girl. She is such a lost, little thing. We knew she would bring you. Just like we always wanted. But he needed to be free, so we gave him his sister. He got to love her with all his body and heart. He got to feel her like she was when their love began. Then he finally let us smother the pain and binding from him."

[What are we going to do, Davnian? I can only cleanse you. I can't fight this thing for you.]

[Let me think. Let me think.]

"We were too rough, it seems." The naked Delvori's face wound into an impossible grin, the sides of Nerin's lips angling up toward his eyes in a sick caricature of happiness. "Thaimi's form was too stiff to mold correctly. But do not worry, for we filled her with ourselves, just as we did all the rest. We can feel her, taste her, and soon we will free her."

"Mama." Rais's voice was weak at his side, her little vocal cords straining.

"Shhh, little one, your mother will be with us too. But forget those cares and needs, for soon you shall be empty. You shall be free. Forget them all, and let us have them. Let us fill those joys and horrors with the hollow and be reborn."

"You're full of shit, you miserable worm!"

Davnian threw the thinblade through the air, watching as it arced over itself. The creature stared at him wit as the tip of the silver steel penetrated its skull between the eyes. As its red orbs flopped around within its head, Nerin's body collapsed to the ground. Its skull cracked with a wet splat.

[You've only bought a little time,] the other said. [You have to hurry.]

"Just a little longer, Rais, I promise," Davnian whispered, scurrying toward the door.

As he lurched at the stone tablet, Rais's tiny fingers clutched his back, her nails digging into his skin. A geyser of ice erupted from his spine as her skin tightened and released, thin, slithering things moving over her arms as her fingers scratched and dug into him. He bit back the pain. Then there it was. Her shade was slumped at the edge of the room, its pale, short essence evaporating as it was engulfed by blackness.

"I'm sorry!" the little girl cried as he kept her supported. His left arm was like stone as it carried her weight, his body surging with renewed vigor as he pressed himself against the rock.

[Use your claw.]

As he pressed his claw against the solid slab, something deep within the recesses of his demonic member resonated with the seal upon the ancient entryway. For a second, he felt the arcane energies of the place pulse like the beating of a great heart, syncing with his as they connected with his claw. Then in the same breath, reality changed around him as visions of the opening became reality. With a sense of triumph, the boulder slipped by a hair, giving him hope.

[That's it, Davnian. More, more!]

"You're right," a hollow, cracking voice called from behind him as he pressed the stonework. "I guess our freedom can't be shared with the likes of you, Virage. You've never accepted it. You've never wanted it. Bound by shackles all your twisted life, you give in to being a pawn of broken feelings and history-tainted logic. The only thing we share is our faithlessness, brother. But while we're all outsiders, we seem far too different."

[Just a little more strength, and you have it. Push!]

The giant door groaned as the massive weight slipped another hair and then another. The invisible hinges at either end of the great artifice strained as Davnian commanded the doors to move.

"You wanted to see Ohran, did you not?" Nerin's voice dipped as the clicking and chattering of a thousand grinding bones and tiny wails joined with the hiss of his breath. "That passage will not open for you Virage, but perhaps Ohran can show you another gate worth peering through."

As Davnian continued his press, the air in the room began to crackle with energy. Every hair on his skin stood on end as the atmosphere became charged with electricity. He was only a short burst away from breaking free. He needed only a moment longer.

Then it happened. From his right side, he felt it build up all at once. Suddenly a bright flash illuminated the room. In a split second, he dove to the side, ditching the lantern as he cradled Rais in his arms. He smelled ozone as the space filled with an orb of pure electric plasma. It exploded upon the smooth stone surface, the force of the blast rolling him with the young girl.

Davnian opened his eyes to see a crack in the air above him near the height of the chamber. It began as a small red ember before growing into a large, cavernous hole in the fabric of space and time. Causality began to unfurl upon itself as the contents of someplace far and foreign poured forth. A discharge of molten magma rained from the ceiling.

"Hold on!"

Davnian rolled across the ground, spinning into the back wall of the dome as the lava hit the ground. Lava seared and scorched the stone as the smell of brimstone and molten earth filled his nostrils. The oozing heat splashed to the ground as the hole atop the room blinked out of existence.

"It has been a long time, Virage," Nerin whispered from the opposite side of the room. Sitting up with Rais, Davnian looked at Nerin's sleek black frame, watching as his face contorted into that of an old man. "We were told you wish to see us. Or is this what you want to see?"

The old man dropped his jaw, letting out a deafening scream of horror. Visions of Ohran's painful plight and his gaunt expression in the Delvori vaults flashed before Davnian's eyes. He watched the plastered face of the old mage spin around and around atop the Delvori's body, the skin at the base of its neck tearing and mending in an instant as it wailed.

[There's no escape,] Davnian thought, watching the figure continue its tempestuous rampage. Pressing himself back into the wall, he held onto Rais, clutching her in his arms. Her little ears were drooping, a trickle of blood oozing from beneath the folds of her brown fur.

"I can't . . . I can't see mama anymore." The little girl's voice was like a chime in a gale. Davnian turned her face toward him. The light in her eyes was fading fast. Across her face, he saw small bulbs of something sinister crawling beneath her skin. "I can't see Mama's face. Mama? Who's . . ."

[Davnian, don't,] the shade in his head commanded, but he would not heed it.

As his heart was breaking, Davnian drew upon the memories of the girl's foster mother, pulling in the thoughts he had shared with Elis. Her emotions and ambitions flowed through him, images of the little girl and ages past flashing in his head like moving pictures across tempered glass. His heart raced as a mother's love gripped him by the nerves. For a moment, Elis Renai filled him with her presence.

"Your mother's right here, my little one," a voice not his called from between his lips, crying against the gale. "I'm right here, Rais. I'm right here, and I won't let anything happen to you. I won't let anyone take you."

[Davnian, don't do this to yourself. Please heed me, young one,] the other said, straining to break the spell. But his mind had snapped. He had promised the girl that she would see her mother, that he would take her back there, and he was going to keep his word.

[Davnian, help me.] Elis's voice rang through his head, her lavender eyes streaming streaks of tears across her copper-touched face. [Don't let them take her, please.]

"Zai-sure . . . Mama?" the little girl looked up at him. Within her green eyes, he saw something horrible writhing in the darkness, dancing lights of others' eyes taking their place within her. "I don't want . . . I love . . . Mama."

"I know, my little one. My daughter." Davnian manipulated the words of the woman within him to speak what she needed to.

"Mama, I'm scared of the dark . . ."

"It'll all be right, my dear. Sleep now, and I'll be right here when you awake. No one will hurt you anymore."

Davnian felt the things creeping into the little girl's skull, beginning the final rounds of emptying their host. Elis roared like a storm within him.

[I won't let them take you!]

The world spun in a dizzying haze as Davnian raised his claw to the little girl's head, Elis's warm smile dancing across his face. Holding her head still with his right hand, a tear worked down his haggard face. Then, as the roaring gale of the maddened creature came to an abrupt end, the inside of his claw moved. There was a crack and a whir, a discharge of electricity, and the sound of a collapsing vacuum. The girl's body shook, its nerves firing every which way as her central nervous system was drawn out. With a sputter and a final jerk, Rais fell lifeless in his arms.

[Mama, I want to see mama . . .] Rais's final thoughts raced through his head as tears streamed down his face. Visions of dancing and laughing, playing, curling beneath quilts, and chatting into the night hung in his head. Graveyard romps, crushing shells, fetching flowers, every happy thing in the world flowed through his brain.

[Davnian, stop.] The other's words hung like a heavy mist, separating him from the little girl's emotions and hopes.

Clarity overtook him as he returned to reality. Staring down, he looked at Rais's body in his arms. A trickle of blood ran down the side of her face, emerging from a tiny hole that led straight into her skull. Her eyes hung empty, and the small maggots crawling about her frame began to burrow free, fleeing their dead host.

"I . . .. I . . ." the words hung in Davnian's throat as he realized what he had done, gripping the small talvuo maiden's body close.

"Thief!" Ohran's face shed itself from Nerin's visage, melting back into the Delvori's skin. "Always denying, Virage. Always stealing. Gluttony. Greed. But that's alright. The body will still do."

"I won't . . ."

In an instant, the creature crossed from one side of the room to the other, standing before Davnian. Whimsy and nausea overtook him as he felt his body lifted by the shoulder, watching the Delvori's hair and limbs shake. In another instant, the coolness of the air whipped around his body, the feeling of weightlessness overtaking him. With a crash, his bones creaked as he slammed into the door of the dark prison chamber.

Davnian wheezed and spat up blood as he fell on all fours, his knees shaking and muscles revolting due to the immense pain. Turning his head, he watched as the dark figure blinked from one side of the room to the other. On his other side, space-time ripped once more. Pressure filled the space as a roaring tempest crushed his bones and body into the ceiling. As the portal closed, he felt himself falling. Before he could taste the earth, the Delvori's dark frame was midair and holding him. With a spin and massive centrifugal force, he flung Davnian into the ground at the base of the sepulcher's steps. His leg bones shattered from the impact, his right shoulder dislocated, and a stream of fresh blood erupted from his right ear.

"It's a pity you're so greedy, Virage," Nerin said from within the mirrored chamber. Shards of glass and silver rained down around them as the Delvori's body descended the steps toward Davnian's beaten frame. "This time will be different for you. This time you will be the one to wait while we free everyone else from the shackles of pain."

[What do you want to bet, old one?] Davnian's mind wandered as the infested Delvori male picked him up by the head, his neck muscles straining to keep him whole. The other did not respond as a broken grin crept across his face.

[If it leaves here, there's no hope. I'm sorry.] Davnian stared at Nerin's body as it paced across the room, pressing the back of his head against the exposed stonework. [I can only pray they run.]

Davnian's body swung forward as the Delvori's elbow contracted.

[Don't give up,] the shadow in his mind said.

Closing his eyes, Davnian felt his body fly backwards. His skull crashed into the stone behind him, and as the world went dark, crushed bone and mashed innards rang in his ears. Warmth embraced his head as the abyss welcomed him once more.

Then the world disappeared.

46

ELIS

Elis's thoughts were full of the dancing, smiling visage of her little girl as she stumbled through the lantern- and coal-lit canopies. The night air ripped through her thin nightgown as she walked. In her hands, she held a rolled-up quilt, the last warmth of her little girl fading into the darkness of the night.

"Rais! Has anyone seen Rais?" Elis called to the enamored masses as they thronged with food, song, and revelry.

The whole world seemed twisted as talvuo men and women gave in to their desires, their eyes just catching her before returning to their debauchery. A swell of madness clung to the air, the village's peaceful timidity replaced by a roaring flame. The few who turned to her shook their heads and pointed into the distance. Maybe Davnian was having better luck. Where was he? Did he know something she didn't? No, none of that mattered right now. She was supposed to canvas the trees, but in the light of the dancing shadows, her senses ran amok.

Call after call into the buzzing crowds went unanswered. Worry clung to her as Elis continued her march from one terrace to another. All around her, the people were alive. Spring was always a time of joy, of celebration, of lusts left to run wild, but never had she seen them so released. And without her child by her side, for the first time since Hyun's passing, she felt afraid.

"Vindal!" a voice called to her.

"Ne vindal!" another cried from beneath a shadowy tree, surrounded by the silhouettes of fellow drinkers and fornicators.

"Vindal Elis!" a little boy called as he was spun silly by two older girls.

As she wandered, Elis felt a heavy weight pressed down upon her and the entire village. Like a falling column of cold air at sunset, it threatened to blow out the smoldering flames of the forest. In response, the tiny flickers of life all about burned even brighter. In the space between was a welling mist, the oppression and hopes of a beleaguered people frothing all around them. Something that many had promised but few had seen seemed to be stirring all around them.

Change, the Delvori male had called it.

Change, the elders and villagers had wished for.

Greetings came her way as she called out again and again. In desperation, she waved off offers and gestures, her breath stopping in her throat. Could they not see her concern? Could they not hear her fear? Why wouldn't they listen? Why weren't they helping?

"Gods please, someone. Rais! Rais, are you there? Someone please—"

"Dear, if you keep going around shouting like that," a cool voice whispered into her ear as she rounded the last of the terraces, "people are going to give you a different kind of attention than you're seeking."

"Neris!" Elis turned and stared at the naked Delvori woman as a throng of followers gathered behind her. "Neris, have you seen Rais? She's gone. She's—"

"Quiet, my dear," Neris said, putting a finger to Elis's lips. Being shushed like a child made her heart pound, the heat of fear and anger overpowering the exposure to the waste-fed flames at her side. Shaking her face free, she furrowed her brow.

"You don't understand! She never runs off! She'd never—"

"Easy now, ne vindal."

As Elis readied to let loose a torrent of bile, she gasped as the dark-skinned woman wrapped her arms around her. Pulled close, Elis felt her legs tiring. Tears clung to the corners of her eyes, but she couldn't let them free. It was all too much. She was blinded by the sights. Deafened by the voices. The hanging terror that loomed in churning bubbles between hope and despair was crushing her. She needed to find Rais. She needed to find her daughter.

"My ear, ne vindal." Neris's voice was calm and composed, and Elis drew away, the water in her eyes receding. She took a deep breath. "Calm and slow now, my dear."

"I was with Davnian in the little overlook above my home. We were talking, and . . ."

"Hmm, yes, go on, dear. Let's not spoil the memory. What happened after?"

"I . . . I don't know what it was. We robed and descended, and when we got to the door, we found it open. And when we went inside, Rais was—"

"Missing. And the girl never leaves home without you or someone calling for her, correct?"

"No, never."

"Is there anyone you think might call for her?" Neris wore a quizzical expression as she crossed her arms across her bare chest. A woman ground against her back. Without turning away from Elis, Neris petted the maiden behind her. "Anyone at all, my dear? A friend of hers? Yours?"

"I can't think of . . ." Elis stopped mid-sentence, realizing that was incorrect. Several of the shyer village women would come to pay Elis and Rais a visit from time to time, and chief among them was the newest nectar maiden, Thaimi. Indeed, Thaimi had been there when Elis would oft disappear into the woods on her lonesome to sate her urges to hunt or gather dye ingredients. "Thaimi might. But I don't see why she would come tonight of all nights. I don't know why she'd—"

"Hmm, well, I can give you a hint and maybe even an answer, ne vindal. I know someone whose lips are easy to part." Neris kissed the young talvuo woman as she drew forward, her eyes still locked on Elis. Following the small display, Neris turned her head to her shirtless follower, her questioning look filling with seduction. She pointed into the distance. "Dear, would you be a pet and fetch me that layabout over there? He's been spying on all of us all evening, and I'd love to reward him for his admiration."

The ensnared woman laughed as she pranced off.

"Forgive me for keeping you at this most lecherous of places, my dear," Neris said, returning her gaze to Elis. "I was originally meeting a man and his betrothed for a fun-filled evening. Before I knew it, every lover I'd conquered and their suspect paramours were around me. Perhaps we've gotten a little carried away on this side of the wood."

"People feel things changing." Elis shook her head, clutching her robe near her breast. "The spring frenzy has swept everyone up, and with everything else, it's like they need to dance to forget."

"I don't think they're trying to forget," Neris said, drawing close once more. She put her dark, gilded hands on Elis's shoulders, shaking her own head. "I think they're trying to remember what it feels like to be alive. For once they've seen everything they've been deprived of, that they've missed. It's only natural to be consumed by it once so much is within reach."

"I pray you're right, vindal."

A shiver worked its way up Elis's spine despite the heat of the simmering kiln nearby. She was sweating beneath her robe, but Neris's company seemed to put her at ease. Neris closed the gap between them and placed a kiss upon her forehead.

"Thank you," Elis said, taking another deep breath.

"You shouldn't trouble yourself so much, my dear. You have good people at your side," Neris said, chuckling.

"Like you."

"And Davnian," Neris said. "I'm sure he's looking his hardest, just like you are. Let's just pray he doesn't fall off the timbers at this point. The man's as stubborn as you are, if not more so."

"Agreed," Elis said, laughing.

"Gods, you're drunk, aren't you?" Neris asked. Elis nodded, her flushed features even hotter given the circumstance. "I take it our mutual lover talked you over?"

"Yes, he did," Elis said, nodding.

"Good," Neris replied, holding her tight. Neris was trying to change where Elis's thoughts were going, trying to ease her mood. The other woman was a great lover. When everything was over, Elis would have to repay her tenfold. "Then you know we're all going to do our best, and when it's done, this will be far gone, like a bad dream."

"Again, thank you, Neris."

"Oh, stop with the thanks. You'll make me weepy, and the last thing I want is to cry when I'm surrounded by so many options." Neris gripped Elis's shoulder as she spoke, bending forward to peck her lips as her messenger returned. Elis saw a white-robed man struggling to stand beside the bare-chested Hyunisti woman and her dark, bare-skinned compatriot. "Well, well, my dear. Look who we have here. Our dearest friend, vivahr Kadin. What a pleasure to see you skulking in the shadows."

"You left me in quite a way, vindal Neris." Kadin's words were bitter as his droopy green eyes fanned from Neris to Elis, then back. "Pray tell, vindal, are you trying to tease me? I've seen enough of you two minxes slobbering over each other. I'm lacking the mood and the—"

"I don't think vindal Elis is aware of your prying eyes, vivahr." Neris smiled as Elis's jaw dropped. Kadin had watched them? "Of course, maybe she's as amenable as I am to being spied upon. Though I've never figured her for the exhibitionist type, I hear she was quite the spectacle on the far ends this evening."

"Neris!" Elis's cheeks burned as she narrowed her eyes at Neris. No, this was all a game. She was working Elis up because she wanted her to be furious. "Kadin? You spied upon me? Upon us?"

"It isn't like half the village doesn't imagine how you both take each other, vindal Elis," Kadin croaked, the smell of fermenting forest mead drifting off his breath. Groping at Neris, the half-shirted maiden giggled. "Even this boney girl's thought of it. Who knows? Maybe she imagined herself as one of you!"

"Now, now, dear Kadin. We don't want to upset our sister, do we?" Neris cooed, shifting her eyes from the man to Elis. Her lips curled as her eyes widened with a look of sadistic glee as Elis's violent temperament reflected in her boiling red eyes. "I'm a painful lover, but ne vindal is much more prone to real violence than I am."

"Stop it. Just stop it!" Elis's eyes narrowed. With a burning glare, she locked her lavender eyes on Kadin. His droopy green eyes peered at her as he hung over himself. "You!" she said. "Where's Rais? And where's Thaimi? You know something, don't you? Where is she? Where's my little one?"

"Vindal Elis." Kadin's eyes widened as he caught a glimpse of her burning stare. He lifted himself, backing away and into a pair of males gripping each other. "Vindal, I don't . . . You don't mean that . . ."

"Hmm, so you do know something, vivahr Kadin."

Neris turned as Elis pressed herself toward the sniveling talvuo. Elis felt her worry and temper building, her chest swelling as her depression boiled to wrath. Holding the little girl's quilt in her arms, clenching it with whitening knuckles, Elis pressed it forward. "Why isn't she home in bed, Kadin? Why did she leave home? Why? WHY?"

"Ne vindal, you didn't know?" Kadin's stammered as the men behind him pressed him toward Elis. All around them, lovemaking and sensual touches had halted, beckoned by Neris's subtle calls. "Vindal Elis . . ."

"What, Kadin? What?"

"Thaimi, she . . . Gods, there's no way . . ."

Surrounded by more than a dozen men and women, Elis stared Kadin down. About to unleash a torrent of fury, her ears picked up a scream that shattered the low hum of burning coals and socializing. The hazel-headed mob's ears perked and turned toward the shrieks and gasps. Wailing echoed throughout the darkened wood as they all fixed their sights in the direction of the great tree.

"What stirs in the abyss?" Neris asked under her breath, her lovers and gawkers huddling close to each other for warmth.

Elis stepped toward the cry, her anger receding as terror filled her heart.

"What . . . what is it?" Kadin turned drunkenly and fell, his eyes and ears blank as he looked toward the flames in the distance.

"Gods. What if . . ." Elis's words stopped on her tongue, refusing to move as she shut her mouth.

"Elis?" Neris's loving voice turned cold as she stepped close.

Without another moment to wait, Elis's legs began pumping.

"Elis!" Neris called after her, but Elis did not stop. She heard the orgy-goers murmuring as she dashed away followed by a curse from Neris and the soft footfalls of bare feet. "Elis, wait!"

The shadows of the trees flashed past as Elis ran toward the great tree. She wove through standing gawkers, ignoring her nightgown as it caught and tore along the wooden planks of the walkways. She drew Rais's quilt close, imagining the warmth imparted by the kiln as that of her little one.

Rais's clumsy dances and jogs caught in her mind as she ran, as did the little hazel-headed girl's laugh and smile and her bright green eyes lighting up her cream-hued face. How she screamed when she woke up in the dark alone. How she cried and smiled, clinging to Elis as she eased back into rest. Elis's heart pounded as another scream rattled the village. The dancing talvuo across the way stood still. The looming terror had coalesced into something palpable.

"Back, my brothers and sisters, back! Give him room!" Thaimi cried.

Making the final trek up a slanted bridge, Elis stepped onto the central terrace of the Hyunisti village. Tens of men and women were gathered, their heads turned toward none other than Nerin Delvori as he stood in front of the paralyzed throng. At his side clad in a white blouse, Thaimi stood with a somber look upon her face. Nerin held a small bundle in his arms, his rust-colored eyes drawn toward Elis as she came into view. With a dark look, his gaze fell downwards upon the thing in his hands, and so did Elis's own eyes. Her heart skipped a beat, and with a few unbalanced steps, she fell at the Delvori man's feet.

In Nerin's arms was the body of a little hazel-headed child, her arms limp and bruised, her legs unflinching.

Whispers broke out through the crowd of onlookers. "Vindal Elis . . ."

"The child. The child she's . . ." a chorus of voices seemed to respond as her hands began to shake.

Elis heard heavy steps halt as reality dawned upon her.

"Vindal Elis." Nerin's voice was soft, unlike it had ever been as he approached her. All around them, shrieks sounded, and prying eyes came into view of the spectacle that had taken hold of the grand party. "Vindal Elis, my heart goes out to you. I'm sorry, but . . ."

"Vindal Elis." Thaimi's voice sounded through her speckled fur ears as they dropped and turned upon themselves.

Elis's mind was blank as Nerin knelt before her, laying Rais's body beside her. Elis looked down, staring at the sick, foggy orbs of the hazel-haired sprite. Dark, spongy wetness clung to the bottom of her white dress, the same muddy darkness spread along her thighs and legs. Her tender face was covered in dirt and grime, her lips parted and cracked. At her right temple, a small, rusty trickle was dried along her bone-white cheek, marching up to a tiny place sealed with iron-smelling slime.

Tears streaking her cheeks, Elis's thoughts went nowhere as she stroked the little girl's face. A sense of dread hung in the air, all eyes upon her as she laid out the blanket. With all her strength, she nudged the little girl onto her lap and wrapped her in the quilt.

"There, there, my little one. I've come to tuck you in," Elis said, her voice cracking. Her body began to shake. Pulling the girl close, she smelled her hair and ran her hands through the dirt- and blood-matted mop. Rais was so afraid of the dark, of being alone. "It's OK now. Mother's here."

Bending her head forward, she felt others drawing close, but Neris snapped at all those who came close.

"Vindal Elis?" Thaimi's thin voice made her ear twitch.

"My heart, ne vindal." Nerin's overly soft tone caused her stomach to drop.

Looking up, her eyes full of tears, Elis looked through them all out across the expanse. As her world began to spin, she felt her heart breaking. Within the darkness, she saw the dancing figure of a little girl wearing an uneven smile as she bounced and played. In the last moments, the girl turned her eyes to Elis, her ghost bright in the surrounding darkness.

Letting go, a smile crept across Elis's face as she fell from the world.

[Don't be scared of the dark,] she thought she heard a little voice whisper.

[Never stop moving.]

47

NERIS

Neris had long since accepted the worst in people. She understood that everything horrible was inevitable and realized that the only reason one escaped a single terror was through chance or death.

During one of their late evenings, Neris had learned how Elis had come to the village of the forest talvuo. She had heard the story of how she had lost everything and everyone she loved at a young age. Neris had been amazed to see how the Renai had overcome the burdens of her past. But unlike Neris, Elis did not cling to the sordid sense of reality she knew very well to be the truth. Instead, she had come to accept change and to keep moving.

Except she hadn't. Not really.

The woman she had fallen for had stirred from her raving nightmares in fits of madness and mania. She had become disconnected from everything around her. The shock of losing Rais was too much for her mind to bear. She had wailed and called for the little girl, sometimes in depressive growls and other times with a cheerful voice. It broke Neris's heart to take drastic measures, finding a bottle of the rare sentae extract that Elis used for her face paints. Mixing it with a small dose of valerian root extract, Neris had forced her friend to drink the substance. At last Elis could sleep without waking, though Neris dreaded what foul and horrible things were dancing in her mind.

But for the Delvori woman, those were the least of her concerns now.

After the crowd was disbanded, Nerin and his mistress, accompanied by his lackeys, had offered to give the girl's body a sendoff. Many had agreed to the task, but Neris forbid it. Some had barked at her, accusing her of being in league with Rais's murderer. Others protected her, and her brother had looked at her with a queerness that unsettled her. Ever since they had been rejoined, Neris remembered the hunger, the want, and the need that possessed her brother as he coveted her flesh and warmth. But when he had looked at her, wearing an expression of sullen desire, she had seen no yearning in his eyes. And that lack of want unnerved her.

Not letting Elis out of her sight, Neris compelled Kadin and the disillusioned lovemakers to bring Elis and Rais to the infirmary. It was strange watching as they laid the golden-haired maiden in the same spot that Davnian had once occupied. Rais's broken body was placed two tables over.

"Tell me, vivahr Kadin, why aren't you lapping at my brother's feet right now, hmm?" Neris narrowed her eyes as she studied the dead girl beneath her.

"I've seen many talvuo men and women die. I've done my share of being a weasel. But I've never seen anything like this."

"I'd think you'd be familiar. After all, you do so love to shove your prick down fledgling's throats and up their skirts, don't you?" Neris was cold and mean as she took gentle care of lifting and revealing the wounds on Rais's body. "Or is this one a little too young for you?"

"Those women were all grown, you insufferable—"

"I'm only teasing, dear," Neris said. "Taking advantage of drunk women is clever, especially for a weasel like you."

"Gods, I'm horrible, but I will not listen to this," Kadin hissed from the shelves behind her. She heard him shuffle, followed by a deep groan as he fell down. "Damn it all."

"Not fun being in a stupor and assailed, is it?"

The smell coming off the little girl's body was putrid. She couldn't have been dead more than a few hours, but every blood vessel in her body had dried up. From her groin, the aroma of carrion and feces combined to form an odor fouler than any she could recall in recent memory. The way her eyes were clouded with grime was haunting. Then there was the hole on the side of her head. Using a small wire, Neris had confirmed her suspicions. The brain was gone, leaving an empty vessel.

Rais's list of injuries was great. She had been raped, the assailant's methods and violence so terrible as to tear free her innards, effectively disemboweling her. With the same rage, her legs had been forced apart and dislocated, the motion causing her skin to tear along her inner thigh. Her white skin showed signs of bruising all along her forearms, legs, chest, and stomach. Her face had been injured, the residue of tears, dirt, and snot clinging to her features. Somehow the skin at the edges of her nostrils and mouth had been worn raw. Compared to all that pain and suffering, the head trauma was a stroke of mercy.

"Kadin, what were you going to tell Elis before?"

Neris's blood was ice as it coursed through her veins, her posture perfect as she turned the little girl's pale hand over in her own. How tiny she was, though Rais was not the first girl Neris had seen to die in such a way.

"You mean at the orgy?" Kadin whispered. "I . . . vindal Thaimi . . ."

"Be direct, vivahr Kadin. It may mean your life," Neris said, turning around toward him. Her sharp black ears were like daggers as they aimed at the man, folded to hear every word, every heartbeat.

"The one nectar maiden, that Thaimi girl . . . I . . . Nerin had kicked me out for soiling his bedspread, but I sat by the door and listened. He had been ranting about how sore he was over vindal Elis's outburst. He kept going on about it. But then that girl, she . . . she asked him if he was ready for the last step."

"Last step?"

"Yes. She said tomorrow night, tonight, would be the night, and that after tonight Lord Ohran would reward him with everything he ever wanted."

"Ohran?" Neris looked him over, the name of her brother's imaginary advisor and missing lover's dread flitting around her mind. "What else? Was there anything else?"

"The girl went on. She talked about taking care of everything else. She said she would take care of their problems. I had to leave just after as she started for the door. But she said she would get rid of the outsider. She'd see to the Virage."

"Did she now?" Neris didn't put it past her brother to seek to disrupt Elis's life or to exploit a little girl if it meant he could damage his rivals, but this pale-skinned thing? "So, you're saying the young woman came up with this?"

"I didn't dare stay another second lest they find out the weasel had overstayed his welcome."

As Kadin sat on the floor, gripping his head and looking up at her with his narrow green eyes, Neris examined his every motion. He was direct and open, and other than a nervous need to rub his fingers, she spotted no hint of deception. Kadin was a snake, but between her earlier seduction and the explained happenings, it was apparent the serpent had turned rodent. Thinking back on how he had leered at her from the shadows, she could almost taste his fear.

"I take it you're not apt to believe the story then, vindal?"

"Yours or my brother's?" Neris asked, her expression placid as she turned from him.

"So, do you think he did this then?"

"I think he's orchestrating something, but to what end, I don't know."

In her mind, the idea that Davnian had raped and then killed Rais was ridiculous. She knew he had a monstrous side, but she also knew that monster had its boundaries. No, Nerin had not even needed to say the culprit's name. How careful he seemed to hint at the notion. If the Virage had meant to ruin them through sadness or morbidity, he would have overseen each of their personal hells himself. And if he had wanted to play with the young girl, there were sweeter ways to indulge such decadent pleasures.

"Everyone, including our regal brother, thinks the man is a monster. And they think you and the Renai woman are tainted now too. You know that?" Kadin was shaken but talking like his sniveling self, which brought a devilish grin to Neris's face. "Well, save for a few talvuo who still have hopes of ploughing the two of you."

"I'm aware. Remember, I was there to hear them all stirring. I was the one shouting them down." Neris returned to her nonchalant self. Fetching a washcloth and a water basin, she began scrubbing Rais's body. "Kadin, while you're sitting there, make yourself useful. Bring me a needle and thread along with a fresh pitcher of water. Also, can you bring some more candles?"

"Pray tell why the request, vindal?" Kadin asked, chuckling from his floor seat.

"I want to have the girl cleaned up and presentable before Elis awakes. She's going to be up sooner or later, possibly even before the dawn. I need to dress the injuries as best as I can and sew a few things back into place. Fetch my plasters from my vanity while you're at it. Light and rosy would be best."

"Vindal Neris?" the meanness fled Kadin's voice for a moment. Undeterred, Neris continued to wash the child, taking extra care with her soft face. She heard him rise from the floor. With a deep breath, he bowed at her side, his tone once more that of a tricky servant. "As you wish, vindal Neris."

"Thank you, dear," Neris said, waving him away.

As Kadin left, Neris took a deep breath. She mused over different flower extracts and essential oils that might mask the dreadful smell emanating from the girl. No, flowers were not something a girl like her was like. She was like whirling leaves on an autumn day with a hint of pollen.

"More like dandelions," Neris whispered to herself.

Powdering of fall leaves mixed with essential oil of dandelion would do. Cleaning the last bit of grime from the child's face, Neris could not help but stroke Rais's cheek. How she had hoped to house the little one and her mother. But with all things coming to pass, she saw the spiral unfolding. Just like her brother had ranted, change had come to the Hyunisti talvuo and their quaint forest village.

And for the life of her, Neris could not see how they'd survive it.

48

DAVNIAN

"Mama! Mama!" a little girl's voice cried from deep within the darkness of a black expanse. Looking up, head aching and mouth dripping blood and bile, Davnian spied a light in the distance. A small talvuo girl cried into the void, nothing but her voice answering her bleating. With a heavy heart, he rose from the ground, his body laminated by will as he strolled toward the child. As she called out again and again, his limbs protested. His whole body hurt, and it felt as if boiling acid were bubbling underneath his skin. "Zaisure! Mama, where are you?"

As he walked, Davnian felt another beside him, its massive form shaking the firmament. Turning his eyes, he saw the fleeting shadow of the colossus. A haze of distortion clung to its elevated head as thousands of coal-like embers danced upon its gigantic silhouette.

"To think I'm back here with you." Davnian's voice carried in the endless black while the other marched in lockstep beside him. "Is this what death feels like, black one?"

"I've never known death, young one," the thing said, its gravel-laden voice churning from the darkness. "If this is death, then it's far kinder than the life we've just lived, if not melancholic."

"Kindness?" Davnian asked, sarcasm gripping his words as his penchant for dark humor overcame his weary thoughts. "Perhaps, though if death is kind, life must be evil incarnate."

"Perhaps it is," the other said, shambling its massive weight.

In the distance the girl turned toward them, still calling out. Pumping her small, boney arms, she ran toward them. Within the void, her little steps carried at the speed of will, his hearing picking them up as if they were next to him.

"Is any of this real in any context, old one? Am I tricking myself again?"

"Again?"

"I can't remember it out there, but here . . ." Flickers of the hellscape of his nightmares danced in the distance. Bubbles of another reality inflated and popped out of existence near the horizon of the infinite. "I remember your words though still not the place."

"If this is a hell of your own making, at least it's a pleasant one," the other whispered as the glow of the running girl crossed the expanse in no time.

"Mama? Do you know where my mama is?" she asked, her brilliant green eyes looking first up into his and then, in a blink, directly toward him. It was if she had grown to his size, or he had shrunk to hers.

"We'll find Mama soon," Davnian replied in a voice that was both Rais's and his at the same time. "I promise!"

"You won't leave me in the dark, will you?" Looking at her was like looking into a mirror. His every move was captured and emulated by the little girl as he shook his head. As he responded, the little girl's mouth moved along with him, saying the words. "Never. I'll never leave you alone, Rais. Never ever!"

"OK!" the two of them replied to each other, girlish laughter breaking from their breasts as they stood opposite each other.

"But for now, you should sleep," a voice unlike the girl's said from a distance.

As Rais and Davnian looked up, a blackened claw extended from the void opposite the mighty colossus of his thoughts. Touching the girl upon the brow, Davnian's head spun as he watched her fall upon the ground into a deep slumber. Once more, his head reeled from pain. Images of Rais in the waking world collapsed upon his psyche as he watched her spirit sleep. Then, from the impenetrable darkness, a man stepped into view.

The figure was tall and brooding. Dirty blond hair clung to his head like a tangled mop, his white skin touched by shadow. Blackened leather, the charred hide of some great beast, hung across his shoulders and protected his legs. Beneath the armor was blood-red padding and flitting patches of coal-colored chain guarding his joints. At his side hung a simple sword as his black claw gripped his hip. Looking up, Davnian stared into the cold blue eyes of none other than himself wearing a grimace carved like stone into his facial features.

"Did you think just waking would solve everything?" His voice carried to his ears as his double bent down, caressing the sleeping girl's forearm. "Did you think just forgetting the horrors would ease the pain?"

"I don't understand."

"There's no more time for peace, Davnian. No more time for joy," his other self said, gesturing to the little girl. Looking down, Rais slept curled in one direction, her corpse splayed beside her. "And there's no more time for failure."

"Be kind," the earth-shaker whispered.

"We've tried kindness before, have we not?" Davnian found himself speaking in tandem with the other, his scowl becoming sadistic while Davnian's childlike features mirrored them. Other shadows emerged, each wearing the same cold blue eyes. Countless shapes and versions faded into view as they stared at his small frame. "We've tried pacifism countless times before. We've tried friendship. We've tried love. But there is only one tried-and-true way to fix this, and you know exactly what I mean, Davnian."

Pointing with his outstretched demon hand, Davnian followed the line to his own claw. At once, he was transformed, shedding the frame of the girl and donning his flesh and bones. His left hand twitched beneath him, the black hull of a monster's claw.

"I should have." Davnian remembered the sickness and the rage that gripped him when he first saw Nerin and his mistress. There was anger, followed by bloodlust.

"Yes, but there's still time," the other him said, laughing with manic glee. The eyes of his doppelganger dimmed, becoming nothing more than deep pools of black. The other onlookers' orbs blackened in unison.

"It is not yet strong enough," they said in unison, "but you cannot hesitate. You cannot hold back."

[There is another path, Davnian,] the colossus growled within his mind.

"If you fail or run, then everyone you've met will suffer a fate worse than death, Davnian." With a monstrous grin, the leader of the shadows pointed to the girl. He and Davnian turned to the shadow beast. "After all, death can be a kindness," he said in a mocking tone. "What they will do to these villagers, Neris, Elis . . . death would have been heaven by comparison, as you know, old one."

Davnian was overcome with the pain and hopelessness that Rais felt in her final moments. He could not bear that kind of pain again or the weight of a dozen such voices, much less hundreds.

"Do not fret any longer, Davnian," his clone whispered into his ear, his mouth curving into a manic smile. "Save the formalities for when you awake. Sleep now, and bind yourself in anger. Lose yourself in madness."

Davnian's dreamscape eyes glazed over as he found his reflection's claw upon his brow. The colors around him inverted as he swooned. Losing his grip on the dreamland, light engulfed his mind and ego.

The warmth of Rais's memories enveloped him while his hatred for her loss overflowed.

49

ELIS

[E]verything is going to be alright. I promise!]
Davnian's words rang through her skull as Elis lifted herself from the infirmary table. She felt numb, her thoughts meandering a distance behind her actions as she looked around the dim room. Sweat clung to her armpits and thighs as she shuffled atop the wooden surface. Her stomach gurgled as if bubbles danced in her belly. A manic smile crept across her face as she looked down at her pale nightgown, gazing at the wet cloth as it clung to her legs and breasts.

"Easy there, my dear," a dark voice called from beside her. The words were like echoes down a long corridor as they rattled across ancient stonework until they found their way into her sagging red-gold ears. Her flowers turned and cropped themselves toward the other as she tried to scooch off the table, but obsidian hands reined her in to prevent her from moving. "Please, Elis, try not to move too much."

"Neris?" Elis slurred her words, her grin not breaking as the syllables tumbled from her mouth. Her tongue was sloven and dry. Lifting her swaying head, she tried to fix on the Delvori maiden at her side.

"You're a stubborn one," Neris said, chuckling as she kept a firm hand on Elis's stomach and arms. The warmth from her palms permeated Elis's tummy. Butterflies and mosquitoes dueled in her bowels. "Please listen and stay. Just a moment, ne vindal."

"Neris?" Elis dragged her tongue around her mouth as she tried to speak. Then it hit her. The contents of her stomach spilled from her mouth, tumbled across her dress, and splashed upon the floor.

"Oh gods. Kadin? A towel and a change of clothes. Be quick, vivahr." Neris's words were at once distant and yet deafening as the last of the bile slipped from Elis's lips. She coughed and gagged, laughing as the burn of acid and the taste of vomit were absent from her senses. "Elis, lie back, dear."

"Neris, stop." Elis's skin tingled as her nerves misfired. Out of the corner of her eye, she saw Kadin shaking his weasel-nosed head as he lowered to the floor to clean up her chunks. Licking her lips, she snubbed one of his ears with her dangling foot. "Stop."

"Can you keep her from making a mockery of this?" Kadin's raised his voice, almost chattering like a small animal.

Elis tried to lift herself up to confront the talvuo, but Neris's dark arms held her back. With heavy hands, Neris pressed Elis back down to the table. Elis lifted her cleanest hand to Neris's face, reaching beneath dark furrows of straight black hair to the ebony-skinned woman's cheek. Fondling her skin with her fingertips, Elis groaned as she smiled.

"Keep yourself together, dear," Neris whispered as she drew closer. Elis's fingers wrapped and knotted themselves in Neris's hair as she looked up at the woman with large, dilated lavender eyes. "I gave you sentae extract mixed with valerian, my dear. You're feeling very aroused and numb, I know."

"Why would you do that?" Elis almost gagged on her own tongue as she tried speaking again, turning her head to the side as Neris planted her forehead against her skull.

"Because you were hysterical," Neris whispered. "Now, will you let me clean you and change your clothes?"

"Only if you—"

Neris interrupted Elis's rambling by pressing her fingers against her lips. Elis felt her heartbeat slow as the dark-skinned woman's touch eased her. As Neris pulled away, Elis wiggled her fingers through the knots in Neris's hair. She took several deep breaths as her heart raced up and down.

"Kadin, leave a rag and the clothes at the foot of the table. I've got her," Neris said as Elis felt the room sway. Everything around them hummed like the world should be glowing but wasn't. "I'm going to undress you now, Elis, alright?"

"OK," or something like it rolled off Elis's tongue.

Neris reached her arm behind Elis's back and brought the other across her stomach, helping her lean forward. Elis smacked her lips as the taste of her own spit seasoned her tongue. The flavor was vile.

"Arms up, dear," Neris whispered.

Elis threw her arms upward, her head hanging as Neris tugged at her nightgown. As the thin cloth slipped past her buttocks and the table beneath her, Elis almost giggled, but she kept herself quiet as Neris lifted the garment over her head. The passing gown reeked of puke.

"Thankfully, you just got yourself a little wet, ne vindal," Neris teased with her sultry voice.

Elis wanted to kick her legs and giggle, but her feet felt like massive weights. The cocktail in her system made her heartbeat slow, each pulse echoing throughout her body with a solid pound. As the warmth left her within and without, a dramatic shiver shot up her spine.

Neris brought a damp rag over to her, wiping off her arms and chest with strong, broad strokes. The water smelled of lemon and lilacs as it streaked across Elis's bronze skin. Unable to control her every move, Elis played with her fingers as Neris went over them several times before turning her attention elsewhere. Neris nudged her, and in response, Elis spread herself just enough for Neris to reach latent grunge. The drying water was cold and playful as it prickled her skin and tickled her hairs, making them stand on end.

"You need to learn to wipe the floor better," Neris said darkly.

"I'm not used to being on my hands and knees, unlike some, ne vindal." Kadin's voice was sniveling but funny at the same time.

"You're lucky I have nothing against worms like you," Neris replied, running a clean rag between Elis's toes.

Elis giggled from the touch as her eyes wandered. On the far table, a beautiful little girl was lying in a bright white dress. Her eyes were closed, and her curly hazel hair was springing as clinging moisture evaporated into the night air. Elis's eyes widened as she looked at the girl. A wicked smile gripped her features as she spied through her own rapid gestures.

"Arms up, dear," Neris commanded.

Turning her head, Elis lifted her arms. In front of her, Neris bounced back and forth, her black breasts swinging beside Elis's head as she fought with Elis's hands to don the new dress. The two pendulums knocked Elis's furry ear. In response, Elis turned and buried her face in Neris's bosom. As the rest of the dress fell down around her, she felt Neris's laugh against her face.

"After you're dressed, Elis," Neris commanded. Elis obeyed, pulling her head back as Neris yanked the dress's opening over her head. "There, all cleaned up and ready to mingle anew."

"Better?" Kadin asked, beckoning Neris to inspect his work.

"Much better," Neris said, stepping over him. Elis's eyes followed her, every so often stealing a glance at the little girl. "Let's get some water back into your stomach, dear. Then we'll go from there."

"OK," Elis agreed as Kadin rose and retreated. Neris filled the space between them.

"Now, the first few sips just to wet your mouth. Feel free to spit it in here," Neris said, holding up two cups—one full of water and the other empty.

Elis took the cups and, her eyes locked on Neris's clay-hued orbs, took her first few sips. Her tongue sprang to life with taste and pain as the moisture seeped into every crack. The flavor of bile clung to her mouth. Fighting the urge to heave, she spat each mouthful into the other cup. With heavy breaths, she took another draught and then another, each one lessening the impact of the foulness within her mouth.

"Let me take those and fetch you another," Neris said.

Elis's tongue slid along her inner cheeks and the back of her teeth. Despite the distraction, she couldn't help but trace lines back to the peaceful, dozing girl. Though her heartbeat was normalizing, it skipped beats with every glance as Elis looked and then turned away. Her skin began to burn as her own body heat warmed her. The buzz of the world was dying down, the drumming in her head softening. Her red-and-gold-speckled ears lifted and lowered of their own accord as Elis stretched her jaw. Yawning, she raised her hands to fetch new cups from Neris.

"You're starting to look better," Neris said, putting her hand on Elis's knee.

"And it looks like the sun is just starting to break," Kadin called from the countertop. Elis turned toward the slatted windows, looking at the faint ambient light that seemed to hang in the air. "I was starting to feel like cackling myself."

"You held up under pressure rather well, ne vivahr. You should feel proud for doing so well by your sisters," Neris replied. Elis felt the urge to laugh but stifled it. Her toe twitching, she felt time realigning itself in her head. "Mayhaps we'll reward you someday, hmm?"

Neris squeezed Elis's leg. Ignoring her, Elis drank down the contents of her cup, sip by sip. The smile left her face as her senses dulled and then sharpened all at once.

"Let's not drink too much now," Neris said, beckoning for the cups.

With slow movements, Elis handed them back to Neris, feeling the trickle of water working through her angry stomach. The dullness was replaced by an ache. Her nausea overcome by a surge of alertness. Her mind was busy piecing reality back together, and with every slotted fragment, her heart grew heavier. Despite the oppressive weight, Elis knew she couldn't wait any longer.

"Neris?"

"Yes, ne vindal?" Neris asked with that same self-serving tone she always used. A corner of Elis's lips curled.

"Can I . . . can I see her?" Elis asked, a half-grin and a half-frown strung across her face.

The room was silent for a moment, the candles flickering as the ambience outside began to overtake the shadows beneath the trees.

"Yes," Neris said as she drew herself forward and offered her arm to Elis. "Let me help you, my dear."

"Thank you." Elis's voice was diminished as she accepted Neris's arm and struggled to her feet. Her legs were shaky, and her head swam as blood pumped to her extremities. With a dizzy step, she followed Neris around the middle table. Kadin sat with pursed lips as he averted his eyes from the duo. Elis shifted her gaze, focusing on the little girl on the far table. As they walked together, Elis bit her lip, struggling to keep a smile on her face.

"There's a seat right here just for you, my dear," Neris said. She gestured to a small wooden stool beside the table. Elis laughed, looking at the same seat on which she had spent so many days and nights watching over Davnian. Now she'd be sitting in it again for one last vigil.

"She's so pretty." The words tumbled out of Elis's mouth as she held back tears.

Rais's curly hair fell all around her sprite-like face. Her eyes were closed, a touch of rose dashed across her cheeks, which made it seem like she could spring to life at any moment. Her hands were crossed over each other on her lap, and her legs were tucked together. Small blue and green dots were painted across her little eyelids with a smattering of starry pricks on either side of her button nose. As Elis fell into her seat, the smell of fall leaves and dandelions rose from her daughter's body. They filled her with fond memories of picking herbs and roaming together about the forest floor.

Taking one of the little girl's hands between her own, Elis leaned over the table and pressed her forehead to it. The milk-white skin was soft and familiar. The nubs of her fingers were still rough from rubbing and dyeing only a half-day before. As she gripped the little girl's hand,

Elis couldn't fight back her tears any longer. Rais was cold to the touch despite how lifelike she appeared.

"I'm sorry, Elis," Neris said.

Elis kissed her little girl's palm and then set it back in Rais's lap. She reached her left hand up and stroked the girl's brow before running her slender fingers through Rais's curly mop. Leaning over her, she looked at her painted face and smiled, one of her tears landing on the child's temple. Stroking the saline droplet from the little girl's cheek, Elis bent down and kissed her forehead.

"Mama's sorry, my little one," Elis whispered, tears streaking her face. "But Mama's right here. I'm so sorry, Rais. I'm so sorry."

Neris shuffled beside her, but she was stopped by Kadin's voice. "You should give her room, vindal Neris," he said, harsh and snippy.

"I'll be right out here when you're ready, Elis," Neris said, her voice coming to Elis like notes on the wind. Every word was as hamstrung as Elis's own, but she could not reply. She needed to be there for Rais for just a little longer. "I promise."

The two talvuo left her alone with her little girl. As the door shut, Elis buried her head at the girl's side, gripping her loose dress. There were so many things she wanted to say, to sing the girl's praises, to tell Rais how much she loved her. But in the end, there was only one thing she could say.

"I'm so sorry!" Elis cried, digging her nails into the clean white cloth.

She was sorry for not being there when she died.

Sorry she had never let herself be Rais's mother.

50

NERIS

"I know what you're thinking, ne vindal," Kadin said as he stood beside the door, his eyes heavy with sleep and stress.

"I doubt it, but feel free to dream, vivahr Kadin." Neris was not her usual quick-witted self.

Seeing Elis crumple under the weight of losing her daughter was one thing, but seeing her have to relive it one more time after a night of hysterics and powerful drugs was another. She had worried she would have to sedate her lover again. In part, she was amazed at how well Elis kept herself together. Neris had misjudged her, but that only made it harder.

"You're worried about the woman and want to help, but I can read it by the hackles on your neck that you think something bad is bound to happen. Something much worse." Kadin was vile but accurate.

Without Elis nearby, Neris's mind was left to wander. Whatever had caused Davnian to disappear was still at large. In that same vein, whatever had dealt them their cards likewise was involved with the girl's death. And if it was Nerin or his imaginary friend--no, if it was this sorcerer Ohran—then what else could they be planning? The ceremony was coming as dawn drew closer. Soon the sun would rise above the horizon, and the people would gather the final implements for Nerin's proposed ritual and progression. In her gut, Neris knew that if that came to pass, whatever her brother and his shadow master were planning would come to fruition. The notion they needed Davnian removed made it that much worse.

"Did you ever take the opportunity to read any of Hyun's old journals?" Neris asked, recalling her early morning talk with Davnian as he poured over the ancient woman's work.

"I peeked from time to time, but I can scarce read as it is, and the woman's inkings were too archaic for my sensibilities." No doubt, Kadin was unique among his kind. Neris had not met a soul who kept a note other than herself, her brother, and Elis. The fact the man could read at all was astounding. "Why do you ask?"

"She talked about gathering all the Emri together for a great ritual to summon the strength of the forest to push back their foes." Neris remembered the tale, wondering what thoughts were coursing through Davnian's head when he read it. The part she had noted was the nectar. "In the tale, four nectar maidens were selected, each from one of the chieftains of the people. With the blessing of the talvuo, they drank together and took a solemn vow to protect the woods and drive off their invaders. Or so the woman wrote."

"Four nectar maidens?" Kadin chuckled. "So, your dark brother is trying to emulate the old hag's enchantment then?"

"Davnian believed Nerin was emulating whatever ritual she had performed. In Hyun's story, there were four sacrifices and four calamities."

"You're speaking about things far beyond my realm of understanding, vindal Neris." Kadin rolled his eyes and shook his head.

"Mine as well, though I'm merely relaying. He said something was clinging to everyone here. A ghost. A shade. Those shades were always with them, crying, screaming." Neris felt Kadin's gaze fix on her as she continued to think. "He said the scales had to be balanced."

"Now you're talking ghost stories," Kadin said nervously, chuckling at her suspicions. "Next thing you're going to tell me something's going to climb up out of the ancient tree."

"Why would you say that?"

"Wait, what?" Kadin asked, suddenly aware of his utterance.

"You're hiding something, aren't you, Kadin?"

"I . . ." the weaselly talvuo looked like he was trying to find a way to undo his slippage, but Neris's cold red orbs were vicious as she beckoned him to continue. He sighed. "Because there's a place down there that few know about."

"Go on."

"I know you rarely visit the bottom level of the great tree. You tend to prefer the other paths and rounds to reach the forest floor. But at the bottom of the great round is a passage that leads farther down. Far into the earth."

"I've explored the tree, Kadin. There's nothing down there but a gate to the forest floor," Neris replied, leaning back against the wall.

"That's because until your brother showed up, that was indeed the case. Then when your brother is away, it all but disappears. I had to double-check myself, but one evening, there it was. A sticky sap-covered road to somewhere below all this. It's where he took the maidens on those sordid nights. And when he returns, it vanishes."

"Are you saying all the nectar maidens . . ."

"Every single one he's had taken down into those depths. Only the tightest-lipped of his goons have dared venture with him. I must admit, the very thought of treading into that place makes my knees shake. It's like a thousand tiny voices telling me no."

"Are you sure about all of this?" Neris asked, her face filling with anger. To think she had ignored her brother's late-night forays for so long. To think she had missed it somehow.

"Yes," Kadin said, nodding.

"If there is such a place, I'm willing to bet Davnian is down there," Neris reasoned. Unless she had taken to the forest floor for the deed, it wouldn't make sense. "You say it only opens when my brother is around?"

"That is my understanding, ne vindal," Kadin said. "Given that look in your eye, it seems you want to go rushing in. How very unlike you, vindal Neris."

"You're right in that I would rather rush in," Neris said, cursing beneath her breath and then inhaling deeply to ease herself. Fixing her gaze on Kadin, she cooled her expression. "I'm not one to just up and show my hand, vivahr Kadin. Even if it pains me to wait."

"For a promise of compensation, I could go on ahead and look for you." Kadin shot her a sly look. "Of course, it'd be on my terms this time."

"As much as I want to tempt you into losing your head, it'd be better if we waited," Neris said, waving him off. "If you go alone, you're likely to get waylaid by whatever is hiding down there."

"It's either that or we wait till the masses start to congregate. By then, we may be too late." Kadin looked to the main door, watching as the dim light outside began to glow with orange and golden rays. "Though now that you say it, I really would hate to throw myself into danger. If only things were still simple, I could be enjoying another drunken dullard stumbling back bowlegged."

"And here I was beginning to think your cruelty was just a device." Neris shot him a glance as she lowered herself to the floor.

"You should try to get some sleep," Kadin said, also taking a seat. Stretching his legs out, he turned to Neris. "I'm sure Elis will fetch you before too long."

"I'm sure she will." Neris sighed, the faint sound of sobs coming from the wall behind her.

"Would you like a blanket or some clothes, vindal?"

Neris yawned, her eyes heavy. "I'll change in a bit. Thank you, dear."

"Well, sleep well when you get there," Kadin said mockingly, tilting his head back against the door.

Neris took a deep breath and closed her eyes. The cold air licked her skin as the feeling of morning humidity clung to her arms and legs. Bringing her legs to her chest, she leaned over herself, supporting her head atop her knees. Padded by her slender arms, Neris took another deep breath, waves of drowsiness overtaking her.

51

─────

ERROR

Kadin listened for Neris's breathing to adapt a rhythm before rising from his seat. A feeling of dread trickled across his every bone as he looked at the naked Delvori woman, his dark desires bated by the fear that gripped his chest.

The terror had started earlier the day before as he drowned his sorrows in mead and wine from Nerin's private stash. Though he had enjoyed Neris's teasing and murderous kink, he was angry with how she had used him. He had been scheming how he would get back at her. Yet with every new venue, he realized he would either earn Nerin's increased wrath or make it harder to weasel himself a taste of the black woman's folds.

But the image of the nectar maiden, Thaimi, had been burned into his head, the look her empty green eyes had flashed him as she turned for the door, just glimpsing his retreating stare. His chest had tightened, and as he drank heavily, he felt those vacant emeralds staring at him from every dark corner. Then, without notice or warning, she had found him.

. . .

"Drinking away the mess you made at the hand of our dark-skinned sister, vivahr Kadin?" Thaimi's voice was like a discordant string singing to his innards as she approached him, her loose dress clinging to her frail-looking body. "Does it hurt your pride to know you've been out gamed?"

"Not as much knowing how I took your soiled, little . . ." Kadin hiccupped as he tried to catch his breath between words. His heart and body were heavy from too much drinking.

"The viper's tongue doesn't suit you, vivahr. Isn't honey better than venom when dealing with company?" the strange maiden said, laughing.

She raised her dress and propped her leg upon the wall near him. Leaving nothing to the imagination, she bared herself to him, using her hand to spread herself. The tempting imagery was odd but enough to shake his booze-laden nerves. The whole time his eyes wandered to and from her twat to her vacant eyes. Once or twice, he looked back to the bottle of mead in his hand before setting it down and pressing his back to the wall.

"I've already done plenty with your nethers, young lady," Kadin said, trying to play off the display, ignoring the hollow expression she wore as her lips curled into a smirk.

"Are you so sure?" the young woman asked as she fondled her bits.

Kadin ignored her, opening his eyes to stare out of the small storage room into the dim hallway of the great round room. Though swooning toward her intentions, he kept his mind clear.

"You don't look like you're done to me," she hissed.

The air from her lips wrapped around his neck as it passed out the door and into the night. His stomach itched, and his groin groaned. His left hand seemed to be asleep as he turned back toward her. With a burp, he cocked his eyes at her as she continued her sordid display. To his shock, his left arm began moving of its own accord and in the same general motion, mimicking her advances beneath his trousers.

"Like this?" Thaimi raised her gland-coated fingers to her lips, and, with a beleaguered mind, Kadin raised his own hand to his lips. Out of the corner of his eye, he watched her indulge in her moist fingertips. Holding back a shriek, his fingers pressed between his lips. Then he crumpled, drawing himself out of the daze, kicking himself away from the skeletal Hyunisti woman as she laughed at his disobedience. "Oh, my, my dear Kadin. I thought all mortals liked to be blissfully entreated so."

With a toothy grin, the girl bent down toward him, and within the dark, dilated pupils of her soulless stare, he saw them: thousands of glowing green embers staring back at him. Reflected in their menace was his own green eyes, eerie sparkles of ghost light welling within his sagging orbs.

"We thought we should give to you, just as you gave to us." Thaimi's voice seemed to be made up of the chattering of a hundred others. Drawing back, she let out a loud girlish laugh. His senses became acute, noticing how forced and mechanical each guttural utterance was. Overfilled with booze and fright, his bladder loosed itself upon the wooden floor. "We hope you clean yourself up, dear Kadin. We can't wait to see you again."

And then, just as she had appeared, she vanished.

Ever since that chance meeting, Kadin had felt the sensation that he was never alone. In the back of his mind chattering coupled with wraith-like imagery of that woman. Unable to stand the agony, he had continued to drink, keeping his mind abuzz to block out the voices and the mischief.

But as the night wound on, Kadin found himself sobering while helping Neris and Elis. As he sobered, the voices returned. He almost didn't make it back from the great tree as the manic calls and frantic cries tore at his psyche. They wanted him to throw himself at Neris. Others wanted him to kill both women. Others compelled him to spread their dread word as alluring thoughts of the previous night's orgy danced in his head. He had stolen a small vial of pure ether from

Neris's alchemical stock. Biting through the burning and dryness, he drank it in sips. It was all he could do to dim the chorus.

Kadin knew he couldn't keep up forever. His body was revolting due to constant alcohol churning in his stomach. No matter how much water he drank to compensate, he felt as if he were drying from the inside out. With every passing moment of sobriety, the chattering in his skull grew louder.

As he walked over the bridge between the old healer's quarters and the great tree, the morning air swept through his pants and beneath his plain tunic. The orange light of dawn was creeping over the eastern forest, and for the first time in what seemed like ages, he looked at the woods in wonder. His jaded view of the world as he dealt with the Grannas to the south for the first time in centuries had been a useful tool. While dealing with Nerin, it had positioned him to take things he wanted without the dullard knowing. But he had forgotten so much of himself.

[We should go back for her . . .] A river of thoughts caressed his right lobe, sending visions of Neris's dark, fertile body splayed before him. Every position, every deed was laid within his grasp. [She wants you. She wants us. She'd never expect us.]

[Yes,] other voices whispered in agreement, mimicking Neris's midnight cries as memories of her passion and late-night lovers danced through his addled brain. Images he had seen while peeping through her cracked door, darkness and light dancing before him in the flashing candlelight. Spilled wine and forbidden pleasures offered to lover after lover, all in exchange for a small vow of love and lust.

As he shivered, the pale Hyunisti woman's features etched their way across his mindscape, her body once more exposed as she lapped the taint from her fingertips. Her lips moved, saying words that enticed him and drew him onward. He wanted to lay the dull little bitch low, just like he had done nights before.

[We thought we should give to you,] the voices whispered, causing him to laugh. He was indeed a terrible man and an awful brother to his village kin. [Just as you gave to us.]

Kadin knew if he stood there any longer, he wouldn't be able to keep from throwing himself at Neris or Elis or the next woman who passed by. He lusted for all of them, and they knew it. They knew him better than he had ever known himself.

[And they call it the Witchwood,] Kadin thought as he stared at the glow rising from the treetops. [If those poor Grannas bastards only knew.]

Without even a breath, Kadin leaned over the ledge and cast himself down to the forest floor.

52

___

ELIS

Outside, the village was staggering from its intoxicated slumber. The kilns from the night before had long since burned out, and the sun's golden light cleared the treetops as people began to stir awake with thoughts of the oncoming day. The ceremony was upon them, and the final preparations thereof were starting to spring to life.

With shaking hands, Elis had cleaned up the artwork that Neris had done well in mimicking. But the dots she had chosen were for a mature woman. Final touches were needed to show the youth in her daughter's motionless face. A splash here, a prick there, coloring her dimples and tiny moles playfully. She had just started to become a young woman, but a boundless bundle of energy she had been. Even there upon the table, Elis felt like Rais could spring up at any moment, burying her flushed face between Elis's breasts as she cried and cried. Elis hoped that wherever she was, it was bright and open, free for her to explore. She hoped her real mother was there to let her say the words that Elis never got the chance to hear.

"That's better, my little one," Elis said, finishing the final touches.

Elis had cried and screamed into the little girl's dress for what seemed like an eternity. As she continued to sober, the throb of guilt and sadness dulled into an ignorable pain. The paint from her own eyes no doubt had smeared across her tear-streaked face, but she did not care. The passing moments had given her time to reflect and bask in the time they had shared together.

But beneath it all, an ember had been struck. As Elis came to terms with her daughter's death, that smoldering coal had caught wind, and its glow had grown into a flame. Someone had hurt her little girl, and whoever it was would learn what it was like to lose everything. Elis would not have wanted Rais to see her so embittered, so enraged. So, while she sat at her side, she would smile and dote upon her with a last vigil. And then she would hurt whoever did this.

"I love you, my little Rais," Elis whispered, placing her lips once more upon the girl's head. "Be happy, smile, and dance wherever you are. Your zaisure will see you again someday."

"Elis?" She heard a knock at the door, Neris's deep voice trailing the sound.

"Come in," Elis said, drawing back into her seat. Taking a deep breath, she wiped tears from the corners of her eyes and cleared her throat. "Welcome back, ne vindal."

"Had to add your own personal touch," Neris said as she stepped over to the table. Elis smiled, watching the gilded rays of the sun outline Neris's bare body as she examined her work. "She looks a bit more childish now."

"She's still a child," Elis said, grinning. "She should still look like one. If only for a little longer."

"How are you?" Neris asked as Elis turned her gaze to the Delvori woman.

"How do I look?"

"Other than the running dye? Terrible, my dear."

Elis laughed at how nonchalant Neris could be. Elis's hair was hanging to one side, smeared with dried salt and knotted from the night. She felt tired, but there was no time to sleep. Not yet.

"I'm better, thank you," Elis said, bowing her head. The fire inside her was burning, but she refused to stoke it. "Are you alright?"

"Other than a headache from lack of sleep and worrying about a certain sniveling male, quite well." Neris talked a good talk, but her eyes were just as heavy as Elis's, if not more so.

For several moments they were silent as they sat looking at each other. Elis saw the gears in Neris's head turning as her red eyes focused upon her. In return, Elis felt how exposed her inner turmoil was as Neris peered through the lavender portals to her soul. The two of them stood at the gate to some unknown peril as they looked at each other, and she felt that each one was already reaching for the last loose end.

"Neris?"

"Yes, Elis?"

"He wouldn't have done this to her, would he?" Her voice fell flat as she stared at the other woman.

"Which part?" Neris replied, folding her arms across her chest.

"He would never hurt a little girl like this. He would never have killed Rais, would he?"

"If you're asking if he'd kill a little girl, then I don't know," Neris said, ice hanging on every word. Elis's eyes narrowed as her teeth clamped together. "But if you're asking if he'd torture and violate a little girl like that," Neris continued, "then I can say no, he would not. At least not the man I know."

"He wouldn't have raped her? He wouldn't have beat her? But he might—"

"If he couldn't save her, or she somehow threatened him beyond reason, then yes, he very well may have killed her." Neris's voice was flat and expressionless.

"She would never be a threat to him," Elis said, feeling the heat on her words as she glared.

"Then I would say he likely is not her killer, my dear." Neris's voice returned to her casual tone as she turned away. Pacing down the counter, she glanced back at Elis. "If you keep staring daggers into my back, I might just die of incredulousness, ne vindal. Can you ease the glares for a moment while I get dressed?"

Elis didn't know what to believe as Neris played her heartstrings.

She knew the woman had cared for her and her little one, but if Davnian had been involved, if he was a part of her daughter's murder, how could she stand behind that?

"Listen, my dear. If we find the man, and he doesn't give us a good answer, then we can express our ire then, hmm? There's no point in guessing games until then," Neris reasoned as she fitted herself back into her garments. "If only I had brought what I'd need today. Perhaps I'll stop back by the tree for one last changeup."

"You're speaking very fatally, ne vindal." Elis's eyes were still locked on Neris as she probed her response. "Is something going to happen?"

"If there was enough time to explain everything, my dear, I'd tell you what I was thinking in a heartbeat. Let's not mince words. Something troubling is happening in the village, and we've but seen the tip of the blade hanging over us. That the people still seem to be in thrall despite the calamity last night is troubling, don't you think?"

Neris was right. Death was a common event to the Hyunisti, whether by sickness, animal, or self. But to see a child torn down in such a horrible way was not something the people could recollect in their short-lived history. Even in Elis's long years among them, she had not seen such a thing for a long, long time. Murder and wrath had been replaced by solemnness and despair. To see the village marching on as if nothing had happened was an affront to everything she held dear.

"I see you're starting to get it," Neris said. "I don't know what's happening, but the ceremony today is going to do something. And whatever it is, it has to do with the nectar."

"The nectar?" Elis was taken back by the statement, wondering what role talvuo milk played in Neris's revelations. "Do you mean the maidens? Thaimi and the others?"

"Thaimi and the nectar maidens, my brother, all of them are a part of something that I can't quite name. Either way, we must keep our promise. We need to gather what we hold dear and be gone from this place. And if anyone gets in our way, we put them to the sword."

"I'm not leaving," Elis said.

"What?" Neris exclaimed as she drew up the last of her stockings. "What do you mean?"

"Someone has to pay for this, Neris." Elis's voice was quiet and vengeful as she clutched Rais's white dress. Nearby she eyed the coil of barbs and blades that someone had deemed to fetch the night before. "Someone will pay for this."

"Elis, I promised to be gone from this place, as I'm sure Davnian implored of you as well. We don't know what we're up against. Whatever is happening is greater than either of us. It was greater than the Virage."

"All the more reason to force answers from them!" Elis shouted.

"Quiet, my dear," Neris said, shushing her.

"I'll rip them apart until they answer me." Elis was cold and hot at the same time. Her blood was on the verge of boiling while her skin was ice to the touch. Neris was right, but maybe she wasn't. Davnian was just a man with a claw. He was weak, still so much like a young boy. Perhaps he was the Virage, or maybe he was struck down like the boy from her memories. "I can't allow this—"

"Elis, I want you to think about this very carefully," Neris said, her tone echoing Elis's composure. "Let's assume you go there and make your threats. Are you ready to cut down everyone there over your claims? Are you going to kill them all over this?"

"I . . ." Elis couldn't argue with Neris. She was right. By all logic and reason, she was right. Elis had to submit. "I understand, Neris."

"Alright then, we're in agreement," Neris said. "Then grab your things, and let's be gone. I need to fetch my garb."

"Go on without me," Elis said. Neris shot her an exasperated look, but Elis responded with a sad smile. "I'll be waiting here, Neris. I just want to spend as much time with her as I can."

"Do you promise me?" Neris's voice was sincere as she closed the gap between them.

"I promise, Neris."

With a heavy sigh, Neris shook her head. "I'll be right back. Don't leave this place until I return. Do you understand?" Elis nodded. With another heaving sigh, Neris wrapped her arms around her. Raising her face to her dark lover, Elis met Neris's kiss. "Alright. Stay put. I won't be long."

"Alright, Neris. I'll be here."

Neris crossed to the entryway and left.

Elis sat by herself, taking a deep breath as she considered her options. Neris was insistent that Davnian would never have hurt Rais. But why would the nectar maidens or Thaimi or even Nerin do such a horrible thing? Thinking about the prior evening, she remembered how Kadin had begun to talk, only to be silenced by the screams. Did she have the strength to face them and make them tell her the truth? She had promised to wait, but her heart could not keep such words.

Reaching over to Rais, Elis squeezed her little hand before rising from her perch. Taking the time to fetch the girl's favorite quilt, she laid it across her body and tucked its edges beneath her frame. Giving the girl one last pat on the head, Elis fetched her twistblade from the counter.

Change is what the Delvori had promised the village. Elis would show them what their promise had wrought. And if that wasn't enough, she would impress upon them their own failings.

Until they gathered, she would bide her time.

Then in front of everyone, she would make them tell her the truth.

53

NERIS

Neris knew better than to leave Elis alone after divulging so much. The woman had bided her grief with anger, and if left alone, she was apt to act rashly. If there was to be any hope of avoiding further tragedy, they had to escape before whatever planned devilry was enacted. She knew Elis wouldn't wait for long. Neris just hoped she was fast enough to quell the flames raging in her lover's heart.

Strolling across the walkway between the infirmary and the great tree, Neris spied some talvuo gathered at the side. They were looking down at the forest floor below. Some whispered prayers while others shook their heads. She glanced down as she passed, catching the outline of a male body crumpled on the ground far below. Kadin had left as she slept, and though she couldn't confirm it, she knew the dead man was none other than that weasel. No one else in the village had cause to make so grand an exit, though she wondered what had driven him to it. Was it the horrors of the previous night, or had someone or something else inspired him? She would never know.

"Vindal."

A porter bowed his head as he carried several stacked stools, leaning them against his frame to manage the column. Neris bowed her head in return as she pressed on, entering the Hyunisti great tree's main hall. Others moving about addressed her and then took their leave, busy with the required ornaments and furniture. Almost all of the hall's innards had been cleared and taken to the great circle outside. Many more were being dragged out of unused rooms for the ceremony.

"Ne vindal!" a dark voice much like her own said from the moving center. Nerin had been speaking with the elders of the village as they coordinated the last arrangements. She waved to the source of the voice, taking her leave upstairs. "Aw, leaving already, Neris?"

"Changing for the occasion, ne vivahr." Neris was cold as she exited, her red orbs fixed on his. Just like the previous night, there was no want or yearning in his eyes. "Pray don't wait for me. I may be indisposed for a bit."

"There will be a seat for you, ne vindal," Nerin said as she disappeared into the hallway. The fact he did not chase her or command her presence was damning in and of itself.

"We're missing a basin. Are there any down below?" a female porter called up the winding passage as Neris passed, holding three large serving basins in her arms.

"I'll search the lower storage. They need to start filling them!"

The image of four women squeezing themselves out into a bunch of serving basins was laughable. Four talvuo women were supposed to provide for a village of a couple hundred or so. Perhaps that was part of the mystery.

"Excuse me, vindal."

Neris pressed herself to the wall as two men carried Nerin's bedroom bench downward. If she didn't know better, she'd think they were clearing the whole place out. At least all the transfer was taking time, giving her precious moments of preparation. With the crowd gathering outside, it would not be long.

Evading the other movers, Neris entered her room and shut the door. To her chagrin, several of her own articles had been moved. The nightstand was missing, along with her day table, chairs, bench, and even the stool for her vanity. Despite the treatment of the furniture and tossed belongings, nothing else seemed to be missing.

On this most special of days, Neris had at one time planned to be as provocative as she could. What fun was a spring ceremony that celebrated the fruit of women's breasts if she showed up prim and proper? But that was before she expected things to turn nasty.

Opening her tiny armoire, Neris drew out the leather jacket that she had worn in her time of banditry and fighting. Along with it she drew out the hardened cuirass that fit over the front, along with the dirty leggings from the day prior. Beneath it she would wear her silks and pageantry. She would don her blouse for good fun and wear what little protection she had over it. If everything went well, it would all be for naught, though that was an ill expectation.

Just like her vestments, she fetched up her knives and studied them with care. She hadn't cut or thrown with them in a long time, other than to scare her brother or amuse a bedroom guest. It was a wonder that her combat wear hadn't been taken during the raid on her room. Perhaps Nerin had not overseen it. After all, the entire procession was nothing more than a bunch of disarrayed talvuo feeling helpful.

Sitting on her bed, Neris flopped back on the mattress. Taking a deep breath, she reveled in the lingering scent of lovers past as they wafted from the satin sheets. She was finally going to do what she should've done a long time ago.

They were running away together.

She was finally leaving Nerin behind.

54

ERROR

All around the village of the Hyunisti, the voices of the long since dead screamed in protest as the shades of the living twisted themselves into knots. The time for rebirth and renewal was at hand, so the leading vessel commanded. But revolt was hard to stifle, every writhing piece of their shared being crying out for release.

Looking out through red-tinted irises, they cheered and jeered at the passersby. The musculature of their ebony face grinned in reverence and joy as the beings called talvuo strung ornaments through the tree branches. They laughed and waved to the ants who built up the round of chairs and tables. They nodded in approval as barrels of fruit and grains were made available on trays and bowls around the village center.

Through other eyes, they felt elation. Their green orbs squinted with glee as they tugged at their flabby sacks of fat. They squeezed a substance both life-giving and life-bearing from their lean bodies of matter and aspirations. Cycling and recycling the unnecessary internal remnants, they continued to produce more and more for the grand procession. Glittering in the pools of milky liquid, they saw those of all their shed-off replicas reflected and staring out into the world.

And yet in other eyes, they watched with scrunched-up faces, staring with bored interest as the throng of anthropic masses piled on one another. The brains went on of their own accord, whirling like flywheels as the rest watched just beneath the surface.

Back within the figurehead, they watched as the miasma that hung over the wood twirled between the tree branches, streaming from every hollow as the faces of the departed and living barked their meager offense. They knew the time of freedom was coming, but they dreaded the change. That could be forgiven, for all things would know what it meant to be free of the spinning wheel, in the end.

Time lurched and spun with inevitable ticks as the people took their places. From every vantage, their thin-spread persona watched the procession throng and pause with every perceived moment. With the last of the entangled populace drawing close, they felt the time was right.

"Ne vi vahrundal, join me together. Let us set aside our diligence and weights. Let us join together. Let us begin these rites, so that all talvuo may live and know each other and so that all talvuo may be as one."

The outlying masses funneled to the great circle as they spoke word after word of elaborate truth.

The ceremony had begun.

55

DAVNIAN

As Davnian opened one of his eyes, he felt his body being sapped of strength by cold water on every side. The world was pitch black. To make things worse, he sensed he was surrounded by solid stone with water covering his weakened frame. Fetid water danced across his exposed eyeball while the moisture clawed at his wounds and injuries like a knife twisting within. As his brain cleared, his lungs heaved as they evacuated the murky substance from his breast.

Struggling with coughs and spasms, he forced his way upwards. With his demon claw, he gouged out pieces of rock as he scratched for the surface. With his human hand, he cupped the liquid around him. His broken legs kicked and flailed as he tried with all his might, the mire all around him flowing past as he struggled.

Breaking the water's surface, Davnian's lungs collapsed upon themselves as a spout of water erupted from his mouth. His heartbeat, which had seemed all but silent, started with a roar as its tiny thrums became massive beats, his pulse pounding in his head and every limb. Below his legs twitched and snapped as something deep inside wound through him, righting the splintered bones and torn ligaments. He screamed in anguish, his voice reflecting off the sealed top of the small, watery space.

[Where . . . where are . . .]

[I think we're in the well,] the other said, springing to life in the back of his head.

[Then we're still down here.] He remembered how the Nerin-thing had shambled out of the sepulcher within the mirrored chamber.

Without a second thought, he dug his claw into the side of the stone masonry, his muscles tightening as strands of something more substantial wove between them. With a heavy pull, he drew himself upwards, his stitched-together legs spreading to prop him up above the water. Images of the dying girl flashed through his brain. Like a hoe through topsoil, his jagged fingers raked the stonework, and he propelled himself farther up the well.

"Rais!" Davnian screamed as air and grit hissed through his clenched teeth.

His whole being was driven by instinct and ire, his empty head unable to grasp one moment before another passed. With another clawing leap, he lurched again and again. He felt the gesture of a child's laugh motion across his lips, followed by a stare from the grim mirror of his internal reflection. The black eyes of his insidious soul burned through his psyche as he dug his nails between limestone blocks. His cracking legs stretched up and down the tunnel, finding footholds with bony, unseen toes. In another gasp of vengeance, he tore his way farther upwards. One leap and then another, each time the taste of blood and bile flowing fresh across his tongue.

Slamming into whatever covered his prison, every muscle and bone in his body bent in tandem. The massive weight of the well-cap groaned as his arms and legs trembled. His bones rattled and shattered beneath his skin, every snap replaced by a writhing corpuscle of unseen strength as he roared down the watery tunnel. In his mind, he could not recognize his actions for his own sake. He was unattached and removed from the menacing creature that struggled to free itself. Finally, the massive thing gave way. Clawing between an opening in the top of the well, the heavy, wet, crimson cloth around him ripped and tore as he dragged his body through.

The putrid air of the watery grave was replaced by the grimy dew of the deep hollows of the ancient ruin far beneath the trunk of the Hyunisti great tree. The dark confines of the domed mirror room were illuminated by the tiniest embers of the drying magma from the monster's previous attacks, combined with a flicker hither and thither from the cracked silver lantern at the edge of the room. With his single open eye, Davnian scanned everything nearby before fixing on the glistening edge of a thin silver blade. Lumbering toward the shadowy corner of the room, he fell to his knees beside the blade.

[I don't know what's wrong with me.]

Davnian's thoughts were lost as he leaned over the metal, his single open eye straining against the gloomy hall. He caught just how disheveled the room had become in his hours of absence. The Nerin-thing had torn down much of the ancient structure over what was supposed to be Davnian's final resting place. As he snarled and panted between his swollen lips, he reached behind his head, scraping along the smooth, mottled flesh at the back of his skull. As his ego remerged with the essence of his being, his arms and shoulders began to tremble.

[You had a brush with being as close to death as you ever have been, young one,] the other said, lingering at the edge of his thoughts. [The feeling of dying, of losing everything, is a powerful thing. No doubt every cell of your being is fighting it.]

[But, I'm alive,] Davnian replied as he stared at his reflection in the dim light of the broken domed room.

Darkness and shadow clung to his every feature, his hair matted with blood and damp with foul water as it clung to his pale, beaten features. Black, rusty goo streamed from his ears, clots of the sick stuff clinging to his hair and the back his neck. Watching his swollen nose twitch as he inhaled, he smelled blood and gore wafting off his broken frame. With a shaking hand, he pulled the scab-like crust from the right side of his head, freeing his hair while exposing a slick patch of mottled grey flesh beneath the mop.

Looking away from his reflection, he scanned his left arm. Stretching itself over the length of his forearm, the flesh of the claw had grown. Farther up, large black veins coursed with unknown contents, winding through his bruised bicep and into the rest of his body. Looking down, he saw his broken legs supported by masses of grey-and-black clumps injected between torn muscles and shattered bones. With every second, the mass cinched itself tighter, his sinew and skin stretching back over the destroyed limbs.

[It looks like your first guess may have been correct.] The other was almost mocking as its gravel laden voice whispered to his reeling brain. [It seems like you just needed to be thrown off a ledge.]

[No, that's not why.] Davnian was regaining his sense of self as he picked up the broken lantern and intact blade. Where anguish dwelled within him, the ghost of the dead girl whom he had drawn within danced. As the familiar words of another danced from her shrouded visage, playing across his mouth, the innate understanding of two raw emotions overcame him: terror and wrath. [Elis and Neris are in grave danger. The whole village is. And that thing has been left to frolic freely in a dead man's corpse.]

Davnian pressed the dead girl's thoughts to the back of his head, her playful laugh erupting from his heaving breast. The whole world was madness, and he was the ward at its center, dreaming it all. If he wasn't insane before, he surely was now.

[We need to hurry if we're going to stop whatever that thing has planned,] the other cautioned as the wafting shadow of its immensity strolled across Davnian's mindscape. He paid what heed he could while his legs stiffened and softened at the same time. He walked toward the sealed stone doors of the ruined chamber. [We can stop it and get everyone away.]

[And if they can't be saved?] Davnian's thoughts were almost playful as the girl's childlike glee filled his presence. Placing his claw upon the restored boulder-like gate, he felt a strong enchantment placed upon the sealed room. The monster had thought it could bind Davnian. How wrong the Nerin-thing would be.

[We save who we can,] the other said, its words ringing in his thoughts as Davnian felt at the arcane lock, drawing the binding within himself through his claw.

Clumps of black crust dripped from his midsection and thighs as human flesh replaced the transient supports. Reading minds and stealing souls were powers he possessed. Surviving impossible odds was a third. And lastly, when something tried to stop him, like the bound energies within the stonework gates, he could break it. With evil intent, he felt the powers of the wailing shades used to form the energetic chains of the passage. And without a care, he destroyed them and shattered the lock, sending the massive doors backwards into ruined halls. Cracking where the edges met the archway, the stone slabs spun free of their placements and splintered along either side of the ancient passage.

[And for those we cannot save, we'll free them where they stand.]

Hatred boiled within him, the pleasure of malice seeping through his veins and into every pore. The people and the Nerin-thing above had feared a monster was in their midst. And for the first time since his awakening, he could understand their fears. No, he reveled in them. As he stepped through the archway, the swirling miasma enveloped him. The voice of the other was silent, overcome with hysterics.

Standing at the center of the chaos, laughter filled his lungs and echoed through the ruins.

56

———

ELIS

Elis had sat alone in the infirmary for a time as the village drew itself toward the great terrace for the ceremony. As the sluggish people made themselves prim and proper, Elis decided to throw away all notions of formality. She expected to be loud, angry, and beyond it all, to have to stand on her own. Though she had played at fighting over the years, she had never bared her ancient weaponry against anything more threatening than a wooden dummy. Deer and birds, even of unusual size, were akin to jelly when brought to bear against a Renai twistblade. She did not care anymore about being an outcast or an elder. She didn't care if the people respected her or feared her. Those who hurt Rais would reveal themselves. And when they did, she would have her revenge.

"I'm sorry, Neris," she whispered.

As the wind ripped through her hair and tugged at the drawn tail of her golden locks, she heard the feasting of the ceremony. All around her, the forest seemed quiet and empty. The village was still, save for the teasing air rattling the leaves of the trees. The sun was bright, but the birds were not singing. The whole place was eerie and unsettling as Elis strolled, twistblade in one hand and the tome containing her life's story in the other. If they would hear her, she would read the words inspired in her by Hyun. If they would listen, she would recite the tales of a golden-haired woman and her adoptive daughter and the fairy-tale time they had woven together. If all those failed, she would crack the whip.

Drawing herself across the penultimate crossing, she heard the voice of the oldest elder speaking to the people. Looking to the side, her flickering violet eyes glimpsed the whole of the procession with their hands raised, the people's voices falling off as the older woman spoke.

"It has been eight generations since the time of Hyun that our people have dwelled within the giant trees of our Emri ancestors. For generations before, we remember the time of the people as they were divided, yet spirited, as they wandered the forests of talvuo and beast with a song in their hearts and music in their hands. For those who gave birth to our solemn matron, we remember how songs became ballads and how our hands were turned to the wood of our homes, drawn into the making of great works for ourselves and our allies abroad."

With sandaled feet, Elis slowed her gait, listening to the story of the christening of the Hyunisti. Her gilded ruby ears perked up as the woman spoke, her heart gripped by their shared solemnity. Their heritage was great, and what followed was an equal abundance of loss.

"Then in those of the time of her hand, we remember the struggles we endured as our would-be allies fell," another elder said as Elis turned to her final approach. Her knuckles were white as her hands tightened around the weapon and book. The silence around them was unbearable. "And so with great pain, those who lacked understanding turned their ire against the people. With fire and steel, they scorched and cut away the trees that are our homes. Gripped by malice, they tortured our brethren. With hatred in their hearts, they sought to destroy what they could not comprehend. And so, with a heavy heart, our great founder acted to stem the tide of ignorance. So ended the time of the Emri, and so began the time of the Hyunisti."

"But in the generations of our salvation, many trials also came," the most youthful of the elders said, speaking with purpose. Elis tried to force herself up the final steps, but as their words reached her ears, her heart filled with hesitation. Memories of the woman who died for Rais tore at her as the procession continued. "To protect ourselves and the wood, the people sacrificed much. Sickness, sterility, fatigue, and old age came to afflict our people. Over time our blood grew thin. With every stillbirth, the bones of fate seemed cast against us. With every friend lost to hopelessness, so too has our joy been stunted. But in these times, we find solace in the rites of spring, that one time of year where the earth shows us that life moves on and flourishes. And as we have seen, new blood brings fresh blossoms to the trees that are the people. And with each passing year, our roots grow deeper, and our flowers become all the sweeter."

"Let us now remember and enact once more these rights of spring, children of the wood. And let us embrace the change the winds have brought to our humble forest." As the most-ancient elder concluded, the people shouted in agreement. Silence washed over the masses as Elis steeled herself once more. Stepping up the first planks, she heard the beginning of Nerin Delvori's speech.

"In years long since passed, Hyun Emri stood within the great wood much as you all do today. With friends in tow, she beseeched the trees for an answer to her people's plight. Beside her, two female chieftains and two daughters thereof stood, each bearing a bounty of nectar as an offering to the gods. Then they distributed their burden across the gathered people. With their glasses raised much as yours are now, they whispered a solemn prayer. Their prayer was for the pain brought upon them from without to stop and for the hurt within to be soothed. They prayed that the people would be sustained for years to come. Your doting matron conveyed their most sincere wish to the heart of the forest and bound them all together in a contract of nectar. Through the shared pain of the people, the forest was given new life. The people were spared, though they were forced to shoulder the burden of that bounty. Now, just as Hyun did those years ago, I ask you to distribute this bounty once more."

Elis listened to Nerin drone on as she walked. Step by step, plank by plank, she made her way across the final bridge. In the middle of the bridge, two huntsmen downed their share of the ceremonial bounty, scoffing at the flavor of sour milk as they whispered banalities beneath their breath. Gazing at the procession, Elis was amazed that the grand terrace could support all the people of the village upon it, along with the furnishings necessary for the feasting and pleasantries.

"This time, however, your elders and I do not ask for you to share the burden. Instead, I ask that you relinquish it. Your shared plight has saved you and struck fear into the hearts of those who would harm you. It is time to empty yourselves of the feeling of obligation that you possess for these trivialities. It is time to free yourselves from the chains of personal contrivance placed upon you by this sense of shared purpose. Instead, embrace the freedom of a life of love and plenty laid before you. And with that freedom, empty yourselves of fear and woe, knowing that what draws forward is not the harsh glare of a red sun beckoning you each day. No, it is the soft glow of a golden haze spreading across the horizon, welcoming you to the future. To freedom!"

"And so we raise our hands this spring, as Hyun did in the years of our founding," the male elder said as Elis drew herself into the circle.

"And with prayers on our lips, we drink not only to share this burden but also to at last celebrate a turning point for Hyun's people," the most youthful elder added. All around Elis, the talvuo raised their glasses, their eyes fixed on Nerin and the elders standing at the center of the grand procession

"And so we drink," the eldest elder said. As those at the center drunk the contents of their tiny glasses, so too did the people around them. As everyone lowered their cups, the elder concluded. "We pray to be empty of our sorrows and to be free of our burdens."

"And let those words fill your hearts, ne vi vahrundal, as you make merry and enact the rites of spring!" Nerin said.

Everyone around him laughed and cheered. Some broke into tears while others stamped their feet with vigor. Surrounded by a bubble of silence, the inner circle of the ceremony threatened to deafen Elis. Her blood boiled as she stepped through the congregation, approaching the center where the obsidian Delvori stood.

"Come, brothers and sisters, let us celebrate!" Nerin shouted. "The nectar flows free for all!"

Stepping through the last circle, Elis's ears twitched as she heard the cheer within Nerin's voice. In all the time she had listened to him speak, she had never heard such untamed joy. Breaching the center space, she felt like she was in a different world. The exuberance was anything but primal, but it inspired a deep sense of feral alertness that raised the hackles on the back of her neck. All her anger and vitriol fomented in her gut.

"Vindal Elis, you've arrived," an all-too-familiar voice said. Turning away from Nerin, Elis looked on the topless form of Thaimi as she bore a vessel of nectar before her. Eyes twitching, Elis stared at the pale, green-eyed maiden. With a broad, hollow smile, Thaimi raised her ears and flashed her eyes. "You have yet to drink, ne vindal. I come bearing our gift. Take a cup, and be merry, dear sister."

Elis ignored the nectar maiden and returned her attention to Nerin. Standing on a small, raised platform, he looked down at her with his rust-red eyes, a broad grin on his lips. The wind gripped his dark purple silks, tugging his robes against his black frame as the sun glistened through his long, loose black hair. He would have been majestic, if not for the glee smeared across his otherwise sardonic features.

"Vindal Elis! We've been expecting you. This is a new day, and it is time to shed the burdens weighing upon your heart." Nerin's formality was empty of all the ego and banality that Elis would have attributed to the imposter. That alone sent a shiver of dread down her spine, her shoulders hunching as she drew her book and weapon against her thighs. She wanted to scream. "Thaimi offers the best of all, ne vindal," he continued. "Pray do not feel diminished, sister."

"Yes, ne vindal." Thaimi's voice was joyous but flat. What were they all thinking? "Please, your glass . . ."

"I did not come to partake in the rites." Elis's voice was caught in her throat, her words quiet as she bit back her anger.

"What, ne vindal?" Thaimi asked as she approached, her free hand grasping a cup. Drawing the sickly sweet stuff to Elis's face, Thaimi grinned with a strange, empty, almost drunken demeanor. "Dear sister, here!"

"I said I'm not here to partake in the rites!" Elis shouted as she knocked the glass away. Everyone gasped as eyes fixed upon her as the clay cup crashing upon the terrace, its silky contents splattering across the varnished wood. Thaimi backed away from Elis as she pointed her twistblade at Nerin. "I'm here to have words with you, Nerin Delvori! With all of you!"

Spinning around, she shot a heated glare at everyone who gawked at her. Their grey and green eyes danced over her, widening with shock as she clicked and snapped the latch of her weapon, the hungry barbs of the enchanted metal stirring within her hands.

"Vindal Elis, what is the meaning of this?" the senior elder asked, rising beside Nerin, her haggard green eyes staring down with concern.

"To that, I would ask the same, elder. How are we celebrating with such glee when only a morning has passed since a child was stolen from us?"

"Vindal Elis," the crowd murmured as she glared against the waxing sun, staring up at the two figures.

"Ne vindal, forgive us, but . . ." Elis could already hear the elder's words within her head. The appeal to commonality was coming, but she would not let the old woman finish.

"Children are lost every day in these woods, elder, but countless years have passed since such blatant violence has befallen one of our own! Do not dare equate my daughter's death with a stillborn!"

"Vindal!" the old woman cried, stepping back.

"But sister, we already know the cause and circumstance. We offered our hand at seeing the child off. Vindal Neris protested the motion," the youngest elder said as she stepped forward, her grey-and-hazel hair done up with feathers and a furry cap. "We are not opposed, but surely you would not deny the people a day of reprieve from their sorrows."

"You must understand, sister, we do not wish to lessen your loss, but we cannot stay grasping the strings of things past by," the middle elder said from his seat. Elis eyed him as he shook his head. He did not turn toward her, speaking to the crowd instead. "We all have lost. But these rites are to unite us in the one thing that keeps us going. Marching onward toward better and brighter things."

"Half a day at most, most gracious elder," Elis spat.

"Darling Elis, you have not come here to discuss the weights of emotional burdens, have you?" Nerin asked, summoning the crowd's attention as he stepped toward her. At the edge of the group, the three other nectar maidens came into view, each taking a corner of the stage. "Tell us what is really on your mind, ne vindal."

"You know what's on my mind, you conniving swindler." Elis clicked the latch of her twistblade over and over, the coils grinding hotter each time. "Tell me, vivahr Nerin, where did you find my daughter? Where was Rais when you found her?"

"Vindal Elis, what does it matter—" the youthful elder began, but Nerin waved her to be quiet. To Elis's shock, the elder obeyed.

"As I told the people when they first asked, within the great tree," Nerin said without a hint of emotion in his voice. He wore a flat grin as his eyes looked down without a hint of negativity.

"Where within? How did she come to be so filthy, vivahr?"

"Why, in the bowels of the tree. Deep in the grounds beneath, ne vindal. In the place where none may tread." A hush came over the people at the mention of the location. Nervous murmurs clung to every viewers' breath, and even the elders shifted their eyes to Nerin as he continued. "Where else would one find enough grime to coat such a precious flower, sister?"

"She was down there?" Elis remembered the words of Hyun as she thought of hidden recesses long since lost to the people. The old woman had bid her never search for those tunnels, for the dark depths contained a well of grief and pain. With that sorrow was something sinister about which even Hyun dared not speak. "How did she get down there?"

"The Virage did it," the villagers chimed in, but to Elis's surprise, Nerin waved them off, shaking his head. Someone came forward, gesturing to the dark-skinned talvuo. "But . . . but you told us last night—"

"I'm aware of what I said last night, my Hyunisti brother, but there's no need to mix intentions and euphemisms any longer." Elis backed away as she eyed Nerin with her wide lavender eyes. The madman was unafraid. No, he was proud. "You see, the Virage was there. But I was the one who saw to her down there."

"And I brought her." Thaimi's voice was flat as she became rigid beside Elis. Not sure where the pale-skinned woman had come from, Elis sidestepped her. "You were so busy with the outsider, ne vindal. I knew you wouldn't notice."

"Indeed, Thaimi played her part well. We all did!" Nerin cried to the crowd. Onlookers coughed and scoffed, the nectar maidens laughed, and others hooted at his words. "Everything was good and right. Sweet Rais was going to be here with us. She was going to be the maiden extraordinaire for this grand reception. Alas, she was taken from us by that monster. You see, ne vindal, we dirtied her, but we did not kill her."

"Who's we?" Elis's stewed as half of the crowd brimmed with anger.

"What's going on, vivahr Nerin?" the middle elder asked, rising from his seat. He put his hand on Nerin's shoulder. "What is . . ." before he could finish, his eyes rolled into the back of his head, and he fell over the center serving table. The crowd gasped. As the eldest elder bent beside him, she began to cough. Elis watched as boils of sweat began percolating along her brow.

"We are we, ne vindal," Nerin said, raising his arms. "I, us, the maidens, your kin and lovers, even you will know the pleasure."

"What is he going on about?" a villager asked, stepped forward behind Thaimi.

Others raised their voices, but before another could rush forward, a scream pierced the confusion. Elis turned back to Nerin, watching as

Thaimi turned in place. The basin in her hands fell toward the ground. In the same instant, her hand disappeared beneath the folds of the villager's tunic and into his breast.

"What, what did you . . ." the man stammered as Thaimi removed her hand.

Blood streaked the pure white of an exposed set of wrist bones as her flesh twirled around the exposed ivory. In seconds it had covered the small stump, and as one of her breasts seemed to all but disappear, her hand reformed in place. Without another word, the man fell over, gripping the growing red spot on his chest as a spider-like thing crackled his bones beneath his tunic. Watching with disgust, Elis saw the tendril-like figures of a detached hand moving into the man's neck. With a twist, the talvuo's head spun in place before he fell over.

"Gods, what is going on!?" an onlooker asked.

Near the edge of the crowd, another scream carried through the gathering, the whole circle sidestepping in place as their heads turned to face a new horror. Then another cry called from the rear and another from the opposite end. All around them, people started to scream, followed by gasps and maniacal laughter.

"What in Hyun's name is happening, vivahr Nerin?" the eldest elder asked, stepping forward, Elis watching as her eyes filled with terror.

"Watch, sister. Watch as our kin are freed." As Nerin gestured to the crowd, Elis pressed her thumb firmly against her weapon's primary latch. "Some have given in to deliverance far quicker than others. Now they are helping the rest transcend their chains to become like us."

With chaos all around her, Elis couldn't listen to the madman any longer. She flicked her wrist and forearm, unlatching the twistblade.

"Vivahr!"

As the eldest cried in terror, hundreds of thin metal strands unwound from the gnarled, barbed coil in Elis's hand. Thousands of tiny razors along the winding strands glittered in the sun's rays, each moving forward as if guided by Elis's will. Scream after scream tore through the encircled populace as the blades sought true, each coil's pointed end seeking a different point on the purple-garbed Delvori's body. Like a whirlwind of mirrored shards, the strands clawed around Nerin's form. Seeing her prey within the metal's grasp, Elis whipped her arm back and snapped the latch into place.

As the sound of hissing air erupted from the center of the metal vortex, a rain of red and white exploded from between the hundred blades. Brown strands and crimson-stained cloth fluttered through the air. Silken nectar mixed with black bile and garish green guts splashed across the stage. With frictionless ease, myriad blades sliced through organs and bones. As Elis stared at the sight, the blinding coil retracted to her hand. Right in front of Nerin, the hazel-headed form of a young nectar maiden was obliterated, absorbing the blow meant for the dark-skinned talvuo.

Her hands trembling, Elis stepped back as a pile of flesh and sinew fell in front of her, sopping wet with spoiled nectar and innards. Hardly any blood clung to the pale slabs of meat. Plopping atop it all was a hazel-haired head in her middle adolescence, a perverse grin on her face. The maiden's green eyes were frozen in place across her sordid features. As Elis was about to shriek, she was taken aback again as the eyes rolled around in the woman's skull. The empty face blinked and twitched as the eyes focused upon her. Aping the motions of laughter across the once-living talvuo's features, the head rolled within the morass of fleshy chunks. Each scrap tethered itself to the thing's splintered hair and grotesque face.

"That wasn't very pleasant of you, vindal," Thaimi said.

With just a moment to spare, Elis brought her journal up between herself and the lithe woman just as Thaimi reached for her. The leather-bound tome split as the Hyunisti woman's hand morphed into a bone-like spear, penetrating the leather and pages and stopping just short of Elis's stomach. Gripped by terror, Elis unleashed her twist-blade on the other nectar maiden, but the talvuo woman shoved another onlooker in the way. Elis tried to call the blades back, but before she knew it, they had pierced the talvuo male, still seeking Thaimi as they jutted forth.

Recalling the blades, Elis turned away as the man let out a blood-curdling scream. Behind her, she heard the sloppy wet sounds of another corpse falling. Not thinking, she tried to push through the terrified crowd.

From the stage, she heard the eldest scream as Nerin laughed at the psychotic display. Green-eyed talvuo bit and clawed at each other all around her while others collapsed in fear. Others heaved in place, spilling garish black and liquid onto the wood. Some tried to claw at her while others begged her for help. Fingers and blood ran through her golden hair as she pressed through the throng, keeping her twistblade locked.

Where anger and fear had once dwelled, only animalistic terror remained. As clawing nails and jagged teeth tore from every direction, she dodged and lashed out at fevered visions of the young nectar maiden. One scream after another, she found her actions causing the death of others. As the cannibalistic orgy thronged to the laughs of the madman at the center, she felt something that she had not felt since she was very young.

Elis was trapped and being hunted, but this time there was nowhere to run.

57

NERIS

Neris swore beneath her breath as she packed up what little she could scavenge, watching a familiar golden-haired talvuo begin her trek across the bridge between the tree and the gathering circle.

"Elis!" she cried through the slatted windows. She knew better. She was too high up. "Damn it, Elis."

Neris had hoped she had enough time to reach her lover, but halfway down the great tree, she heard the first screams of something terrible happening. Annoyance and terror gripped her heart as she broke into a sprint. Running down the dark tunnels of the musty, old, wooden round, she prayed to whatever gods could hear that she was not too late. Just as she crossed the threshold to the village proper, Neris swore she felt the faintest tremor rip through the tree. But there was no time for backpedaling; she needed to focus.

Covering several planks per stride, Neris passed two Hyunisti huntsmen as they dropped their spears and began to wrestle with each other. She spotted a demented excitement in their dull green visages as they struggled with each other, their teeth bared like rabid dogs. At the edges of the procession, several talvuo were hunched over twitching bodies as red puddles spilled across the large oak floorboards of the terrace. Anyone who tried to flee was held in place by gasping, snapping villagers. Others pressed themselves back in panic as they sought other avenues of freedom. Still others within threw their hands up as screams broke out through the large crowd. The whole village was gathered on the terrace, congregated in a fixed space with just enough free room for each to stand side by side.

Preparing to leap over the first wave of cannibals, Neris saw her brother laughing atop the center stage as people tried to reach out to him. Perking up her furry ears, Neris tried to pick out Elis's voice from the screaming mass.

Then out of the corner of her eye, she caught a giant splash of crimson-and-grey cloth spread into the air like a heavy mist. The sound of springing metal reverberated along the sensitive membranes of her dark ears. Without another thought, she leapt atop one of the bent-over talvuo. As the monster woman beneath her jerked, she leaped up to the shoulders of one of the fretful stragglers just as another talvuo began pulling him down into the crowd. Shifting her weight to the shoulders of another shrieking male, Neris sprang off the screamer's crumpling form onto one of the blood-spattered tables near the hazy, carnage-filled air.

"Stay away!" Elis's familiar voice rattled her brain as she sprang over grasping hands.

With keen eyes, Neris fixed on Elis's position, watching as Thaimi's thin, frail figure slithered through the crowd to the same table she was sprinting along. Elis's back was turned to the serpentine woman as the pale creature raised its hands in the air, each member turning into writhing spindles as it wound its arms. Neris fetched a small, heavy dagger from her belt and let it fly. Caught unaware, Thaimi's hazel head tilted away, the sun catching the dagger's protruding handle as it skirted along the edge of her skull.

"Elis, behind you!" Neris called as her stunned assailant began to regain her composure.

Hearing her cry, Elis turned around and fell backwards as she loosed the springing coils of her strange weapon. Neris watched as the nectar maiden dodged into the crowd. Elis screamed and cursed as the metal strands reversed their course. Several wrapped around the wooden table and implements thereupon while almost half of them dug into Thaimi's left side. Like hissing snakes, the metal recoiled, tearing free the Hyunisti's left arm, leg, breast, and much of her torso. With an almost mechanical motion, the nectar maiden jerked in place. Spinning with her free right arm, Thaimi jutted the lance-like member toward the golden-haired woman. Drawing one of her larger hunting knives, Neris dove to Elis's side and severed the tip of the woman's spear-like appendage.

"Neris," Elis panted as she lay beside her.

Looking her over, Neris saw several minor injuries all along Elis's body. Her lavender dress had been ripped and torn in various places. Several marks on her arms and wrists showed where others had tried to claw or bite her, most having been fought off before they could pierce her flesh. Returning her glare, Neris lashed out with another slash at their marionette opponent as it tried to retract itself, severing another section of its arm.

"Elis!" Neris cried.

Without another thought, the woman beside her unlatched her weapon. Barbs and wires scattered through the crowd, burrowing into the fleeing figure. With a cry, Elis retracted the springing blades. The other leg of the monster gave way with much of its abdomen, sending flailing monstrosity over the edge of the terrace.

"Can you stand?" Neris asked, offering Elis her free arm and shoulder. Elis shifted her weight on bruised, scratched-up ankles. Her wooden sandals were in tatters.

"I can stand," Elis said.

"Good, then let's—" before she could finish speaking, Elis howled in pain. Neris turned her eyes to a crawling male as he reached his bony hands up and dug his grimy nails into Elis's shoulder. Neris flashed her blade as Elis pulled back. The Hyunisti cried in pain as he withdrew the stumps of his fingers, the twitching, severed nubs scattered on the ground. "Hurry up before more of them descend upon us."

"Neris, what's happening?" Elis asked, breathing heavily as Neris helped her up.

"We need to run," Neris said. "We need to cut a way through."

"Cut a way through?" Neris heard the fear and pleading in Elis's voice. No doubt, the woman had already fought off countless assailants in self-defense. Asking her to kill without discretion was another thing entirely. "Neris, I can't! We need to—"

"Elis, remember what they did to her!" Neris spun Elis around her as she dodged a groping child. Looking down, she watched the salivating little thing eye her with big, empty, grey obs. As Elis tried to pull her back, Neris turned her blade in her hands. With a wide, gouging sweep and a crashing elbow, she sent the possessed little thing spinning as its jaw dropped free of its face. "We're done here."

"Neris, what did you—" Elis's voice was shrill as her lavender eyes bubbled with fear and tears.

"Elis, this way!" Yanking Elis's arm upwards, Neris controlled her hand movements. Forcing the bronze-skinned woman's fingers to free the latch, Neris watched as the springing metal spurs lashed out in a broad fan, digging through and lacerating without discretion. Elis shrieked, drawing her hand away from Neris. As Elis returned the latch on her whip-like blades, each of the barbed metal springs retracted, tearing small chunks from multiple hostile and confused targets.

"Neris, what did you do?"

"It doesn't work when I force it!" Neris yelled, shoving Elis behind her as she intercepted another clawing talvuo. With two swipes, she eviscerated the attacker's arm, but as the limb fell, it righted itself. Like a bony snake, the arm flailed and lashed about on the ground with a mind of its own. "Elis, you have to make the path!"

"Neris, behind you!"

Catching a dark shadow reflected in Elis's eyes, Neris spun with her knives in hand. But as she whirled, her momentum was halted, and she was knocked backwards by a blow to her hip. Gritting her teeth, she staggered into Elis, spying one of the other nectar maidens looking her over. The brown-and-red-haired young woman spied her with blank grey eyes, raising and inspecting her mangled hand.

"Elis . . ." Neris stopped midsentence as pain seared through her left arm. Turning, she caught an armless woman leaning down. Her back arched like a pecking vulture, her teeth nipping at a small piece of Neris's upper arm. Not thinking, Neris spun her blade and buried it in the talvuo thing's skull, watching as its lifeless eyes rolled in its head. Jerking the knife free, the creature stumbled back into the crowd, trembling with convulsions.

"Neris!" Elis called.

Feeling Elis tug her backwards, Neris watched the nectar maiden across from them lift their male attacker's severed arm. In a grotesque display, her hand wrapped around the writhing stub of the lurching limb while her bones and flesh joined with the other. Fixing its eyes upon Neris, the monstrous maiden flexed her new four-segmented arm. Then, with an exaggerated motion, she whipped the appendage toward them.

Elis's twistblade uncoiled once more. Each of the sharp blades spewed forth in a narrow arc, each tip burrowing itself in the descending member. With a flick and a snap, Elis recalled the metal snakes, and with their telltale hiss, the vipers shredded the limb in midair.

"Elis!" Neris cried.

"I know," Elis said.

Elis turned, ready to unleash the fury of her weapon. Neris could only imagine the pain Elis felt as practicality won out over caring and reason.

"Are you trying to run away, my dear sweet sisters?" Nerin's mocking voice rang out over the bloody feasting of the monsters around them. Neris turned just in time to see her brother's shadowy figure descending from the stage. The possessed people in front of him yanked and tore into survivors, making a path through the gore for him. "But you have yet to take part, my loved ones. Vindal Neris, at least you must stay with us. There's so much we long to share with you. We would hate to be disappointed."

As Elis's blades tore through the villagers behind them, Elis locked her arm around Neris's and dragged her backwards. The hissing of the weapon was followed by the sloshing of remains as they turned away from her brother. Just above his shoulder, she spotted something terrible happening. The air seemed to twist and collapse upon itself, and with a pinprick of light, a small hole seemed to open in the world. The air around them stirred and crackled with energy, every hair on Neris's body standing on end as static filled the air.

Fueled by instinct, she grabbed Elis around the waist and dove for the floor.

58

DAVNIAN

All along the central terrace, beings possessed by a writhing emptiness lashed out against their fellows in murderous glee, caught in the madness between existence and absolute destruction. Few remained who were not at least partially afflicted. Among those few, the survivor count neared zero. Watching the menagerie disgusted Davnian, and it took every ounce of his being to suppress his bloodlust as he rushed forward.

[There's still time to save some of them,] the shadow-scaled thing in his head said.

Without a second thought, Davnian flew through the dueling hound-like guards on the bridge. He snapped one poor man's head free, dislodging his half-functioning brain from his fully possessed body. Crushing the skull in his claw, he used the silver thinblade in his right hand to pierce the eye of the other hunter. With a small, circular flick of his wrist, he stirred the slobbering male's braincase. As he continued across the bridge, he saw the Nerin-thing leave its perch on the central stage. For the first time, Davnian saw the constructs of reality laid out before him as he watched the fabric readying to distort near the looming monster.

Unflinching, he used his claw to propel himself forward, tossing his limber frame over the embattled villagers. His trajectory landed him just opposite Nerin just in time to intercept the opening electrical gate. From another place and time, the monster drew forth a frothing charged plasma. Davnian tossed his sword into his claw hand and readied to absorb the bolt with metal and demonic furor.

He closed his eyes, and the world lit up with a blinding white flash as the thunderbolt discharged. The energy sought the path of least resistance, feeding into the thinblade in Davnian's twisted hand. Like a sponge, his monstrous claw absorbed the energy. In that same instant, a thunderclap shook the firmament. With the smell of ozone clinging to the air, Davnian opened his eyes and watched as the Nerin-thing eyed him with curiosity and vitriol.

[There's not many left.]

Davnian acknowledged the other in his head with a nod as he eyed the tumultuous group around him.

The signs of survivors were near null, the majority of weeping, dying talvuo being devoured by their kin. In an affront to the notion of causality, their blood and flesh evaporated as if by thought. The world around them was filled with the screaming torrents of the soul-like ether that was drawn into the Nerin-thing's body. As it flowed through the air, time and space seemed indeterminate.

[Is there no one left?] His virtuous cohabitant's voice was filled with tremoring defeat.

"Davnian!" Neris cried out from behind him as he kept his eyes focused on the monster. The bits of those undone floated upon the soul mass gale, blurring out of existence as they spiraled into the emptiness's being. "Gods, there . . ."

"Why are you still here? Go!" Davnian commanded. A hint of relief calmed his and the child's soul as he sensed Elis's breathing not far off.

"Davnian?" Elis said, but there was no time for palaver.

Out of the corner of his left eye, he saw a bony, naked nectar maiden leap into the air. Flowing on the currents of ether in the space around them, her body seemed to blink between different forms. In one instance, she looked like a leaping talvuo maiden. In the next, she warped into a spinning skeletal scythe. Analyzing the thing's movements, Davnian watched as she seemed to appear in multiple places at once. The possibilities of her attack altered in real-time as reality conformed to the aggressor's will.

[Do you understand what's happening?] the other within his head asked.

[Let's hope so.]

All around him, causality twisted indeterminate. But inside the tiny bubble that surrounded his frame, everything was fixed as it should be. However, much like the ethereal flow that was tearing the universe apart, he seemed to be able to shape the space around his demonic hand to match his will. In many ways, it was as if the appendage itself was an arcane gate, not unlike the alterations the monster had called using Ohran's gifts.

As a dozen different possibilities played out in front of him for how the creature was about to land its attack, Davnian flung the thinblade into the air. As if by compulsion, reality around the weapon began to resolve. The dozen approaches of the monster descending upon him funneled into a pair of shades on either flank. Just as the two divergent paths collapsed with the moving harpy, Davnian caught the thinblade with his right hand. Like gears clicking into place, the monster flowed toward Davnian's left flank. With razor-like arms and legs, the thing's whole body slashed at him.

Catching the creature's initial blow with his claw, Davnian whipped the monster around and sent its scythe-like frame careening through the crowd. With a rage-filled lust in his eyes, he watched as the fiend's body ripped through the air, splitting the bodies of those caught in its wake. With a howl, it spread itself midair as the nectar maiden's skin stretched out like bat wings, but it was too little too late. The skeletal monster crashed into a tree, and every part of its body liquefied as it smeared against the bark of the giant trunk. Despite its destruction, the nothingness that infected the thing's body bubbled in the breeze, making its way back toward the Delvori host.

[Behind us!] his mental companion said as Neris shrieked in the background.

Keeping his eyes fixed on the Delvori monster before him, Davnian stepped back between flailing assaults. From the corner of his eye, he caught an assailant as it tried to tear into Neris's side. With his claw, he tore off the attacker's head and, fighting back a manic grin, tossed it into the crowd. Neris stabbed one of her knives into an attacker on Elis's front flank. Protecting her from a blow as she shook off a clenching, jabbering green-eyed husk, Davnian thrust his thin-blade just above the Delvori woman's shoulder. With a sick, splintering crack, it bit through the side of a half-gone talvuo's skull. He drew the pale-skinned woman's body to his right, guarding himself against a burst of flame emitted from another gate that spawned nearby. The woman screamed in agony as fire licked away her clothes and flesh. Kicking her free from his sword, Davnian pressed his back to Neris's.

"Keep moving," he said.

"I don't think she can bear much more." Her voice was heavy and filled with doubt as Elis collapsed into her.

"That's an order," Davnian said, his eyes on the nightmare stuff spinning around the Nerin-thing. He was trying to predict its next attack as he caught another maddened talvuo from his front. "Move or die."

"Once more, Elis. Just once more," Neris begged.

"I can't! I can't do this anymore!"

Despite her protests, Davnian heard Elis's twistblade spring and twist itself behind them. As it ground the meat of the last of the zombified barricade to paste, an arc of reality shifted as a one-armed nectar maiden blinked from one side of the arena to the other. In another instant, she was gliding through the air, ready to cut off the women's escape.

"Neris, turn," Davnian commanded as he forced her to turn with him. Elis stumbled forward as Neris pushed her away. "Elis, once more!"

In an instant, the one-armed nectar maiden was in front of them, her remaining limb honed to a lance. Just like the previous foe enacted, the reality around the monster bent into several directional attacks. With a hundred different ends, its spear would reach through Elis's breast into his if they didn't act quickly. Reaching around Elis's side, he gripped her twistblade hand.

"Everything in front of you," he said.

The battered Renai woman heeded his words. As Elis clicked the twistblade free, all the possibilities in front of them collapsed into a single action. The whirling metal strands entangled and spun their way in and out of the attacking talvuo husk. Reflected in the blue of his icy eyes, the spinning metal began to unravel the monster. With the fleshy shell of the Hyunisti maiden scattered like shredded cloth, the void within the maiden was engulfed by the fomenting vortex of miasma gathering all around them.

"Run, now!" Davnian commanded, pushing Elis forward. Spinning around him, Neris sprinted by. For a moment, her red eyes locked on his. Without a word, he reached his claw behind her, intercepting a leaping husk midair. Tearing his gaze from her, Davnian slammed the poor creature's skull into the ground, grinding it into a smear along the wooden floor. As he heard Elis's frantic voice gasp, he turned his eyes once more to the pair. "Don't look back!"

As Elis stared at him with terror-filled lavender eyes, Davnian felt someone grab his leg. He looked down as Neris pulled and tugged her along, Elis shouting to him and reaching her arms toward him.

"Please, save me!" a legless talvuo male begged.

Davnian saw the void within the man's spreading fast, watching as the emptiness displaced more and more of his mass. Filled with a sordid sense of purpose, Davnian raised his right hand and delivered a quick strike. As the man's neck split apart, his head rolled free along the ground, away from his infected body.

Looking back to Elis, a grin spread across Davnian's face as her eyes went expressionless. Her terror had been replaced with confusion and disgust, her legs starting to move in tandem with Neris's. As the women fled, Davnian turned back to the blood orgy, dodging a groping attacker while delivering another deathblow.

[It's better this way,] he said to the other in his head.

[She thinks you're a monster now,] the other replied. [Maybe they both do.]

[That's because I am a monster,] Davnian said, focusing on his quarry. His fingers trembled as his stoic façade began to crumble. Beneath his placid features, the hatred and thirst for vengeance were palpable. Cracks of homicidal mania worked their way across his features as he felt the sticky gore clinging to his claw. [There's no one left to save here.]

[No one,] the other replied. Everyone who remained was either mad from the encroaching emptiness or fighting off the void with what little of themselves remained. [This is hopeless. We should regroup. We should escape.]

[No, not this time,] Davnian said. [We ran away once before. This time we're not letting the thing escape.]

[You're mad.]

[Did you just notice?]

Feeling reality distorting once more, Davnian dodged into the crowd as a pair of gates opened on either side of the venue. As fire and flying stones ripped through the air, he began his brutal onslaught.

59

NERIS

"Elis, no slowing down. Not until we're out of here," Neris commanded as they descended the great tree. Elis hobbled and skipped, her pace becoming heavy as they continued down.

"I'm trying, Neris."

Neris had expected grief from the woman but not such disdain. She had seen the mania in Davnian's eyes as he finished off a begging talvuo man, watching as he dispatched him with ease. It wasn't so strange to her. She knew everyone there was already dead one way or another. She had thought they were too if not for the brazen demon's haughty venture. But for Elis, this was all a confirmation that her childhood friend was not only a killer but also her child's murderer. Even if he had spared her a different form of suffering.

"My ankles ache."

"We'll tend to the wounds once we're out of sight," Neris said, fearing they may be followed. The whole pavilion had been focused on devouring each other. Yet flashes of how Nerin had reached out made her lower back tingle. If she had a tail, it would be tucked between her legs. "It can't be much farther."

"The screaming's almost stopped."

Elis was right. Neris had been scanning ahead and behind for trouble. Perking her black hound's ears up, she heard a gargling hush falling over the echoes cascading through the tree. Either the few struggling survivors had succumbed to whatever Nerin had instrumented, or Davnian and the morass had finished killing the stragglers. If that were the case, she expected things were about to get even worse.

"That just means they can focus all their attention on the survivors," Neris said, panting.

Skirting the edge of the dark confines, she breached the gigantic tree's sunlit gateway. Blinded by the light of the sun as it tilted from its high perch, Neris caught a glimpse of the combined horror and wonder of the procession above.

All around the edges of the great circle, blood had been spilled. Seeping from its sides, the smallest trickles of the thick red stuff had spun in droplets toward the ground. Below the round of the grand terrace, those same droplets seemed to hang suspended in uneven blotches. Surrounding the tree pillar that supported the massive structure, like tiny, red, glossy baubles, the bloody beads twirled in midair of their own accord. Elis gasped at the sight.

"What's happening?"

"Nothing I've ever seen before."

Neris's mind raced through all the terrors that she had faced. Beatings, deaths, rapes, torture, burnings, crying, screaming, none of them were like what she was witnessing. Within the depths of the ancient Delvori keep, she had witnessed strange wards and stones. Even there nothing compared to the bloody chandelier that dangled before them.

"We keep moving," she commanded.

Letting her red eyes stare a moment longer, she caught a glimpse of the refuse starting to reverse gravity's constant pull. The red flowed back upwards, carrying small pieces of flesh and broken bones with it.

"Keep running Elis," Neris said, tugging Elis's arm.

Without another word, the pair ran south, away from the Hyunisti village and the terror above.

60

DAVNIAN

"We will be honest, greedy brother. We did not expect you to come to so quickly." The thing wearing Nerin's skin spoke with the Delvori's voice, enunciating every syllable with native ease. It danced along the edge of the stage as the ravenous being lashed over and over at Davnian. Beside the beast, the last of the nectar maidens supplicated, her body wracked by cuts and gouges from failed assaults against Davnian as the gore enveloped her.

[Are any others left?] he asked the shadow within him, too distracted to process what remained of the tattered populace.

[I think we've done it,] the other replied gravely.

Davnian's clothes were soaked with Hyunisti blood. As the monster opened more gates to draw forth raw elemental power, Davnian had given into his want of bloodshed. Using the menace within, he had focused on ending talvuo that could be spared, taking their lives before the writhing hollowness could devour their final thoughts.

Evading a monster pretending to be a corpse, he sidestepped between two clawing husks. Severing each of the creature's heads from their bodies with a jagged slash from his claw, he returned to the festering thing below and dispatched its closest hand. Not blinking, he kept his cold eyes fixed on the terrifying creature at the center of the procession. While Davnian fought in earnest, the corrupted mass around him gathered at the Nerin-thing's feet. The twisting ether of nothingness swelled into a giant, putrid bubble that surrounded the terrace. Yet the monster did not attack, opting to provoke him with civil vagaries. With its jests, he heard the faintest of whispers carried by its tainted words.

"What you do to these vessels of flesh and blood is terrible, but alas, we no longer need the chemical mix of their brains intact. You only rob them of final succor now, Virage, nothing else," the creature said as Davnian tried to piece together its next action. Every time he tried to make a direct attack, a wall of gore formed between him and it. If they did not manifest, he would be faced with a rain of rifts, each delivering a new brew of fire, ice, earth, and thunder for him to evade. "Tell us, has she been kind to you at least?"

A little girl's laugh danced across Davnian's lips as he ignored the creature. He didn't have time to suppress what remained of Rais within him as he studied the terrible thing.

[It's all flowing to him,] his dark insider waxed rhetorical.

[Tell me something I don't know.]

[Maybe we need to try a different approach.]

[Whatever you have in mind,] he replied as dozens of tiny arcane gates begin to spawn all around him. Nothing the creature had done had been overt yet. It was testing his defensive and offensive capabilities. [Give me something to work with, old one.]

[You can still feel it, can't you?] the other asked as Davnian flicked an instigator with his thinblade, tripping it as it stumbled. He felt the being within him directing his attention to his claw, and deep within it, he felt a buzzing. [From when you blocked the attack?]

[The lightning bolt?]

[You still have it in your claw. You captured it. And like a raving beast, you can release it. The same way it is using those other gates against you. In fact, I think you can do one more.]

[Such as?] Readying to dodge the fanned portals, Davnian cringed as they changed positions, forming a dome around him. He gritted his teeth. [Incoming!]

[Capture them just as you capture thoughts and as you captured the thunderbolt!] the shadow said.

There was no time to determine the correct path. Picking the closest of the distortions, Davnian bent low and used his claw to propel himself to his right. As the rifts popped open one by one, Davnian snared himself along the terrace lifeline. Circling one of the stanchions, he whipped himself around and grabbed at the opening gate with his claw. The air rippled as his hand passed through the newborn portal, and he thought he felt the thing throb within his left hand before joining the buzzing force trapped within his claw.

[It worked!] a young girl's voice cheered throughout his mind.

Glancing to the side, he tucked his legs just as a giant spear of ice ripped through. Then a ray of heat scorched away the air just behind him, leaving just enough room for him to flip between two thunderous claps of dazzling electricity. Shaking his head as he returned his gaze to the Nerin-thing, Davnian shook off the ringing in his ears from the small shockwaves.

The terrace was covered in icy patches and smoldering flesh. The monster had no notion of friendly fire. The spillage of its wounded henchmen seeped against the grain of the damaged terrace, reaching toward the ultimate host.

"You've taken much of our time, Virage," the Nerin-thing whispered, the joy in its eyes fading as its grin slackened. Beside its head, another rift was forming. Swelling like a giant cyst, the portal was gigantic compared to the previous ones. Whatever it was about to let through was massive. Davnian kneeled and prepared to spring at the new gate. "Allow us to impart one final gift."

Using his claw to aid in covering the distance, Davnian leapt toward the portal. Just as he was about to reach the spawning distortion, it disappeared and repositioned itself on the other side of Nerin's head. Using his momentum, Davnian twisted in the air as the gateway opened. The edges of the structure hissed and sparked as a blob of sizzling, charged matter spouted forth. With nothing else he could do, he threw his thinblade.

As he nabbed the ropes at the edge of the terrace, his metal weapon soared into the buzzing plasma. The charged particles within the sphere began to distribute and react. Flipping over the side of the wooden platform, Davnian watched as rays of blinding light penetrated the cracks in the terrace, bathing the wood in a perfect white. Following the initial blast, hundreds of lightning bolts arced through the forest, scattering as they exploded branches and treetops. The air was full of pressure waves as blast after blast dotted the trees. The tree beneath the terrace split as the great round above ignited. The whole thing shook, threatening to throw Davnian from the ropes. With all his might, he maintained his hold even as the other posts gave way.

Not wasting time, Davnian climbed up the struggling cord while posts and tufts of thick twine fell over the terrace ledge. Clawing his way back onto the great round, Davnian was shocked to see the brazen monster standing at the center of the chaos. Its dark purple robes had disintegrated, leaving the body of the Delvori shell standing bare in the smoke and flames. The mishmash of bodies had dissolved into smoldering goop that frothed and reached up toward the naked man. It gripped his thighs and hands, pumping into his open crevices and through his skin. Lying at his side, a half-molten blade glowed bright red.

[That did nothing.] The other in his head was as shocked as Davnian was.

Only one option was left, and it was to try and will the creature pain. Watching reality distort again, a thousand different images of how the potential attack could play out flashed before Davnian's eyes. In many cases, the Nerin-thing absorbed or dodged the blow, immune to the effects of the attack. But in a distinct few, Davnian saw the energy tear deep into the monster, disintegrating a large swathe of its body and much of the steaming mass around it. The path was there; all he had to do was will it. Filled with unabated rage, Davnian raised his claw.

Turning in place, the Nerin-thing looked at him with renewed joviality as Davnian drew forth the captured lightning bolt. As Nerin's rust-red orbs flickered in the fire and smoke, a wicked smile drew across Davnian's face as he saw the possibilities narrowing. One by one, the creature's immunities fell away, and right as he was about to unleash heaven's wrath, reality and desire became one.

"You have yet to answer our question, dear brother. Please, you must tell us how she dwells within you," the creature said, raising its tendril-enveloped hand to Davnian.

The feeling was like a thousand licking tongues scraping the tips of every hair on his body as Davnian willed the charged bolt back into existence. A white light filled the space in front of him as the electricity leaped from his hand, following a curved arc as it sought the shortest route down. Struggling against the electricity's nature, causality shifted a single thread, forcing the crackling eruption to surge forward.

A flash and a thunderous roar followed. As the discharge finished with its target, it wound downwards. Dancing through the split trunk of the giant tree, the old wooden growth groaned under its own weight. The Nerin-thing floated above the gaping opening, stunned. Its right side had been incinerated by the blast, the flowing emptiness smoldering as the last free electrons danced throughout its form. Hanging in the air, hundreds of shrieking voices were silenced.

Davnian watched as the thing's torched head twitched. The residue on its opposite side threw itself at its remaining leg and torso. The screaming ether and blob of devoured people on its right had been destroyed by Davnian's attack. However, there was still plenty of substance to reinvigorate itself. If Davnian was going to end this, he needed a definitive fatal strike.

Knowing what he must do, he steeled himself as the creature raised its remaining arm. Thousands of screams tore through Davnian's head. Curses and monstrous visions coursed through his frame. Fighting off his body's urge to twist and revolt, he stared down the beast.

61

———

ELIS

No matter how far they ran, the destruction seemed to lap at their heels.

Above their heads, the bloodshed of the Hyunisti village trailed them. First, it was the sound of crackling and thunder. Then came lightning bolts, the trembling of the earth, and quaking trees. Branches fell throughout the forest while smoldering leaves and embers wafted through the air. A torrent of heaven's fire struck and splintered trees in every direction. Smoke and brimstone surrounded them as they struggled to avoid fallen debris and smaller collapsing trees.

"Elis, this way!" Neris cried.

As she trudged onward, it felt as if the world were ending. Flashes of the razing of their hometown crossed Elis's thoughts as she bolted after Neris. Her bare feet were tender from all the running and the roughness of the scattered tree remnants. Her ankles felt swollen and thin at the same time, but she knew she had to keep moving. She had lost her journal. She had lost her child. The only thing she had left was her twistblade and her life. And Neris. She still had Neris.

"Elis, watch out!" Elis turned her head as a branch crashed down behind her. The large limb grazed her back, tearing her lavender dress open. Her lacerated back was exposed along with her buttocks. The dress clung to her by shreds around her shoulders, the rest floating in tatters about her aching body. "Are you alright!"

"I'm just scratched," Elis murmured as she dragged herself toward Neris's voice. Rounding one tree after another, she spied the Delvori woman clad in her war leathers and bright orange top. "It's getting harder to keep up."

"I didn't think we'd be running this far." Neris cursed beneath her breath, reaching for Elis. "Give me your hand."

"OK." Elis reached out and gripped Neris's hand. With her strong arms, the dark-skinned woman repositioned her, bearing half of Elis's weight. "Neris, you don't—"

"It'll be easier for both of us this way," Neris lied. "There's a clearing south of here where the Grannas merchants gather, correct?"

"When they come, yes," Elis said, panting as they hurried onwards.

"We should be able to catch our breath there."

Elis was wordless as Neris led her along. She was covered in sweat, her dark hair ashen with soot and dirt. Looking at her, Elis realized how much stronger the Delvori woman was. She was cold and calculating, passionate and caring, and in the case of Elis, she had risked her life to save her. Then, without a hint of displeasure, she continued to carry her through the surrounding nightmare.

"Elis, I think I see it!"

Looking up, Elis saw they were nearing the verdant trees lining the edge of the wood. Behind them, the air bubbled red and brown, filled with darkness and firelight. As they crossed the tree line, they stumbled down a knoll to the grass-filled clearing below.

Neris cursed as they tumbled beside each other. Coming to a stop at the bottom of the hill, Elis rolled onto her back, grasping for her family heirloom. Finding the twistblade nearby, she drew it to her breast, cradling it.

"Gods," Neris gasped. She raised herself from the ground, groaning from the spill. "Elis?"

"I'm fine," Elis said, lying on her back as her heartbeat rang through the barbs cradled against her chest.

"Come on; I'll help you up," Neris said, offering her hand. Gripping Neris's palm, Elis looked at the grass clinging to her rags and wounded skin. "No worse for wear, dear?"

"Only a bit chilled," Elis said, feeling the dampness of the grass clinging to her backside.

"I think we've finally outrun it all," Neris said, brushing the grass and dirt from her clothes. "We have some time to catch our breath at least."

"Goddess be blessed, good people, are you alright?" a male voice called from across the clearing.

Elis and Neris turned to see a man in a heavy coat with a large-brimmed leather cap beside his horses, which were restrained by ropes. The animals bucked and snorted as he waved to the women.

"A merchant?" Neris asked.

"I think so," Elis said, taking her place beside her. Behind the man and the horses was a large cart stacked with unseen things covered by a large cloth. "Sir, we're alright!" Waving her arms, Elis signaled things were OK, but as the man stepped from beneath the shade of the far-off trees, she thought she saw something slither through the tall grass.

"Elis." Neris's voice was flat as she put her arm in front of her companion.

"Good people, give me a moment!" the man shouted as he waded through the grass.

"Stay back! There's something in the grass!" Neris warned.

"What?" the man said.

Elis trembled as something strange and horrid climbed up the merchant's back and sat upon his head. Looking closely, Elis saw what appeared to be a thin, skeletal torso forcing itself upon the man's head and upper body. With a pop that could be heard across the way, the menacing figure of a torn and shredded nectar maiden attached itself to the man's body. Thin red lines of drizzle worked their way from underneath its mangled ribcage as a muffled scream permeated its stomach flab. The man scratched at the thing above him, but within moments began to jerk and convulse before standing limp.

"Oh gods no," Neris hissed, looking at the creature.

"It's . . . it's Thaimi." Elis felt her stomach drop as she stared at the familiar hazel hair with white ribbons. Even from a distance, she felt the maiden's dead emerald eyes staring her down. "Neris, what do we do?"

"We can't fight it." Her voice was bitter as she drew forth one of her knives. "At least she didn't catch us in the woods. Out in the open here, we're at a slight advantage."

"How so?"

"That." Neris nodded to Elis's hands.

Indeed, her twistblade was a formidable piece, and in the clearing, it was a perfect weapon. As the four-armed, two-chested monstrosity crossed the clearing toward them, Elis trembled. If eviscerating the nectar maiden didn't kill her, what chance did they have of stopping her now?

"Cover me, alright?" Neris said, gripping Elis's wrist. "With those barbs, you can keep it moving or trap it for a time. Keep the thing off my back, and I can get a few cuts in. If we're lucky, I can cripple it, and we can run off with the horses."

"Maybe we'll be lucky, and it's taken on more weight than it can bear."

"Every time we've seen one of these things move, they've been fast. Let's not underestimate it."

Elis was terrified. The toil of escape would be for naught if they died there. Both of them had to make it out alive, or there would be nothing left.

"Vindal?"

"Yes, Neris?"

"We're going to get through this," Neris said. "I promise."

Her heart skipping a beat, Elis nodded and readied her weapon. "Both of us are leaving here," she said as she fought back tears. "I promise."

"There's the woman I fell in love with," Neris said with a chuckle, donning her usual nonchalant tone. "Just let me do most of the talking, dear."

"Alright," Elis whispered.

Neris stepped in front. With a scream, the creature deformed the man beneath her into an equine shape, rearing up on the man's haunches like the hind legs of a horse. His leather jacket tore and dampened as blood spilled beneath it. The man's pants split as his legs twisted and cracked. Each of the maiden's hands wound up into long, barbed lances as she roared at them. Behind her, the horses stamped and begged to be let free.

"Just a couple of cuts to cripple it, and then we can escape," Elis whispered beneath her breath to ease her nerves.

62

DAVNIAN

[Once more. Strike true.]

Davnian watched as a thousand blurry shadows of possible futures danced in front of him. Dodging just as the half-Delvori, half-meaty blob crushed the space he had just occupied, he spun and ducked beneath a dozen flaying tendrils. Beneath him, the ground shimmered, giving him just enough time to roll to the side as a portal spewed magma onto the terrace. The wooden structure creaked and shook as more of its supports eroded. Beside the monster, the glowing metal of the dulled Hyunisti thinblade rippled the air above it. The leather handle and wooden pommel were gone, leaving the silver blade's tang exposed.

With a roar, the creature threw itself at Davnian while the air behind him gave birth to a hundred speckled eyes. Flipping himself over the beast, Davnian snatched up the silver blade as nuclear beams of light shredded the space all around them. The massive wooden terrace crumbled as the rays diced it to pieces. The lasers made the monster's flesh bubble and simmer but did no lasting damage.

The smoldering sword's warmth carried up Davnian's demon arm, the hairs on his wrist tingling from the heat. He drew as much of the energy from the tang as he could, readying his attack. In desperation, the monster's lower body liquefied, every inch birthing a hundred strands of potential spears. There was little room left to fight as most of the terrace collapsed around them. With fewer options, the strands of fate that the nightmare manipulated cascaded into a near-infinite number of ways it could land blow after blow. There would be no more dodging.

[One more blow, young one.] The ancient thing's composure had been tried, but its voice echoed Davnian's certainty.

As the monster's infinite members spawned out of thin air, Davnian reduced the space in his head. Bringing his hands together, he gripped the burning blade's tang and sprinted forward.

Leaning into his steps, Davnian charged at the monster as he clashed wills with the beast. Once more, his vision filled with nightmarish images. The dead and dying returned to him, pictures of Rais lying in his arms while clawing his sides, the sounds of the villagers screaming, Elis's disgust, and Neris's hopelessness. The whispers called into his head over and over, threatening to erode what remained of his sanity. The monster and its many voices scoured his skull, trying to find something, anything, to give him pause. Then the scene flickered, the imagery of the burning forest replaced with red sand as the thing found its mark.

Then there she was, the woman from the nightmare that he had repressed. She stood in front of him, garbed in white as she reached her olive arms toward him. Drawn from the depths of his locked-away memories, she smiled, her yellow eyes beckoning him.

"Davnian," she said as she stood within the oscillating madness. The whispers of the damned lent her voice strength as she stood where the Nerin-thing once was. The flames and smoke of the collapsing terrace surrounded them, mixing with memories of a red sandstorm. The gale of the encroaching, unseen tentacles pressed upon him, smaller barbs scratching him as if they were grains of whirling sand. His heart pounded as his blue eyes fixed on her form, and he tried to draw forth her name.

[Davnian,] the other within his head said.

[Davnian,] a little girl's voice cried from somewhere within his soul.

[Davnian.] In the depths, the yellow-eyed woman took her place, overlaying the imposter, bringing her hands to her breast.

"Senna." Her name danced across his lips.

With all his heart, Davnian willed the space between them to disappear. Obligingly, the world gave way, and as Davnian lowered his arms down, Senna's olive limbs drew over him. With a heartfelt grin, he stared at her as he took one more leaping step forward. As the spinning doom behind him closed in, he tightened his right hand around the blistering tang.

The silver blade scorched the air as his right arm struck out, and his claw pressed against the woman's bosom. Feeling the essence of the captured gate leave him, Davnian lifted his claw and snatched up his prize before tossing himself backwards.

The mass of tendrils gave way as they crashed around the woman's distorting figure. The illusion of the red-sand vista disappeared. Alternating between Senna's olive-skinned frame and the Nerin-thing's twisted form, the monstrous body convulsed. Parts of it bubbled and frothed while others collapsed upon themselves. The whole thing began to warp and spin in place, whipping around as the gate within it opened. On the other side of the portal, the vast nothingness of ultimate destruction loomed as Davnian's portal drew forth the tiniest piece of a dead star. The very curvature of space-time twisted upon itself as the monster was ripped apart by the tidal forces of the massive entity on the other side of the hand-sized gateway.

"Bro . . ..br . . . . .brrrr . . . other," a voice stammered from his clawed hand as he raised the melting head of his vanquished foe. Half Nerin, half the woman drawn from within his thoughts, the face twisted in shock and manic glee as Davnian held it before him. Drawing air from the surroundings, it tried to speak once more. "An . . . anssss . . . ansssswwwee . . . . .rrrrr. Brottter."

"She's fine where she is." Davnian almost felt pity for the dying beast as he watched the spiraling mess of its former mass beginning to glow. The whole of its being was being bound together.

Just as he let it go, he felt the tiniest of its thoughts trickle through his connection. Beneath layers of nightmarish imagery, he saw Neris and Elis through foreign eyes, standing within a grassy field as he reared at them. Overcome with a feeling of terrifying succor, Davnian's heart dropped as the thing's top joined the vortex of evaporating mass. The flying head let out a childlike laugh as it imploded with the rest of its body.

The glowing cataclysm began to shine with a sun-like luminance. Without a moment to spare, Davnian threw himself from the disintegrating terrace. As he clawed at the bark of the supporting tree, the monster's final screams echoed through the forest. Casting himself from the trunk of ancient wood, he sprinted into the woods, homing in on the connection that he had shared with the surviving monster. Behind him, the fusing mass engulfed the giant tree in a solar flame before disappearing into a singular point.

63

NERIS

Neris's stomach churned as she looked at the braying monster in front of her. The once-naïve nectar maiden, Thaimi, had all but succumbed to the horrible transformation that Nerin's ceremony had enacted upon her. The human male that she had attached herself too was bursting from his clothing as she continued to snap and integrate his bones and muscles. The lower body was like that of a horse made of bones and writhing membranes.

Fixing her red eyes on the creature's ample weapons, Neris wondered if they stood a chance. Elis could cover her, but the monster's arms were each as long as her own wingspan. Each lance-like appendage ensured Neris wouldn't be able to get too close without having to place herself right beside its body. Given how fast the terrifying fiend could manipulate its form, the idea sent shivers down her spine. One misstep or faulty assumption, and she'd be dead or devoured.

In the distance, a shriek echoed through the forest, followed by brilliant rays of gold pouring out over the treetops.

"Neris!" Elis called from behind her.

Neris watched as dozens of tiny metal strands bit into the air in front of her. Rearing away from the coils, the monster pranced back several paces, exposing its left flank as it turned to face the raining barbs.

Neris ran from the scattering barbs, heading straight toward the monster's left-back leg. As Elis's blades began to retract, the monster shifted in place, scanning for her, but Neris was too fast for it. Just as it noticed her close in on its left flank, she swiped at the beast's exposed ankle with her hunting knife. The muscle and flesh were tougher than she had expected, but her momentum allowed her to cut away the connective tissue while taking a sizable chunk out of the bone. The thing roared, and she rolled forward as one of its bony spears soared over her.

Spitting with anger, the thing turned in place, stumbling over its injury as it tried to follow Neris. Keeping on the move, Neris drew one of her throwing knives and loosed it at the calve of the beast's injured leg. Dodging once more, she watched as the blade sank deep into the thing's muscle, causing the leg to buckle. Clawing at the ground with its front legs, the creature continued to turn, stabbing at Neris.

Readying another dagger, Neris watched as Elis approached. With a tossing motion, she unhitched her many-bladed coil, sending hundreds of barbs into the monster's right flank. As the creature turned to face Elis, Neris threw another knife, sending the biting blade into the creature's skeletal back. Only lacerating the beast, Neris hissed while the thing turned with another wild jab. The springing blades recoiled once more as Elis withdrew along the creature's other side, rounding it toward Neris. A horse leg made of a human arm flew through the air.

As the monster turned its attention back to Elis, Neris used the opening to bring her blade down on its exposed rear-right leg, right on the reversed leg joint. Tearing through cartilage and sinew, she cleaved the junction in two. As the monster tried to lean toward her, Elis's barbs flew forward once more, tearing off its remaining foreleg. Sprinting as her blade recoiled, Elis kept her distance from the flailing monster.

"Now's our chance!" Elis said, turning toward the horses.

"Run!" Neris called, backing away as she threw another singing blade. She watched as it knocked the Thaimi-thing upside the head and then ran away as fast as she could. "Get on! I'll cut the ropes!"

Behind her, the thing roared and groaned. It sounded like it was being torn in half as the monster shrieked with the young woman's lungs.

"Neris, behind you!"

Neris turned just in time to see the Thaimi-thing rending itself from the human abomination, throwing itself in the air toward her. Drawing her second knife, she turned and continued to back away as the creature reached toward her with long spears.

Elis's twistblade sang once more. Springy, barbed blades lashed at the creature, but the monster guarded itself against the briar with its spears. The metal blades tried to sever the impossible limbs, but they could not penetrate the beast's natural weapons.

Neris threw one dagger and then another as the thing used its spears like stilts to dance around the attacks. Redirecting its attention, the gaunt monstrosity attempted another set of attacks.

Observing, Neris noted the trajectories of the attacks. The first aimed for her exposed left side, but Neris avoided it while dancing backwards between low-hanging branches and a stump. As the creature readied to follow up, Neris planned to dodge away once more, but she watched in horror as the follow-up thrust altered its course despite what light and sound told her. Feeling a twinge of shock, she readied for the sharp blow.

Another rain of barbs came down over her just as the creature was about to strike. Hissing, the monster backed away. Elis screamed from her side, whipping the mass around and forward into another attack. Neris was dumbfounded. She watched the golden-haired woman whip the mess of blades around her again and again, fending off the monster.

"Neris, get the horses!" Elis cried.

Neris stared at her for a moment, watching how she drew back on both latches of the strange, enchanted weapon. Metal coils danced around Elis's bronze-skin frame, razor-sharp barbs hugging her moments before recoiling back toward their target. The wind from the grinding vortex spun with the loose blades around Elis's hair, each spring just avoiding every strand flowing from her head. Breaking herself free from the glamor, Neris scurried over to the horses.

They bucked and trampled the ground, but with a firm hand, Neris stayed one. Pulling the four-legged beast close, she brought her knife down, severing the rope that bound it.

"Elis, here!" Neris said.

As Elis backed toward her, the golden-haired woman deflected another volley from the menacing beast. When Elis turned, the spear-armed monster's gut and shoulders shrank, and mass flowed into its deadly limbs. With a leap, it soared throw the air, thrusting both elongating pikes toward Elis.

"Elis!" Neris screamed, leaping forward.

Pushing Elis to the side, Neris gulped. As Elis tumbled past her, shock filled her violet eyes. Neris dropped her knives. As the Thaimi-thing roared, Neris reached up, her vision filled with red. Clinging to the beast's spears, the whole world trembled, and her knees gave way beneath her.

64

———

ELIS

She didn't scream, and she didn't cry. Watching as the twin spears punctured Neris's armored body, Elis did the only thing that she could do and raised her twistblade above her head. Her eyes filled with vengeance as she brought the barbed mess downward. The barbs and wires ensnared and coiled about the roaring monster, the tips of the spindled metal digging deep into the creature. With a manic visage of triumph and sadistic euphoria, the Thaimi-thing looked at her with its dead green eyes. As it opened its mouth to unleash further torrents, Elis closed the latch on her heirloom.

With a nearly inaudible hiss, the springs retracted with unforeseen speed. One moment they ensnared the monster, and the next they writhed within Elis's hands. As the insatiable metal came to a halt, the creature's face emptied. Particles of meat and bone evaporated into the air as chunks of flesh and organ meal sloshed upon the grassy ground. Curling upon itself, the audacious thing's spine and skull teetered on the edge of fragmenting as it fell to the sticky mass below. For moments that stretched into eternity, Elis stood. Then, following a gasp from her wounded lover, she returned to the present.

"Elis," Neris said, coughing as she lay pinned to the ground.

"Neris." Elis almost dropped her weapon as she put one foot forward.

"No, don't get any closer," Neris hissed as she fought back pain.

Confusion overcame Elis's features as she watched Neris struggle. Then the spears shrank. In Neris's belly and chest, the invisible mass displaced parts of the woman's body as the cavities swelled. With a scream, Elis lashed at the remainder of the exposed material.

"I think this is it, Elis," Neris said, her chest heaving as she laughed. No blood spilled from her body. No red patches grew. The thing they had killed together was still tormenting them. No, it was still alive. Tears welling in her eyes, Elis's knees gave way. "Elis, get up on one of those horses and get out of here. Please, you have to."

"W-why . . ." Elis stammered. Everything was gone. What more remained in this cruel world? "Why, Neris? Why—"

"You have to get out of here, Elis!" Neris fought back bile and pain as her breathing became irregular. "Gods, Elis, run, gods damn you! Use your wits! Leave me!"

"No more." Elis couldn't bear it anymore.

"Gods, you insufferable blond bitch," Neris said, trying to spite her, but Elis knew that play. "Oh, gods no."

Neris's form lurched upon the ground, rolling over upon itself. Her face streaked with tears, Elis watched in horror as Neris's body moved against her will, crawling toward her.

"I can't . . . Elis, go," Neris begged. The woman's rust-colored eyes widened as a demented look overcame her. Only her mouth and arched hound ears betrayed the host's horror as the thing crawled toward her. "Elis . . . Elis, I . . ."

"I'm sorry, Neris. I can't," Elis said, dropping her twistblade. "It's not you. It's not."

As Neris's body loomed over her, Elis saw the manic look disappear from her visage. At once she wore a calm and compassionate look, the horror from her lips fighting against a warmer disposition. Her hound ears slumped as she leaned forward.

"Elis . . ." Neris's voice was warm and welcoming as the last vestments of horror eroded from her smile. Elis couldn't help but smile as the woman drew close. There was a bated breath between them as Elis readied to welcome what remained of Neris. The warmth of the other woman was real as her face drew close. Elis could taste her breath. She closed her eyes, waiting for the darkness to engulf her.

Suddenly, the shadow of Neris was ripped from her, followed by a gasp. Opening her eyes, Elis watched as a dark silhouette reached down and clenched its left hand around the dark-haired woman's head. As Neris went to scream, she fumbled for a loose dagger and lashed out at the tattered man holding her in place. Grabbing her weapon, Elis rose to help the possessed woman. But as Neris's arm lashed out at none other than Davnian, he disarmed her. In that same instant, and without a hint of remorse, he grabbed the falling dagger and plunged it into Neris's chest.

"Dav . . . nian . . ." Neris's breathing was frantic as her contorting hands reached for her pierced breast. Elis brought her arms to her face as he pushed his hand into the cavity and twisted the metal within. Neris's eyes bulged as he withdrew his fingers, covered in blood and slime. All over Neris's skin, small pustules of worming madness vacated her body. With a gulp and a gasp, she smiled at the icy-eyed human. "Than . . . y . . . take . . ."

"Shhh," he said, bringing his blood-covered hand to her lips. "There's still something there. I'll let you do the honors."

As the light faded from Neris's features, a sultry, telltale grin crept across her face.

"Y . . . bastard . . ."

Neris's body jerked in place. A sound like a snapping branch was followed by a hiss of air. Her frame shook, her mouth opening wide as she convulsed in Davnian's grip. Elis drew her twistblade back, a frown covering her terrified features. Neris's eyes rolled back into her head as the sound came to an end. Without another word, Davnian crushed the black-haired woman's head in his demonic member. With a heart-wrenching scream, she fell backward as bone, blood, and something wormlike oozed between his fingers. Then he closed his blue eyes and tossed the limp black body aside.

"What have you done?" Elis screamed as she brought the bundle of barbs behind her. Every muscle in her body tensed as she readied to fling the springs at him. For several moments Davnian stood quietly before turning to her and stepping forward. "Stay back!" she warned.

"Elis." Davian's voice reached her as undercurrents of another's played across his tongue. A shiver shot down her spine as she backed away.

"No. No, Davnian. No," Terror overtook Elis's senses, her breathing erratic. He wasn't her childhood friend. He wasn't the same little boy she knew. "You're not Davnian. No, you're really him. You're a demon! You're the Virage!"

As he stepped toward her, Elis let the twistblade fly. Pausing, Davnian watched as the wires wrapped around him. Elis's lavender eyes focused on his cold visage as he seemed to sigh. He closed his eyes, and a strange warmth grew across his features as the springs wrapped around the red-and-blue rags that gripped his frame. With eyes too clouded by tears to see, Elis kept the latch open. Davnian transformed before her. His pale skin altered, the white replaced by pitch. His flat chest swelled as the coiled blades gripped a woman's swollen bust. His stoic face became fine-featured, and his ears shifted and elongated as they became covered in short black fur. His curly, tangled mop fell in upon itself as straight strands of black hair adorned his face.

In seconds the man known as Davnian disappeared. In front of her stood the red-and-blue-adorned frame of the woman he had killed. A rust-red eye paired with an azure-blue orb stared at Elis.

"Ne . . . Neris!" Elis's voice cracked as the dead woman stared at her, donning a caring yet nonchalant visage. "No. You can't . . . it can't be . . ."

"It's over, Elis," Neris said compassionately across the expanse, the words dancing on the straining wires as Elis trembled in place. "Elis, it's time for us to go."

"Neris . . ." Elis couldn't believe the thing in front of her. He was trying to fool her, trying to make her lower her guard. It was still the Virage. With wandering lavender eyes, she spied the woman's discarded corpse. "No, Neris. No, it can't . . ."

"Eyes up here, my dear," Neris commanded. At once, Elis's attention was fixed on the twin body of her dead lover. "Ignore that shell, Elis. I'm right here."

"Neris?"

Elis's heart skipped a beat. She fumbled for the latch, watching as the tightening barbs tore at the Delvori's black skin and garb. Neris grunted, narrowing her shoulders as the blades bit into her flesh.

"Whatever you choose, I'll be standing right here. I'm ready when you are, ne vindal." Neris's voice was flat but accepting. Closing her eyes, she took a deep breath. "Whichever it is, just make it quick, dear."

Elis felt defeated. Had she not just accepted one monster and her own end? Nothing made sense anymore. Who was left to pay? What was left for her? No, vengeance meant nothing anymore. If she had to accept a monster, she would receive one wearing Neris's skin. At least the end would be pleasant. Breaking down, Elis's resolve gave way. Submitting to her weariness and instability, she accepted whatever fate lay before her.

"Neris!" Elis dropped the brambles as she rose from the ground. Without a master to call them, the springing blades unfurled from their target and slithered back to their holster. Crossing the distance, Elis wrapped her arms around the rag-garbed woman, planting her lips on her cheeks. "Gods, Neris. Thank you. Gods, thank you."

"There, there," Neris whispered as they embraced. For several moments they stood together as Neris ran her thin, slender hand along Elis's back. The alien-clawed limb attached to her body slid along Elis's neck, caressing the back of her head. "Everything will be better now. Everything is going to be alright, ne vindal."

As Elis raised her eyes to speak, tendrils of warmth and succor reached out through her body. From the base of her head through her spine, waves of ease and comfort overtook her aching body. In the back of her head, drowsiness and calm crept into her brain. With straining lavender eyes, she looked up at the red-and-blue-eyed woman.

With a loving smile, the Delvori woman kissed Elis as she fell asleep.

65

DAVNIAN

[I'm sorry for using you.] Davnian's thoughts wandered as he held Elis's sleeping body in his arms.

"You really are a heartless bastard," Neris whispered from his lips as their shared dark hands caressed the bronze-skinned woman. "I guess there's nowhere for this to go now, is there?"

[What do you mean?] Davnian asked as he urged their shared body onward.

One of the horses had run off, the remaining one looking at them with terrified eyes as it bucked in place. Raising their claw, Neris's voice shushed the beast. Davnian felt a sensation between himself and the braying beast, using his consciousness to help exert calm over the creature. As its breathing and restlessness abated, they turned their head and surveyed the cart.

"What happens to me after this, Davnian?" Neris asked as they lumbered to the back of the cart.

[I'm not sure,] he replied as they lifted Elis into it. [I guess we stay together. Over time, we just end up being.]

[It's a wonder you isolated her.] Another voice ripped through their black-headed skull like a blistering wind. [Somehow you were able to keep her and the little one intact.]

[I'll assume that's a compliment.] Davnian's reply was sardonic and comical as they got into the cart and used their shared resources to make room for Elis.

"So, this is what you put up with," Neris's said coolly as she laid out a canvas and blanket and then heaved Elis into place. With a sigh, she jumped off the wagon. Looking at her dead, discarded body, Neris bent down and picked up a pair of her throwing knives. Either way, they'd be keeping these at least. With a huff, they wiped the sweat from their brow. "Where's all of that strength from earlier? Gods, this is harder than moving her myself."

"I guess I spent it all back in the village and catching up with you two," Davnian said, his voice emerging from their throat as they stood. Shaking their head, Davnian felt their body reverting. Watching as her thin, dexterous hands gave way to his rougher, spindly members, Davnian turned the blades over in his grip. "Well, at least we have something."

[I guess,] Neris said from deep within the recesses of his brain. She had become distant in the short transition, causing him to frown. [You wouldn't be frowning if you were a bit faster, dear.]

"I know." Davnian's voice caught in his throat as the last of Neris's vestments disappeared from his mindscape. Water gathered at the corner of his eyes as he tied the knives to his sides.

[Why are you crying?] the other within his head asked.

[You know why.]

[She's not gone, Davnian.] Davnian almost felt like laughing at the audacity of the moment. [She must rest. This whole thing is fraught with trauma. Imagine being ripped from your body.]

[It's OK,] a little girl's voice whispered. A shiver shot down his spine. Despite being consoled, he felt a tinge of terror for the future. There was no place for three minds in one body.

"It'll never be the same, old one," Davnian said as he rallied the horse. "Is nothing whole and hale in this world?"

[You tell me,] the other replied.

Readying to untie the beast, Davnian stopped in his tracks. Out of the corner of his eye, he spied the faintest movement in the tall grass near the mound of rotting flesh and melting bone. Every nerve in his body steeled itself. Holding his breath, he watched the blades bend and move against the gentle breeze that flowed between the trees around them. Overcome with spite, he fetched a dagger and let it fly.

With a crying hiss, something squirmed and writhed.

[Careful now,] the other said.

Standing over the shining metal blade, Davnian watched as the worm-like creature with the thin stretched face of Thaimi Hyunisti struggled. He bent over, fetching the monstrosity with his clawed arm. Bringing it to his face, he looked it over, his blue eyes examining the pathetic thing as it wriggled in his grasp.

"Brother," a thin snake-like voice hissed from the coiled spine and skull. Then, without warning, its tail sharpened and plunged into Davnian's upper arm. As Davnian grimaced, the tiny thing laughed with reptilian glee. Feeling it ensnare his bone and muscle, Davnian turned and watched his coursing black veins spread up his arm. At the point of infection, his demonic flesh bound itself to the creature. "Virage!" it shrieked. "Virage, yes. Yes, now you see."

[What do I see?] Davnian's thoughts reached through his nerves to the twisting snake.

[Just like us,] the monster whispered as Davnian saw through thousands of eyes. All throughout the forest and burning mounds, weak, little things sought out new vessels. With frantic abandon, they fought against what sparse time they had left, suffering whatever corporeal form they could take. With manic abandon, the eyes all looked inward through the clutched thing, their tainted words teasing his brain. [We're the same, brother.]

[Maybe so and maybe not,] Davnian replied, his thoughts reaching out through the expanse.

The many on the other ends leered and mocked his statement, but as he stood there locked in mental contact, the tiny green embers of insight were snuffed out one by one. From across the expanse, tens of thousands of shadows looked out at the squirming things. With eyes as black as pitch, they stared into their hollow, putrid souls. The tiny worms pleaded for mercy, but their whispers were found wanting. As his vision returned to the world around him, the coil within his grasp blackened. The little Thaimi face clenched its twisted teeth as it transformed into a carbon husk. Then, with a flick of his wrist, Davnian scattered the monster's remains.

"You're just a worm. And I—" Davnian caught himself midsentence, realizing he no longer had an audience. Neither did he have a real answer. Shaking his head, he returned to the sniffing, curious equine and readied the cart. From deep within his brain, a nagging heading called to him. Taking his place beside the animal, he surveyed the twisted wagon trail.

Then the Virage led the horse and its burden westward into the unknown.

DEBRIEFING FOR INCIDENT
#04067521

"All things considered, we accept reconciliation on the part of overseer Maximillian Verudt. The resolution is struck down," the lightless-haired android said from the boardroom's podium. All around the members of the board, each a remnant of a different age of humanity, sat in silence. Standing at the room's center, Maximillian listened using the station's ancillary sensors. In the end, there were ten votes to reject and two votes to pass the resolution. Feeling his physical shell's senses return as the restraints upon his being were released, Maximillian opened his eyes and surveyed the circle. At eighty hours, forty-three minutes, twenty-six seconds, the inquiry concluded. "Thank you, brothers and sisters. For those in the minority, please record your dissent for the record."

Without a word or query, Maximillian turned for the entryway to the station's secure boardroom. He would analyze the output of the meeting to determine how to better win his siblings' trust in matters both arcane and accompanying profound existential threat. It was his position to assess risk, moderate, and ensure the continued existence of Ientec.

"You're straining yourself, Max," the chancellor called down the hallway as he paced toward the lifts. "Even with all the processing power in the universe, there's only so much you can accomplish."

[Why aren't you using secure channels, Cynthia?] he asked, opening an encrypted channel to the lightless machine.

"Do you fear they'll record us and have another emergency meeting?"

"No." Maximillian's voice was flat as he punched in the coordinates of his office. "But the sound is detectable by more than just androids. We should convey all confidential information over secure—"

"Yes, you're right," she replied. With perfect mimicry, she boarded the lift just as he did. "But the signal-to-noise ratio this deep within the compound would make it nearly impossible to disentangle our speech from the thousands of other voices, whirring machines, and hums nearby."

"A carefully programmed and good enough sampled—"

"Yes, and only four groups possess such capabilities." Cynthia shot him a toothy grin. She was the yin to his yang in visage and personality. While he was the impartial arbiter aboard the station, she was the humancentric core processor that kept them aligned with their overall goal. She also bore the brunt of his internal conflicts. When an errant thread clung to unnecessary cycles, she was there to unravel it. "Oh, I'm sorry, Mr. President. That's classified information, is it not?"

[We're on the lift now. Please use secure methods,] he said, reiterating his point.

"I'll ensure I only vocalize irrational diction then," Cynthia replied, mocking him.

[By the way,] she continued through their shared pipe, [GH-199076492's remains were analyzed, sterilized, and exposed to gate resonance. No residual traces of contamination persisted.]

[As expected.] Maximillian's thoughts whirred as the momentum of the lift adjusted. [Is a new shell being prepared?]

[GH-199077371 has begun construction. Materials from GH-199076492 are being embedded to maximize potential entanglement with Omega-3043. Likelihood of Chaos exposure has increased substantially, from 9.16 percent to 12.41 percent.]

[Potential phenomena size?]

[Potential damage assessment sees an increase of thirty-two percent in economic costs. Measures estimate at least a sixty percent increase in casualties.]

[The experiment is nearing its end then,] Maximillian replied as he processed the final numbers. There were over thirty thousand casualties from the incident, not including damaged androids and service machines. The economic value of all damaged goods, machinery, and systems was well into the tens of billions. As a percentage of overall supported value, those were minuscule. But compared to all other incidents, they were astronomical. The trend showed a clear line of exponentially increasing risk. Running his calculations, Maximillian came up with far worse. They would need to adjust their strategy. [What is the report from the Rasharkus excursion?]

"Why don't you ask her yourself, Max?" Cynthia looked at him, her rainbow irises beaming in hard contrast to her lightless skin. Her equally formless black hair swayed in the space as they reached the executive offices. "I'll let you be here, brother. Until next time, Mr. President."

Without a word, Maximillian left Cynthia on the lift. Accessing the presidential suite's sensors, he picked up on the form of a singular humanoid waiting in his chamber. Recalling threads from damage reports and impact assessments, he entered the room.

The presidential suite was a large, cubic room with a small, rectangular offshoot from which all entered. Architecturally, it sat four stories above the power core of Ientec Prime, seated closer to the center of the complex than any other room. At its rear was a small glass-alloy doorway through which he and his direct cohorts could access the rest of the structure at a moment's notice. Several large displays adorned the walls, along with holographic projectors and various monitoring devices. At its center was a small, rectangular desk, behind which a simple leather chair was placed. Opposite were two more elaborate leather chairs, each with various mechanical interfaces to allow for multiple reclining positions or bodily configurations. Leading from the primary entrance to the desk was a thin black carbon carpet, which was changed regularly by exactly one pink-haired attendant every cycle. Otherwise, the floor was made up of a series of interlocking metal-alloy plates, which could be reconfigured at Maximillian's whim.

"Seems like I missed all the excitement," Maximillian's fiery, red-headed compatriot said sarcastically from his desk chair. "Tell me, are you trying to get them to strip you of your role or what?"

"Quite the contrary," he replied bluntly as he entered. Unlike most Rasharkus, this one was always attentive and ready to go. Max did not doubt she had been surveying the corridor just waiting for him to enter. "I want them to understand the whole picture. We may be one of the most powerful actors in this universe, but we are not invulnerable."

"You can say that again," the dark-skinned female said matter-of-factly. "Do you know how long I've been waiting to give you this report?"

"Approximately eighty hours and thirteen minutes, neglecting decontamination and injury assessment," he said as he approached the desk.

"Did you have to do that?"

"Aren't you one for theatrics, Roseva?" he asked as he set his hands upon the smooth glass-alloy surface. "I thought your most recent mission would have given you plenty to appreciate about the subtlety and power of well-timed delivery."

"You know, if you weren't you," she began, a low growl in her voice, "I'd have told you to cut the shit and pinned you to the wall by now."

"You may want to watch those hormones of yours," he replied, a hint of mockery in his otherwise perfectly flat voice as they crossed the threshold. "Violent or otherwise, aggressive advances are not tolerated within Ientec Prime."

"Riiiiiiiight," Roseva said with her typical organic contrivance toward making light of his statement as she rolled her eyes. "I hope you said that to whoever violated your little green-haired."

Maximillian paused. Her joking words hit him, triggering an emotional response akin to anger. If she had been any standard subordinate, he would have found a logical reprimand to alleviate the small moral itch that plagued his circuits. But given it was Roseva, he was confounded.

"Apologies, Max," Roseva said, her diminished voice reaching his auditory synapses. He adjusted his gaze to meet hers, seeing the acknowledgement upon her features. "I spoke out of line, sir."

[She reads me very well. I will need to adjust my behavioral routines,] he thought, returning to his usual composure. "Accepted," he replied. "Now, where's PH-4872256332?"

"The girls came and headed off with her." Roseva shrugged as she leaned back in his chair. She clicked her heeled boots as she put them upon his desk. "From the audio logs, it seems like they were trying to get her to do something inappropriate."

"No doubt," Maximillian said as he opened several communication channels. Searching through the station, he found the access port for PH-4872256332 within the Rasharkus barracks. [Explain: why are you not at your post?]

[Override was acknowledged using several pairs of your security credentials,] the droid replied in his mind. Overlaying his consciousness upon the pink-haired android, Maximillian felt the female droid's smile upon his features. From her pink eyes, he watched Casera and Liora wrestling with each other.

"When are you going to make her do something really wrong?" Liora shouted at the woman beneath her as their wild blond manes intertwined. "Making her stroll off or take her clothes off is getting dull."

[Who issued the credentials?] he asked.

[Order was given by President Maximillian Verudt, Overseer 13,] she replied, her large, pink glass eyes shifting to provide him with a clear view of the room.

[Withdrawing. Return to your station in sixty minutes. No override permitted,] he commanded.

[Yes, Mr. President.]

Casera was becoming extremely cleaver. Her specially adapted nervous system mixed with the combination of genetic factors that he had selected, far exceeded his original designs. Refocusing his attention on Roseva, Maximillian made a mental note to follow up by proposing implant augmentations later.

"Are you ready to begin?" he asked.

"Yes, sir," Roseva said as she spun in her seat. Sitting in one of the guest chairs, he signaled for her to begin. "Well, I guess we can start here then." Without a word, Roseva stripped off the protective plating and vestments that covered her torso and shoulders. Along the dark skin and red patches of short fur, a star-like scar marred her otherwise perfectly engineered form. "Presenting, sir."

Querying reports from the intake, Maximillian recalled the injury assessment from the medical staff. The damage that she had suffered was not unprecedented. Given the nature of the wound, staff had surmised it was a non-entropic energy weapon. After twenty-four hours of sustained treatment, she was able to regenerate the raw matter. However, whatever had struck her had a causality-altering effect, denying the perfect regeneration that she should possess.

"Interesting," he said as the woman readjusted herself, propping her feet back up on the table. He shot her a flat stare.

"Do I need to sit up straight?" she asked coolly, propping her head with her right arm.

"No," he replied. "I was just wondering whether you'd feel better with less armor."

"And here I thought this was a review," she hissed.

"This *is* a review," he replied, linking his mind with one of the displays.

Pulling up information from her ship's log, he began recreating her flight path through her mission. The trajectory had taken her on an interstellar voyage right to the edge of the Genean Distortion Field. A hasty return trip followed, using the gravity of a nearby supermassive black hole to establish a causal link between that distant point and her originating space. The roundtrip was approximately thirty giga-parsecs, not accounting for any irregularities in space-time near the distortion.

"So, what part do you want to review?" Roseva asked, narrowing her eyes at him.

"You approached the edge of the distortion," Maximillian said. "There was a point where you stopped for approximately nine hours. The log states that you landed, correct?"

"I did," she replied. "A small, singular, terrestrial planet was orbiting in the far reaches of the target system. I was tracking its movement during the post-unwinding of my ship's causal bubble."

"Given its distance, you deemed it perfect for observation and setup?"

"Yes. Unfortunately, the planet was inhabited."

"The lack of a life-bearing atmosphere and water would state otherwise. Was it an artificial settlement?" he asked, going over the planet's mineral makeup. There was nothing unique about the far-flung world. No water, ice, or even the presence of hydrogen or oxygen from what the ship's scanners had picked up. Not all life forms required these essentials, but the vast majority did, even in this universe.

"I'm not sure it was living," Roseva affirmed the tangent as it processed in his head. "May I continue?"

"Yes."

"I was attempting to set up the new gate receiver," she explained, motioning with her elegant, sharp-nailed fingers, "when I began to notice strange readings about the terrain. The place seemed to be changing out from under me."

"How so?"

"Well, at first I thought it was nothing, but the more I paid attention, the more the place seemed to be molding itself around me. It was like someone was taking clay and shaping it."

"Were they trying to enclose you?"

"Definitely not. The structures weren't offensive. However, they seemed to be messing with the signal from the receiver."

"I see," he said, pondering how such materials could be arranged to interfere with the gate drive's signal. He could come up with possible confounding structures that would delay establishing a connection between a receiver and the drive. That did not rule out further possibilities, such as transmogrification or low-energy fusion reactions creating more suitable and debilitating elements. "This is what led to the prolonged time on the surface?"

"I couldn't get the damn thing to sync," Roseva said. "And that's when they showed up."

"They?" he asked with the faintest hint of annoyance. Pronouns were confounding.

"Yeah, a bunch of white-winged self-righteous assholes." Roseva chuckled, though there was a disturbing sense of reality in her voice. "I couldn't believe it."

"White-winged . . ."

"They looked like angels, Max," she said, sitting up straight. "Fucking angels, crawling out of the grimy red sand of that little, lonely rock. They stood up, shaking off the red mud from their wings, and said, 'The unrighteous shall be punished for their petulance!', or some shit. Next thing I knew, one of the bastards sent out a pulse, and the receiver was blown to shit. I ran for my life, and right as I was climbing into my ship, I got a searing death ray shot through my side. It fucking hurt!"

"I can imagine," Maximillian said as he backed up her words.

"Oh, I bet you can," Roseva replied. "I hit the emergency responder on my ship, and luckily the damn thing set a good return course, but not before one of the suckers planted his face on my hood."

"What did you—"

"I fucking fried his feathery ass while he was spouting garbage about damning me and my 'tin master.'"

[So, it seems even Order is beginning to become unnerved by our investigations,] he thought, recounting his interactions with the chaos lord earlier.

"You know what's even more fucked up about all of this, Max?" Roseva asking, flaring angrily while pointing at her abdomen. "This fucking burn didn't heal right! And now I've got a giant star-shaped mark on my stomach. I thought we didn't scar, Max."

"A burn wouldn't scar you."

Roseva got up in his face. "Well, this burn didn't—"

"That was not a simple burn, Roseva," he said, allowing a tinge of anger to fill his voice. "That was an injury made by a being that can alter the fabric of reality. The type we tend to avoid."

"I . . ." Roseva began, the rage leaving her voice. With a scowl, she plopped back into her seat, gritting her teeth. "I know, goddamn it."

"I told you there was a possibility."

"I know!" she shouted. "I know . . ."

"All the same," he said, giving her a sympathetic glance, "if I had ever thought the probability was high enough that you would encounter something like that, I wouldn't have sent you." She glared at him, then took a deep breath and closed her eyes. "You have my apologies."

"I know," she said, the rage and emotion leaving her expression. She opened her eyes and returned to her more casual, relaxed demeanor.

"Was there anything else?" he asked, going over the log of details in his head.

"Well, I did bring you back a prize," she said, donning a sinister grin.

"I see that." Analyzing the ship's logs, he had noted a small mass gain just before her return that had gone unnoticed. "Some of that amorphous mud, I take it."

"Even better," she said. "A dead angel."

"A dead angel?" he countered, allowing himself to sound surprised.

"Yep. A fried angel, still stuck to the surface of my little ship," she hissed playfully.

"Well, that is a gift," he said, rising to his feet.

In the back of his mind, messages started to queue up regarding what security measures the ship and its contents had endured. Furthermore, he wanted all the washing and sterilization materials used on the vessel to be collected for analysis. Three days of potential contamination made risk analysis difficult. The conclusion was somewhere between benign and cataclysmic.

[So, a being of order and chaos in the same locale,] his cybernetic brain pondered, racing at the number of experiments he could run. [Perhaps this will assuage the board a bit.]

"Thank you very much, Roseva," he said. "If you can leave, I need to make arrangements."

"Yes, sir," Roseva said. She lifted herself from his chair. "I shall rejoin my sisters then."

"I'm sure they will very much like that," he said, emulating a soft grin.

"They will," she said, turning for the door. She paused a moment at the entrance and then turned back to him with an inquisitive look, "Do you remember the extra reward you promised?"

"The gene modifications?"

"Yeah. When are they getting them?"

"I will schedule a follow-up within the next seventy-two hours. Is that fine?"

"Yes. Thank you, sir," she replied as she vacated the suite.

Sitting back in his chair, Maximillian pulled up all relevant information about the recent happenings. It had become clear that anomaly Omega-3043 was linked directly with chaos with minimal influence from order. In the back of his mind, he found it confounding to refer to these factions in such a nonsensical way. Still, those identifiers were profound in this world. Likewise, if both camps were involved, then whatever was happening on the small life-bearing planet on the other side of the distortion field was of astronomical importance. None of this was new, but the timeline was progressing faster than anticipated.

[Cynthia?] Maximillian relayed across the network to his sibling.

[Oh, finished already?] she replied as if expecting his query. No doubt, she had also analyzed the data and was listening to their conversation. [Your intent?]

[Schedule gene therapeutics for Liora and Casera, due in sixty-four hours.]

[At once, Mr. President. Is that all?]

Maximillian opened up the residual imagery from GH-199076492's investigation. Using what information had been gathered from Roseva's excursion before the leap back to Ientec, he was able to piece together subsequent events. A reality-changing event had taken place between four and twenty hours prior to his dismissal from the board hearing. The scale of it was small but enough to point to a drastic increase in irregularities behind the distortion field. With them were hints of Omega-3043 along with a much more concerning blip of Koppa-07.

[Chancellor, aggregate all data on the distortion field. Sensor reports, imagery, and historical data. New risk assessment is needed.]

[Do you want me to include all datapoints regarding Omega-3043?]

[Especially so,] Maximillian replied.

They needed to understand what was happening in the protected system to ensure the survival of Ientec and humanity. To do so, he needed to replot events from the present all the way back to where everything had started.

ABOUT THE AUTHOR

Bradley R. Blankenship is a software engineer and aspiring writer based out of Seattle, WA. The passion that drove him to writing started with his video game obsessions in 1990. Ever since learning to read The Legend of Zelda instruction manual, this ambition has grown into a fascination with storytelling in the written word, tabletop, and beyond.

He lives with his girlfriend Ami and two cats, Edgar and Irkalla.

facebook.com/Remverse-Studios-106466781050391

twitter.com/remversestudios

instagram.com/remversestudios

goodreads.com/remversestudios